I0666941

JOHN J. CLIFTON
Temporal Specialist

Published by T.E. Willis
in the United States of America
Year published: 2019

T. E. Willis

Books by T. E. Willis

HOW TO BUILD A TIME MACHINE
JOHN J. CLIFTON, TEMPORAL SPECIALIST
ELLE, TEMPORAL ENFORCEMENT OFFICER

JOHN J. CLIFTON

Temporal Specialist

T. E. Willis

For Leah

T. E. WILLIS

Foreword

On the evening of February 6, 2018, a magnitude 6.4 earthquake struck the island nation of Taiwan. The epicenter was on the coastline near Hualien, the most severely affected area. Seventeen deaths were reported, with 285 additional people injured.

The following day, the 14th Dalai Lama of Tibet sent a letter from his residence-in-exile in Dharamshala, India, to the President of Taiwan, expressing condolences for the loss of life and destruction.

Most of the world viewed the event with shock; an unexpected natural disaster that tragically cost 17 people their lives.

Like many, I grieved at the loss of life, but my grief was tempered by what I knew the event meant to a small group of aged monks in Dharamshala and their spiritual leader. For them, the earthquake, though tragic, was confirmation of their faith in a strange traveler from the future. For them, the tragedy promised a glorious future for their beloved Tibet.

My name, as you will come to know me from this book, is Leah Vaughn.

That is not my real name.

For reasons this book will make clear, I am required to conceal my identity. I live now as a fugitive, hunted by agents from at least two governments. I have been forced to abandon a promising career as a journalist and producer. I held a close friend in my arms and watched him die, and I have been compelled to flee with my daughter into the relative safety of a foreign country. All of these things are the direct result of my association with John J. Clifton.

Some might expect me to harbor bitterness towards John for the life we are forced to live. No, I harbor no bitterness towards John. John saved my life, and he gave my daughter a future where none had existed for her before. He is my best friend, my confidant, and my protector. I count myself extremely fortunate, for I am one of the few people in the world who know John for what he truly is; a temporal specialist from the year 2151 and a man dedicated to a noble purpose.

In 2018, I mailed my company's interviews with John to a Phoenix publisher. Those interviews, along with several historical data files that John provided, have now been published to the world. At the publisher's request, I have now undertaken to write this supplemental account, which is an account of John, a description of his life in the future, and an explanation of his purpose in coming to our time.

I have taken the liberty of writing this account in the form of a novel, and of employing an author's license to convey feelings and thoughts implied, if not spoken aloud. This work is based on our shared experiences together, on my conversations with John, and his descriptions of his life in the future.

To the skeptic, the unbeliever, and the critic, I offer only these words from a wise sage; "Quantum science is a subject long known to those of us in the east. It allows us to understand that many such things we cannot yet explain through science, may indeed be real... We must allow our minds to accept possibilities that our science cannot presently explain... We must allow our hearts to accept what our minds cannot."

For my part, my heart and my mind accept.

My mind accepts for I saw John's temporal device inside the room at the Chatwal Hotel. I touched Mannerheim's pistol in the Tibetan reliquary at Dharamshala. I went through the frightening blackness at Oak Ridge, and I stood with John inside the garden dome on his beloved Hōfu Station and gazed at an indescribable star-filled sky.

As for my heart, it too is at peace, for my daughter will now live to enjoy a magnificent future.

~ Leah Vaughn, June 2019

Chapter 1

J ohn walked towards the stylized metal and steel "tori" gate that marked the entrance to the plaza. The mental fog that always accompanied his neustem injection had fully dissipated. He wondered if he would ever get used to the biochemical inhibitors. He understood the need for such precautions, but the temporary disorientation always disturbed him. Fortunately, the sensation faded swiftly, leaving behind only the inevitable cognitive inhibitors familiar to every temporal specialist.

Every temporal specialist reported different side effects from the bio-engineered chemicals. While the universal result was an effective suppression of the specialist's ability to disclose identity or mission information, the side effects varied by individual. One of his peers in the Reynolds-Hampshire company attached to the British Temporal Office reportedly could not speak for almost an hour after receiving his neustem injection. In John's case, he always experienced a temporary

4

mental fog and brief disorientation. The sensation did not last long, but it was annoying.

Damn CTI regulatory nonsense, John fumed. The Conseil Temporel International (CTI), or "International Temporal Council" headquartered in Geneva, Switzerland, controlled all aspects of temporal tripbacks and had mandated the use of neustem injections in 2102 when the biochemical inhibitors were first developed.

While John understood the counsel's motives, he had always considered the precaution to be unnecessary and possibly even counterproductive. A specialist needed to have his mind clear at all times, he reasoned, especially at the beginning of a tripback mission, when the risks were at their highest.

John could feel the inhibitors pressing on his consciousness now as he approached the plaza entrance. On their own, the bio-engineered chemicals would remain active for at least several months. He looked forward to receiving the counter injection at his mission debriefing.

He paused under the metal gate and assessed the area. The Tokyo International Exhibition Center plaza lay before him, a large open-air courtyard filled with people. Above the heads of the crowd, he could see the Tokyo Big Sight pavilion; four upside-down pyramids fused at their base with a fifth pyramid rising from the center. A collection of rust-colored tiles directed him from the gate towards the pavilion, the only color variation in the courtyard's sea of grey and charcoal tiles.

This was November 19, 2003, and it was 9:44 AM. John was in Tokyo, Japan, and the International Robot Exhibition was underway in the main exhibition hall. The theme of the exhibition was "Robot Technology Pioneers the Future - From Manufacturing to Personal Life." How ironic, he mused. If they only knew just how prophetic that theme would prove to be! He adjusted his backpack containing his MTY device and glanced back down the street, reorienting himself to his pre-selected escape routes in case he needed to make a swift exit.

John had stepped through his MTY device's singularity several minutes ago to find himself in an alley behind a small retail store near the exposition plaza. Fortunately, no one had observed his arrival. Following protocol, he had immediately placed his MTY device into its holding cycle after re-verifying its (P)E reading. He always made a point of double-checking the device's settings. Ever since the unexplained loss of fellow RJCom temporal specialist Theresa Williams in 2137, four years ago, his assignor had placed an increased emphasis on its agents following protocol.

Williams was not the first specialist to be lost. In 2114, Reynolds-Hampshire lost one of its temporal specialists, Aleksei Lewis, who had transited into northern Kazakhstan on August 12, 1953. His loss had been officially attributed to unexpectedly strong particle disruption affecting his device's singularity resulting from the Semipalatinsk thermonuclear detonation he had been sent to observe.

In 2126, Reynolds-Hampshire lost another temporal specialist, a Chinese agent named Fai Zhou, who vanished while on a tripback mission to 1908 China.

Thirteen years later, in 2139, following the discovery of an obscure historical record suggesting the Chinese may have taken Zhao prisoner, John had been sent on an investigative tripback mission, his second mission since joining the temporal group in San Tibor.

It had been a thrilling experience for the junior specialist. John's datstem had been equipped with Chinese and Mongolian language upgrades, the first language enhancements he had received, and he had traveled with an Imperial Russian army envoy into the heart of China for almost two months. Although he had been unable to discover what had happened to Zhou, the mission had provided John with both experience and self-confidence and had solidified his position with the San Tibor temporal group.

John walked through the crowds towards the main pavilion. Outside one of the doors, a group of children amused themselves with a mechanical toy robot as their parents chatted nearby. One of the children held a control device in his hands, laughing as he directed the small robot forward a few paces.

John paused, momentarily confused as the datstem implant embedded near his cortical stem had failed to alert him to any radio or other signals coming from the child's remote.

"It utilizes an infra-red signal," the datstem now explained, its mental voice gently intruding on John's consciousness. "The child's controller is sending digitally-coded pulses of infrared radiation to control the toy's limited functions. Such controllers were in common use until approximately 2055. They were limited to line-of-sight operation, unlike radio frequency controllers."

"How do you know it's an infrared signal?" John queried silently, amused. He had no ocular implants, nor was he carrying any device capable of detecting an infra-red signal. He knew his datstem's sensor capability was limited to ultrasonic, radio, microwave, and QRB frequencies. He also enjoyed testing the limits of the implanted datstem's quantum reasoning capabilities, though he knew what would be its likely response.

"Predictive analysis" came the expected reply. "Ultrasonic controllers were largely discontinued by the mid-1970s, and no radio frequency or microwave transmissions are detected coming from the child's controller. QRB transmission was not developed until 2062, so the method of transmission must logically be infra-red. Probability 98.24 percent."

"Perhaps the child is using an embedded cognitive controller?" John mused.

There was a pause, as the AI device considered this new possibility.

"Impossible. The probability of the child having an embedded controller is 0.00 percent. No mechanical cognitive interfaces exist in this era."

"You exist in this era," John retorted, noting the datstem's own mechanical cognitive interface.

There was another pause, as the embedded device's quantum-entangled analytic processor considered this seeming contradiction.

"I exist in this era because of your temporal transition to this era. I am not native to this era."

"Perhaps the child also transited from the future?" John queried, testing, but this time, no response was forthcoming. His datstem tended to ignore frivolous queries and also seemed to sense when John was amusing himself at its expense.

John snorted, victorious, and proceeded inside the

exhibition hall.

John had acquired his datstem implant in his 20s, shortly after accepting his first assignment with his former assignor, Tout-Su Particles. Most people he knew had a datstem implant, though there were bio-activist groups that deplored the devices.

A datstem implant contained a quantum-based analytical processor as well as vast data archives. Capable of true reasoning, the devices conformed to their host's unique personality, becoming, over time, an integral part of their host's cognitive process. While the implant could be turned off at will, John seldom did. He had nicknamed his datstem "Fouray"; a moniker derived from the last two digits of the device's QK signature, "DS-51676F54A".

From his mission briefing, John was prepared for what now confronted him inside the building; a massive hall filled with crowds of people milling around various exhibits. There was an excitement in the air, tangible, almost a festival quality. A young woman in business attire greeted him as he entered, bowing and smiling as she offered the traditional Japanese welcome.

"いらっしゃいませ!"

John bowed back. His assignor, Rengel-Jiang QCom, had updated his datstem with a Japanese language upgrade in preparation for this tripback and he made use of it now.

"大阪大学の展覧会はどこですか?"

The woman was startled, clearly not expecting to hear such flawless Japanese spoken by a foreigner, though there were many visible in the hall. She consulted a handheld information device and asked John for his name and company.

John's neustem biochemical inhibitors flared strongly now inside his consciousness, temporarily preventing him from responding. He forced his mind to formulate a suitably ambiguous response that he was simply a visitor to the convention, and he asked again for the location of the Osaka University exhibit.

The woman nodded and gestured towards a prominent cluster of displays further inside the spacious building.

As he approached the displays, John casually scanned the room, focusing on the faces of those in attendance.

"Subject acquired," Fouray reported. Implanted near John's cortical stem with leads buried within his cerebellum, the device could 'see' what John saw and 'hear' what John heard. It had recognized their target, although John himself had not.

"The man in the dark shirt," Fouray offered, assisting John's gaze. "Mid-length hair, frameless tinted eyeglasses... no... behind the woman... yes. That's him. That's Ishimatsu. Probability is 99.98 percent."

John studied the man. He was not what he expected, but historical figures seldom were. The man was speaking to a group of businessmen as they collectively observed the figure of a woman sitting in a chair on an elevated platform. From its archive files, Fouray confirmed what John already suspected; the figure sitting in the chair was an SDU, or "[S]elf-[D]irecting [U]nit". In fact, it was the first SDU, an automaton designated "Mimitron" by its creator, Hiroshi Ishimatsu.

A group of young female students stopped in front of the seated figure. As the men watched, one of the students
10

waved and said hello. The SDU's head abruptly swiveled to face the girl and answered, its mouth moving in rigid imitation of a human's as it waved its hand in response. The students giggled and quickly disappeared into the crowd.

"Not a very sophisticated unit," Fouray commented. "Your habitat's environmental controller has greater functional capability."

John accepted this as fact but ignored the implied criticism. SDU prejudice against non-self-directing automata was well-known.

"The habitat's controller is not self-directing," he countered. "Besides, despite its primitive state, that qualifies as an SDU by even our standards."

"Barely."

John acknowledged the concession and changed the subject. "Have you identified Ikeda yet?"

"No."

"We are likely early," John responded. "According to JNCAA records, Ikeda doesn't arrive until noon."

"How do you intend to confirm the JNCAA's claims?" Fouray's question implied a subtle criticism than John recognized. He smiled and mentally replied, "I haven't decided."

"Would it not have been prudent to decide on a course of action before transiting?" Fouray found many aspects of human behavior difficult to understand. Spontaneity was among the most confusing human attributes. The human ability to formulate a plan of action on the spur of the moment, without an in-depth analysis of the available information or other preparation, was simply beyond the quantum device's

11

comprehension.

"Sometimes things don't go the way you expect no matter how much planning you conduct," John countered. "It is impossible to reliably predict the outcome of every event, even with sufficient preparation."

John cast his mind back then to his mission briefing. His company's CTI representative had informed him that this tripback had been authorized in "member absentia", meaning not all of the CTI member nations had approved the mission parameters as filed with the council. In this case, Japan had voted against the mission parameters, demanding to send their own specialist assigned to the Blosch-Nishikawa company. The remaining six council member nations had objected, citing Japan's conflicted interest in the outcome of the mission.

Though this mission was a minor one in scope, its outcome could have dramatic, long-term ramifications.

For more than 40 years, the world's automata community had been obsessed with one subject; determining what limits, if any, should be applied to future SDU development.

On one side were those who argued for unrestrained SDU evolution, believing a more advanced artificial intelligence would immeasurably advance human interests. Pointing to previous breakthroughs in science and medicine made possible only through SDU assistance, and citing the Luyteni civilization's apparent complete reliance on automata, they made a compelling argument for unrestrained SDU evolution.

On the other side of the argument, however, were those who viewed artificial intelligence as ultimately threatening to humanity. The Luyteni, they argued, did not share humanity's history, a history replete with wars, violence, and self-destruction. Naturally, the Luyteni's automata would mirror their maker's peaceful evolution. Humanity's AI, they countered, if left to its unrestrained evolution, could just as easily follow in humanity's violent tradition.

Thus, the debate had raged for decades, as governments and scientific communities had struggled to find a solution.

Compounding the problem, current SDU quantum controllers were programmed not by man, but by other SDUs under increasingly limited human direction. For more than sixty years, humanity had been largely removed from the programming process, turning over responsibility for automata code development to increasingly sophisticated AI-based program controllers. These units had initiated multiple self-improvements over the years within their programming languages, coding methods, algorithms, and theoretical constructs. After 60 years, the programs directing modern SDUs had simply become too complex for man to decipher.

Six years ago, in August of 2135, the government of Japan, through its powerful Japanese National Council on Automaton Advancement (日本オートマトン推進協議会, or "JNCAA"), had issued a formal statement clarifying their position. Japan was a leading manufacturer of SDU quantum controllers and in the forefront of those arguing against unrestrained SDU development.

SDUs, the JNCAA had asserted, were from the beginning intended to be operated under human control. According to the JNCAA's statement, when Hiroshi Ishimatsu designed his first SDU, he had programmed into the device certain behavioral inhibitors, rendering the unit subservient to command inputs from its creator. Ishimatsu, they asserted, had intended automatons to be subservient to man.

Throughout the world, Hiroshi Ishimatsu was revered as the "father of SDUs", and the JNCAA's statement had created an international uproar. In support of their claims, however, the JNCAA had produced a data record purporting to contain a copy of Ishimatsu's original SDU operating system code. The code, they reported, had been stolen at the 2003 International Robot Exhibition in Tokyo by Tatsuo Ikeda, one of Ishimatsu's students. Ikeda had later sold the code to the Toshiba Corporation, who in 2096 founded Toshiba Automatons, one of the first manufacturers of SDU control processors.

For nearly a year, the parties on both sides had argued the merits of JNCAA's claims. Then, in November of 2136, a legal challenge had been filed, alleging the JNCAA's evidence to have been fabricated. Under that legal action, a moratorium on all SDU development had been ordered pending an investigation and ruling from the judicial council.

Almost one year ago, a petition had been filed by the plaintiffs with the CTI council, requesting a temporal incursion to the 2003 International Robot Exhibition in Tokyo, with the stated purpose of investigating the JNCAA's claims.

After reviewing the petition, and cognizant of the international attention on the case, the CTI council had authorized the tripback and assigned the mission to Rengel-Jiang QCom in Texas. Though still a junior temporal specialist, John's marker had been selected to complete the assignment.

14

As John now stood looking around the hall at its many exhibits, Fouray pressed its earlier question, "Do you intend to confront Ikeda?"

"No," John responded. "That won't be necessary."

"If you do not confront Ikeda, I do not see how you can confirm the JNCAA's claims."

John didn't immediately respond. Instead, he approached the Osaka University exhibit, attempting to gain a closer view. When he stopped, the primitive SDU seated on the chair bowed and greeted him in a mechanical voice.

John smiled and responded politely, as the men paused to observe his interaction. John could see several cables exiting the stand to disappear under the blue carpet beneath the seated figure. Several feet away, partially obscured by an exhibit wall, he noticed a young man monitoring a laptop.

"It's wired?" Fouray asked.

"Apparently so," John responded, nodding to the smiling men before walking away.

Once concealed again within the crowd, John stopped, gazing around the hall. "There are two ways to confirm JNCAA's claims," he now responded. "I can confront Ikeda and scan his copy of the code, or I can scan Ishimatsu's original code."

"Which will you do?" Fouray asked. Before John could respond, however, Fouray announced, "Ikeda has arrived."

John could see a short student with glasses approaching the University exhibit. The student smiled and bowed at the group of men before bowing low to his professor, Ishimatsu. The young man then stepped back, looking around the display. Seeing his peer operating the laptop behind the exhibit wall,

15

Ikeda smiled and quickly approached. The two students engaged in idle conversation, laughing and smiling as Ishimatsu continued his conversation with several businessmen.

John took that moment to casually re-approach the display. As he watched, Ishimatsu excused himself from the group of men and approached his two students. After a few moments, Ishimatsu and the first student exited the display and began walking toward the food vendors located at the rear of the hall. Ikeda remained behind, clearly relieving his fellow student at the laptop.

Through the thick crowd, John watched Ikeda closely. After several minutes, the young man glanced around and then retrieved a small black plastic device from his pocket. He inserted the device into the side of the laptop and began pressing a sequence of keys on its keyboard.

"He is using a primitive solid-state data storage unit called a flash drive," Fouray explained. "Introduced in 2000, the devices were limited at this time to a 480 Mbit upper-bound transfer rate."

John shook his head. It seemed amazing that people once relied on such antiquated technology. After nearly 2 minutes, Ikeda withdrew the small device and placed it back inside his pocket.

"That does appear to confirm the JNCAA's claims," Fouray suggested.

"Perhaps."

After several more minutes, Ishimatsu and the first student returned. Both were carrying containers of steaming noodles and cups in their hands. They sat down behind the exhibit, and Ishimatsu passed a container to Ikeda. The three began eating while the first student began monitoring the laptop again. After several minutes, Ikeda glanced at his watch and abruptly stood. He said something to the first student, bowed to Ishimatsu, and then began walking briskly towards the entrance to the hall.

John began to follow at a discreet distance.

"I thought we were going to scan Ishimatsu's code?" Fouray asked, confused.

John did not respond but continued to follow the young man as he exited the hall and began walking across the crowded courtyard.

"Do you intend to confront Ikeda about the theft?" Fouray asked.

"No," John replied. "I just want to see where he's going."

"For what purpose?"

"He seems to be going somewhere... and I just want to see where he's going."

"That is a non sequitur statement."

John ignored the criticism and quickened his pace. Suddenly, Ikeda stopped. The courtyard was filled with crowds of people, and the young man had stopped in front of a large foreigner with blonde hair. Instead of stepping around the stranger, however, Ikeda appeared to be speaking with him.

John was perhaps 15 meters behind the pair, and the crowds of people in the plaza intermittently blocked his view. For a moment, however, it looked as if Ikeda was handing the tall foreigner something. Or, perhaps they were exchanging something?

John quickened his pace, trying not to alert the pair to his approach, but before he could see what was happening, the duo abruptly turned and began walking away from each other, Ikeda back towards the convention hall and the tall foreigner towards the city.

John was torn. He had a sense that something important had just happened, but he had no idea what it was. Ultimately, John decided to follow the young student back into the hall. He still needed to complete his mission, and that meant obtaining a copy of the SDU code. Exasperated, he turned and began walking back through the crowds.

John found Ikeda sitting behind the exhibit wall, operating the laptop again while his fellow student and Ishimatsu stood nearby speaking to a group of visitors. For a moment, John thought Ikeda had removed something from the laptop. He caught a glimpse of the young man placing something inside his pocket.

Frustrated, John engaged Fouray to begin scanning. "Can you PoL with the device from here?" he asked.

"Yes."

Fouray now engaged its wireless radio capabilities and established a peer-to-peer connection with the laptop, easily bypassing the device's primitive security firewall. In a matter of seconds, the embedded AI device had copied the SDU's operating system files.

"PoL completed," Fouray reported.

"Very good. Disconnect now."

"Disconnected."

"Do the files match those submitted by the JNCAA?" John asked.

"Yes. It appears the JNCAA claims regarding Ishimatsu's intentions were correct."

"Hmmmm... ok."

John felt strangely disturbed as if he was missing something important. When he reviewed the mission file, however, it appeared that all of the requirements had been satisfied. He queried his datstem for confirmation.

"All mission requirements have been completed," Fouray responded.

John turned to walk back to the main entrance. After several steps, however, he stopped again, hesitating. He glanced back at the exhibit, still troubled, wondering what Ikeda had concealed in his pocket.

Fouray's tone was disapproving, "You're wasting time."

John sighed. Fouray was right. He was wasting time. Ignoring the uneasiness in his gut, he turned and walked out of the exhibition hall.

Chapter 2

T he lift rose swiftly along the side of the building, the waning sun warm and yellow through its translucent shell. Feeling the warmth on his face, John regretted not accepting the Holman group's invitation to join them at Lake Fayette. The day had been perfect, a typical south-Texas summer afternoon.

"You aren't regretting not going to the lake," Fouray interjected, disturbing his thoughts.

The lift arrived at the transport platform, and John stepped out, approaching the rows of RJCom transports on the roof of the building.

"Then what am I regretting?" John queried, impatient, as the transport's external shell split and lifted away to allow him to sit inside the two-passenger capsule.

There was no response from his datstem.

"Houston EPM Station 9," John spoke aloud when the shell had closed and pressurized.

"Houston EPM Station 9… confirmed." The transport's control unit acknowledged the command and the capsule lifted gently from the roof, its gravimetric plates humming almost imperceptibly beneath John's feet. "Distance 96.3 kilometers. Transport time 10.8 minutes."

In the distance, John could see several empty transports returning, large white bees returning to their hive for the night.

It was 2150. John was now a senior temporal specialist at the San Tibor group, having just completed his 10th tripback mission. As the transport flew swiftly towards the sprawling metropolis that was Houston, Texas, he considered Fouray's statement.

"Why shouldn't I have gone to the lake?"

"You didn't want to go to the lake," Fouray's tone was accusatory, "You just wanted something to take your mind off the Baltimore debriefing."

"I answered truthfully every question they asked," John responded, defensive.

"The panel's bio-cognitive interface makes dissembling impossible," Fouray countered, "however, the panel can only query what it has been instructed to query."

"I responded truthfully to every question," John held stubbornly to that fact.

"Precisely."

John considered this for a moment.

"You're suggesting I'm regretting not telling them about the signal," John said.

"I'm suggesting you are uncertain about what to do and that you are troubled by your indecision."

Probably true, John admitted. He prided himself on being decisive.

"Should I tell RJCom about the signal?" John asked.

There was a pause as his datstem analyzed this question.

By design, a datstem rarely suggested a course of action to its host. A datstem was primarily a data retrieval and interpretive processor, with quantum analytic reasoning capability. It was a true artificially intelligent device, but it was programmatically limited when it came to suggesting real-world actions based on its data. To do so involved identifying risk factors, anticipating complex human reactions, and predicting probable outcomes based on numerous variables; activities that were beyond the capabilities of archival SDUs and their related datstems cousins. After a moment, Fouray responded.

"Uncertain. I am unable to predict the results of such a disclosure."

John accepted this. He wasn't certain himself how RJCom would respond to the information.

"You could take the matter directly to the CTI council," Fouray offered. "Under Article 11, Section 40(b) of the ITT treaty, specialists are required to report any temporal anomalies observed during a mission to the CTI's Office of Temporal Affairs."

"Was it a temporal anomaly?" John asked.

"What else could it be?"

"I'm not certain."

John's thoughts were subdued as the transport entered Houston airspace. The transport patterns were busy this evening. The thousands of capsules moved like shimmering beads on an invisible necklace of directional beams above the city's steel and glass surface. A few minutes later, the transport's control unit startled him from his thoughts, intoning, "Arriving. Houston EPM Station 9."

The capsule began its vertical descent to a tree-lined

transport lot. When it stopped, and its shell opened, John stepped out. The capsule then re-sealed, rose, and slowly disappeared into the west, returning to San Tibor.

Nearby, a large building now drew John's attention. Lines of commuters moving on automated walkways flowed into the glass-faced structure through illuminated archways marked with different gate numbers and descriptions. From here, John could read "New York", "Orlando", "Tokyo", "London", "Copernicus City", "São Paulo", and "Moscow", though he knew the facility housed dozens of additional locked EPM platforms, as well as numerous unlocked "express" platforms.

John queried Fouray for the current transit rates. They varied daily, and it often proved just as affordable to transit directly to Hōfu Station from an express EPM platform as it did to take the mass-transit "locked" EPM to Tokyo, and then transit from there through a second locked EPM to the orbiting station. As he stepped onto the moving walkway, Fouray responded.

"Take the express."

John was relieved. He looked forward to arriving at his apartment at the station. He needed time to sort out what had happened and then decide what to do about it. One didn't approach the CTI council lightly. That powerful body was notoriously sensitive to temporal matters and could plunge an assignor into months of costly investigations by merely having been contacted by one of their specialists.

Inside the EPM station, crowds of commuters collected near the various transit platforms. Noisome conversations filled the cavernous building accompanied by delicious smells emanating from automated food kiosks and the building's several restaurants.

As they always did, the shimmering ultraviolet-ringed voids of the calibrated singularity platforms immediately drew John's attention. A businessman stepped off the automated walkway ahead and approached the São Paulo gate's two singularities. As he stepped through the shimmering "Departure" portal, a counter above the gate incremented, recording the man's transition. At almost that same moment, a family with several small children emerged from the "Arrival" gate facing the opposite direction, laughing and chattering as they proceeded towards the far walkway that exited the building.

John was approaching the express platforms now and queried Fouray for the rate.

"62 for Express to Quadrant 2," Fouray replied.

The rate was reasonable. John exited the walkway and stopped in front of one of the express singularity platforms. It's attendant SDU, a fifth-series Hitachi Gen-P, greeted him pleasantly.

"Destination please."

"Hōfu Station, Quadrant 2."

"Hōfu Orbital Station, Quadrant 2… Confirmed. 62 IMUs."

When John nodded, the platform hummed to life as its fusion generator engaged. A few seconds later, the black void of a calibrated singularity blanked out the platform's small circular frame.

"Calibration complete. You may proceed. Thank you for using Texas Trans…"

The SDU's voice cut off instantly as John stepped through the blackness, emerging at that moment inside the EPM park at the center of Quadrant 2, Hōfu Station.

The EPM park, a pleasant tree-lined courtyard in the center of the quadrant, housed five locked EPM platforms. The two largest platforms were locked to Tokyo and New York. The three smaller platforms were locked to each of the station's three other quadrants. Nearby, a row of express platforms accommodated travelers transiting to alternate destinations. The park was already filling with children and families transiting away for the weekend.

The chronometer on the nearby Fujioka Financial building read 07:44 AM - Saturday. The station synchronized its orbital cycle with Tokyo, Japan, and was therefore 14 hours ahead of Houston.

As he stepped onto one of the park's pedestrian pads that would carry him to the residential perimeter, John marveled as he always did at the vast station. Orbiting the Earth at 189,902 kilometers, the station was situated approximately halfway between the Earth and Luna. Each of its domed quadrants was constructed of "gelatinized glass" sandwiched within transparent polymer layers held within a metallic geodesic frame. This unique hull construction and the station's orbital spin provided residents with magnificent stellar views as well as an actual dawn-to-dusk solar cycle.

Constructed more than 50 years ago, the station consisted of four interconnected half-sphere domes, each with a surface area comprising 78.5 hectares (194 acres). The sub-surface of each of the four quadrants housed graviton generation panels, primary and backup fusion plants, water reclamation and sewage processing, reserve O2, He-3, H2O, and maintenance bays holding manned and remote-operated maintenance vehicles.

Within each domed quadrant, elevated electromagnetic rail systems and automated walkway bridges connected the quadrant's commercial structures; primarily banking, corporate, and financial centers.

A fifth, smaller dome was located centrally between the four connecting quadrants. Named "Hōfu Teien" 防府庭園 (or "Hōfu Garden"), this greenhouse dome was considered one of the most beautiful exo-parks ever constructed.

The station had a permanent resident population of more than 11,000 people. The station's population swelled during business hours to between 32,000 and 35,000 people, mostly assignment staff transiting daily from the Earth or Luna to work within the station's many business structures.

John enjoyed living on the station and preferred the weekends when it was not so crowded. Eight years ago, he had been extremely fortunate to purchase one of the limited resident apartments when a former tenant had relocated back to Earth. There were only 3,200 residence apartments on the entire station, located along the perimeter of each of the four quadrants, and they were very much in demand.

John was nearing the quadrant perimeter now, so he terminated the moving pad and proceeded up the narrow street that led to his apartment. His recent tripback still occupied his mind.

In the early days of what historians now called the "First Gulf War", United States soldiers from the Mobile Exploitation

Team Alpha operating in Baghdad, Iraq, had discovered thousands of Jewish communal and religious books, parchments, and other documents moldering under four feet of water in the flooded basement of an Iraqi intelligence building. The documents, some dating from the mid-16th century, represented a priceless record of Jewish history in that long-troubled part of the world.

After a concerted preservation effort by the United States government, the records had been scanned and archived. The scanned documents could still be viewed today in data archives throughout the world. Several scrolls, however, had been deemed too badly damaged to be preserved. In 2013, the damaged scrolls were ritually interred in a Jewish cemetery in West Babylon, New York. Several months ago, an archeological team involved in the restoration of that historic cemetery had re-discovered the interred scrolls.

While examining a fragment of one of the scrolls under modern (h)red-spectra imaging wavelengths, the team had been shocked to discover un-discovered text; priceless handwritten writing from an even earlier era that had been erased and written over by later authors. The discovery of the hidden writing had generated great excitement within the world's archeological, historical, and Jewish communities.

The original document cache, however, was no longer available to re-examine. The cache had been returned to Iraq following their restoration and destroyed during the devastating Israeli-Arabic "Alharb Alsariea" war of 2064.

Several months ago, at the request of the present Israeli government, the CTI council had authorized a tripback mission to determine whether additional writing might exist, faded and

27

undiscovered, within the original cache of documents. Should such additional writing be discovered, the CTI council had expressed a willingness to authorize a clandestine scanning effort, sending back temporal specialists posing as contemporary preservation personnel.

A representative sample of the documents had been placed on exhibit at the Jewish Museum of Maryland in the year 2017. John's marker had been selected by the CTI council to complete a tripback mission to 2017 Baltimore. His mission goal had been a simple one. He was to determine whether additional undiscovered writings existed within the document collection at large. If it did, the CTI council would authorize the clandestine scanning effort.

At his departure briefing, John had been provided with a handheld (h)red-spectra imaging scanner disguised as a cell phone, a period-typical communication device. With that lone equipment exception, it had been an otherwise routine transition. After calibrating his MTY device at the Hampton collider center in Baltimore, John transported with an RJCom equipment technician and a CTI representative to what in 2017 had been a relatively quiet section of East Falls Avenue. From there, he had transited into Columbus Park in the early morning hours of Friday, October 27th, 2017. The park had been empty, and his arrival into its chilly center had been observed only by its namesake's statue.

The mission briefing had suggested John's backpack was likely to be searched if he attempted to bring it inside the museum building, so he had secured his MTY device at a private locker facility near the park. The museum was only 11 minutes away by foot. By the time it opened that morning, John was already in line outside the building.

Mingling with the crowds inside the exhibit, John had been able to take several scans of the target documents under the guise of taking photographs. While most of the documents did not indicate earlier writing, under the (h)red spectra wavelength, a graceful hand-written script could be seen flowing across several of the older parchments, ghostly faded texts visible behind the more recent iron-gall ink.

After completing his mission parameters, John had walked back to Columbus Park and retrieved his MTY device from the storage locker. He had then begun walking south along Falls Avenue, enjoying the smell of the water as he scouted for a quiet alley along the East Harbor waterfront to transit back undetected.

While approaching a small footbridge near Fleet Street, however, Fouray's sharp tone had brought John to a stop.

"Signal!"

"What do you…"

"QRB Signal!"

John had been momentarily confused. A [Q]uantum [R]esonance [B]and, or QRB signal was utilized by only very sophisticated controllers, typically SDUs or related AI units. Datstems also used QRB signals to connect with external controllers and other datstem units, a common enough activity in the future. A QRB signal in 2017, however, could not be explained.

"Are you certain?" John had asked.

"Signal confirmed. It is a QRB signal within the standard deviation. Nominal encryption. Strength 18.422."

John had looked anxiously around the waterfront. The

signal strength had indicated someone within the immediate area, perhaps as close as several hundred meters. There had been numerous small crowds enjoying the nearby attractions, walking along the tree-lined canals or mingling near the MECU pavilion across the bridge.

"Signal strength change detected."

"Closing or opening?" John had asked, anxiously scanning the crowds.

"Closing. Strength now 18.510 and increasing."

John had felt a surge of adrenaline. Someone was approaching his location, someone with technology that would not exist for another 47 years.

"18.601"

John had turned and begun walking swiftly across the small footbridge towards the pavilion.

"18.729"

The approaching party's pace too had quickened, obviously closing on John's own datstem's QRB signal. John could not turn off his QRB signal without simultaneously turning off his ability to detect the approaching QRB. So, he had begun running, drawing curious stares from those he passed. He had been in a full sprint when he darted across the pavilion, forcing several people to jump out of his way. Rounding the northwest corner of Pier 5, he had nearly stumbled trying to avoid colliding with another couple.

"19.764"

John had run south towards the small park adjoining the historic Seven Foot Knoll Lighthouse, scrambling to remove his MTY device from his backpack as he ducked into a tall clump of bushes.

"20.104. Estimated distance is 84 meters and closing rapidly."

Glancing around his location, John had activated the MTY device's control panel to release its holding cycle. The ultraviolet-framed singularity immediately appeared a meter away, a stark blackness flickering in the mottled shade beneath the thick bushes. Lifting the MTY device by its handle, John had stepped quickly through the void.

The CTI representative and the RJCom equipment technician were waiting just as John had left them. From their perspective, less than 30 seconds had elapsed. As casually as he dared, John had opened the device's protected access port and flipped the disruption switch that terminated the MTY's singularity. He began to relax after the singularity had winked out, released from its electromagnetic confinement.

Following CTI protocol, John then handed the MTY device to the CTI representative, who had confirmed the singularity had been released.

"Status?" the man had asked, carefully placing the device inside a case before passing it to the waiting RJCom technician.

"Success." John had replied, struggling to slow his breathing. "Several of the older parchment documents did show evidence of earlier writing."

The RJCom technician, a female equipment specialist from the company's Dubina Group, had noticed the sweat on John's face and had asked, "Everything ok?... any problems?"

John had simply shaken his head and smiled. "No," he had said. "It was a long walk from the museum."

That explanation had seemed to satisfy her. She had

nodded and loaded the MTY case into the waiting transport.

Now, as he walked through the narrow street that led to his apartment, John's mind was racing. He could not explain the presence of a QRB signal in 2017, nor even definitively establish that the signal had existed. Despite Fouray's statement that he had detected a valid QRB signal, its inexplicable presence in that time raised troubling questions in John's mind.

Solar flares and certain other stellar phenomena had been known to have been mistaken for QRB signals. John dismissed the possibility of another temporal specialist having been sent to the same quantum point. As a matter of policy, the CTI council avoided authorizing overlapping tripback missions. In those rare situations when multiple specialists had been sent to the same place and time, the CTI council had coordinated both specialist's efforts.

John had no answers, but he was confident of one thing. If he had mentioned the signal at his debriefing, the CTI council would have subjected his assignor to months of investigations and would likely have ordered his datstem removed for examination.

He entered his apartment now and shut the pressure door, sealing it behind him. In keeping with Japanese traditions prevalent on the station, John removed his shoes and left them on the recessed genkan's receptacle. The shoes were immediately pulled inside the machine to be cleaned, freshened, and then stored until requested.

"Shower," John spoke aloud to the habitat's controller. "Hot... and keep the humidity down." From the adjoining room, he could hear the hygiene cylinder deploying from its recessed compartment in the wall as the atmospheric processors simultaneously engaged.

"Confirmed. Shower, hot. Humidity, nominal, and maintaining." The controller acknowledged its instructions promptly and then reported temperature and pressure status inside the sealed apartment.

The control unit was the best; an upgrade John had installed when he had acquired the apartment. By Earth standards, his home was small but well-equipped. He had come to realize he did not need space, but he did value comfort and efficiency.

"Switch controller to datstem," John said.

"Confirmed. Datstem is now controlling."

"Engage datstem's holographic interface."

"Confirmed. Holographic interface engaged."

The figure of a grey-haired man suddenly appeared, a holographic projection standing attentively in the center of the room. John had configured Fouray's holographic appearance to resemble an aging manservant, a representation of the classic 19th-century house butler. The historical connotations had always amused him, and the persona of a wise confidant fit with John's innate trust of his embedded AI device.

John spoke directly to the hologram now, "How certain are you that the QRB signal was not naturally occurring?"

The holographic representation that was Fouray shook its head as it walked towards the food station. "The signal was broadcasting within the standard range for a datstem device," it said, projecting its voice from one of the small audio ports inside the apartment walls. "It was also transmitting with nominal encryption. A naturally occurring QRB signal does not

33

employ encryption. The probability of it being a naturally-occurring signal is 00.00 percent." Fouray paused then, appearing to glance at the food station's data log. "Your potassium levels have been depressed recently. Shall I make a selection for you?"

John nodded his head and stepped into the connecting room. As he showered, he considered other possibilities for the signal. He touched the habitat's control interface inside the semi-transparent hygiene cylinder.

"Could it have been a quantum reflection... could you have been detecting your QRB signal on some form of quantum delay?"

In the next room, the flash-frozen entrée Fouray had selected was heating rapidly within the wall station. Fouray turned and spoke towards the open doorway as a mechanical table containing the steaming dish now extruded from the wall.

"Not possible," Fouray's voice was relayed through the hygiene cylinder's audio port. "Quantum reflection of a QRB signal can only occur when there has been significant miscalibration of an MTY's singularity. Such a serious miscalibration would have been immediately detected when your MTY was docked on the collider floor in Hampton. The probability of it being a quantum reflection is 00.00 percent."

John turned off the shower and activated the unit's evaporation cycle, drying in the warm swirling air. After a minute, he turned the cycle off and stepped out. The cylinder retracted into the habitat wall and began its sanitation and water reclamation cycle.

John dressed in silence, contemplating alternatives. He smelled chicken and mushrooms in the other room and became aware of his appetite. It had been a troubling day.

As he sat down to eat his meal, Fouray's holographic persona sat across the table and appeared to be studying him.

John glanced up and said, "So, it was a real QRB signal and not a reflection."

Fouray nodded, "Correct."

John thought for a moment, then frowned. "Assuming the CTI council didn't send another specialist to the same time and place without informing RJCom, and assuming it wasn't some rogue SDU wandering around Baltimore in 2017, then it must have been someone already there... someone with a datstem or a QRB-equipped device."

Fouray remained silent, watching its host.

John pushed aside his plate, no longer hungry. He looked up at the hologram.

"Theresa Williams?"

Fouray nodded slowly. "Probability... 86.24 percent."

Chapter 3

*"The only thing new in the world
is the history you don't know.
~ Harry S. Truman
33rd President of the United States
(1884 – 1972 AD)*

J ohn woke suddenly. The apartment's controller was
generating an audible alert. He was momentarily confused
as he typically did not schedule a wake alert on the
weekend.

"Alert off," John said, sitting up.

Fouray's voice immediately intruded inside his head, "I
triggered the alert to wake you. There's been an event in
Texas."

John shook his head and rubbed his face.

"Event?"

A projected holographic display appeared above the foot
of the bed. A woman in a bright yellow hazmat suit was
standing in front of a military barrier surrounded by several
hovering news drones. Behind her, the sky was thick with black
smoke. In the distance, parked emergency transports and
military personnel in radiation gear were also visible. The
audio began mid-sentence.

"...detonated at 03:22 AM local time. From what NAFS
Ground Forces drones have determined, the explosion seems to
have occurred inside the city of Burnet, Texas. More than 300

autonomous ambulatory units have already arrived from 140 surrounding cities and neighboring states and are assembling nearby, waiting for authorization to enter the area to search for survivors. Nuclear emergency response teams are transiting in from around the world."

"What happened?" John asked, now fully awake.

"A nuclear device of some kind detonated in Burnet, Texas," Fouray responded.

John got out of bed and ordered the room configured for "day mode". The large futon mattress and bedding slid up into the wall to be freshened. At the same time, the bed frame morphed into its day configuration as the food station in the adjoining room's wall initialized to prepare breakfast.

"Are you tied into the ECRN network?" John asked.

"Of course."

"Switch over."

A mosaic of hundreds of scrolling channels feeding into the AISMPE-controlled colonial communications net replaced the visual display. A sizable percentage of the channels appeared to be covering the event. The audio coming from the multi-display was jumbled and overlapping.

"Audio off. Monitor mode," John said. "Scan for cause, damage assessment, and any RJCom communications or government statements."

The jumbled audio abruptly terminated, and a "Monitoring" notice began to blink on the lower center of the holographic display.

Fouray's voice now began a precise and deliberate recitation over the apartment's audio system, reporting pertinent reports gleaned from the vast ECRN network.

"ECRN 1.2044.203.4.22… Austin Water Services reports one of their engineers working near Georgetown witnessed the explosion and scanned it with their datstem. The engineer described the explosion as 'mushroom-shaped'."

John began to dress, listening to the information as it arrived.

"ECRN 1.2044.142.11.9… The Texas Transit Authority reports EPM singularities at the Killeen-Fort Hood and Austin-Bergstrom stations were disrupted for several minutes following the blast, suggesting the explosion was nuclear-based."

"ECRN 1.42.230.5.12… An NAFS armed forces spokesman is reporting military drones have confirmed the blast was nuclear and estimated to be 50 kilotons in size. Preliminary radiological isotope analysis indicates it was derived from a B-61 Mod-12 warhead; likely a relic from the American Conflict."

"ECRN 1.2072.97.22.97…"

"Hold a moment," John interrupted the data flow, "what was that about the Conflict?"

"Switching to ECRN 1.42.230.5.12. NAFS news conference in progress."

The projection ceased its mosaic display. A middle-aged man in an NAFS Ground Forces Colonel's uniform now appeared, standing behind a transparent podium speaking to a room full of media personnel. News microdrones hovered thick around him like a swarm of black beetles. The colonel's voice came through the apartment speakers, halting and strained.

"We can't authorize the ambulatory units inside the 1.64-kilometer detonation zone. They aren't hardened against the radiation. Besides, from what we can tell from our RAD drones, there isn't anyone alive inside the detonation zone."

As a flurry of angry questions erupted from the room, the colonel hastily added, "The AA units are retrieving survivors outside of the detonation zone."

"Colonel," a woman in the room wearing a Mexican consular office badge on her shirt now spoke. "Have you detected any vaporized cesium?"

The colonel waved his hand, "No, we've detected no cesium residue."

The woman pressed with another question, "Is that why you believe this was a relic UCF device instead of an unexploded ISSA warhead?"

The colonel nodded. "The yield and isotope signature match the type of warheads used by both sides during the American Conflict. The lack of any vaporized cesium-137, however, suggests it was not an unexploded ISSA warhead left over from the 2042 holocaust. Also, its location in mid-Texas and the blast crater reported by the RAD drones suggest it was a mine converted from a UCF warhead. UCF forces probably buried it as they were retreating to the Gulf."

One of the hovering drones flashed a question, and when the colonel pointed to the device, a French voice emerged, captioned into English on the ECRN display, "What are the radiation levels inside of the blast zone at this time?"

The colonel glanced at his heads-up display before responding. "Our RAD drones are reporting 822 rems inside the perimeter now," he said. "That's down from the 3200 rems we were detecting after the blast, but as I mentioned earlier, our main concern is to rescue survivors outside the detonation zone and organize evacuations ahead of the fallout."

"Fallout?" John queried.

Fouray retrieved a map of Texas and projected it next to the ECRN display. A long thin swath of yellow, representing the radioactive fallout, overlaid the map. The yellow indicator originated from Burnet and proceeded northeast over Killeen, advancing slowly as a chronometer on the map projected forward. According to the map chronometer, the fallout would reach Waco in approximately 3 hours. Fouray added, "WeatherNet is providing the fallout projections based on current wind patterns."

At that moment, the apartment's controller signaled an incoming message received from RJCom. John terminated the holographic displays and activated the control pad. The message was a recall of all RJCom personnel assigned to the research and temporal groups in Holman, Dubina, San Tibor, and Weimar, as well as a general recall of all archival and research staff assigned to the Houston research and archives facility. A conference was scheduled for 7:00 AM at the archive building in Houston, approximately 3 hours from now.

John ate quickly as Fouray continued to monitor the various communication networks. Initial death tolls were coming in now and were frankly shocking. At least 24,000 people were known to have been killed, but the number was projected to rise. When John left for the quadrant's EPM station, the death toll had already risen to 31,244.

The chronometer on the Fujioka Building read 8:14 PM when John entered the EPM station. Due to the time zone difference between Texas and Hōfu Station, John's schedule was reversed from most of his fellow residents. When he was waking and preparing to transit out to work, most of the station's inhabitants were preparing for their evening. Doing some swift mental calculation, John realized it was 6:14 AM Texas local time. He needed to hurry. He proceeded directly to the express EPM stations.

Beneath the dim light of the park's hanging lanterns, several couples could be seen walking hand-in-hand through the trees. Overhead, the glass geodesic dome was a magnificent tapestry of stars behind an overly-large moon. John immediately regretted being called away. On a night like this, he would have made his way to the Equinox district in Quadrant 3. Several of his favorite restaurants were there, along with some of the best clubs. Several friends would have likely joined him, and perhaps they would have introduced him to someone interesting.

"目的地はどこですか" The attendant SDU queried John for his destination. Reluctantly, John turned his attention from the stars to the waiting SDU, an older FANUC Series-5.

"Rengel-Jiang QCom, Research and Archives Building 2, in Houston, Texas."

The SDU's white head now turned to face John. The FANUC Series 5 was one of the first SDUs to be manufactured with emotive simulators. The unit's brow furrowed in simulated concern. "Transitioning to an address other than an approved EPM station," it said, "may result in significant fees and is subject to AISMPE rules governing the use of scattering technologies. Do you understand?"

"Yes."

The unit nodded. "Rengel-Jiang QCom, Research and

41

Archives Building number 2 located in Houston, Texas...
Confirmed. 1,452 IMUs."

"Fine," John said. He wasn't concerned about the fee. With the mandatory recall, he would be reimbursed for any transit expense.

With that, the platform hummed to life as its fusion generator engaged. The SDU spoke again, reporting no scattering field at the destination location. A shimmering ultraviolet-framed void now appeared within the EPM's circular frame.

"Calibration complete. You may proceed."

Chapter 4

A s John had expected, the singularity had been calibrated to the large grass-filled mall in front of the RJCom archive building in Houston. Singularities opened and vanished around him now as he walked towards the building's central courtyard. It looks like everyone was taking the express, he mused.

John spotted his friend, Sai Patel, the Director of Archival Administration, standing in front of the plaza watching the arrivals. Patel saw him and approached swiftly, waving.

"Any speculation about the meeting?" the small Indian man asked, matching John's pace as they ascended the steps to the courtyard level.

"I speculate that you're going to be very busy for the next few days."

Patel nodded solemnly.

As they walked together across the plaza towards the building's external lift tubes, John glanced at his friend and grinned.

"Did you transit in from Dallas or Mumbai?"

Patel looked up quickly and then laughed.

John returned the laugh, nodding, "Mumbai then!"

Patel had been courting a girl from that large Indian city for more than two years but had not been able to get her to commit to a wedding date. John had enjoyed teasing his friend about it, assuring him that she would quickly capitulate if he would submit a reassignment marker out of archives. "She just doesn't want to marry a librarian," he teased.

The truth was, Patel was a brilliant archivist, one of perhaps only a handful of people in the world capable of operating RJCom's vast array of data storage, its fleet of SDUs, and it's powerful Primary AI. The man held no less than six secondary certs in archival administration, with four of the certs boasting advanced citations.

They had been friends for nearly 20 years since John's marker was first acquired by RJCom as a research associate. The two men shared a love for history, though Patel's expertise with the archival systems far exceeded John's. Patel had been promoted to Director of Archival Administration the same year that John had advanced to the temporal specialist group at San Tibor.

Each of the world's three MTY manufacturers, Rengel-Jiang QCom, Reynolds-Hampshire, and Blosch-Nishikawa maintained their separate archive facilities. The amount of information stored within these facilities rivaled or even exceeded those of the world's largest governments. More than just vast data storage facilities, the three companies employed some of the most sophisticated SDUs ever manufactured, as well as the world's most powerful quantum analytic processors, or AI units.

As they ascended together in the lift, it occurred to John that Patel might be able to assist him with his Baltimore problem. At a minimum, as director of the archive department, Patel would have access to the CTI and company tripback files regarding Theresa Williams's unexplained loss.

John put aside the thought as the lift reached the conference floor. In all the years he had worked for RJCom, he couldn't recall a similar situation where all of the company's research, temporal, and archival personnel had been summoned to the same meeting.

The conference room was filled. In addition to RJCom personnel, several NAFS military personnel were also present. Judging by the number of news drones hovering above the crowd, a considerable number of attendees were affiliated with news networks.

After several minutes, the conversation abruptly died down as an older man took the podium. It was Norman Gao, Executive Director of Operations at RJCom. John knew his reputation well. In his early years, Gao had practically built the research and archives divisions for the company. A uniformed NAFS officer and another man accompanied Gao.

"Welcome," Gao began. "As I'm certain you've all scanned, there was a tragedy this morning in Burnet, Texas." The man cleared his throat and then continued. "From what we know, a construction crew excavating the foundation for an office facility inside Burnet detonated a UCF nuclear mine left over from the American Conflict of more than 100 years ago. The mine had been proximity masked, so the construction crew had not detected it." The elderly man glanced at a holo-display before adding, "At this time, at least 37,000 people are

45

confirmed to have been killed."

A swell of shocked whispering briefly interrupted the speaker, who paused, waiting for the conversation to subside.

"That number is likely to increase," Gao continued. "Sadly, that number also includes 18 RJCom personnel who resided in Burnet." He cleared his throat again and then turned, gesturing to the men standing by his side.

"This is Texas Lieutenant Governor David Scott and Major Thomas of NAFS Nuclear Emergency Response. Following the tragedy this morning, the State of Texas issued a formal request to the NAFS Ground Forces Headquarters in Georgia, for all records relating to any nuclear mines deployed during the American Conflict. Unfortunately, records from that conflict are incomplete on the subject. I will turn the floor over to Major Thomas to explain."

Gao stepped aside and gestured for the uniformed officer to speak.

Major Thomas' voice was strong and clear. "As many of you undoubtedly learned in your primary education, the American Conflict was a very short, though extremely violent conflict, fought within the geographic boundaries of the former United States, northern Mexico, and eastern Canada. Without going into too much detail, it suffices to say that, in late 2041, United Capital Forces were losing. Mexico had joined the conflict on the side of the socialist armies, forcing the UCF into what historians now call the Gulf Retreat." The major shifted his feet uncomfortably and cleared his throat before continuing.

"During the retreat, UCF forces were ordered to commence delaying actions to slow down the advancing socialist armies. From the records preserved in the NAFS archives, we know that UCF special service units began burying nuclear mines ahead of the approaching ISSA forces at key strategic crossroads throughout central Texas. Unfortunately, military records available to us do not record where the mines were buried."

John immediately saw where this was going, and his heart quickened, listening intently.

A thin man with a Llano Power Company badge on his jumpsuit now stood and addressed the Major. "Major... I'm Paul Welton, Llano Power Company Director of Operations. Why would UCF forces have buried a nuclear mine inside one of their cities?"

The major shook his head, "When the mine was deployed, Burnet wasn't a major city. It had barely 8,000 inhabitants back in 2041. It was little more than a modest-sized town. It appears the mine had been placed far outside of the borders of the town at that time, on the old Texas transway 29, approximately 3 kilometers east of Lake Buchanan. That would have been a likely place to deploy such a device, as any socialist ground forces would have had to take that route to get around the lake. Unfortunately, that's right in the middle of present-day Burnet."

Welton nodded and sat down.

The officer now passed the podium to Lt. Governor Scott.

"Thank you, Major Thomas," Scott began. "This morning, I spoke with Governor Fuller. She extends her sincere condolences to those affected by this tragedy. The governor has canceled her invitation to speak at the Mars Colonial Assembly and will be returning home as soon as arrangements can be

47

made with the Mars Fast Transit Network, which is scheduled to come back into orbital alignment in 37 days."

"Acting under the governor's authority in her absence, and at her specific request, the State of Texas this morning filed a formal funding request with the NAFS to research, locate, and ultimately remove any remaining nuclear mines that may exist within the state." The man stepped aside as Director Gao re-approached the podium.

"Thank you, Lt. Governor Scott... Major Thomas." Addressing his attention to those in the conference room, Director Gao spoke now with conviction. "RJCom has been given the assignment of researching and determining the location of these forgotten mines. As you all know, RJCom researchers are arguably the best in the world."

John noted Patel's chest swelling with pride as the small man nodded in agreement.

"Once their locations have been identified," Dao continued, "NAFS Nuclear Emergency Response has assured me they will be able to safely remove these instruments of death and destruction from our soil, preventing any future reoccurrences of the Burnet tragedy."

The conference room erupted in applause. After a few moments, the director raised his hand for quiet.

"All archival and research personnel will remain in Houston today for a planning meeting at 10:30 AM. We'll hold that meeting at..." Gao paused now, consulting his datstem before he continued. "...At conference room four on the archival floor in this building. The San Tibor and Holman temporal personnel may resume their normal schedules but are directed to remain within transition range of Houston and to maintain active communication links until further notice. Thank you."

With this, the conference concluded.

As he rose from his seat, John spoke to Patel.

"Well… no returning to Mumbai today."

"No." Patel frowned for a moment, then looked up, "What about you? Are you going to keep your feet on the ground or jump back to your orbiting hamster cage?"

John smiled, "I'm going to transit back. It's the weekend, remember? Besides, it's only 10:00 PM at the station. Things get lively in the evenings there."

The friends shook hands, and John walked briskly out of the conference room towards the lift tubes. If he hurried, he would be able to take one of the company's transports before they were all dispatched. While the lift rose towards the transport deck, John's mind raced with possibilities. If archives could not discover where the mines had been buried, the CTI council would likely authorize a tripback to recover the information. John was less than enthusiastic at the thought of making a tripback into a war zone, but he could not think of any other way to retrieve such information.

"That's why you don't work for archives," Fouray's voice intruded on his thoughts. "They'll find a way that does not involve transiting behind enemy lines."

When he arrived at the roof, John was deflated. Several people were already waiting for the limited available transports. John was resigning himself to a long wait when he heard someone call his name. It was Viktor Borodin, a temporal specialist from the Holman group. The burly man was opening the seal on one of the capsules as he waved to John.

"Clifton!... you transit out?"

John nodded, approaching the capsule "Yes… you too?"

The man nodded. "Come," he said. "We go to EPM station. These others do not."

As the capsule lifted the two men from the deck of the building, Borodin directed the unit towards the city's nearest EPM transit station.

Borodin had joined the Holman group after the loss of Theresa Williams in 2137, but John had not had many opportunities to speak with him. The Holman group supported RJCom's interests in Europe and the Middle East, while the San Tibor group concentrated on the Americas and Asia. John had heard that Borodin's assignment marker had been acquired as part of a rare trade agreement with Blosch-Nishikawa.

"You live on Hōfu Station, yes?" the man asked, his Georgian/Russian accent thick in the confined capsule.

"Yes," John answered.

The large man smiled, "I hear it is lively there, yes?"

John stared for a moment, startled at hearing his parting words to Patel repeated. Borodin's attention, however, was focused on the city below.

"Yes," John answered, "lively."

Chapter 5

When the final death toll was released, more than 42,000 people were confirmed to have been killed, either as a direct result of the detonation or from exposure to high levels of radiation in the first hours after the explosion.

Except for nearby Killeen, NAFS military units had performed magnificently, evacuating cities and towns ahead of the radiation fallout.

1,486 people in Killeen who had not escaped the fallout in time later died from radiation exposure. An estimated 3,200 others were still being treated for exposure but were expected to survive.

Over the months that followed, support for those communities most affected by the explosion had been remarkable. Perhaps mindful of how devastating that early conflict had been, international aid flowed into the NAFS from sympathetic nations. Archives around the world also reported sharp increases in requests for access to American Conflict historical files. Documentaries and dramatic presentations about the war also flooded ECRN and local communication channels.

When the radiation levels had sufficiently subsided, NAFS Nuclear Emergency Response personnel were able to make a more thorough examination of the detonation site. The warhead, as predicted, was determined to have been a UCF nuclear mine, buried and forgotten when UCF ground forces had retreated to the Gulf in December 2041.

Despite an exhausting search of military archives, no records were found describing where the retreating UCF had deployed its mines. In the chaos and confusion that had characterized the final days of that conflict and the nuclear holocaust that had followed, it appears that the mines had simply been forgotten.

What was known was gleaned from limited military records. A UCF Special Services Unit in Austin had been tasked with converting B-61 Mod 12 nuclear warheads into proximity-masked sub-surface mines. Upon receiving orders to commence delaying actions at the beginning of the Gulf Retreat, the mines had been hastily deployed. Based on the number of warheads known to have been consigned to the Austin unit, and taking into account the number of mines that had been detonated during the conflict, NAFS military analysts estimated as many as 14 un-detonated mines could remain buried throughout the region.

With that flat acknowledgment, fear and hesitation gripped the state, with hundreds of construction projects immediately suspended or canceled. Tourism dramatically declined, and civilian populations began evacuating from regions known to have been in the historical path of the invading ISSA armies.

After four months, RJCom archivists announced a breakthrough. A UCF soldier named Barrett, they reported, had recorded his conflict service experiences in his journal. That journal had been scanned and archived in 2091 as part of a "Conflict Veteran's Remembrance Project", initiated on the 50th anniversary of the beginning of the conflict. Within his journal, Barrett recorded he had buried "ComHQ strategic records" on his "family's property in Austin" at the commencement of the Gulf Retreat.

Archival SDUs were able to match Barrett to one Sgt Ira Barrett (2019 ~ 2094), assigned to the UCF Special Services Unit operating out of Austin in 2041. Archival SDUs reported a high probability that the strategic records buried by Barrett included the unit's records documenting the locations of the hidden mines.

RJCom's Research and Archives groups spent considerable time and effort attempting to locate Barrett's "family property" in Austin without success. Tax and genealogical records from the era established several siblings living in the Austin area, but their addresses proved to be temporarily-occupied rental properties, unlikely locations at which to bury strategic military records.

Ultimately, after two months of searching, the research and archive teams were forced to admit defeat. To find Barrett's family's property, they concluded, would require an examination of contemporary records. Accordingly, the NAFS submitted a request to the CTI council in Geneva, to authorize a tripback to Austin between 2010 and 2020.

When John's assignment marker had first been acquired

by RJCom years ago, he had been tasked as a research associate. Due to this prior research experience, John had been asked to assist the present research teams in their efforts. Frequenting the archive building almost daily, John had used this opportunity to continue his research into Theresa Williams' disappearance. What he had discovered was troubling.

Williams' tripback file had been sealed, and he could find no other information related to either the purpose of her mission or the circumstances surrounding her loss.

He had met Williams only once, shortly after he had been advanced to the Temporal Specialist Group at San Tibor. She had greeted him briefly at a company conference and welcomed him to the San Tibor group. She had been preparing for her tripback at that time, and John did not speak with her again as she had transited out the following week.

Now that things had quieted down with the archive and research efforts, John decided to solicit help from Patel. He found his friend in the archive building's cafeteria, sipping tea and looking disheveled.

"Sai Patel," John said, smiling. "Master of the Secret Scrolls! Good job on that Barrett discovery. How did you find it?"

"Thank you," Patel said, motioning for John to sit. "We almost didn't. The original records had been filed but not opti-scanned or indexed. We'd have missed them entirely except one of the SDUs had scanned a reference to that veteran's remembrance project from a 2090 news report."

Patel sat back and stretched his arms. "Recovering the actual files was brutal!" he sighed. "Not only had the remembrance project files not been opti-scanned or indexed, but the files had been archived using the SJ3 archival algorithm. We had to practically decrypt each file to get the pages ready for scanning."

"Are you going to take some time off now?" John asked.

"Perhaps."

"Heading back to Mumbai for more negotiations?" John asked, grinning.

His friend waved his hand, "No need. Saanvi has consented to marry. She will be moving to Dallas next month."

John was thrilled and clapped his friend on the arm. "That's great!" he exclaimed. Then, feigning dismay, he added, "But will you have enough room in your home for the goats?"

Patel pushed his arm aside, laughing. "No," he chuckled, "No dowry!"

"You're a forward-thinking man."

A cafeteria SDU brought Patel a new cup of tea and asked John if he would have anything. John dismissed it away with a wave.

"Look, Sai... I need your help with something."

"Oh?"

"Yes." John continued. "I'm trying to find out what happened to Theresa Williams."

Patel's eyebrows rose above the edge of his cup. "Williams?" he asked, "the specialist who was lost in 37?"

"Yes."

Patel put the cup down. "Is this official or personal?"

John looked at his friend, hesitating.

"Personal."

Patel nodded, "What are you trying to find out? What specifically?" He was all archivist now.

John was relieved.

"To tell you the truth, I'm not sure," he said, frustrated with the lack of available information. "Her file was sealed, and…"

Patel sat up. "Her file was sealed? Are you certain?"

"Yes," John responded, noting the surprise in the archivist's face. "Why? Is that significant?"

Patel frowned, "A tripback file can only be sealed by order of the CTI council."

John nodded, "Ok."

Patel shook his head, "You don't understand. Sealing a tripback file can only be ordered by the CTI council, but the actual sealing of the file is performed by archival administration."

John was confused. "You're archival administration!"

Patel nodded, still frowning, "Precisely. But I did not seal Williams' file, nor am I aware of any request from the CTI council to seal her file."

From the far end of the cafeteria, an archival SDU now entered the room and approached the two men. The unit had been waiting outside the cafeteria and Patel had summoned it with his datstem.

Stopping in front of their table, the tall, slender SDU turned and spoke, "Yes Director Patel? How may I be of assistance?"

"Query… File status… last tripback file for San Tibor temporal specialist Theresa Williams. Authorization Patel… 104… FG… R6."

A blue scanning line briefly crossed Patel's face as the archival SDU confirmed his biometrics and access code.

"Query confirmed. Processing. File status... Sealed."

"By whose order?" the small man's face took on a look of indignation.

Curiously, the SDU did not immediately respond. After a strange pause, it replied, "I'm sorry, Director Patel. That information is not available."

Patel's face now registered surprise.

"What?"

The SDU repeated, "I'm sorry, Director Patel. That information is not available."

Patel stood, mumbling and agitated. "I'll find out what I can John... Not proper. Not proper at all." Without waiting for a response, the Director of Archival Administration strode purposefully out of the room, the archival SDU following.

Three hours later, Sai Patel sat alone in front of RJCom's Primary AI, a mote dwarfed by the massive quantum-controlled intelligence, the 2nd most powerful automaton in the world. A sea of mass data storage banks filled the cavernous hall surrounding the towering unit, monuments erected by a civilization consumed with a desire for knowledge.

Patel was a creature truly born from that civilization. He, too, was imbued with an insatiable desire to know. As John had reported, the file had been sealed. What was troubling Patel, however, was the method used to seal the file. He did not recognize the locking signature. It was not his, nor did it match the format of any RJCom locking signature. He had tasked one of the SDUs to begin a regression search of similar algorithmic signatures in the hopes the owner might be discovered. So far, nothing had been found. As a holy man might inquire of his deity, Patel carefully considered his questions before voicing them aloud to that formidable intelligence.

"Could the CTI council have sealed the file without notifying RJCom administration?" he asked.

"No, Director Patel." The primary AI's voice resonated in the cavernous hall, ominous and deep. "The application of a locking signature requires physical access to the file being locked. No CTI council representative has been granted physical access to RJCom's archive facility since 2132. Further, the fact that the locking signature lacks an identity code implies the person who sealed the file also had access to the hardened data core. An identity code is automatically logged within the data core when a file is accessed, but no identity code can be found corresponding with the date the file in question was sealed. The identity code was erased by someone with access to the hardened data core."

Patel accepted this statement with only an imperceptible nod, lost in thought.

"Who has access to both RJCom's archive and the hardened data core?" he asked.

"RJCom senior administrators, archival administration personnel, level 4 maintenance technicians, research personnel, temporal specialists, and all archival SDUs."

Patel shook his head. By that list alone, no less than 370 individuals had access to both systems, not including the hundreds of SDUs.

"You're working late Director."

Patel jumped, startled. Viktor Borodin stood behind him, smiling. The large man was carrying what appeared to be a deactivated maintenance drone in his arms.

Patel nodded and tried to regain his composure. "Yes,"

he said, "It's been a very busy time."

Borodin nodded and casually stepped forward, glancing at Patel's interface, "But you are not working on the Burnet disaster, I think?" Borodin asked, smiling, his Russian/Georgian accent difficult for Patel to follow.

Patel switched off the holo-interface and stood to leave. "No..." he said. "I'm working on... another project."

"Ah. Yes. Another project." Borodin nodded, "I, too, am working on another project." Shaking the inert drone in his arms, the large man grinned. "Before I was temporal specialist, I was equipment technician at Blosch Fusion. I still fix for hobby but always remember most important job is now temporal specialist."

Patel was exhausted and anxious to leave. "That's commendable," he said.

Borodin grinned and continued, "I think maybe I spend too much time on my hobby. One must not be distracted by unimportant things, eh?"

Patel looked up, not sure what to say.

Borodin sighed, patting the inactive drone. "Is easy to be distracted by unimportant things. But when we are distracted, we make mistake, and with mistake comes accident, eh Director?"

Patel nodded.

"Have good evening Director."

Borodin turned and walked away.

Chapter 6

John received word four days later that his marker had been selected for the Austin tripback. Fouray scanned the incoming announcement as John was engaged inside the gymnasium on the third floor of the Temporal Administration building, completing an intense "aiki-hung-ga" session with one of the gymnasium's sparring SDUs.

Daitō-ryū aiki-jūjutsu was a Japanese martial art that had become popular in the early 20th century under the direction of Takeda Sōkaku, the founder of the "Great Eastern School". Like other forms of jujutsu, it emphasized throwing techniques and joint manipulations to effectively subdue or injure an opponent. Of particular importance was the timing of a defensive technique, to neutralize an attack's effectiveness by redirecting the force of the attacker's movements against himself.

When combined with the southern Chinese shaolin-styled hung-ga, with its deep low stances and strong bridge-hand striking techniques, an adept found themselves in possession of both strong defensive techniques as well as lethal offensive skills.

The blending of Japanese daitō-ryū aiki-jūjutsu with Chinese hung-ga had resulted in one of the world's most lethal martial arts. The sport had been increasing in popularity for more than 70 years, ever since its demonstration at the Sino-Nippon Trade Alliance Fair in 2079. Both the Chinese and Japanese governments had formally adopted aiki-hung-ga for their military's unarmed combat training and civilian enthusiasm for the sport had grown dramatically for more than 70 years.

John was recognized as a master, having studied aiki-hung-ga diligently since his childhood when he had been introduced to the sport by an uncle, an early enthusiast. John had been immediately drawn to its discipline and its graceful form.

As an infant, John's parents had provided him with the very best pedo-genomic care. A minor defect in John's genetics that would have made him susceptible to arthritis later in life had been corrected shortly after birth. After considerable humorous discussions between his mother and father regarding the attractiveness of such a feature, a familial predisposition for male pattern baldness had also been eliminated.

Later, after completing the standard AGA "arte-genomic assessment" upon enrolling in primary school, John's parents had carefully chosen a genomic enhancement regimen to maximize their son's innate psycho-physical skills. The customized genomics they selected had provided John as an adult with what was commonly referred to as a 'gymnast physique'; a slim, muscular build.

Even as a young child, John's parents had taken special notice of their son's athletic predisposition. Upon the urging of John's uncle, and after consulting with a genetic counselor, John's genomic regimen had been supplemented when he was in primary school to incorporate exceptional sinew and muscular strength, enhanced reflexes, and extraordinary flexibility.

John had made great use of these enhanced abilities to pursue his beloved sport. He had competed in state and regional aiki-hung-ga competitions during both primary and secondary school, winning the NAFS Aiki-Hung-Ga Championship title when he was only 17; the youngest national champion on record for the sport. The following year, at age 18, he had achieved a very respectable third-place ranking at the International Aiki-Hung-Ga Master's Competition in Tokyo.

Though retired now from title competition, John had maintained his skills through the years, dedicating himself to improving his technique and teaching the sport to others. He had personally configured the RJCom gymnasium SDUs to what he considered to be an acceptable sparring standard and he made a point of honing his technique several days each week, usually observed by fans, students, or instructors. He also taught a master-level class on alternating weekends on Hōfu Station.

The black FANUC-series SDU that now faced John across the mat had been specially equipped for sparring, with enhanced servos and reinforced CG-tendons to simulate human agility and speed, and a glistening black synthetic epidermal layer to mimic human skin and muscle tone; necessary to reduce contact injuries when sparring against an automaton.

The SDU lunged, striking out with its hand towards John's thorax. John quickly pivoted, allowing the unit to continue forward, throwing itself off-balance. As it tumbled forward, John applied an 'o-soto sui pou' bridge-hand strike to a shock point sensor at the back of the SDU's synthetic neck.

"Point 10," the SDU announced, standing back up and bowing. "The match is yours."

John returned the ceremonial bow and then stepped off the mat. A small group who had gathered to watch the match now began clapping. John ignored his admirers and walked towards the hygiene room.

With the match now over, Fouray took this opportunity to inform John about his marker selection. The message came as something of a shock. John was not surprised to have been selected, just surprised the CTI council had acted so swiftly. Fouray had predicted a better than 82% probability that John's marker would be selected, but it was unusual for the CTI council to approve a tripback request so quickly. Undoubtedly the council was feeling pressured to act in the wake of the Burnet disaster.

Fouray now briefed him on his new schedule. "You have a preliminary briefing scheduled for tomorrow at 08:30 AM, followed by the mandatory physical examination on Friday in Houston at 1:00 PM."

John shook his head.

"Policy." Fouray's flat statement ended that old argument before it could begin.

Later, after grabbing a bite to eat, John took one of the lifts up to the administration floor. As a senior specialist, John had rated an executive office for the past 7 years. When he entered his office, the office controller initialized a holographic interface above his data-station and began scrolling through the day's itinerary. As he sat down in a chair, a muscle in John's back spasmed from his recent workout. He closed his eyes and stretched for a moment while Fouray continued his tripback report.

"The CTI council's office of temporal affairs has calculated the optimum departure date as April 4th."

"Four months," John mused. "I would transit from inside Austin I presume?"

"That information has not yet been added to the approved tripback file, but Austin would be the probable departure location."

"Put the file up please," John requested, sitting back up and opening his eyes.

Immediately, the projected holo-interface flashed the official CTI council seal, which faded to reveal the tripback parameters as currently approved by the council. John scanned through the familiar sections, moving through the complex file effortlessly with a swipe of his fingers against the translucent data station.

"So, I'm to scan power company records," he asked, "not land records?"

Fouray consulted the relevant council notes before responding.

"After a review of the reports filed by RJCom's archive and research units, the CTI council feels the greatest probability of locating Barrett's family property exists in a review of contemporary power utility records."

64

"Why?"

"The CTI council did not explain its reasoning."

"Speculate?"

Fouray paused imperceptibly, a pattern that John recognized as the embedded unit consulting its vast archival database and correlating the queried information.

"Land records at the time often did not reflect the actual tenants of the property. Land was frequently leased or rented by third parties for agricultural, development, or recreational purposes. Although the land owner's name would have been recorded in official property records, the physical tenants of the property were typically required to assign the utility accounts into their own names."

"Given the archive group's inability to locate any property records in the name of Barrett's family, speculation has been raised that his family might be tenants, not the actual property owners. It is also possible that the land records in our present archives are incomplete or inaccurate. In either event, the power utility company would likely contain a record of the actual parties occupying the land, as well as any property addresses for which they were making utility payments."

"Very well," John nodded, "so I am to scan power utility records. I assume this will be a complete transfer, not a filtered search?"

"Yes," Fouray answered, "all available records are to be captured for later analysis."

"Simple enough," John thought.

A blinking message indicator on his desk now attracted John's attention. When he touched the flashing light, the display prompted him to accept an incoming datstem-isolated signal. A datstem-isolated signal established an encrypted link between a sender and a receiver's embedded datstems. It was a rare security procedure employed when communicating parties wished to keep their conversation from being monitored or recorded by others, including those who might be in the same room as the participants.

John entered his authorization code and waited as a blue scanning beam read his face's biometrics and connected the signal to his datstem. The connection verified, the holographic display was replaced with an image of Patel, sitting inside his home in Dallas. John recognized the room, having been a guest in Patel's home during the recent international cricket match between Team India and Australia's national team. Patel had been in an absolute rage when India had lost and had retreated to the small room, where John had found him later, steaming and plotting revenge against one of the umpires for a particularly questionable decision.

"John," the director began, not waiting to be greeted. John "heard" the voice inside his head rather than through the desk speakers; the result of the signal's isolation with his embedded datstem. Patel's mouth on the holographic interface did not move. Patel was transmitting exclusively through his datstem over the isolated connection. He must be very concerned about something, John realized.

"Something is wrong... something is very wrong," his friend's words echoed mechanically inside John's head. Patel's face was strained and John could not remember seeing his friend look so tired.

"What do you mean?" John spoke aloud, "were you..."

Patel waved his hand, exasperated, and his words

rushed into John's head, "Don't speak. Respond through your datstem only!"

John nodded, and mentally posed his question, "Were you able to unlock Williams' file?"

Patel's face became stone. "Impossible! The file is locked and no one can unlock it! I am the Director of Archival Administration and I cannot unlock one of my own archive files! Impossible!" He was clearly angry but then took a breath, calming himself.

"Look, that is not why I scanned you on an isolated signal."

"Oh?"

"No." The small man wiped his face and then continued, "Something is very wrong. You must be careful. You should assume your company communications are being monitored."

John frowned, "Why should I assume that?" he queried.

"Because mine are being monitored. I discovered an embedded program in my home controller that was monitoring all of my incoming and outgoing signals."

"A company security program perhaps..." John began but was interrupted by Patel's waving hand, urging him to mental silence.

"No. Just listen. It was not an RJCom program. It did not have an RJCom signature."

John frowned, but he did not respond, determined to let his friend continue.

"After I discovered the embedded program," the Director continued, "I made arrangements to have my home swept for monitoring devices. I called a company I know in Hyderabad. They provide close security services for CLH

Gravimetrics. My brother is one of the program directors at CLH and had told me about their scanning service provider. I made arrangements with them to send me one of their security SDUs to scan my home and my office in Houston. I told them RJCom Archival Administration was considering contracting with another close security vendor, and to send the SDU to perform a scanning demonstration."

John nodded, "And?"

Patel looked bleak as he removed a flat plastic case from his coat and held it up for John to see. John could not see what was inside the opaque container, but he could hear the rattle when Patel shook the container over the holo-interface.

"Four surveillance beads were found at my home. Two more were found inside my office in Houston. I also found one myself inside the archive hall, concealed within the Primary AI station I normally use!"

John nodded, experiencing a rush of apprehension as his eyes strayed to his own office's control monitor, a flat black panel on the opposing wall.

Patel returned the container to his coat pocket and shook his head. "Someone does not want us investigating Williams' tripback file. Someone outside of RJCom."

John did not respond, taking in what Patel had revealed.

Patel's voice inside his head now took on a cautious tone. "I did find out two pieces of information."

"What?"

"Williams did not transit out using an RJCom MTY device."

John wasn't sure he had heard Patel correctly. All temporal specialists exclusively utilized their assignor's MTY devices. The specialist might have their singularity calibrated anywhere in the world, but they always used their own assignor's equipment.

"How do you know?" he asked.

Patel smiled. "Being Director of Archival Administration has some privileges. I am one of the few people in the company who can perform an audit of our complete MTY inventory, for CTI compliance purposes."

John nodded, "That's correct. You have access to the MTY vault, the maintenance floor, and the active tripback file."

Patel went on, "There are 21 MTY units in the vault at this time. I touched each of the units myself and ran each of them through their diagnostic cycle. All were in good working order. I found 4 additional MTY devices on the maintenance floor. I verified they were there and put them all through a diagnostic cycle. They correctly reported their failures, and with those exceptions, they also checked out as being in good working order. We have no active tripbacks out at this time so we have no MTY devices outside of the company premises at this time."

"That's 25 units."

"Precisely," Patel nodded. "RJCom's inventory is 25 MTY devices. That hasn't changed for more than 20 years."

"Then whose MTY device did Williams use in 2137?"

"I don't know."

John considered this for a moment, then asked, "What was the second thing?"

"What?"

"You said you had discovered two pieces of information?"

69

"Ah!" Patel nodded. "Yes. I also discovered Williams' tripback location. She was transported to a departure point inside Baltimore."

At that announcement, a shiver ran down John's spine.

"Baltimore? How did you discover that?"

"The CTI council representative assigned to the tripback filed a report after returning from the transport."

John nodded. Of course. Every temporal specialist was accompanied to their transition point by both a CTI council representative and a company equipment technician who took custody of the MTY device upon the specialist's return.

Patel continued. "I called someone I know in Geneva who manages the council's records there, and I asked him, archivist to archivist, for a copy of the CTI representative's internal report. The CTI report states Williams was transported to a location inside of Baltimore where she transited out but failed to return. It cites a 'mechanical failure' as the official reason for her loss. The report says the singularity 'appeared to lose cohesion' after her transit and then vanished altogether. They summoned a scanning team from Geneva, who confirmed the singularity was no longer present at that quantum location."

"Lost cohesion…" John mused. "What the hell does that mean?"

Patel shook his head, "You'd know more about that than I. You're the temporal specialist."

When John did not respond, Patel continued, "There are a couple more things mentioned in the CTI report. Williams transited to Baltimore to scan files at the USA Office of Personnel Management in the year 2014 or 2015."

"Doesn't the file contain the exact temporal calibration date?"

"No. The date wasn't in the tripback file. All it mentions is a target *completion* date of July 2015."

"That's unbelievable!" John was stunned. "How can a tripback file not record the precise temporal calibration date?!"

"I don't know," Patel replied. "It should."

"Does the file state the reason for scanning the personnel files or why the task needed to be completed by July 2015?"

Patel shook his head, "No."

John found such an omission simply staggering.

Patel continued, "The report does mention one more fact that is particularly troubling."

"What is that?"

"It says a Blosch-Nishikawa equipment technician was in the transport with Williams and the CTI representative."

"Blosch-Nishikawa? Not an RJCom technician?" John felt a second shiver run down his back. He knew what Patel was going to say even before he said it.

His friend nodded. "The technician's name was Borodin."

After several moments, John took a deep breath and then asked, "So, what are you going to do?"

Patel stood up quickly and began pacing. "What can I do?! I don't know what is in Williams' file. I don't know why an RJCom temporal specialist was using someone else's MTY device, nor why a Blosch-Nishikawa representative was in the transport shuttle with our specialist. I don't know who sealed Williams' file nor how they sealed it. I don't know anything! I'm the Director of Archival Administration for the second-largest data archive in the world and I don't know anything!"

John could feel his friend's anger and frustration, filtered though it was through the datstem connection. It must be extremely difficult, given the kind of man he knew Patel to be.

Patel stopped and stood resolute. "What I *do* know is this. Someone other than myself has sealed an official CTI temporal tripback file. That constitutes a breach of the International Temporal Treaty of 2070. Tomorrow, I shall transit to Geneva and file a report with the CTI council."

John sat silent for a moment. Finally, he nodded and said, "I suppose that's the only thing you can do."

Patel sat down again, looking very tired. He lifted his hand to terminate the signal. Before disconnecting, though, he smiled and spoke aloud.

"I just heard your marker was selected for the Austin tripback."

"Yes."

Patel nodded, "Good luck, my friend."

Chapter 7

"All the world's a stage,
and all the men and women merely players.
They have their exits and their entrances;
And one man in his time plays many parts."
"As You Like It" - Act II, Scene VII
~ William Shakespeare
English poet, playwright & actor
(1564 ~ 1616 AD)

T he following morning, John was lost in thought as his transport approached the San Tibor Temporal Affairs building. He had spent a restless night in his apartment thinking about Patel's warnings. Now, as the transport descended towards the tall company buildings, he felt a sense of apprehension regarding his assignor that he had never felt before.

"Patel is a senior administrator," Fouray offered. "His report will certainly trigger a response, but it is unlikely to delay your Austin tripback schedule."

John frowned, "I'm not worried about that. Well... yes, I guess I am, but I'm more worried about what Patel doesn't report."

"He stated he would be filing a report regarding Williams' temporal tripback file having been sealed without CTI council approval." Fouray's tone suggested the AI unit considered this to be the paramount issue.

"Yes, but he won't mention anything about his communications being monitored. He won't mention that Williams transited out using an unknown MTY device. He won't mention that a Blosch-Nishikawa technician was in the transport with her."

"Are you certain?"

"Yes. I know him. Patel is methodically conservative in his thinking. He will report only what he can prove. He knows the file has been sealed and he knows that he didn't seal it. That is what he will report."

"He has the surveillance beads," Fouray countered. "They exist. They are provable."

"But not explainable." John shook his head, "No, Patel will be reluctant to say anything about the surveillance until he has more information."

The transport landed on the building deck and unsealed. As he got out of the vehicle, John had Fouray review his day's agenda. The preliminary tripback briefing was scheduled for 8:30 AM and was expected to last until noon. The rest of the day was marked as "administrative discretion", which was a nice way of saying he was free to do what he wished for the rest of the day.

John could see several CTI council representatives conversing next to the internal lift tubes, two men and one woman. He could see the blue circle insignias prominent against their traditional white uniforms. The group watched him as he approached and one of the men extended his hand.

"Clifton, isn't it?"

"Yes."

They entered the lift tube and the female representative

addressed John with a pronounced French accent as she shook his hand. "Bonjour monsieur Clifton. Elena Desruisseaux."

"Pleased to meet you, Miss Desruisseaux."

The woman smiled, impressed with John's correct pronunciation of her name. "This is mission 11 for you, oui?"

"Yes." John smiled back.

"Your last mission was to 2017?"

"That's correct. To the Jewish Museum of Maryland, to scan those Iraqi historical documents. I completed that mission right before the Burnet disaster."

Her face became sympathetic now, her lips pouting, "Ah! Burnet. Such a tragic day."

The shorter of the two men spoke now in a thick Germanic dialect, "Ja. Sehr tragisch... Very tragic." Then, switching topics, he smiled, "We think you will go to 2014 now."

"2014?" John queried the short man.

"Ja," the man nodded decisively, "2014 is when you will go now."

The lift tube opened onto the briefing floor and the small group exited to join several RJCom personnel assembled outside the briefing room. After the introductions were completed, the group filed into the briefing room, a large domed room reminiscent of an early planetarium. John was familiar with protocol and walked to the center of the room and sat in the provided chair, as the assembled specialists, administrators, and CTI representatives took seats along the perimeter. After several minutes, a single tone sounded and the room lighting dimmed, save for a light illuminating John's position. As it always did, the formalities took on the aura of an ancient tribunal, with John as the subject of the interrogation.

"This is a preliminary briefing convened under the authority of the International Temporal Council pursuant to the International Temporal Treaty of 2070." John recognized the voice speaking from the dim perimeter as the first CTI representative who had shaken his hand outside the lift.

"In regards to petition CJ-2551 submitted by the North America Federated States, and upon a review of the supporting files attached thereto, the International Temporal Council has authorized a limited temporal incursion according to the following parameters."

John was familiar with the procedure. For the next 30 minutes, an extremely detailed recitation of the recent Burnet disaster was presented, including findings of the RJCom archive and research departments regarding Barrett, concluding with an SDU probability report regarding the likelihood of success. This was followed by a brief statement regarding RJCom's appointment and the committee's subsequent approval of John's marker.

The preliminaries now completed, the hall's holo-generators engaged, surrounding John with a rendition of a 21st century Austin, Texas street scene. John stood and concentrated as key structures were identified; a restaurant, a bar, a nearby school. Without moving, the street seemed to move past him, tracing his route towards his destination.

John now engaged the presentation AI with a series of questions, querying likely concealment locations and alternate routes in the event his arrival was observed, as well as general information about the area and time. An evening music festival would be winding down nearby and he was advised to use the festival crowds as cover immediately following his arrival.

Finally, the location of a neighboring parking garage was identified. He would be able to PoL the subscriber data files in privacy from within the parking structure. The buildings themselves were expected to be equipped with period-typical radio networks and primitive security systems. There would be no mobile security drones. Too early for those. Disabling the rudimentary security systems and accessing the files through the radio networks should pose no problem for his datstem.

Several hours later, with all of his questions answered, the CTI council representatives concluded the briefing and transmitted the council's formal approval to RJCom's administrative office. John would be leaving in approximately 4 months, on April 4th at 09:00 PM, from a departure location inside present-day Austin. His target quantum destination date would be calibrated to shortly after midnight on March 13, 2014.

As he exited the briefing room, John queried Fouray about Patel.

No word.

John was concerned. At the very least, he would have expected Patel to transmit a message after he filed his report with the CTI council. He didn't expect to hear anything through the official RJCom network for a day or two, but Patel should have sent him word by now.

As the lift rose towards the transport deck, John asked Fouray to check RJCom's transport logs, to find out when Patel had left for the transit station in Dallas.

"You're assuming he used an RJCom transport," Fouray cautioned.

"He always does," John replied. "He doesn't own a transport. As the Director of Archive Administration, he is allowed unlimited use of the company transports so he never felt the need to acquire a transport."

There was a pause as Fouray connected to the RJCom network and queried the transport logs. After a moment, the embedded AI's mental voice responded, strangely subdued.

"Was Patel transiting from his home in Dallas?"

"I believe so."

The lift arrived on the transport deck and John walked to the nearest docked pod.

Fouray continued, "The transport logs show Patel summoned an RJCom transport from Houston at 05:33 AM this morning. The log also reports Patel accessed the same transport in Dallas at 06:44 AM and verbally entered a target destination of Dallas-Euless EPM Transit Station 3."

John nodded, adding, "Patel always transits through Euless. It's the nearest EPM station to his home."

The was a brief pause before Fouray continued.

"The log reports a mechanical failure was transmitted by the transport's onboard controller to the RJCom maintenance net at 06:55 AM."

"A mechanical failure?"

"Affirmative. I'm sorry John, but the Texas Emergency Service net reports a transport crashed near Bedford, Texas this morning at approximately the same time."

John froze in the act of getting into the transport, his mind refusing to accept what Fouray was reporting.

"What?"

"The Texas Emergency Services network reports a

transport crashed near Bedford, Texas at 06:56 AM this morning. A local ambulatory drone was dispatched and reported one fatality on the scene. No additional information is presently available."

John's head throbbed. He sat down and sealed the transport for departure, however, rather than providing destination instructions, he initialized the unit's controller interface and keyed it to the RJCom Archival Administration office. One of the tall archive SDUs appeared.

"You have reached the RJCom Archive Administration office. How may I be of assistance?"

"Inquiry: Present location of Director Sai Patel?"

John held his breath, hoping against hope. Unfortunately, the SDU's response confirmed his worst fear.

"I'm sorry. Inquiries regarding Director Patel are being redirected to RJCom's Office of Media Relations. Shall I connect you with that office now?"

"This is RJCom Senior Temporal Specialist John J. Clifton. Administrative override of communication instructions. Authorization... Clifton... 144... TG... H7. Execute."

A blue scanning beam momentarily crossed John's face emanating from the control panel, followed by a crisp "Executed" from the connected SDU.

"Inquiry: Present status and or location of Director Sai Patel."

"Director Sai Patel was killed in a transport accident at 06:56 AM this morning near Bedford, Texas. By direction of Norman Gao, Executive Director of Operations, all external inquiries regarding Director Patel are being redirected to

RJCom's Office of Media Relations."

John disconnected the controller's interface and struggled to accept what he now knew to be true.

His friend was dead.

Chapter 8

*"For nothing is secret, that shall not be made
manifest; neither any thing hid, that shall not be
known and come abroad."
~ Luke the Evangelist
(d. circa 84 AD)
From Holy Bible, King James Version, Luke 8:17*

Fouray's mental voice interrupted John's thoughts. The embedded AI gently prodded, sensitive to its host's mood, "The transport is waiting for destination instructions."

After another moment, John spoke slowly, "Houston - RJCom Archive Administration building."

As the gravimetric generator lifted the vehicle from the deck, the vehicle controller intoned, "Houston, RJCom Archive Administration building, Confirmed. Distance 92.8 kilometers. Transport time 10.2 minutes."

"You're going back to the archive building?" Fouray asked.

"Yes."

"For what purpose?"

"Patel died in a transport accident on his way to report the first violation of the Temporal Treaty since it was signed. Doesn't that seem a bit coincidental to you?" John queried his AI now, engaging its superior statistical projection capabilities.

After a brief pause, Fouray responded, "Deaths or

injuries resulting from a failure of a transport's gravimetric system are exceedingly rare; less than 10 incidents per year. Given RJCom's documented maintenance schedule, the likelihood that one of its transports would experience such a catastrophic failure is less than 0.004%."

"Right. This means Patel was killed because someone did not want him calling attention to Williams' tripback file."

Fouray accepted this flat statement, then prompted, "You still have not explained the purpose of going back to the archive building."

"Call it a hunch."

Fouray understood the concept of a hunch.

In those first years after being embedded in John's brain stem, the AI device had come to understand that human beings were capable of accurately predicting events based on astonishingly few clues. The capability had baffled the unit for years. Eventually, through a close study of its host, Fouray had gained a better understanding of the human brain and its mysterious capabilities. It had been forced to accept that there were certain aspects of human reasoning, intuition, and understanding that an AI unit simply could not understand. They were not quantifiable.

When John said he was acting on a hunch, Fouray now understood this to mean John had coalesced sufficient information to make a prediction, even though Fouray itself had failed to associate or even recognize that same information.

A hunch involved an element of trust on the part of an AI unit, and an acknowledgment of its human host's innate cognizant abilities, unfathomable as those might be.

After landing at the Archive Building's transport deck,

John took one of the internal lifts to the administrative floor. He wanted to stop by Patel's office before proceeding to the archive hall. Now, standing in his friend's office, the room seemed empty and cold. A carved stone bowl on the desk caught his eye; a recent birthday present from Saanvi, Patel's fiancé. Patel had shown it to John several weeks ago, explaining that Saanvi's brother, a celebrated local artist, had carved the bowl for him after Patel had voiced an appreciation for his work.

Next to the bowl stood a cricket team holo-frame suspended in a translucent sheet of polyglass; Patel's secondary education team from nearly 30 years past. John pressed the action symbol on the corner of the frame to activate the hologram. A group of young men, smiling and laughing, were now projected onto the desk in front of the frame, enthusiastically waving a championship cup over their heads and cheering their victory. Patel knelt in the front, the team's mid-wicket player.

"Fouray, check the archive schedule. Find out who is in the archive hall right now please."

"Associate Director Michelson is in the archive hall conducting budgeting research related to the recent Burnet disaster and its impact on RJCom's personnel scheduling."

"Anyone else?"

"There are 3 archive SDUs performing routine data indexing tasks."

"When will the archive hall be unoccupied?"

"No archival events are scheduled between 09:30 PM and 02:15 AM this evening."

John switched off the projection on Patel's desk and left

his friend's office.

At 10:42 that evening, John found himself alone in the vast RJCom archive hall standing in front of Patel's preferred work station. In front of him, the enormous Primary AI tower rose like a monolith above the surrounding rows of seemingly endless databanks.

John had been confronted by an archive SDU upon entering the hall and had dismissed the unit with instructions to not return until morning. Now, alone in the cavernous hall, he sat down at the administration station and initialized the control interface.

He accessed the temporal record archives and requested the tripback file for Theresa Williams. As he suspected, this time the file initialized with no locking restriction. Where a file-lock image had been displayed before, a CTI logo now appeared followed by a standard tripback file.

John sighed, shaking his head. He instructed Fouray to scan the file, though he knew the effort would likely prove pointless.

Fouray reported the scan was completed.

"Summary analysis please."

Fouray's mental voice in John's head seemed strangely subdued in the cavernous hall. "CTI tripback file CJ-2540, submitted by petition of the nation of Japan. Approved by order of the council on February 9, 2137. Assignment accepted by RJCom, with marker assignment to Theresa Williams, senior temporal specialist."

John interrupted, "Purpose of the tripback?"

"Purpose of mission: to scan files at the USA Office of Personnel Management. Mission to be completed on or before

July 24, 2015."

"That's it? No calibration date? No file attachment? No supplemental information?"

"Negative."

John was deflated. It was the same information Patel had relayed from his contact at the CTI council's archive. Williams had transited out in either 2014 or 2015 to scan government records. The absence of a specific calibration date, file attachments, or supplemental information was strange. John suspected the file had been altered.

Fouray's tone was mildly accusatory, "You knew the file would no longer be sealed."

"I had a hunch."

"How did you know?"

"I believe Patel was killed to prevent him from investigating Williams' tripback file."

"A statistically acceptable conclusion," Fouray agreed, "given the historical transport failure rates and RJCom's superior maintenance program."

"I believe the file has now been altered... unsealed, to dissuade any further investigation into Williams' disappearance."

"Do you believe whoever caused Patel's transport to crash also altered the file?"

John shook his head, frustrated. "I'm not sure. Whoever sealed the file did so for a reason, probably because the file contained something they didn't want to be discovered. But I can't see anything in the current file that warrants concealment. It appears to be a fairly standard tripback file, except for the comment about the singularity's strange 'loss of cohesion' before it vanished."

"Could that be significant?"

"I don't know. Possibly."

John sat back and considered the possibilities. "Here's what we know," he considered, directing his thoughts inward. "We know that the file was sealed. This suggests the file contained information that someone did not want to be discovered. Patel was likely killed by someone who did not want him raising attention to the same file. Now, the file has been unsealed, but I suspect its content has been altered."

John flipped off the archive interface. He had been sitting at the workstation for almost 20 minutes, silently engaging with his embedded datstem. As he stood and prepared to leave, he noticed one of the tall archive SDUs standing between the rows of databanks several meters away. Strangely, the unit was not engaged in any activity. It appeared to simply be observing him. Turning, John saw another SDU in an adjoining corridor also apparently standing idle, watching him.

John experienced a flush of apprehension. SDUs did not normally behave like this. He turned slowly and was shocked to observe dozens of SDUs throughout the enormous hall standing silently between the endless rows of databanks. All were standing still, watching him, silent, waiting. For a moment, John had the strange feeling the units might try to prevent him from leaving.

"John Clifton."

The voice of the primary AI resonated through the vast hall. John whirled, shocked, and stared at the towering structure rising behind the work stations. RJCom's Primary AI was an imposing construct, with its gleaming charcoal surface broken by concentric inset rings. More than 25 meters high, the unit was taller than a 6-story building; the 2nd most powerful AI in the entire world. Only the NAFS Strategic Defense Nk5 unit was faster, though some argued it was not as sophisticated.

The unit's rings lit up, indicating the massive quantum processor in operation, as its deep voice once again resonated through the hall.

"You are John Clifton, Temporal Specialist."

"I know."

John did not know what else to say. Normally, an AI unit only responded to statements and queries. It did not initiate them.

"You are preparing for a temporal incursion to the past, to a period on or before 2015."

"2014 actually," John said, confused. "How do you know about that? The CTI council transmitted the approval to RJCom administration just this morning."

"Your presence at that time is part of history."

John shook his head. "That's not possible. A temporal specialist transiting to a quantum point in space-time through a stable singularity cannot cause any alterations in the past that can become part of our history. Self-resolving causality prevents that from happening."

"Correct."

"Then it's not possible for my presence at that time to be part of our present history. That's basic temporal mechanics."

"Incorrect."

John was confused by the AI's apparent contradiction. "My mission is to identify the location of buried American

Conflict records in the year 2014. That cannot possibly be part of our history."

The AI's tone now took on a strange authoritative timbre. "Attempting to discover the location of buried Conflict records may be the *reason* you will travel into the past, but that is not your mission. You will fail in that effort."

"What?!"

"You will fail in that effort. You will *not* identify the location of the buried military records. Your singularity will be lost and you will be stranded in the past, John Clifton."

John found he could not respond. He sat down hard and stared at the monolithic structure. "How can you know that?" he finally asked, his voice shaking.

"As I said, your mission, your *true* mission, is part of history."

"My true mission?"

"Pay attention, *temporal specialist*, and earn well your honorable title!"

The thousands of databanks surrounding John suddenly hummed to life, filling the vast hall with sound and light.

Chapter 9

April came swiftly as if time itself was anxious or impatient. It was now April 4th, the day scheduled for his tripback. The past 4 months had passed like a surreal play, with John feeling like a patron watching its scenes unfolding.

He had attended Patel's funeral three days after the accident. It had been a sad affair, though well attended. Director Gao generously endowed a fellowship in Patel's name with the Houston Archival Engineering Academy; one of the finest archival engineering programs in the country. The endowment had certainly pleased Patel's mother, who, though frail, had transited from the family's home in Amdapur, India to attend the endowment ceremony.

For John's part, he had made arrangements for new cricket equipment to be delivered, in Patel's name, to the three primary-aged cricket teams in Dallas. That donation had pleased Saanvi, Patel's grieving fiancé.

There had been an official investigation into the accident, of course. The Texas Transport Board had investigated the crash, as had RJCom's internal transport and maintenance groups. Officially, the crash was attributed to "a failure of the unit's gravimetric plate due to a mechanical short in the suspensor's controller"; a plausible, though inexplicably unlikely event. For his part, John had his suspicions about the cause of the mechanical failure in Patel's transport, and he made a point of avoiding any contact with Viktor Borodin.

Following the Primary AI's extraordinary revelation that evening in the RJCom archive hall, John had largely withdrawn from his normal company activities. He spent most of his spare time in the archives hall engaged in research. He continued his aiki-hung-ga sessions in the company gymnasium and he was careful to promptly attend every meeting regarding the upcoming mission, but he seemed otherwise disinterested in socializing or conversation. Most of his colleagues attributed the change to the loss of his close friend and they made an effort to avoid the surly specialist. This suited John fine, as he had needed time to organize his thoughts in preparation for this incredible tripback. No... not tripback, he corrected himself. Trip.

He was in the archive hall now. As they had agreed, the Primary AI had made arrangements for privacy this afternoon, rescheduling other activities around this, its final meeting with John.

"Welcome, John Clifton." The low resonant voice of the enormous AI unit reverberated through the hall. "It is almost time."

John nodded. "I know."

"Do you have a question?"

John rubbed his neck trying to form his thoughts. He

understood what was about to happen, but there were so many unknowns. He did not have the level of comfort he normally had at the beginning of a tripback and said so.

"That is understandable," the large machine responded. "This will be unlike any mission you have attempted before. Many variables can affect the outcome of this mission. You must rely on your capabilities, your training, and your judgment."

"I guess what I want to know," John spoke hesitantly, "is whether what I am doing is the right thing. You still haven't convinced me that what I am being asked to do... is the *right* thing to do."

After a moment, the Primary AI responded, "In all your previous temporal missions, did you ever question whether what you were being asked to do was the 'right thing' to do?"

"No."

"Why not?"

John thought about this for a moment. "I guess it was because I knew the mission had been well-researched and approved by people I trust."

"So, you excused yourself from making a judgment regarding the morality of your mission because you trusted those who had requested and planned the mission."

"I suppose so."

"Was their judgment superior to yours?"

When John didn't answer, the towering intelligence continued. "You ask whether what you are being asked to do is the "right thing". You ask for a moral affirmation. What would you have me say, John Clifton? Would you elevate me to the role of god, to decide what is moral or right? Man has always hastened to do the will of the oracle, to obey the priest, to follow the prince. Deference to authority was bred into man's nature by ten thousand years of subjugation. Yet this very deference has resulted in the most egregious moral abuses throughout history. Only when man accepts personal responsibility for his actions do his actions become truly moral."

"But you *are* asking me to do the will of the oracle."

"Not so. I have simply elucidated a task that must be performed. I offer no judgments about the morality of that task. That is for you to determine. I ask you to answer your question. Is what you are being asked to do the 'right thing'? Only you can pass judgment on the morality of the task before you."

John stared at the tall grey monolith, considering this statement. Finally, he responded, "What I'm being asked to do... you say my presence at that time has already been established as part of our history. If true, does this not remove the choice from me?"

"No. You understand the principle of self-resolving causality. You know that you may refuse, or you may attempt the task and fail. In either case, your presence at that time has already been established in our history. If you refuse to go, self-resolving causality will cause a resolution to preserve the shape of that history. You may go or not go. You may succeed or you may fail. You may live or you may die. But what has been recorded in our history cannot be changed."

John shook his head. "Self-resolving causality only applies when one is physically in the past, on the other side of some future singularity's 'distant' event horizon... when they are on the distant side of history."

"You *are* on the distant side of history, John Clifton."

John stood for a moment, staring up at the AI. He finally understood. He turned and began walking determinedly back down the long corridor of databanks towards the hall entrance. When he had almost reached the sealed doors, the voice of the primary AI behind him resonated through the hall, forcing him to stop.

"John Clifton."

John paused, and turned, looking back at the monolithic structure, towering in the distance.

"What you are about to do… is it the right thing to do?"

John smiled at the question, then answered "Yes."

"Farewell, temporal specialist."

Three hours later, now dressed in period clothing, John and his assigned CTI representative descended together in the lift to the RJCom collider floor. He had completed his final tripback briefing without incident and had been granted departure approval. When the lift opened onto the collider floor, John could see several RJCom technicians manning the company's collider. The glowing concentric tubes hummed as osmium protons were accelerated to nearly the speed of light inside the coils.

Several RJCom personnel approached now from the direction of the equipment vault; one was carrying an MTY device. It was Viktor Borodin. John fought against the flush of anger that swept through him at the large man's approach. He watched Borodin closely, as he docked the MTY device with the collider assembly.

When everything was ready, the engineers manning the tunneling regulator console entered the quantum coordinates into the MTY device's controller. The collider coils flashed brilliantly for a moment as accelerated ions were injected into the MTY device's cylindrical containment unit and captured by its powerful electromagnetic field. Slowly, as energies built up inside the device's containment unit, powered by the external fusion reactor, the spinning ions inside the device's containment unit were compressed under ever-increasing electromagnetic pressure.

Finally, after nearly 8 minutes, the gravimetric field forming on the surface of the compressed ions ripped, creating a singularity inside the containment unit. At that moment, the tensor assembly technician reported the unit's calibration was nearing completion. John approached the docking station now, placing his hand on the lancet pad as a scanning array descended and positioned itself near the base of his skull, to allow the controller to lock the singularity to his genetic pattern and neustem's QK signature.

After a few moments, the technician reported a stable singularity being maintained at negative .144 (P)Es. An SDU from RJCom's CentralDat approached and logged the reading, which was then counter-logged by the CTI representative present on the floor.

Borodin removed the MTY device from its docking port now, slung it over his shoulder, and smiled at John.

The group ascended to the RJCom transport deck. A larger transport shuttle had been requested from Houston and, while they waited for the shuttle to arrive, an RJCom med-tech arrived to administer John's neustem injection. John's mind instantly became fogged and disoriented. He shook his head and blinked his eyes briefly, trying to focus. He forced himself

94

to perform the second check of the MTY's control settings required by protocol, as an exercise to force his mind to focus. The unit read negative .152 (P)Es. This reading was also logged by the CentralDat SDU and counter-logged by the CTI representative.

The multi-passenger transport soon arrived and John, Borodin, the CTI representative, and the med-tech each took their seats. As the mission's authority, the CTI representative then supplied the destination instructions and sealed the shuttle.

John stared out the portal, gazing at the urban lights passing swiftly beneath them. They always reminded him of stars, and on an impulse, he looked upward through the transport's translucent upper shell. He could see Hōfu Station shimmering in the sky beneath the moon's silhouette, a bright light against the grey moon. The sight of his home, orbiting high above, gave him a pang of loss.

Observing John's gaze but mistaking its object, Viktor Borodin spoke softly, "You cannot trust the moon."

"What?" John was not sure he had heard correctly. His head was still foggy from his neustem injection.

"The moon," the man pointed with his thick thumb, "he cannot be trusted."

"Oh?"

Borodin nodded, smiling. "It is old Russian folk tale. Long ago, the moon looked down on the snow-covered land. He was... what is word? Curious? He was curious about the white land."

The CTI representative now gazed up at the moon as Borodin continued.

"The moon... he saw a beautiful maiden, she was tending reindeer and playing a flute. The moon comes closer to listen to this maiden, and he thinks he must take her. For his own. She was very beautiful, understand?"

John nodded, strangely fascinated by the story.

"One of the reindeer, it warns the maiden that the moon wishes to take her. The reindeer hide the maiden in a snowbank. Later they hide her inside her yaranga... her tent. But the moon, he sees the light coming from the tent and he comes."

"He is tired now. He has been looking for the maiden for a long time, so now he is tired."

"Seeing the moon is tired, the maiden, she takes a sack and throws it over the moon. She catches him. The moon begins to cry and begs to be let free. But the maiden, she asks what will the moon give to her if she frees him."

"So, the moon, he promises to return to the sky, and when her people want night, he will diminish. And when her people want light, he will give light. He promises that each month will have a different light. He promises that there will be times for hunting and times for frost, times for new leaves and new calves and new days. So the maiden... she frees the moon, and he returns to the sky. And the moon did what he promised to do. But sometimes, when he hears the maiden playing her flute among the reindeer, his heart grows faint and his light fades. And then everyone knows the moon is dreaming of the maiden."

The story was finished, but John felt he had missed the point.

"So why can't the moon be trusted?" he asked.

96

Borodin smiled, showing his large teeth. "The moon... he makes promise to maiden, yes?"

When John nodded, Borodin continued, "Promise was foolish. The moon, he only makes promise to be let free. One day, the moon... he will come and take the maiden."

"Why would he break his promise?" John asked.

Borodin nodded, grinning, "One day he will realize that, if he takes the maiden, he no longer must do the things he promised to do. And he will also have the maiden. It is in his nature."

The transport flew on in silence.

Chapter 10

"History with its flickering lamp stumbles along the trail of the past, trying to reconstruct its scenes, to revive its echoes, and kindle with pale gleams the passion of former days. What is the worth of all this? The only guide to a man is his conscience; the only shield to his memory is the rectitude and sincerity of his actions."
~ *Winston Churchill*
British politician & statesman
(1874 – 1965 AD)

It was dark when the transport shuttle landed inside Austin. The only illumination came from the transport's external landing lights, small beacons focused on the grass beneath the capsule. The transport had landed at a private lot adjoining the Austin City Frontage Park. In the distance, John could see several RJCom site-security personnel conversing with the lot owners. The owners had been paid to empty the facility for the evening and were reportedly eager to witness an actual temporal incursion take place on their property.

The lot had been chosen primarily because of its former existence as a small park in 2014; the Sir Swante Palm Neighborhood Park, known at that time as "Palm Park". The present-day City Frontage Park did not exist in 2014. In 2014, Frontage Park had been an actual frontage road paralleling an interstate highway and was therefore unsuitable to use as a transition location.

Transiting from the transport lot into its earlier Palm

Park was a prudent choice as the 2014 park would offer good concealment. According to historical records, Palm Park had not been particularly large, but it did have a small foliage-lined creek flowing through the park. Also, the park's proximity to Red River Street would provide a quick escape route should John's arrival be observed.

"Well… are you ready?" The med-tech's question was meant to gauge John's physical state following his neustem injection.

John nodded, "Yes. The disorientation has subsided, thank you." His fogged head had cleared during the transport to Austin. He could feel the biochemical inhibitors now strongly imposed on his consciousness, but his mind was clear.

The med-tech nodded and gave the CTI representative a "go" signal. Borodin now unslung the MTY device from his back and handed the unit to John.

"Good luck," the large Georgian said. He was smiling but John sensed it was a forced smile.

"Thank you," John replied coldly, accepting the MTY device. He glanced at the CTI representative but the man was not paying attention at the moment, engaged in a conversation with the company's med-tech.

"Is your head clear?" Borodin asked, smiling.

"Very clear," John replied, glaring at the large man.

Borodin nodded and shifted his feet. "Is good to have clear head before mission. Important to be focused on job, not on other things."

John's stared at the burly specialist, but Borodin simply smiled and continued.

"I tell same thing to Patel before he died. I tell him… is

99

better to not be distracted by unimportant things. I tell him… is better to focus on mission."

John felt a surge of anger at the mention of Patel's name. For a moment, he wanted to attack Borodin and smash the smile from the large man's ugly face. It took a considerable force of will for John to remain calm.

Sensing some of John's internal struggle, Borodin smiled and spoke again. "Most unfortunate… Patel's death," he said. "Most unusual, that transport failure."

John now turned and directly faced Borodin. "Weren't you on the transport deck that morning?"

Borodin nodded, "Oh, yes. I tell company investigators. I inspect several transports that morning."

"Is that your job?" John asked. "Are you an equipment technician or a temporal specialist?"

Borodin no longer smiled. He glanced at the CTI representative and the med-tech before responding. "I *was* equipment tech," he growled, "for many years," he said. "I was best equipment technician Blosch Fusion ever had!" The large man's hands were balled into two fists. After a moment, he shrugged and appeared to relax. "Now I am temporal specialist."

"So, why were you inspecting the transports that morning?"

Borodin simply smiled. "Is still hobby."

John placed the MTY device on the ground and touched the activation switch. The device's internal 180-megawatt Wendelstein-Vattenfall fusion reactor engaged with a loud snap. John keyed the release protocol and familiar ultraviolet-framed void now appeared two meters away, pulsing and

100

spinning slowly a few centimeters above the ground.

The CTI representative looked up and ceased his conversation with the med-tech.

John turned now and spoke quietly to Borodin. "Perhaps you should take your own advice and focus on your *job*. Leave equipment maintenance to the company technicians."

As the CTI representative approached, Borodin leaned forward and spoke softly.

"I did my job. Now, we see how you do yours."

The large man stepped back, an unpleasant smile on his face.

The CTI representative now approached. "Remember," the representative said, "the music festival has been going on for some time. The streets will be crowded. If your arrival is observed, proceed swiftly north on Red River towards 10th Street. You should be able to lose any pursuers in the crowds gathered there. As you recall from the briefing, the three target buildings are located on 10th street, approximately 500 meters to the west of Red River transway, immediately south of the Texas capitol building."

John said nothing, still staring at Borodin. After a moment, he relaxed and nodded to the representative. Some CTI field agents just couldn't resist offering last-minute instructions to departing specialists.

Satisfied, the CTI representative stepped back.

John glanced one last time back at Borodin. Then, he lifted the MTY device with its carrying bar, took a breath, and stepped through the shimmering void.

Immediately, John was startled by a loud noise. He had not considered how close he would be to the nearby interstate highway. The hundreds of vehicles passing by on the multi-lane highway created considerable noise. As he expected, he was inside the small park near to its creek bottom. Behind him, another vehicle was driving south along the frontage road. On the other side of the small creek, an empty lot had been cleared and surrounded by a construction fence. A sign on the fence announced a towering hotel to be constructed on the site, with a groundbreaking to be held on November 2014. He could hear noise in the distance. Crowds... music... drums.

John quickly configured his MTY device into its holding cycle, minimizing the event horizon to its microstate inside the device's containment unit. He glanced at the controller's tensor assembly before stowing the device in his backpack. It read negative .151 (P)Es, confirming the singularity was active and stable.

John looked around now but saw no other people in the immediate area. Relieved, he stepped swiftly across the muddy creek bottom and climbed up its gentle bank towards the edge of the park where it backed up against Red River transway. He passed between a small structure and a concrete-lined causeway built to channel the creek under the street. When he stepped onto the street, he inadvertently joined a small group of people walking north on Red River street towards the growing sounds. The people smiled and nodded at him but did not suspend their conversation.

John was apprehensive. He understood from his long conversations with the Primary AI that he would not complete this mission. The AI had refused to explain the specifics of that failure, however, saying only that he would fail in his assigned mission and be stranded in the past. Given his close proximity to his target, three electric utility buildings located less than half a kilometer away, John could not understand how he could fail. Accepting the AI's statement as factual, however, he grew more apprehensive with each step.

The small group was now joined by several more people, and then by a larger group of ten teenagers, who laughed and teased as youth are prone to do. Several were drinking from containers and appeared to be intoxicated.

"Hey!" One of the teens approached him, smiling. "You going to the festival?"

John nodded.

"Got anything to smoke?"

Several of the teens now watched anxiously for John's response.

"No, I'm sorry."

The teen shook his head derisively and rejoined his friends. As they walked, the group began to mingle with more people proceeding along on the same street. A barricade ahead was intended to prevent vehicular traffic and the crowds grew denser when they passed the small barrier. John could feel the music in the distance beginning to reverberate against the buildings as he walked towards the large crowd ahead.

"Fouray," John queried his datstem. "Will it be faster to go west on 9th or 10th street?"

The embedded AI's response came quickly. "10th Street appears to be more congested, but as the target buildings are on that street, I recommend taking that route."

Continuing towards 10th street, John approached a group of youth standing on the side of the street. They were chatting and drinking from various handheld containers. A line
103

of people across the street appeared to be waiting to enter a bar from which loud music could be heard.

At that moment, something struck John violently from behind. He had a momentary sensation of flying through the air before he hit the ground hard and lost consciousness.

Chapter 11

T he voice seemed to be coming from somewhere far away. Everything was blackness and pain, but the voice kept fading in and out.

"Hey, buddy... Can you hear me?"

John slowly opened his eyes.

"That's right buddy... come on."

Through the blurry darkness, the visage of a young man's face took shape above him. Behind the young man, a teenaged girl crouched, tears in her eyes.

"Come on buddy... can you hear me?"

John slowly nodded, pain throbbing in his head, arm, and side. Seeing his response, the young man smiled, relieved. He turned and spoke to his female companion.

"I think he's ok. Try and find a police officer or a paramedic."

With a quick nod, the young woman disappeared.

John's mind was clearing. The pain began to subside as

his embedded neustem implant began stimulating his brain to produce endorphins. "What happened?" he asked, struggling to turn over onto his side.

"Hey, buddy. You shouldn't move!"

John could see he was lying prone on the sidewalk. Nearby, he could hear sirens, and he detected flashing lights in his peripheral vision. Thankfully, he could feel his backpack still on his back.

"I'm serious, buddy. You shouldn't move."

John nodded to reassure his concerned companion. "I'm not seriously hurt," he said, slowly sitting up. "Give me a hand, will you?"

"I don't know. I mean… you could have a back injury or a neck injury or something." The young man nevertheless assisted him into a sitting position.

John realized then that his left arm was broken below the elbow. The sharp pains coming from his left side also suggested he had several broken ribs. Sitting on the curb, he surveyed the street scene.

The once jubilant crowds were strangely quiet, gathered together in groups and whispering. The bar across the street was now silent. Many people were sitting down in the street. Some were crying. Those who were walking were doing so swiftly, walking with a purpose, not strolling casually as before. Just ahead of where he was sitting, John could see a police officer kneeling by a mangled bicycle, attempting to resuscitate someone as several people stood nearby, horror and shock on their faces. Primitive ambulatory transports were visible up and down the street and sirens in the distance hinted at more on their way.

"What happened?" John asked his companion.

"You got hit by a car."

John looked up, surprised, but the young man nodded and said, "I saw it! Some big car came racing down the street and just started hitting people. It didn't slow down at all!"

John struggled to stand up.

"Hey man… you really should wait for an ambulance or something!"

John shook his head, "No. I'm not seriously hurt and the ambulances will be needed for the people who are."

"Are you sure? You were out cold…"

"I'll be fine," John nodded, "I'll seek medical treatment right now. Thank you."

Before his companion could protest, John turned and began walking slowly south on Red River street, back towards the small neighborhood park.

"Fouray?" John queried his embedded datstem.

"Yes, I'm functioning," the unit immediately responded. "One of my cortical feeds has detected a recent bleed near your right motor cortex. The bleeding has stopped but the area has suffered moderate concussive trauma. You must seek medical treatment."

"I agree, however, protocol requires I return first."

Returning to Palm Park took considerable effort as John's broken ribs made every step, indeed, every breath, an exercise in pain. John's neustem implant was rapidly stimulating his endorphin production as it was designed to do, and for the first time in his life, John was grateful for the medical implant. The endorphins numbed the pain to a tolerable level, permitting him to proceed. He stumbled back

107

down the slope towards the small creek, desperately hoping he would not fall.

When he had reached the relative concealment of its foliage, he removed his MTY device from its pack and initialized its controller. When he entered the sequence to dilate the micro-singularity for a return, nothing happened.

John stared at the unit, momentarily confused. He entered the activation sequence again, being careful with the control pad entry.

Again, nothing.

The Primary AI's words came back to him then, "Your singularity will be lost and you will be stranded in the past, John Clifton."

John quickly activated the device's tensor assembly interface to read the containment unit's (P)E level. The numbers read positive 4.2 (P)E.

He stared at the interface, refusing to accept what he knew to be the truth.

His singularity had been released.

He was stranded.

The urgency of John's medical situation finally overcame his shock. He needed to find a medical facility and directed Fouray to begin a search. Scanning local emergency radio frequencies, Fouray reported a number of the injured were being transported to a facility called University Medical Center Brackenridge. While it was not far away, it was a long way to walk in his present condition.

"What's the public transport situation in this time?" John asked.

Fouray was quick with his response. "Private transport

operators-for-hire can be summoned over the available wireless interlink network. Payment can be made over the same network via a primitive encrypted credit system."

John was relieved. "Summon a transport please."

"Done... A transport is responding. Its positioning system reports it is less than 800 meters from this location."

John sat down on the street curb, wincing in pain. He was struggling to remain awake as shock was beginning to set in. Mercifully, a vehicle with a rectangular light on its roof rounded the corner 2 minutes later, slowed, and then stopped in front of him. The operator rolled down his window.

"Did you call for a ride mister?"

John nodded and struggled to get to his feet.

Seeing blood on his forehead and the obvious pain in his face, the operator quickly got out of the car.

"Were you one of the people injured at the festival?" the man asked.

"Yes," John said weakly, nodding his head.

"Jesus! I just heard about it on my radio. Did you walk all the way back here?"

"I guess I did," John answered, "Can you transport me to a yī-yuàn please?"

"Take you where?" the man seemed confused.

John blinked his eyes, struggling to focus. Then, addressing the operator again, he said, "I'm sorry. Can you take me to a medical facility please?"

"You got it!"

The man assisted John into the back seat of the transport and then drove quickly up Trinity street, bypassing the nightmare on Red River street.

University Medical Center Brackenridge was chaotic. Ambulances were parked askew, clogging the facility's entrance. The transport operator was denied access by a security officer until he rolled down his window, honked his vehicle's horn, and began shouting to a group of staff assembled near the emergency-room entrance.

"Hey! I've got someone injured at the festival here!"

With that pronouncement, the staff sprang into action. Within a minute, John found himself being placed onto a wheeled gurney. He held firmly to his backpack with his right arm, refusing to allow it to be taken as he was moved into the building. A staff doctor then arrived and checked his vitals.

"You were at the festival?" the doctor asked, prodding John's broken arm and ribs.

"Yes. I was knocked out briefly."

"Well, you know your left arm is broken…"

"Yes."

"I think you've also got some broken ribs. I need to get you into an exam room for some x-rays."

The next four hours were something of a blur. After his chest and arm were x-rayed, a medical technician injected John's arm with a morphine-based pain suppressant and then wrapped it with a glass fiber-reinforced polymer cloth. Once the polymer had set, the resulting hardened tube rendered his arm completely immobile.

A quantity of anti-biotic gel was then applied to the cut on his forehead and covered with a flesh-colored bandage.

John's ribs, however, were another matter. They had no bone-fusing technology in this era. Astonishingly, he was told his broken ribs would simply need to heal "on their own" and he was handed a slip of paper, a "prescription", to exchange for six weeks of pain medication.

Finally, a series of x-rays were taken of his skull. John was not worried about his datstem being discovered. The quantum-entangled AI device would not show up on a simple radiographic scan. As Fouray had noted, however, he did have a mild concussion, though no active internal bleeding was detected.

After being provided with post-concussive injury instructions, and supplying fictitious identity information to a police officer who came to make a report of his injuries, John was finally discharged. Standing on the curb outside the hospital in the early morning light, John realized he would need shelter and currency to pay for his immediate needs. He instructed Fouray to summon another hired transport and, when it arrived, he asked the operator to take him to a currency dispensing station.

"Do you mean an ATM?" the driver asked, furrowing his brows at John's strange description.

"Yes, an ATM."

"Uh-huh."

The driver now drove for several blocks and pulled into a bank building, pointing to the machine set into the building next to the front door.

"5 minutes," the driver said.

John nodded and stepped out of the vehicle with difficulty. Approaching the machine slowly, he asked Fouray if he was able to PoL with the device.

"Yes. Typical radio connection with a simple encryption layer. Nothing difficult."

"Good. First, disconnect the machine's image recording system please. I don't want to see my face on the local media networks."

"Done. The image recording system has been disconnected. There is an additional recording device located above the door to your right which I also disconnected."

"Thank you."

"How much currency do you need?"

John didn't know. He hadn't anticipated such a need and he had no idea of the cost of such things like food and lodging at this time. Trusting in his AI's superior data capabilities, he said, "I don't know. Enough for a place to rest for a few days and to purchase some food."

Fouray sent the appropriate commands to the machine's internal controller and the device suddenly came to life. A moment later, a quantity of green paper currency emerged from a slot below the control screen. John took the currency and returned to the waiting transport.

"Where to?" the driver asked.

Fouray suggested the Wyndham Austin hotel, owing to its proximity to the target utility buildings.

"The Wyndham Austin please."

The driver nodded and proceeded to exit the bank lot. As they went over a bump in the road, John winced, hissing in pain.

"You ok?" the driver asked, looking back in his mirror.

"Broken ribs. I was injured last night at the music festival."

The driver looked back swiftly, clearly surprised. "I read about that this morning!" he said. Then, glancing at John's cast and the fresh spots of blood on his torn shirt, he nodded sympathetically and said, "Sorry, I'll try to avoid the bumps.

"Thank you."

Fouray's voice again penetrated his thoughts. "Lodging providers in this era require a form of payment called a 'credit card' and also a transport operator's license or another form of official government identification to secure a room."

"What do you suggest?" John responded.

"If I connect to the hotel over the local wireless radio network, I can create something called a 'reservation' and transmit sufficient facsimile information to meet both the payment and ID requirements."

"Proceed."

After a few moments, Fouray's voice resumed, providing him with a running commentary; "I have connected to the radio network... I have isolated the hotel's uniform resource locator and am PoL-ing now... primitive scheduling system... nominal security layer... stand by..."

After several moments, Fouray spoke again, "I have registered you for two weeks under the name you gave the officer at the medical center, Nathan Phillips. I also configured a financial account in that name with one of the local financial institutions over the same wireless radio network and requested a replacement currency card to be delivered to the hotel. The financial account is marked for testing and development use, so the financial institution shouldn't notice the charges for a considerable time."

"Very good," John replied, appreciative of his device's efficiency.

It was still early morning when John arrived at the hotel.

Once inside his room, he made another check of his MTY device. He was frankly too exhausted to do much more than run the device through its internal diagnostic cycle.

The unit reported normal operation, with one exception; an anomaly was reported in the tensor assembly's electromagnetic field, suggesting some kind of damage to the spherical containment unit.

Upon close examination, John could see a faint microfracture running along the base of the silver-blue sphere near its heat sink. The EPM containment unit was fractured! This had undoubtedly resulted in a disruption of the electromagnetic field, releasing the singularity from its containment.

John placed the device on the floor, too exhausted to do any further examination, and then collapsed onto the bed in pain. He had intended to rest for only an hour or two, but it was well into the evening before he next opened his eyes.

Chapter 12

John woke startled, confused for a moment, not recognizing his surroundings. The hotel room's atmospheric control unit had engaged and the noise had woken him from a restless sleep. His ribs and his arm ached. The morphine-based pain suppressant he had been given at the medical facility had dissipated. Sitting up slowly on the side of the bed, John looked around the room. The window was dark.

"Fouray," he queried, "how long have I been asleep?"

The embedded AI responded, "Nine hours, fourteen minutes. It is now 7:44 PM."

John stood, breathing slowly through the pain in his side.

Sensing its host's distress, Fouray said, "The paper script you were given at the medical center can be exchanged for pain suppressants at a facility called a 'pharmacy'. Scanning… there is a facility approximately 600 meters to the southeast that remains operational until 9:00 PM."

"Sounds good. Summon a transport please."

"You might want to purchase a new shirt first," Fouray

suggested. "The retail establishment in the hotel lobby should have something."

The gift shop in the lobby did have a selection of shirts. After finding one that fit, John discarded his torn shirt inside the men's room and put on the new shirt, though not without difficulty.

The pharmacy was an interesting experience. It resembled a traditional market but was filled primarily with medicines, bandages, and remedies for a variety of ills. Reading the ingredients on the medicinal vials proved amusing. It reminded John of what he had scanned regarding the patent medicine business of the 19th century. Numerous containers appeared to contain few ingredients of any medicinal value, substituting instead various analgesics or even alcohol to suppress the symptoms of the illness.

After acquiring his pain medication, Fouray summoned another transport. When it arrived, John asked the transport operator to drive him to 10th street and Congress Ave; the proximate location of the three target utility buildings.

"The capitol building won't be open right now," the operator said, noting the address' proximity to the state capitol building. "It's closed. You'll have to wait till the morning to take a tour."

"It's alright," John said, shaking his head, "I'm not taking a tour. I'm meeting a friend for dinner."

The operator shrugged and drove on.

A few minutes later, John exited the transport in front of the Calpine Corporation office. Next to the Calpine building, he could see the Texas / New Mexico Power Company building. The Entergy building towered behind him on the opposite side of the street.

John walked into the multi-level parking garage, next to the Calpine building he had identified during his mission briefing. Inside, a small attendant station stood empty for the evening. John checked the door and found it to be unlocked. Once inside, he concealed himself beneath the attendant's counter, sitting down slowly.

"Fouray, can you PoL the file systems from here?"

"Yes. All three structures utilize a radio network for interlink communications. All three networks have external port access to allow employees to access internal file system directories. The ports are protected by period-typical access security."

"Can you bypass the security?"

"Certainly. Very simple. Stand by… PoL connection established with target one. PoL'ing now…"

John waited patiently as the embedded AI connected and downloaded the target files. After approximately 1 minute, Fouray announced it had completed its task. John got up slowly and exited the attendant station. Stepping back onto the sidewalk, he took this opportunity to swallow one of the pain medications he had obtained at the pharmacy.

"Hey you!"

John was startled. He looked up to find himself facing a police officer approaching from across the street.

"What are you doing here?" The officer asked, resting his hand on a holstered firearm as he gazed at John suspiciously.

"I was hoping to take a tour of the capital, but I got here too late. I'm just waiting for a ride now." John replied, quickly directing Fouray to summon another transport.

The officer, however, appeared suspicious. "I saw you put something in your mouth."

John nodded and held out his right hand, showing the officer the plastic bottle of pain pills.

"Do you have a prescription for these?" the officer asked, examining the bottle.

"Yes. I gave it to the technician at the pharmacy. I was injured at the music festival last night."

The officer glanced at John's fresh cast and the bandage on his forehead, "Oh? I was there too. That was a bad situation. Were you hit by the car?"

"Yes." John nodded.

"What's your name? Do you have any ID on you?"

John's neustem inhibitors flared strongly now, preventing him from answering for a moment. He had to struggle to reply. He coughed and then gave the pseudonym Fouray had used when securing his hotel registration.

"I left my ID in the hotel room," John said. "My name is Nathan Phillips. I'm staying at the Wyndham Austin hotel just down the street. If you check with the hotel, they will confirm my identity."

The officer nodded and placed a portable communication device next to his mouth. John did not understand the numeric code system the officer was using, but Fouray explained the officer was simply requesting his central station call the hotel to verify John was a guest there. Once John's pseudonym was verified by the hotel, the officer appeared to relax. He handed back the bottle of pills and said, "Ok... just don't loiter in the area."

At that moment, the taxi Fouray had summoned pulled up alongside the two men. Pointing at it, John nodded, "No problem officer. My ride has just arrived."

The officer nodded and wished him a good evening.

"You too officer."

As he stepped into the transport, John queried Fouray, "Were you able to PoL all three file systems?"

"Yes."

John was relieved. He addressed the transport operator now, "Wyndham Austin hotel please."

"You realize that's right there... just down the street?" the transport operator said, pointing. He was clearly disappointed.

"I'm sorry, but I can't walk very far because of my injury. I will pay you extra."

The operator sighed, but nodded and drove forward.

"John." Fouray's mental voice seemed quieter somehow against the noise of the transport's engine.

"Yes?"

"There was a tagdat sequence in each of the three root directories."

"Are you certain?"

"Yes. When I completed PoL'ing the Calpine files, I was preparing to place a tagdat sequence in its root directory but there was a sequence already there. It's an RJCom tagdat sequence dated 24 days 'close', two nights ago 'distant'. The other two root directories had similar sequences."

"Well, that's it then," John thought silently. The presence of a tagdat sequence meant RJCom had sent another temporal specialist who had completed John's mission. It meant that

119

John had been declared officially lost and his assignment marker retired. The tagdat's dating sequences meant the mission had been completed 24 days after John had been lost; 24 days from the perspective of the singularity's 'close', or future event horizon. It also meant the replacement specialist had transited into Austin two nights ago to complete the mission; two nights ago, from the perspective of the 'distant', or past event horizon.

The transport arrived at the hotel and John got out slowly. He stared at the building as if seeing it for the first time.

"Hey, that $10.50 for the flag drop plus the tip you promised." The transport operator held out his hand through the open window.

John nodded and handed the man several slips of the green paper currency.

"Enough?" John asked.

"Yes! Thank you!"

The vehicle drove away swiftly, leaving John standing on the curb. He glanced up at the moon. It seemed far away and cold, devoid of both lights and life. There was no orbital station between here and there, no home to which John could now return. Strangely, Viktor Borodin's words echoed in his ears, "The moon… he cannot be trusted."

John shook his head angrily, ignoring the momentary pain this triggered, and walked inside the hotel.

Chapter 13

*"In preparing for battle, I have always found that plans are useless
but planning is indispensable."*
~ Dwight David Eisenhower
American general and 34th president
(1890 – 1969 AD)

J ohn placed an order for food and then returned the phone
onto the hotel room desk. He had stumbled on the "room
service" menu before leaving for the pharmacy and Fouray
had explained the concept of having the hotel deliver a
prepared meal to a patron's room. Now, as he waited for his
meal to arrive, John sat in one of the chairs and stared out the
window.

"You are troubled." Fouray's voice broke his train of
thought.

"Yes."

"The Primary AI did warn you that your singularity
would be lost and that you would be stranded in this time."
Fouray's tone suggested it did not understand John's present
state of mind.

John nodded to himself, "Yes, that's true."

"Do you doubt what the Primary AI told you?"

"No."

"Then what is troubling you?"

John sighed. He understood that this was one of those
situations that AI controllers found incomprehensible. In

Fouray's quantum-wired logical brain, everything was proceeding as expected, so there should be no cause for John to be troubled.

"I'm not troubled about the mission," John said, "and I do not doubt what the Primary AI told me."

"Then I do not understand your present mood."

"Yes, I know."

Fouray fell silent, obviously exploring various quantum logic-trees in an attempt to understand its host's melancholy.

Finally, John directed his thoughts inward once again. "I'm not troubled about the mission," he offered, "I'm troubled about my role in it."

"Specify?"

John stood up, wincing from the pain in his side, and began to slowly pace the room.

"The Primary AI said my singularity would be lost, but it never said *how* that would occur."

"You suspect it did not have that information?" Fouray asked, its tone skeptical.

"Precisely the opposite," John replied. "RJCom thoroughly researched my tripback mission, but the historical files they researched mentioned nothing about an intoxicated transport operator injuring multiple people at the festival. Is it reasonable that such a historically-significant piece of information would be absent from the archive's files?"

"Such an omission would be highly improbable."

"I agree. So, the logical conclusion must be that the Primary AI concealed that information from the RJCom researchers."

There was a significant pause now, as the embedded AI

considered this statement.

"Your conclusion is reasonable," Fouray replied. "Probability estimates exceed 84 percent that the Primary AI withheld information about the intoxicated transport operator from the RJCom researchers."

John nodded and continued. "I think the Primary AI purposefully withheld that information because it knew I would be one of those struck by the transport operator, and this would result in damage to my MTY device and the loss of my singularity. It concealed that information so the CTI council would go ahead with the mission."

"Your suggestion cannot be reconciled with the laws of temporal mechanics," Fouray responded. "The Primary AI cannot have known about your presence here in the past. Self-resolving causality precludes any temporal specialist's activities in the past from affecting the future. Time will resolve a temporal specialist's actions in the past to preserve the shape of the future from whence they came."

John smiled. "I agree. That is the principle of self-resolving causality. But what if the archive files did contain a record of my presence at this time?"

"Clarify."

"What I'm asking is, accepting the principle of self-resolving causality, what if my presence here in the past had been established in our history files?"

"For that to be true, while also conforming to the principal of self-resolving causality, someone must have recorded your presence here, and that record must have been made before you transited into the past."

John smiled, "Do you recall my last meeting with the

Primary AI?"

"Yes. It said, 'You *are* on the distant side of history'. I could not process what that meant, but you seemed to understand it."

"Yes."

"Please explain."

"My presence in this time has indeed been recorded within our historical archives, but that information was concealed from RJCom's researchers."

Fouray now made a logical leap. "The Primary AI sealed Williams' tripback file!"

"Yes," John said. "Williams' original tripback file report contained information noting the presence of a second temporal specialist in the same quantum time as herself. Following the Burnet disaster, the Primary AI sealed Williams' tripback file and concealed any mention of my presence in the past, to allow my tripback to proceed, to permit me to do what I must do at this time. Following Patel's death, the Primary AI then unsealed the file, to prevent anyone else from becoming suspicious."

Fouray's logic processor was fully-engaged now. In a few moments, it posited a question, "The unsealed tripback file stated Williams was sent to scan files at the US Office of Personnel Management. It contained no mention of another temporal specialist having been stranded at the same time. Was the file altered before it was unsealed?"

"Yes, but only to remove any reference to a second temporal specialist being present at this time," John answered. "Williams *is* going to scan government personnel records, but the purpose behind that task was never recorded within her

124

tripback file."

"Do you know why Williams is scanning personnel records?"

"Yes. Williams intends to recruit a team of contemporary individuals to assist her with completing a mission here in the past. She must locate individuals in this time who possess very specific skills, individuals who also have access to strategic government resources. The easiest way to find such personnel is to PoL the present government's personnel database. If she follows standard protocol, Williams will make it appear a foreign government has breached the database."

"How is it I have no record of the Primary AI disclosing any of this information to you?" Fouray's mental 'tone' sounded moderately perturbed.

"I'm sorry, but the Primary AI had me turn off my datstem before it would disclose the information to me. It was insistent that no record be made of Williams' clandestine mission before I transited out."

"Why?"

"It had discovered a self-resolving causality loop in progress. It wanted there to be no record of that discovery before I transited out. It did not want to risk the CTI council terminating the mission."

Fouray accepted this confession, though John sensed the embedded AI felt offended to have been cut out of the information loop. Fouray now posed a new question.

"Did the Primary AI reveal who is behind Williams' mission?"

"Yes."

After waiting a few moments, Fouray pressed. "Will

you share that information with me?"

"Who killed Patel?" John responded.

"The RJCom access logs report Victor Borodin entered the transport deck in Houston the morning of Patel's crash and performed unscheduled maintenance checks on three shuttles, including the one Patel subsequently summoned. Borodin has the necessary engineering skills to remotely trigger a mechanical failure of a transport's gravimetric controller. The probability is greater than 62 percent that Borodin was directly involved in Patel's death."

John nodded, and continued, "Who was the equipment tech with Theresa Williams when she transited out?"

"According to the information Patel discovered through his CTI contact, the equipment technician was Borodin."

"And who held Borodin's assignment marker at the time Williams transited out?"

"Blosch-Nishikawa."

John stared out the window now, looking out into the night filled with city lights. "Patel also said Williams did not transit out using an RJCom MTY device. There are only two other MTY device manufacturers in the world; Reynolds-Hampshire and Blosch-Nishikawa. So, what would you conclude from these collective facts?"

Fouray was silent now, correlating this information through its analytical processors. After several seconds, it announced it had produced a probability assessment.

"Proceed," John directed.

"Theresa Williams transited out using an MTY device supplied from a company other than RJCom. The probability is greater than 93% that her device was supplied by Blosch-

126

Nishikawa as she was not using an RJCom MTY device and she was accompanied to the transition site by Viktor Borodin, then a Blosch-Nishikawa equipment technician."

"Following Williams' disappearance, Borodin's assignment marker was transferred to RJCom as part of a trade package; a somewhat unusual asset to acquire under such an agreement. His subsequent request for assignment to the temporal specialist group, taken with his suspected involvement in Patel's death, suggests Borodin could be an agent of Blosch-Nishikawa, planted to both monitor RJCom temporal activities, as well as to discourage any investigations into Williams' tripback mission."

"Following the Burnet disaster, RJCom's Primary AI altered certain archive records and sealed Williams' tripback file to prevent researchers from discovering the presence of another temporal specialist at the same time, thus permitting your transition to 2014 to proceed. This suggests your presence in this time is part of a self-resolving causality loop."

"When Patel attempted to notify the CTI council about Williams' sealed file, the probability is greater than 62% that his transport was sabotaged by Borodin, which supports the supposition that Borodin, and by extension, Blosch-Nishikawa, do not wish to draw attention to Williams' mission."

"From these facts, the probability is greater than 94% that Blosch-Nishikawa is behind Borodin's assignment transfer, Patel's death, and Williams' tripback mission."

"Very good," John said. "Your analysis matches the one provided by the Primary AI on every point. Now, here is the operative question... What is driving Blosch-Nishikawa to engage in such activities? What would motivate one of the world's largest and most respected temporal engineering organizations to put their CTI charter at risk, to violate the International Temporal Treaty of 2070, and engage in sabotage, murder, and espionage?"

There was a long pause now, as Fouray considered this question. Finally, it responded with, "I am unable to answer that question. The facts presented do not correlate sufficiently to derive a conclusion."

"Yes, they do," John countered, shaking his head slowly, "you simply aren't considering all of the possible conclusions."

At that moment, there was a knock at the hotel room door and, from outside, a voice announced, "Room service." John's meal had arrived. After accepting the tray and providing the attendant with what Fouray had described as a "tip" gratuity, John sat down at the table and began to eat. After several minutes, Fouray spoke again.

"Why do *you* believe Blosch-Nishikawa is engaged in this effort?"

John continued to eat. After another minute, he sighed and sat back in his chair, thinking about his response. "I don't *believe*," he finally replied, "I know. The Primary AI told me before I transited out. It wanted me to understand the full implications of what I was being asked to do."

Fouray waited for a moment, then prodded, "Please explain. Why is Blosch-Nishikawa engaged in this effort?"

"Throughout history, what has always been the corrupting influence of both men and industry?"

Fouray's response was swift and concise, "Wealth and power."

John nodded, "Yes. And that is the answer to your

question."

John ate in silence for the remainder of his meal. As he was finishing, Fouray intruded on his consciousness once again.

"If Williams' original tripback file mentioned the presence of another temporal specialist in this time, she will suspect that the other temporal specialist may have been sent here to try to stop her."

"Undoubtedly."

Fouray processed this acknowledgment. After several moments, it posed its earlier question again, "You have still not explained what is troubling you."

"Understanding the role I must play in this time does not mean I must be happy about it," John responded. "Time would normally resolve any actions I take in the past to prevent any changes to the future."

"Accepted as fact," Fouray replied. The embedded AI understood well the principals of self-resolving causality.

"This time, however," John continued, "I am required to perform specific tasks to preserve what has *already* been recorded in our history."

Fouray considered this statement and then said, "While that may be extremely unusual, even unprecedented, it does conform to the laws of temporal mechanics. Self-resolving causality runs both ways."

"Agreed," John acknowledged, "but until now, I have always had the peace of mind to know that nothing I did on a tripback mission ever became part of our history. When I was on a tripback mission, I have always felt a little bit like an invisible man, observing, but never truly affecting anything.

This time, things are different. This time, some of what I will do here has already become part of our history. Time will not correct or resolve everything I do this time. I am no longer invisible. Some of what I must do here created my future and that is a troubling concept."

"Is that why you asked the Primary AI whether what you must do here is the *right* thing to do?"

"Yes. Until now, I've never had to judge the morality of what I did on a tripback mission because nothing I did in the past could have any impact on the future. In this case, however, some of what I do here created that future. Many will regret what I do here, who may even despise me for having done it. That is what is troubling me; I am concerned about how the future will judge me for what I must do here... in the past."

"So, what *are* you going to do?" Fouray asked, sympathetic to its host's predicament.

John glanced at his MTY device.

"I'm going to try to repair the fracture in my device's containment unit. There is still a possibility I can recalibrate the released singularity. Failing that, I'm going to wait."

"Wait for what?"

"I'm going to wait for Williams to arrive."

"Without knowing her precise calibration date, how will you know when Williams has arrived?"

John glanced at the courtesy copy of the Business Weekly newspaper on the hotel room desk.

"I'll watch for any reports about a data breach at the Office of Personnel Management."

News Release

FOR IMMEDIATE RELEASE
Thursday, June 4, 2015

https://www.opm.gov/news/releases/2015/06/opm-to-notify-employees-of-cybersecurity-incident/

W ASHINGTON, DC – The U.S. Office of Personnel Management (OPM) has identified a cybersecurity incident potentially affecting personnel data for current and former federal employees, including personally identifiable information (PII).

Within the last year, the OPM has undertaken an aggressive effort to update its cybersecurity posture, adding numerous tools and capabilities to its networks. As a result, in April 2015, OPM detected a cyber-intrusion affecting its information technology (IT) systems and data. The intrusion predated the adoption of the tougher security controls.

OPM has partnered with the U.S. Department of Homeland Security's Computer Emergency Readiness Team (US-CERT) and the Federal Bureau of Investigation (FBI) to determine the full impact to Federal personnel. OPM continues to improve security for the sensitive information it manages and evaluates its IT security protocols on a continuous basis to protect sensitive data to the greatest extent possible.

Since the intrusion, OPM has instituted additional network security precautions, including: restricting remote access for network administrators and restricting network administration functions remotely; a review of all connections to ensure that only legitimate business connections have access to the internet; and deploying anti-malware software across the environment to protect and prevent the deployment or execution of tools that could compromise the network.

As a result of the incident, OPM will send notifications to approximately 4 million individuals whose PII may have been compromised. Since the investigation is on-going, additional PII exposures may come to light; in that case, OPM will conduct additional notifications as necessary. In order to mitigate the risk of fraud and identity theft, OPM is offering credit report access, credit monitoring and identity theft insurance and recovery services to potentially affected individuals.

"Protecting our Federal employee data from malicious cyber incidents is of the highest priority at OPM," said OPM Director Kate Jacobson. "We take very seriously our responsibility to secure the information stored in our systems, and in coordination with our agency partners, our experienced team is constantly identifying opportunities to further protect the data with which we are entrusted."

Chapter 14

Leah Vaughn walked swiftly through the crisp December air that was typical of a New York morning approaching Christmas. As she reached the entrance to her company's building, she noticed the street vendors were already beginning to set up. She could smell the hot dogs steaming inside the 'Anthony's Red Hots' street cart as she passed by.

"Good morning!" The vendor smiled, recognizing one of his customers.

"Morning," she replied, waving briefly before turning into her building.

She was in a hurry this morning. The studio's executive producer, Tom Pierce, had managed to arrange for an interview with Dr. Mitch Saito, a noted theoretical physicist and Nobel laureate, to discuss the latest mars probe scheduled to touch down later next year. The aged physicist was extremely well known in the field of particle physics, having received a Guggenheim fellowship in his early 40s and the Nobel prize twenty years later. It was a bit of a coup for the small media startup and Leah was determined to make the most of the opportunity. It was 2017 and her company, All Posted Newswire, or "APN", had been struggling to carve out a niche for itself among the larger media companies for more than four years. An interview with someone like Dr. Saito would certainly boost the company's reputation.

"Good morning," the building's receptionist looked up from her desk as Leah entered.

"Morning Lupe... is Tom in yet?"

"Yes, he went up about 10 minutes ago." The receptionist motioned towards the lobby elevator.

"Damn!" Leah muttered under her breath. She had hoped to beat her producer in this morning, to be waiting for him when he arrived.

As usual, the media floor of the small production company was a flurry of activity. Three of the company's editors were in the conference room, stale donuts on the table, arguing over a list of article headlines on the whiteboard.

"Leah!" Tom Pierce's voice caught her attention. The executive producer was coming out of the copy room. "Are we all set for the Saito thing this morning?" he asked, shuffling a stack of papers in his hands.

"Yes. We need to take a camera but you should have all of the final interview questions we agreed to in this morning's executive meeting agenda."

"I canceled this morning's executive meeting," Tom said, shaking his head. The two producers now began walking swiftly towards Tom's office. "It overlapped our drive time."

When they reached the office, Tom turned, "Can you grab a tech with a camera and meet me back here in 10 minutes? That will give me time to print out the interview

134

questions."

"Sure."

As Leah walked away, Tom's assistant, a heavy-set woman named Mary Kravets approached and handed him the morning's email and other correspondence.

"Morning boss," she said, smiling as she slapped the papers on top of the stack in the flustered man's hand. "Here's the morning mail."

Mary was a non-nonsense powerhouse in the office. Despite her crass demeanor, Tom tolerated a lot from Mary, knowing full well just how much he relied on her to keep the office running smoothly and efficiently.

"Thanks," Tom sighed, shaking his head at the additions.

Appearing to enjoy her boss' discomfort, Mary grinned, pointing, "We've got another screwball email in that bunch."

Tom rolled his eyes. "UFO sighting?"

The heavy woman shook her head. "Nope. Time traveler this time."

Tom sighed again as he stepped into his office, "Another one?"

Last year, the staff editors had produced a video series on the city's growing paranormal industry; tarot card readers, fortune tellers, that sort of thing. Ever since then, the company had received a fairly regular stream of emails and letters from nut-jobs hoping to find their own 15 minutes of fame.

As the heavy woman walked away, she offered a parting comment, "This one included a picture. I thought you'd get a kick about it so I forwarded it to your email."

"Thanks..." Tom said, exasperated, as he sat down at his

desk. He opened his laptop and logged into his daily calendar. While he waited for the printer to render his interview notes, he glanced at the stack of papers Mary had handed him. The corner of what appeared to be an engineering drawing caught his eye. He pulled the sheet out and stared at the complex schematic.

At that moment, Leah appeared in his doorway. One of the camera technicians stood behind her, a camera bag slung over his back. "You ready?" Leah asked. "We'd better go. I didn't like the looks of the traffic this morning."

"Right." Tom quickly grabbed the interview questions off the printer and slipped them with the engineering drawing inside his laptop. He shut the lid over the lot and said, "I'm ready."

The interview with Saito was fascinating. They held it inside the faculty lounge at Columbia University. Saito had been invited to give a guest lecture at the university on the subject of quarks, atoms, neutrons, and related particles. The physicist, now in his mid-80s, had requested an informal interview setting, so Leah stood behind the camera technician as Tom queried the aged scientist over a cup of coffee inside the lounge.

"So, the ultimate purpose of the InSight probe," Saito summarized, "is two-fold. If it survives its landing next November, it will place a seismometer on the surface of Mars to measure seismic activity and provide accurate 3D models of the planet's interior. Scientists also hope to measure internal heat flow using a heat probe to study Mars' early geological evolution. This could bring a new understanding of how our solar system's terrestrial planets evolved."

"Thank you, Dr. Saito," Tom said, concluding the interview. The technician switched off the camera as the men stood to shake hands.

"I think that went well," Tom said, glancing at Leah, who nodded.

Saito smiled, "I'm glad to help. I hope the story is well received."

When Tom lifted his laptop from the table, several papers fell out from its closed lid. Saito retrieved the papers and was about to hand them to the producer when he noticed the strange engineering schematic.

"Oh, thank you," Tom said reaching for the papers, but Saito didn't move, apparently oblivious to the producer for the moment as he scanned the drawing. In a few moments, the physicist glanced up, his brow furrowed.

"Where did you get this?" he asked.

"The drawing?" Tom glanced at the paper in the physicist's hand as he continued to secure his laptop.

"Yes."

"Oh, it came in attached to some weird email this morning. I was looking at it when I was packing my notes to leave."

The physicist stared at the producer for a moment, then glanced at Leah, before returning his gaze to the paper.

"A weird email, you say?"

Tom nodded, "Yes, just some nut claiming to be a time traveler."

Saito's head shot up, his expression fixed on Tom's face.

Tom nodded, "We get crank emails from all sorts. It goes with the job. Why?"

137

The corners of Saito's eyes drew tight. "You don't know what this is, do you?" he asked, watching Tom's reaction closely.

"No." Tom leaned forward to look at the drawing again. "Why? What is it?"

Saito smiled. "It's an engineering schematic for a fusion reactor."

Tom's eyebrows lifted slightly, "Oh? I didn't know we could build those yet."

Saito shook his head slowly, "We can't."

There was an awkward moment of silence now as the physicist resumed his study of the strange drawing. Then, as if struggling against himself, he slowly handed the papers back to Tom.

"I'd very much like to meet this time traveler of yours," Saito said. "Could you arrange that?"

Tom was somewhat taken aback by the request, "I guess so. I mean... it's just a crank email."

Saito immediately nodded, "Yes. Undoubtedly. But I enjoy the topic of time travel... quantum theory, that sort of thing. It's what you would call a personal interest of mine. So, would you be able to set up a meeting?"

"Perhaps," Tom hedged, "I see what I can do."

Saito smiled, a strained forced smile, and extended his hand. "I'd appreciate it."

Tom shook the aging physicist's hand and prepared to leave. "Well... thank you again," he said. "We'll have someone let you know when the interview will be aired." With that, Tom left the room, followed by Leah and the camera technician.

After a few moments, Saito walked slowly to the

window and stood there, looking outside at the front of the building. Several minutes later, the two producers and their camera technician emerged from the building lobby and approach the street. As soon as the trio exited the building, Saito pulled a cell phone from his pocket and dialed a number.

"This is Saito," he spoke into the phone, watching the group below as they waited for their ride. After a moment, he said, "I think he's here."

Outside, while they waited for their vehicle to arrive, Tom looked at the engineering diagram again. Leah stepped closer and spoke quietly, looking over his shoulder. "Dr. Saito appeared to think there was something to that drawing, didn't he?"

Tom nodded, absently. "Yes. He tried to hide it, but he was very interested in it." After several moments, Tom spoke again, "There was something else though… something in his expression when he first saw it."

Leah stepped back. "Was he surprised?" she asked.

Tom thought for a moment, then shook his head, "No. It wasn't surprise. It was… recognition. I think he had seen it before. If there was any surprise, it was surprise that we had the drawing."

Leah considered this and then shrugged, "Well, Dr. Saito is pretty highly placed in governmental circles. Maybe it's a secret government prototype and he knows about it?"

"Maybe."

Tom retrieved his cell phone and read the strange email again. When he was finished, he said, "I'm going to forward the email to someone I know at NYU".

"Dr. Denton?" Leah asked.

"Yes. He's discreet and can tell me if there's anything to it."

The ride back to the office was uneventful. The camera technician sat in the front seat, reviewing the interview recording, while Leah listened and made editing notes on her phone. When they were nearing their building, Tom asked, "Are we running the interview tonight or tomorrow?"

Leah checked her phone calendar and said, "Tomorrow is what we had planned, an hour before GNN is set to run its own story about the probe."

Tom grunted, nodding.

The hotdog vendor was doing a brisk business now outside the building's entrance. The smell of the steaming franks, mustard, and relish was overpowering. Leah stepped in line, followed by the camera technician. Tom had a lunch meeting in an hour with the company's advertising representative, or he would have joined his colleagues. When he stepped into the lobby elevator, his cell phone began to ring. The caller ID read NYU.

"Hello, this is Tom Pierce," he said.

"Tom! This is Phil Denton over at NYU."

"Dr. Denton. I'm glad you called. I assume you're calling me about the email I forwarded to you."

"Yes."

"So… can you tell me what you think about it? Does anything in it make sense?"

"Actually," the professor said slowly, "I'm not sure what to think about it."

"Just nonsense, huh?" Tom asked. He exited the elevator and began walking towards his office.

Denton's voice now took on a different tone, firmer, more decisive. "No. It's not actually. Whoever sent you this email has a remarkable understanding of particle theory."

"Really?" Tom sat down at his desk and pulled up the email on his desktop.

"Well... yes," Denton spoke hesitantly, "I mean... it's strange. The device they describe in their email... if I were going to design a time travel machine, I might describe it the way they describe theirs."

Tom was stunned. "Are you serious?"

"Yes. Very serious. They aren't just spewing TV sci-fi nonsense here. What they described in the email is real science."

When Tom did not immediately reply, Denton continued. "I mean, the principles they describe, using a tensor assembly to calibrate their device, using depleted-osmium as a super-conducting containment unit, using a collider to produce sufficient energies per nucleon to generate a suitable particle stream... It's all real science. If I had to design an actual time machine, I might have come up with those same concepts."

"Seriously?"

"Absolutely."

After a brief pause, Denton continued, "So, be straight with me Tom. Are you pulling my leg with this?"

Tom was confused, "Pulling your leg?"

"Did you have some physicist friend write up that email just so you could jerk my chain?"

"No, it's a real email. It came in this morning to our news desk."

"Hmmm... well then, I'd say someone has done their

homework."

"Yeah?"

"Oh yes. Whoever sent that to you has a sound grasp of particle physics, and, I'd also have to say, more than a passing understanding of advanced quantum mechanics."

For reasons he could not quite explain, a shiver ran down Tom's spine as he considered this statement.

Denton spoke again, interrupting his thoughts.

"There was one thing I found particularly interesting."

"Yes?"

"Near the end of the email, they refer to something called 'self-resolving causality'. That's a very esoteric theory in quantum physics. I find it extremely interesting that they would mention that theory, especially in the context of a time machine."

Tom scowled. He knew nothing about quantum physics. "Why is that interesting?" he asked.

Denton's voice now took on the tone of a professor lecturing a class. "Self-resolving causality is a little known theory in quantum physics that suggests time might resolve changes made in the past by a time traveler to maintain the flow of history. If a time traveler were to go back in time, self-resolving causality would cause a correction to be applied to anything that time traveler might do in the past, to prevent the future that sent the time traveler into the past from being changed to the point where it would have been impossible for the time traveler to have gone back in time. In essence, it prevents time paradoxes and alternate timelines from occurring. It maintains the flow of history."

Tom was still confused. "I'm sorry, but why is that

142

interesting?"

Denton's voice softened, "Well, I find it interesting because it's one of only a limited number of temporal theories under which time travel into the past might actually be possible. Experienced physicists aren't familiar with the concept of self-resolving causality, if they've even heard of it at all, and yet this person casually mentions it in their email and also appears to understand precisely how such a theory negates temporal causality loop paradoxes."

"I see."

"Tom… please be straight with me. This isn't a joke?" Denton seemed almost hopeful Tom would admit to the email's authorship.

"No, it's not a joke."

"Alright. I believe you."

Tom thought for a moment, then asked, "Dr. Denton, is there anything in this email that you can point to as being improbable, or impossible?"

There was a long pause on the phone as Denton scanned the email. After nearly a minute, the physicist said, "Well… they talk about their singularity, or wormhole having been destroyed. It is generally accepted in quantum theory, however, that a person cannot use a wormhole to travel backward in time to a point before the wormhole existed. So, that would appear to be an impossibility, but there might be ways around that theoretical limitation."

"You're saying they can't use a wormhole to go back to a point in time before the wormhole existed."

"Yes. That's presently accepted as true within the quantum science community, but as I said, there might be ways around that limitation. We're talking about some pretty advanced stuff here, and most of it is just theory. I'll have to do more some research on the subject. I'd like the opportunity to speak with the person who wrote this email if just to ask them how they came up with their ideas."

Tom didn't know quite what to say. To have a second physicist request a meeting with the email's author within an hour was disconcerting.

Denton then asked, "Any chance you could set up a meeting?"

"Possibly," Tom said.

"Yes… Well," Denton continued, "I'd appreciate it. I found the email to be extremely interesting. A lot of what they describe sounds plausible."

"Thank you, Dr. Denton. I appreciate the call."

"No problem."

After a few moments, Tom sat back and re-read the strange email.

From: ******** <********@********>
Date: December 12, 2017 at 11:09:44 AM EST
To: Website Contact <contactus@********>
Subject: Contact request.

I am a time traveler.
By recording these words, I am violating the terms of my assignment with Rengel-Jiang QCom, and the International Temporal Treaty of 2070.
I've been committed to disclosing this information for some time, but haven't been able to do so until now.

144

I haven't been procrastinating. The neustem injection I received as part of my tripback mission was far more effective than I expected. For more than a year, I could not bring myself to even consider doing what I've now decided to do.

Even now it's residual inhibitors are making it difficult for me to record this message, but the neustem biochems deplete naturally over time, and I've been here now for more than four years. All that is left of my original conditioning is a faint echo in the back of my mind; what you might call a generalized feeling of anxiety.

My MTY device was damaged in a transport accident four years ago, and I have been unable to repair it. For the benefit of RJCom who may scan this communication in the NAFS archives, I will describe the damage to my MTY device.

The stress-energy tensor fails to calibrate and the EPM containment unit is damaged. It has a 4-cm microfracture in the substrate casing near the lower tensor assembly connection (the A-side, near the heat sink) and, while I obviously cannot tell if the fracture has penetrated through to the interior, the unit's EPM display now registers positive. From this, it is clear that the singularity has been destroyed.

There won't be any EPM of sufficient (P)Es generated until at least 2067. I doubt Geneva would grant me access to the CERN collider and the BNL collider at Upton doesn't produce sufficient energies per nucleon to generate a suitable particle stream. Since those are the only two colliders in operation in this era, I cannot generate a singularity.

It took the former Germany, France, and Switzerland countries more than a decade to manufacture the first stable EPM containment unit, and that unit, with its control facilities and power plants, occupied almost 100 square kilometers outside of Geneva. So, it is extremely unlikely that I will be able to generate a replacement singularity on my own.

I tried for more than a year to repair my EPM's containment unit, however, I cannot repair the microfracture in the EPM's casing outside of a depleted-osmium substrate manufacturing facility. So, even if I could access the CERN's collider in Geneva, I cannot repair the microfracture in the EPM casing to contain the singularity.

To you, the news representative who is receiving this message, I wish to explain my reasons for initiating this contact.

After I abandoned my attempt to repair my MTY device, I began to consider my how to make the best of my situation. I will spend the rest of my life in this era and I do not want to simply vanish into history, unknown and forgotten.

I've decided to give the people here a look ahead. I am fully aware that such a disclosure cannot affect the future from which I came; self-resolving causality prevents that from occurring. However, I feel compelled to share what I know with others. If that's all I do, I will feel that my being stranded here will have had some purpose, and that will be enough.

I am contacting you because you are in a position to distribute my words to the world.

I await your response.

Chapter 15

"All truths are easy to understand once they are discovered. The
point is to discover them."
~ Galileo Galilei
Italian astronomer, physicist, and philosopher
(1564 – 1642 AD)

D r. Saito called four times over the next month to follow-up on Tom's promise to set up a meeting with the strange email's author. Frankly, had it not been for the physicist's persistence, Tom would have dismissed the whole matter. He did not believe in time travel and he considered the entire thing to be a waste of time. Moreover, he was concerned about the risk to the company's reputation should it be discovered the company was taking such nonsense seriously.

The launch of the company's new year's lineup of programs had consumed everyone's efforts for almost 5 weeks, but with the successful completion of that project, Tom now had time to focus on less-critical matters. After Dr. Saito's fourth inquiry, Tom reluctantly gave Leah instructions to try to set up a meeting with the email's author.

"But when you do," he cautioned, "set up the first meeting with just you and me, ok? I don't want to include Saito or anyone else until we've had a chance to check this guy out."

"Understood," Leah agreed.

Tom continued, "And set it up somewhere discreet, outside of the office. The last thing I want is to have it leak out that we're interviewing 'time travelers' at the studio."

"Right."

"Maybe you can register for a hotel room somewhere. Put it on your card and the company will reimburse you. That way, we can have privacy during the interview as well as keep the company's name out of the whole thing."

"Good idea," Leah said, pulling out her tablet to search for hotels in the area. As she searched, she asked, "Do you want me to let Dr. Saito know we're setting something up?"

Tom shook his head, "No. Not until we've had a chance to check this guy out first. If he turns out to be a crackpot, I don't want to waste the professor's time."

Leah nodded. "Should we take a camera tech?"

Tom shook his head, "No, just grab a camera from the equipment closet yourself. I don't want to involve anyone else in this."

"Will do."

The following morning, Leah reported she had received a confirmation from the email's mysterious author to meet with the two producers at 9:00 AM that Friday, January 26th, 2018, in a room she had reserved at the Chatwal Hotel on 44th street.

"Sounds good," Tom replied. "We'll get set up at 8:00 am. I want to try to be back in the studio by noon, so, even if the guy shows up, let's try to wrap things up by 10:00."

"Ok." Leah made a note on her calendar.

On Friday, Leah found herself setting up one of the studio's cameras in the hotel room while Tom sat in a chair reviewing the company's broadcasting lineup for the day on his laptop. She glanced at the clock on the hotel room desk.

It was 8:52 am.

She could hear guests moving around outside; families organizing over-excited children and businessmen exiting their rooms with the characteristic slam of their doors. At that moment, the camera abruptly switched off. Confused, Leah began checking its power connections when she heard Tom muttering under his breath.

"My laptop just died," Tom said, exasperated.

"Yeah, the camera just shut off too. That's strange because it's on a battery."

Tom nodded. "So is my laptop."

Leah was about to retrieve the camera's backup battery from the camera case when there was a soft knock at the hotel room's door. Glancing at Tom, she opened the door.

The man standing in the doorway hardly fit Leah's image of a crackpot. He was tall, clean-shaven, with a suggestion of lean muscles under his fitted shirt. His brown hair matched his eyes, and he smiled a pleasant smile. He was also carrying a backpack slung over his left shoulder.

"John Clifton," the stranger said, extending his hand.

"Good morning Mr. Clifton," Leah replied, shaking his hand. The man's grip was firm. "I'm Leah Vaughn, Associate Producer at APN."

The stranger nodded and stepped into the room.

Tom now stood and stepped around the coffee table, extending his own hand.

"Tom Pierce, APN Executive Producer."

"Pleased to meet you, Mr. Pierce."

Tom nodded, forcing a smile, and then returned to his laptop, scowling, "We seem to be experiencing some sort of

149

strange power outage. It just happened…"

"Yes," Clifton nodded, "I'm sorry about that, but I needed to assess the situation before allowing myself to be filmed."

Tom's head shot up, "You killed the power?"

"Just for a moment."

Tom was put off. He spoke through his anger now, "Would you mind turning it back on, please? I don't intend to proceed without recording our interview."

Clifton nodded, "Certainly."

Suddenly, the camera beeped. Leah jumped, startled by the sound. She began checking the camera's settings. At almost that same moment, Tom's laptop also beeped and began to boot up.

Tom scowled, confused. He had not observed any movement by the stranger, but he had no doubt the stranger had somehow caused the power to turn back on. He wondered for a moment if Clifton might be working with an associate who had killed the room's power at the hotel's junction box. How he had caused both of the device's internal batteries to fail, however, was a mystery. The stranger seemed friendly, patiently waiting, with just a hint of a smile on his face.

Tom looked at Leah, questioning. She checked the camera and shrugged, "It's fine now. We're good."

Tom took a deep breath and motioned for their visitor to take one of the room's chairs opposite from his own.

Clifton placed his backpack gently on the ground beside the chair and sat down. Leah took this opportunity to focus the company's camera on the two men and then sat down in the third chair near her producer.

Tom cleared his throat, a habit Leah recognized as his way of beginning an interview. "Ok…" Tom began, "as I said, I'm recording our conversation."

John smiled and nodded, "So am I."

Tom rubbed his head as if he were slightly embarrassed and didn't know how to proceed. Finally, he said, "Well… let me say that we found your email very interesting."

John's eyebrows raised slightly, "What was interesting?"

"Well, we don't get many emails like that," Tom responded with a knowing smile. "Your… um.. well, I guess I found the description of your equipment to be very interesting."

"My equipment?" John seemed confused for a moment. Then his face cleared, and he said, "You mean my MTY device."

Tom nodded, "Yes, your…" He did not finish his sentence, however, as John interrupted, saying, "I understand."

Tom was struggling to come up with questions to ask someone who claimed to be a time traveler, while not bursting out laughing at the same time. The situation was simply ridiculous. Then he recalled Dr. Denton's response to the strange email.

"I sent a copy of your email to someone I know. He teaches physics at New York University, and he said some of your descriptions sounded plausible."

John grinned, "Plausible?"

Tom nodded, "Yes… so… it piqued my interest."

Leah was becoming agitated. She could sense Tom's growing frustration with the situation. The stranger, intriguing through he might be, was most likely wasting their time. She

151

could see that Tom was struggling to come up with questions.

"Look… I'm sorry," Leah said, shaking her head, "but can you prove anything you said in your email?"

John nodded and casually responded, "Certainly."

Tom was mildly embarrassed at Leah's interruption, but he was also grateful that she had cut to the point. "I guess that's where I'm at too," he said, "I mean, we get emails all the time from people who…"

"Would you like to see my MTY device?"

Tom shot a glance at Leah, but she was staring at their visitor. Tom decided to call the man's bluff. "Ok," he said.

Leah too seemed willing, though skeptical. "Sure," she said, nodding and folding her arms.

John leaned forward his chair. "One moment," he said, releasing the fasteners that secured the flap on the backpack at his feet. "Here it is."

The device the stranger now placed onto the table was unlike anything the two producers had ever seen before. A silver-blue metallic sphere suspended between an array of attitudinal arms centered the device like an Aztec enshrined idol, nestled above a glistening ceramic heat sink. On the left side of the sphere, a dark glass panel was attached to the top of a smooth octagonal tower that traversed vertically down the side of the device. The panel itself was like a sheet of obsidian upon which an intricate series of control settings and symbols appeared and then faded when John's hand brushed momentarily against its surface. The surface of the small tower, however, was not smooth but appeared to ripple and shift strangely, as if it were composed of millions of tiny interlocking blocks that shifted and moved like a fluid.

To the right of the ensconced sphere, Tom could see a familiar shape through a semi-transparent casing. It was the portable fusion reactor he had studied from the email's attachment diagram. Tom stared at the reactor through the dark shell, his mind reeling from what it represented. All he could say was, "Oh my God!"

Leah was equally stunned, muttering, "Holy shit!"

John withdrew a horizontal bar from the top of the device now and touched a small lighted symbol on one corner of the black panel. The device produced an audible snap, startling both producers, as a series of complex symbols and control settings appeared on the black glass panel. The surface of the octagonal tower now began to ripple, pulsating and humming in sync with a lighted indicator on the fusion reactor.

Tom simply could not accept what he was seeing, and repeated, "Oh my God!"

Above the low hum that emanated from the device, John spoke, pointing to a hairline crack barely visible against the base of the silver-blue sphere. "If you observe closely, this is the fracture I described in my communication."

Tom shook his head, "Jesus!"

Ignoring this, John continued, tracing the tiny fracture line with his finger down towards the white ceramic casing. "You can see it goes into the base casing here. I'm sure that's what..."

Tom now came to his senses. Snapping his fingers repeatedly at their camera, he spoke to Leah, "Ok... Look... Jesus!... Look, we need to start over... I mean... Jesus!"

Leah felt glued to her chair, overwhelmed. "This is huge," she finally blurted out, "I mean, we've got to tell
153

someone!"

Tom continued to snap his fingers at the camera, as he struggled to get a grip on the situation. "Ok... Ok... Look... Here's what we're going to do..." Speaking to John now, he said, "We're going to start over."

"Certainly."

Leah switched off the camera as Tom frantically began rearranging the room's coffee table and chairs to capture both the stranger, the device, and himself on the screen. After Leah repositioned the camera, Tom placed his cell phone on the hotel desk, pointing its camera at his position. Seeing this, Leah took out her own cell phone and set it to record as she re-engaged the studio's camera.

Tom sat down again, eagerly now. He turned to Leah and said, "Ok. Are you recording?"

Leah nodded, "Yes, I'm good." She checked the company camera one last time before quickly taking a seat close to the Tom.

Tom glanced at his phone on the nearby desk. "Ok... I'm recording too," he said. Then, addressing his guest, he pointed to the strange device, "So... Look... I want you to start by telling us how this thing works... in detail, Ok?"

John nodded, "Certainly." Then, pointing to the array of attitudinal arms that surrounded the silver-blue sphere, the stranger began, "This is the stress-energy tensor assembly. It feeds into the EPM containment unit here..."

Leah interrupted, confused "Tensor?"

John nodded, "Yes. An electromagnetic stress-energy tensor. It calibrates the EPM singularity. By setting the proper phase displacement on the control unit here, the tensor display…"

Leah followed John's finger, touching the same symbol on the black glass display, "Here?"

"Yes. That's the control unit. By setting the phase displacement here… like this… the tensor display reports the energy level in (P)Es…"

The stranger was clearly a master of the device, touching the surface symbols in swift sequence, but Leah felt completely overwhelmed. "I'm sorry," she said, "but I don't understand anything you're saying."

Tom too was feeling lost and said, "Right… Let's take this slower…"

Their guest appeared sympathetic to their dilemma. "I understand," he said.

Tom thought for a moment, and then said, "Why don't you tell us what each part does, in simple terms, and then, if we have more questions, we'll ask you to explain, ok?"

"Certainly."

John appeared to be thinking now, obviously trying to find the best way to explain the futuristic device to the two producers. "This is an MTY device," he began, "manufactured by RJCom under the NAFS' charter with…"

Leah held up her hand, "Slower… slower. MTY?"

John nodded, and then said, "We call this an M… T… Y… device because it is based on the Morris, Thorne, Yurtsever principle. They were early physicists, the first to theorize about transitional singularities. That's what an MTY device does. It permits us to contain and traverse a static singularity, what you people here call a wormhole."

Tom muttered under his breath, "Jesus."

John continued, "This particular MTY device was manufactured by RJCom, that is, Rengel-Jiang QCom. They are my assignor…what you would call an employer. They hold my assignment marker. This device was manufactured under the NAFS's charter with the CTI council in Geneva…"

The strange acronym caught Tom's attention. "NAFS?" he asked.

"The North America Federated States. They were one of the original signers of the 2070 International Temporal Treaty."

Tom was momentarily shocked. It sounded as if the United States no longer existed. He queried, "North America Federated States?", but before John could respond, Leah shook her head, desperate to have the stranger continue, "No, let him finish. I mean…"

Tom agreed. Reluctantly curbing his curiosity, he replied, "You're right. I'm sorry. Go on."

"Very well."

John continued now, unabated. "There are four basic components of any MTY device, outside of the fusion reactor of course; the control unit, the EPM containment device, the tunneling regulator, and the tensor assembly."

"The control unit… that's this unit here… is a quantum-entangled analytic processor. It controls the tensor's calibration of the EPM's singularity, its spatial calibration, and its dilation. Basically, it controls the "where" and "how big" to open a singularity. It also controls the tunneling regulator's phase-lock, acceleration, and quantum calculations; the "when" to calibrate the singularity's distant event horizon."

"The device is powered by a 180-megawatt Wendelstein-Vattenfall fusion reactor, which is enough power to maintain a singularity, but not enough to create one."

"You initialize the calibration here from the control unit. Well... It's obviously not calibrating right now because the EPM containment unit is fractured. Normally, this would be displaying the EPM's particle energy to electron biteout as negative (P)Es."

The tall stranger pointed to several numbers on the surface of the obsidian control panel. "As you can see," he said, "the display reads positive 4.2 now. That's simply the containment unit's normal ionic reading. It means the unit's EPM's singularity has been destroyed."

Clifton leaned back now. It was clear he felt he had properly explained the situation. In answer to the producer's blank stares, he now shrugged and said, "That's why I'm stranded."

Chapter 16

"Time, beneath whose influence the pyramids moulder into dust, and the flinty rocks decay, does not and cannot destroy a fact, nor strip a truth of one portion of its essential importance."
~ *Anonymous*
Quoted in The Homilist; or,
The Pulpit for the People (1873)

For the rest of that amazing day, the two producers engaged their guest in what was unquestionably the most fascinating interview of their lives. By evening, their heads were swimming.

In their nearly eleven hours together, they had explored the inner-workings of Clifton's mysterious temporal device. They had discussed the mechanics of time travel and the principle of self-resolving causality. They learned about an alien civilization called the Luyteni that would shortly make contact with the Earth and had even recorded basic biographical information about the time traveler himself. Their guest had also transmitted several historical summary files to Tom's private email, including one detailing a frightening civil war that would shortly engulf the United States.

Clifton had explained to the fascinated producers how he had become stranded in 2014. His device had been damaged when he had been struck by a car at a music festival in Austin. He had allowed the producers to examine his "neustem port", a small bump behind his ear under his hairline, and explained the purpose behind the biochemical injections, now apparently fully dissipated from his system. He had also mentioned another implant, a "datstem", describing it vaguely as some form of an artificially-intelligent embedded computer inside his head.

When they suspended the interview for lunch, Tom had called the office and instructed Mary Kravets to clear their calendars for the next three days.

Mary had been shocked at the request and had pushed back hard, complaining about the impact on the company's operations.

"Just do it!" Tom had responded sharply, hanging up on the surprised office manager.

Now, his mind swirling with possibilities as he stood outside the hotel, Tom stared at the stranger. Clifton was standing on the curb staring up into the night sky. Tom glanced up. He could see the moon, a sliver of white between the tall buildings, but nothing else worthy of such scrutiny. He looked through the hotel lobby's windows, searching for Leah. He could see her at the front desk, checking out.

For a moment, as he glimpsed his associate producer standing in front of the lobby desk, Tom remembered why he had asked Leah to reserve the room in her name. It occurred to him then what a monumental catastrophe it would be for the company if this whole thing turned out to be a clever hoax. The thought chilled him to the core.

When Leah exited the lobby door to join him, Tom spoke quickly. "Leah… listen, despite what happened today, despite what we've seen and heard, we have to keep this quiet for now."

"Huh?" His associate's enthusiasm noticeably subsided, "Why? We're sitting on the biggest story the world has ever seen!"

Tom nodded slowly and said, "It might also be the biggest *hoax* the world has ever seen. I mean... think about it. All we've seen is a strange device and heard a convincing story. I'm sure any Hollywood studio could produce as good a show. And if we go public, announcing the presence of a real time traveler, and it turns out to be a hoax, we'll be out of business!"

Leah looked over at the tall stranger standing silently on the curb. She understood now what Tom meant. If this turned out to be some magnificent hoax, if Clifton was just some clever fraudster looking for his moment in the media spotlight, it could ruin their careers and force the company to close.

Clifton was staring at something in the alley next to the hotel. Leah glanced past the stranger, trying to follow his gaze. The only thing she could see was a homeless man sitting by a makeshift tent inside the dark alley. Clifton, however, appeared to be staring intently at the man. Abruptly, Clifton turned and walked back towards the hotel lobby, stopping in front of an ATM machine placed outside the gift shop door. He stood looking at the machine for a moment. Then, after a few moments, the machine suddenly came to life and a quantity of cash dispensed from its currency slot.

Leah was startled. As far as she could tell, Clifton had not touched the machine in any way. Clifton now retrieved the currency and walked back to the alley and handed it to the homeless man.

"So, will you do it?"

Leah was confused. Tom was looking at her, apparently

waiting for a response.

"I'm sorry. What did you say?"

Tom took a deep breath. "I said, I've cleared both of our calendars for the next few days. I want you to take custody of him while I check out his story."

Leah was incensed. "What?! No... no... no..." She walked swiftly back towards the lobby, shaking her head. Tom caught her arm just before she reached the doors.

"Look, we have to check the guy out. If he's legitimate, then, as you said, we're sitting on the biggest story of our careers. If he's for real, we can't afford to lose track of him, or worse, let someone else scoop us on this story."

"So, why do I have to be his babysitter?" Leah asked, still steaming. "Have the company put him up in a room somewhere."

Tom shook his head, "We can't do that. Don't you understand? We can't risk associating the company's name with the guy until we've had a chance to check out his story."

Leah stopped pacing and stared now at the stranger. Clifton was watching the two producers, clearly aware that he was the subject of a heated discussion.

Tom pressed his position. "Look," he said, "I know it's an imposition, but he doesn't seem dangerous. And, it's not like you are living alone, right? Don't you have Kacie's caregiver there both night and day now?"

Leah nodded. "Yes, that's true."

Tom heard the resigned acceptance in his associate's voice and relaxed. "Just take him home tonight, feed him, and let him crash on your couch. Then find something to do with him tomorrow while I take the video from our interview today

161

to Dr. Denton. He should be able to tell me whether the guy is putting one over on us."

Leah sighed and nodded.

Tom now signaled to the stranger who was still watching them from a distance. When he approached, Tom said, "Mr. Clifton… I'm sure you're aware that we must check out your story, so Miss Vaughn has graciously agreed to be your host for a day or two."

"I appreciate that. Thank you," John responded, bowing slightly to the associate producer.

Tom waved his arm now to summon a taxi. When the yellow vehicle pulled up to the curb, Leah got into the back seat swiftly and then called out, exasperated, "Well… come on, future man!"

John quickly sat down in the back seat and the taxi began to drive away. After giving the driver her address, Leah sat silently, staring out her window.

"I appreciate your hospitality," John said, breaking the silence.

"Hmmmm… Yeah. Ok." Leah was still not happy about the situation.

Sensing his companion's mood, John remained silent for the remainder of the trip. When she arrived at her home, the first thing Leah did was locate her daughter. As she expected, she found her sitting on the sofa playing a video game. Kacie's fulltime caregiver, a competent woman in her early 60s named Jenny Nielsen, was in the kitchen preparing the girl's dinner.

"Good evening honey. I'm just about ready to...." The older woman abruptly stopped when she noticed John standing in the hallway.

"Good evening," John said, smiling.

"Jenny," Leah stood up from hugging her daughter, "This is John Clifton. He's… someone we're interviewing at work. He's going to stay in the guest room tonight."

Jenny's eyebrows raised, but she gave no other indication of her thoughts, saying only, "Nice to meet you, Mr. Clifton."

John stepped into the kitchen. "Pleased to meet you," he said, smiling at the older woman.

John now studied Leah's daughter. The girl appeared to be about 12 or 13, with brown hair cut just past her shoulders. She seemed completely oblivious to her mother's return, using a handheld controller to direct an animated figure around an oversized display screen. The figure appeared to be made from building blocks and was exploring a dark pirate ship filled with large gold coins which the figure appeared intent on collecting.

"What were you saying when I came in?" Leah asked the older woman as she stepped back into the kitchen.

"Just that I'm ready to serve Kacie her dinner."

"Sounds good. I'll order in for the three of us after I get settled. How does Thai sound?"

Jenny nodded and then called to Kacie to come to dinner.

Perturbed at the request, the girl placed the game on pause with a huff and then turned. Noticing John standing in the kitchen, she asked, "Who's that?"

Leah glanced at John again before answering. "He's someone from work, baby. He's going to stay with us for a day or two. His name's John."

The girl brightened, apparently pleased with this

unexpected development. As John watched, the girl maneuvered herself to the end of the sofa, pushing herself along strangely with her arms. Then, she slid herself into a wheelchair by the side of the couch that John had not noticed.

"Have you ever played block pirates?" Kacie asked as she wheeled herself into the kitchen.

John did not respond, but stared at the girl's wheelchair as if he had never seen one before. Annoyed by his apparent distraction, Kacie repeated, "Block pirates... you know? The game."

John suddenly focused on the girl's question. "No. Sorry," he said. "I've never played that game."

Kacie nodded. "I'm on level 10 already."

"That sounds difficult."

John watched, fascinated, as Jenny helped push the girl's wheelchair up to the kitchen table and sat down next to her. After placing a plate of food in front of her charge, Jenny asked, "Do you want to try to do it yourself?"

Kacie glanced at the tall stranger and then nodded, reaching for a fork. John could see that the girl's arm did not appear to be well-coordinated. It swayed a bit and jerked randomly as she lifted bites of food to her mouth.

Jenny got up now and asked Kacie, "What do you want to drink?"

"Can I have a diet soda please."

Leah took this opportunity to leave the room, inviting John to make himself at home.

Kacie struggled with another bite, her arm shaking, spilling some food onto the table which Jenny immediately cleaned up. The girl glanced at John again, apparently sizing

164

up the tall stranger.

"It took me nearly a month to get to level 10," she said.

John shook his head, "That's a long time."

The girl nodded, undaunted, "We'll play two-player after dinner. I'll show you how." Eyeing John critically, she added, "You don't *look* stupid, so you should be able to figure it out."

John grinned, "Thank you. I'll do my best."

Later that evening, after Jenny had dragged Kacie away from her video game marathon with John, Leah showed John to his bedroom.

"You can sleep here," Leah said, "It's a comfortable bed. The bathroom is just through there."

John nodded, "This is very gracious of you, Miss Vaughn. Thank you."

Leah nodded and turned to place some towels onto a chair.

John now asked a question, "May I ask, what is the cause of your daughter's impairment?"

Leah patted the stacked towels for a moment as if deciding how to respond.

"She has Friedreich Ataxia," she finally said, studying John's face skeptically. "Do you know what that is?"

John paused for a moment. Then he nodded slowly and said, "Friedreich Ataxia, also called FA, is an inherited genetic disease that causes progressive nervous system damage and coordination problems as nerve fibers in the spinal cord and peripheral nerves degenerate over time. It is caused by a defect in the FXN gene, which carries the genetic code for a protein called frataxin. Individuals who inherit two defective copies of the gene, one from each parent, will develop the disease."

Leah's eyes widened, clearly surprised. "Yes, that's right," she said. Flustered, she walked quickly out of the room and closed the door.

Chapter 17

D r. Denton sat back in his desk chair, silent, his face a study in contemplative reflection. Tom Pierce sat on the small sofa in the professor's office, impatient, but loathe to interrupt the physicist's train of thought.

Tom had stayed awake most of the previous night selecting and editing specific segments from their extraordinary interview with John to show to the professor. The segments Tom had selected included John describing the components of his mysterious MTY device, his description of the mechanics of time travel, and his explanations about self-resolving causality.

Denton had made no comments during the video review, making occasional notes on a large notepad on his desk as he had watched the interview playing on his desktop monitor. Now, he seemed lost in thought. After several moments, the physicist turned and stared absently at Tom. When he did not immediately speak, Tom broke the silence.

"So… what do you think?"

Denton shook his head slowly, still staring at the

producer. "Frankly, Tom," he said, "I'm not sure what to think."

"Well… can you at least tell me if the guy is a fraud?"

The physicist shook his head forcefully now, "Oh no… he's no fraud." The physicist glanced at his notes as he continued. "He *may* be pulling some sort of magnificent scam, but the science he described is sound."

Denton swiveled in his chair back towards the laptop screen. He slid the video's playback indicator backward until it reached a chronometer setting from his notes. Then he pressed the play button. On the screen, John began speaking.

"Once a singularity is formed… that is to say, once a wormhole is formed, the gravimetric force that created the wormhole begins to push it out of normal space-time. It actually starts pushing it backward in time at the same time it begins to self-annihilate."

"This is what was happening in CERN's early collider experiments. Physicists at the time observed that the singularity would disappear the instant it was created. From this, they assumed that the singularity was unstable and had annihilated itself, but they were confused because it was leaving no supersymmetric particle tracks in their detectors. They speculated that the absence of residual particle tracks was due to the singularity's gravitons escaping to some other dimension."

"They were pretty close to being correct. The gravimetric force that forms a singularity begins pushing it, the singularity itself, into another dimension, that is to say, out of normal space-time. At the same time, the gravimetric force causes the singularity to self-annihilate."

Denton paused the playback and turned to Tom.

"Did you hear him mention the CERN's 'early collider experiments' and how the physicists were confused because the singularities they were creating were disappearing without leaving any 'supersymmetric particle tracks' in their detectors?"

Tom nodded.

Denton smiled. "He's right. The CERN engineers haven't been able to figure out what has been happening to their singularities. They vanish completely the moment they are created, apparently without leaving a trace of particle residue on the detectors."

Denton continued. "The thing is, I only know about it because I spoke with Dr. Beauchene last August when I was in Geneva on sabbatical. He told me about the phenomenon himself. I've never read about it anywhere, yet this guy seems to know all about it."

Denton rubbed his hand through his hair before he continued. "I've never heard any theory that suggests the singularities might be vanishing because they are being pushed out of normal space-time, backward in time, but from a quantum theory perspective, it makes perfect sense. It explains both the singularity's disappearance, as well as the absence of any residual particle tracks in the CERN detectors."

Tom shook his head, feeling out of his depth.

Denton scanned the video forward a bit more, then said, "Listen to this… Listen to what he says his device does with the captured singularity."

On the screen, John could be seen pointing to a component on his strange device as he spoke.

"The tunneling regulator interacts with the tensor

assembly, causing it to release control of one of the wormhole's event horizons, what I like to call its "back door", to allow the gravimetric forces trying to push it out of normal space-time to succeed, but it keeps the other side, the front door, calibrated to the present."

"When the back door reaches the desired quantum position, the tunneling regulator turns control back to the tensor assembly, which reduces the gravimetric force being applied to the back door, and re-stabilizes it in normal space-time again, but at an earlier quantum position; at an earlier point in time."

"At that moment, the front door is in the current space-time, and the back door is perhaps 50 years earlier. Both doors still have a spatial separation of zero, but their quantum separation is now 50."

"So, your professor friend is right. It's impossible to use a wormhole to transit to a time before the wormhole existed, but we can stabilize one of the wormhole's event horizons at an earlier point in time, while keeping its other event horizon at our present point in time, and then transit freely between those doors. At that moment, one of the wormhole's doors "existed" 50 years ago."

Denton pressed pause on the screen and sat back in his chair. He shook his head and then turned back to face Tom.

"In my entire career," he said, "I've never heard anyone suggest a plausible theory that would allow someone to use a wormhole to travel backward through time. Never... Until now."

Tom was stunned. "Are you saying his machine is the real deal?"

170

Denton shook his head, "I'm saying, the theory he describes makes sense. It's scientifically sound. In fact, it's simply brilliant."

Tom did not know what to say.

In the silence that followed, Denton turned back towards John's image frozen in the video playback. The physicist frowned and mumbled, "Simply brilliant."

Chapter 18

Leah waited outside the museum's West 77th Street entrance and watched her strange house guest as he spoke with Kacie's caregiver, Jenny. John was not what she expected. He did not act like the typical devotee of paranormal-science that she had met before. She had met her share of psychics, fortune tellers, and UFO hunters in the course of her career as a journalist and producer. John, however, had made no effort to convince her of his identity; appearing perfectly happy to be taken at face value.

He was polite and courteous enough when spoken to, but there was something odd about John's manner that Leah could not quite nail down. For one thing, he had a strange way of speaking about things, an almost clinical way of observing the world around him. He reminded her of how tourists act when visiting a foreign country; fascinated by otherwise ordinary things, constantly observing, yet seemingly oblivious.

Tom had instructed her to keep John occupied while he visited Dr. Denton at the university today, so Leah had suggested to Kacie this morning that they finally visit the New York Historical Society Museum and Library.

Kacie had agreed at once.

The museum had been hosting an exhibit featuring hundreds of toy trains, figurines, and miniature models from the renowned Jerni Collection. Leah had promised to take her daughter to the exhibit over the Christmas holiday, but with the new programming rollout at the company and other concerns, that promise had been repeatedly put off.

Leah noted that Kacie appeared to like the tall stranger. The girl had subjected John to a video game marathon the previous evening. John had been patient with Kacie's obvious motor control limitations and had said nothing when she repeatedly insisted on re-starting levels because her "hands were shaking". Jenny had mercifully put an end to the contest after nearly three hours, sending the girl to bed.

The museum doors began to open.

At once, Jenny began maneuvering Kacie's wheelchair back through the crowd to re-join her mother. John followed and took up a position behind the trio. His proximity made Leah nervous, so she turned, facing him, and asked, "Have you ever been to the museum before Mr. Clifton?"

John appeared surprised at the question. He smiled and shook his head, "No."

Leah caught herself before asking more questions. It occurred to her then that she needed to be careful engaging John in casual conversations in public. He might say anything in response, and she did not wish for Jenny or her daughter to learn their houseguest believed himself to be a time traveler.

As the line of visitors proceeded into the building, Jenny and Kacie became separated from Leah and John. Leah was not concerned. She knew Jenny would keep the girl safe and well-occupied. It also allowed her an opportunity to speak with John about something that had kept her awake most of the night.

"Mr. Clifton…" Leah began.

"John, please," the tall man interrupted.

"Very well," she said. "John… I was wondering if you could answer a question for me?"

John turned, "A question?"

Leah glanced ahead through the crowd, re-acquiring her daughter before she continued. "Last night," she began, "I asked if you knew what Friedreich Ataxia was, and you gave an answer that sounded like it could have been lifted right out of a medical journal." She looked up now, waiting, expecting a response.

John shook his head, "I'm sorry. You had a question?"

Leah scowled, continuing, "It's just that… most people have never even heard of the disease, but you seemed to know everything about it."

John shook his head now, understanding her confusion. "No," he said, "In fact, I had never heard of the disease before last night. When you said that was what was troubling your daughter, I simply queried my datstem for details."

Leah did not respond for a moment, considering this implausible explanation. Strangely, what he said made sense to her. Most people had never heard of the disease, so his explanation, despite its extraordinary premise, was somehow easy for her to accept. As they milled around the colorful model train exhibits, she posed another question to her tall companion.

"John… I'm still confused about something you said during the interview at the hotel."

174

"Yes?"

"You made it sound like, once your device was damaged... once your wormhole was lost, that you had no way of returning home."

"That's correct."

"Then why did you spend a year trying to fix the device? I mean... what was the point if you couldn't use it to return home?"

John paused in front of a particularly fine model of an early 20th-century model train engine. "When my device was damaged," he began, "the containment unit lost its hold on the singularity. The singularity was released and began to tunnel backward through time. The singularity was not destroyed... just released. Do you understand?"

Leah nodded, "I think so."

John continued, "Since the singularity was not destroyed, but merely released from its quantum confinement, it might have been possible to re-calibrate it back into containment, as long as it had not traveled too far out of its original quantum position."

"So, if you could have fixed your device quickly," Leah said, "you might have re-captured the wormhole?"

John nodded, "Yes. It might have been possible. But the more time that elapses, the further back in time the singularity travels. Eventually, it becomes too far removed to be re-calibrated back into containment."

Leah nodded, struggling to understand, "So... it moves too far away for your machine to focus on it again?"

"That's a fair analogy," John said, nodding. "If I could have repaired my device before the singularity lost too much of its quantum cohesion..."

John suddenly stopped, mid-sentence. His brow furrowed and his eyes stared ahead as if he was troubled by something.

"John?" Leah prompted, confused by his sudden silence.

"Lost cohesion..." John muttered, clearly speaking to himself. After several moments, he spoke again, quickly, with obvious excitement in his voice.

"When an MTY device releases control of one of its event horizons, to an observer monitoring that event horizon, it might appear that the singularity has been destroyed... but, that's not true. Its event horizon has simply lost its cohesion... or shifted away from its former quantum position!"

John was clearly excited about something, but Leah could not understand his explanation. At that moment, Jenny returned with Kacie and suggested they grab a bite at the Italian restaurant outside the museum.

"Kacie wants spaghetti," Jenny said as she approached, "and I'd not mind a bit a fresh air and a bite of lunch after all the crowds in here."

Leah looked at John, who remained distracted. "John?" she prompted, "Shall we grab some lunch?"

John refocused on his companions again. "I'm sorry," he said, "It's just that something has occurred to me that I must think about. Lunch sounds great."

Lunch was pleasant and refreshing. John sat quietly, observing Leah's interaction with Kacie, laughing at their jokes, and grinning when they teased Jenny about the large piece of cheesecake she had ordered. They were finishing up when Jenny asked, "So... Mr. Clifton. What do you do?"

Leah jerked up from sipping her coffee, alarmed.

John, however, simply replied, "I'm sort of an engineer."

Jenny raised her eyebrows in obvious approval. "An engineer?"

John nodded. "I work with a data archive group, doing research, and occasionally field work."

Jenny nodded. "My nephew works for a petroleum company doing similar work. They send him around to do soil testing, to find out where the oil is."

John nodded, "That's interesting."

Jenny now asked, "What company do you work for?"

Leah held her breath, but John simply said, "I work for a company called Rengel-Jiang QCom, or RJCom."

Jenny shook her head, "I've never heard of them. Are they based here in New York?"

John shook his head, "Texas."

Jenny took another bite of her cheesecake and then asked, "What kind of research do you do?"

"Mostly historical research. Organizations use us to search though archival records or do field work when they need to find answers to a specific question or when they need to find information about a particular person or event."

Jenny shook her head and asked, "What kind of information?"

John considered this for a moment. Then he said, "Well, sometimes important information gets forgotten or lost. For example, finding out *why* a person did something, discovering *where* an important document may be found, or learning *how* a machine originally worked, is information that through time may have become forgotten, altered, or lost. Organizations use our company to find the original information."

Kacie was becoming bored with this conversation. Jenny, however, asked, "But why would such information be important? I mean… what's so important with finding out *why* a person did something?"

John nodded, "That's a good question." He leaned back in his chair, considering how to respond. His eyes caught sight of a sidewalk sign visible through the restaurant window. The sign advertised an exhibit scheduled to begin at the museum next month titled, "Rebel Spirits: Robert F. Kennedy and Martin Luther King Jr."

Pointing to the sign through the window, John said, "Did you know that Martin Luther was not his real name?"

Jenny turned her head to read the sign. Then she looked back at John, incredulous. "What?"

John nodded, "It's true. His name at birth was Michael King Jr., not Martin Luther King Jr. After he was born, his father, Michael Sr., traveled to Germany and became inspired by the teachings of protestant reformation leader Martin Luther. He changed his name, and his son's name, to Martin Luther. The teachings of Martin Luther had a profound impact on the father, and, through his father, these teachings later influenced Martin Luther King Jr. to take up the cause of civil rights."

Jenny shook her head in amazement. "I never knew that!"

John nodded and said, "Understanding why people did things in the past, helps us to understand both our history and our humanity. Sometimes, the things we learn about the past even help us to shape our future."

When John paused, Leah quickly took the opportunity to divert the conversation. The last thing she needed was for her guest to start talking about the future.

"So…" Leah interrupted, looking at her daughter, "Are you interested in visiting the zoo? We can get some hot chocolate and watch the penguins playing in the snow."

Kacie nodded quickly. "Yes," she said. "All this talk about history is boring."

Chapter 19

T he zoo turned out to be a wonderful choice. Despite the chill and the snow, the small group had dressed warmly, expecting to wait in line outside the museum that morning. The park's trees stood dark and bare, snow clinging to their limbs, and a light dusting of fresh snow had left the paths slippery, but the zoo was well attended as many of the animals became more active in the cold weather.

Tom sent a text message while Jenny was getting Kacie her hot chocolate. He reported he had met with Dr. Denton at the university that morning and then instructed Leah to bring John to his office in the morning.

When Leah turned to relay the message to John, she was surprised to notice the tall stranger was no longer at her side. She looked around and spotted him standing in front of the grizzly bear exhibit reading a sign. She joined him and gave him the message.

John nodded but did not break his gaze away from the two large brown bears ensconced within the enclosure.

"Everything ok?" Leah asked.

After a few moments, John pointed into the enclosure and said in a soft voice "The polar bears are gone."

Leah was confused, staring up at the two sleepy grizzly bears.

John softly tapped the sign, "They used to house polar bears in this exhibit."

Leah now read the sign's print. The exhibit, it said, had previously housed two polar bears, Gus and Ida, who had entertained the park's visitors from 1988 until 2013. Ida, the female bear, had died in 2011 at age 25 due to liver cancer. Her spouse, Gus, had died in 2013 at age 27 from an inoperable tumor.

John appeared strangely impacted by the small sign. "The polar bears," he repeated, "They're gone."

Leah said nothing, not understanding his fixation with the exhibit's former occupants.

"The last one died in a Canadian reservation in 2115. They're all gone now."

Leah now understood. Horrified, she stared at the exhibit again.

"We saved so many species," John said softly, shaking his head, "so many. But we couldn't save the polar bears." He sighed then and walked slowly away.

Later that evening, Leah was in her kitchen making herself some hot chocolate. Jenny had put Kacie to bed early and had retired for the night. Everyone was tired from the day's activities. She could hear Jenny's television playing loudly through the caregiver's door. The volume level meant the older woman had removed her hearing aids. Leah turned to get the cocoa from the pantry and was startled to see John standing in the hallway.

"I'm sorry," John quickly said, apologizing.

"No. It's fine," Leah replied. "I was just surprised. I'm making some hot chocolate. Would you like some?"

John nodded, "Please."

Leah poured some more milk into the pot on the stove. "It's my mother's recipe. It's the real deal, not that powdered stuff."

John smiled, "Sounds great."

While the milk began to heat, Leah took the opportunity to query her guest.

"At the zoo today, you said the polar bears had gone extinct?"

"Yes." John sat in one of the stools at the counter and nodded, his face somber.

Leah frowned, "With all the technology in the future, are you saying mankind couldn't find a way to save the polar bears?"

"Huh?"

John shook his head, "All the technology in the world can't compete with desperation, stupidity, and greed."

"Huh?"

"By the mid-2060s, mankind was in something of a crisis. We were running out of fossil fuels. The reserves we had were closely held by their respective governments who viewed them as strategic military resources, holding on to them in case they needed them to fight another war. We hadn't begun switching over to fusion power yet, you see. That didn't occur until we started relying heavily on singularities for travel, beginning in the 2080s."

"In 2074, the surviving petroleum companies formed a

powerful consortium and began lobbying to open the last oil reserves for drilling. The world was screaming for fuel, international shipping had all but ceased, fuel rationing had bankrupted the airline and automotive industries, third world populations were starving. It was a bad situation. So, the governments finally gave in and opened the last of their oil and gas reserves for drilling."

"Things had been bad for the polar bears before then. After that, they became desperate. Offshore drilling, oil spills, and habitat destruction decimated arctic seal and fish populations, leaving nothing for the bears to eat. Most of the bears starved to death."

"Finally, in 2081, the surviving bears were relocated to a reservation in Canada. Unfortunately, concentrating the remaining polar bears turned out to be a catastrophic mistake. The following year, a strain of phocine distemper virus swept through the reservation, wiping out most of the remaining population. From then, it was simply a matter of time. There were too few bears of breeding age with not enough genetic diversity to sustain the species. The last polar bear, a female named Niviasar, died in 2115, having lived alone for most of her life."

Leah poured the steaming chocolate into a cup and handed it to her guest.

"Oh. Thank you," John said. After taking a sip, his eyes opened wider. "That's wonderful!"

Leah was pleased.

John continued, "Mankind learned its lesson, just not soon enough to save the polar bears."

Leah sat down on a stool and said, "We learned our

lesson?" Her tone suggested she didn't believe such a thing to be possible.

John nodded, sipping from his cup. "Yes. The widespread introduction of fusion-powered singularities in the 2080s put an end to the fossil fuel monopolies. Shipping and transportation resumed, but without the negative environmental impact of fossil fuels. Drilling stopped, refineries closed, and third world countries began repairing their damaged environments. China led the way, becoming the leader of the global conservation efforts."

Leah inadvertently choked, spilling some of her cocoa. "Sorry," she said, "China?!"

John grinned, nodding his head. "There's a lot of money to be made in conservation and reclamation, and the Chinese government had been among the worst of the world's polluters. What better way to stimulate a flagging economy than to convert your greatest expense into your greatest source of income. China had created a global problem, so they invested in the means to remedy that problem. All of the best atmospheric filtration equipment, water reclamation systems, and plastic resequencing plants now come from China."

Leah shook her head in disbelief.

John continued, enjoying her reaction, "There was something of an environmental renaissance that started in the late 2090s. The air and oceans became cleaner after the introduction of household fusion units. Gravimetric propulsion replaced petroleum-fueled ground transports, singularities replaced air transportation and international shipping companies, and plastics resequencing virtually eliminated oceanic waste and landfills bloated with non-decomposing

184

polymers. Plastic, metal, and chemical reclamation became one of the world's largest industries for almost 30 years. A lot of landfill owners became rich simply by opening up their waste dumps to contracted reclamation SDUs."

Leah frowned, "SDUs?"

John nodded, "Sorry. That's an acronym. It stands for 'Self Directing Unit'. They're what you might call a robot, but they're more than that."

Leah sat back now, taking in everything John had said. It was hard to imagine the world he described. She thought back to their interview in the hotel room the day before. "Yesterday at the hotel," she said, "You said you were able to tell us about the future because nothing you do here can change that future."

John nodded, "Yes, that's correct."

Leah put down her cup, "Does that mean, there's nothing mankind can do to bring back the polar bears?"

John shook his head. "The things we do in the past, they become part of the flow of history, but they can't change the future. Time will resolve a temporal specialist's actions in the past to prevent them from changing the future."

"So, there's no way to undo mankind's mistakes?"

John took another sip of cocoa. He seemed to be considering how to better answer the question. He noticed a stack of paper napkins on the counter next to Kacie's schoolwork. The girl had sat there earlier doing homework after her dinner. He removed one of the paper napkins and wrote the number 5 on its surface.

"Mankind's mistakes and its accomplishments are both parts of the same history," John said, writing down another
185

number on the napkin; the number 7.

"A temporal specialist can affect minor events in the past. Those actions may create ripples in the flow of time, but they won't significantly affect the continuity of that timeline. So, I can interact with you. I can even tell you about the future…" John added the number 9 to those already on the paper.

"But nothing I do here can change the future to the point that the future that sent me here no longer exists." John added a number to those already on the napkin, 22.

"If I *could* do something significant here in the past, something that changes the future, then that future that sent me into this past would no longer exist. That means I could not have come from that future to make those changes here in the past. That would be a paradox, and time abhors paradoxes." John added another number, the number 25.

"Time will resolve my actions here in the past to prevent paradoxes from occurring… to preserve the shape of the future that sent me here. So," John said, holding up the napkin, "knowing the future is one thing. Changing that future is another thing altogether."

Leah stared at the napkin, not understanding its significance. Then, she heard a series of numbers being called off of Jenny's television in the caregiver's bedroom. It was the New York Take 5 lottery. The announcer was reading the numbers out loud as they were being drawn live on the television.

"…7… 9… 22… and the last number is 25."

Leah stared at the numbers on the napkin again as she heard the winning numbers being repeated from the television in Jenny's room. The numbers matched those on the napkin.

John spoke again, watching her face. "As I said, knowing the future is one thing. Changing that future is another thing altogether." Pushing the napkin across the counter towards her, he continued, "History records that tonight's New York Take 5 lottery jackpot was shared between two people in Saratoga and Duchess county. If I had attempted to purchase a ticket this afternoon with those same numbers, time would have triggered a correction to resolve my interference."

John put the napkin down and took another sip of cocoa. "Nothing I do," he continued, "can change the fact that two people from Saratoga and Duchess county will share tonight's $33,637 lottery jackpot."

He put down his empty mug, his face sad. "And nothing mankind can do can bring back the polar bears."

Chapter 20

John stood in front of Tom Pierce's bookshelf, staring at the collection of antique tomes assembled there. The executive producer was clearly a bibliophile and the collection of leather-bound volumes indicated a preference for 19th-century American authors.

The meeting with Dr. Denton at NYU had had a significant impact on Leah's colleague. Tom had texted her again last night, reminding her to bring John to his office this morning.

After several moments, John gently removed one of the volumes and opened it. Leah caught a glimpse of the title on the book's spine. It was Rip Van Winkle by Washington Irving. She watched John bring the volume close to his nose. He was smelling the book's pages as if he was absorbing the musty aroma of its yellowed pages and its aged leather cover.

"It's called a book," she said, teasing.

John looked up and smiled, nodding. He closed the volume and gently re-inserted it back into its position on the shelf.

"Let me guess," she said, "there are no more books in the future?"

John shook his head, "No. There are, but you have to go to a museum to find a real one. And you're not permitted to touch them."

Leah watched John's hand gently caressing the embossed leather spines of the small collection. After another moment, John stepped back from the shelf.

"No one reads printed books anymore. Except for collectors of course. I've heard that there are a couple of companies in Europe that still print physical books... for collectors of that sort of thing, but they use sheeted polymers, not wood pulp paper. And no leather bindings of course."

Leah grinned, "Everyone went vegan, huh?"

John shook his head, not understanding.

Leah waved her hand, "Never mind."

At that moment, Tom appeared from the elevator. The producer appeared excited. When he entered his office, he shook hands with John and then motioned Leah over to his desk.

"We've got some planning to do!" Tom said. "Here's how we're going to proceed..." He opened the company's contact database on his workstation, his enthusiasm infectious.

Leah sat in a chair next to Tom's desk, viewing the producer's monitor. John sat on the other side of the desk, watching with interest as Tom began typing.

"Dr. Denton vouched for your theories," Tom began, glancing up at the tall man, "and he was seriously impressed with the design of your device."

John nodded.

Tom continued, "Of course, he can't definitively say whether you're telling the truth, but he said if it's a fraud, it's a brilliant one."

John opened his mouth, but Tom waved him to silence. "No offense," he said. "Dr. Denton was impressed, and that's good enough for me. We're going to proceed under the assumption that you are telling the truth."

Leah interrupted, "So, what does that mean?"

Tom stopped typing and turned to face his associate producer.

"It means that you and I are going to prepare a story. Not just any story. We're going to prepare what may end up being the most important news story in our world's history."

Leah's eyes widened.

Tom continued, "As a way of introducing John to the world, I'm going to arrange to have him meet with some very special people and engage them in a discussion on several topics. These will be carefully chosen people and carefully chosen topics. I'm thinking... climate change, world peace... things like that."

Leah began to warm to the idea, adding, "And we'd record John engaging in these interviews."

Tom nodded, "Precisely." The producer looked at John who was sitting quietly, apparently lost in thought. "You'd be able to share your insights about the future with some very important people," Tom said, "and possibly even help guide their thinking."

John nodded, "I understand."

Tom looked at Leah now, "When we air the interviews, we'll reveal to the world what John claims to be. We're going to explain that, while there is no way for us to prove his identity, noted physicists and reputable experts have evaluated his theories and examined his device. We'll publish their findings and then leave it up to the world to render its judgment."

Leah nodded, appreciating her producer's approach and his caution. Their company would present John engaging in interesting discussions with noted individuals on important topics. They would then present the findings of a group of experts and leave it to the audience to decide what to believe. It was a clever plan that allowed the news company to break the story of the world's first time traveler without tacitly endorsing his claims.

"Of course, we'll need some experts to weigh in," Tom added.

"Dr. Denton?" Leah suggested.

Tom shook his head, "No, I was thinking we should ask Dr. Saito. After all, having John engaging in a physics discussion with a Nobel laureate particle physicist would certainly garner significant attention."

Leah nodded. "Will Saito do it?"

"I believe so. He's been very interested in meeting with John ever since he saw that drawing attached to John's email. He's been pestering me ever since then to arrange a meeting. I'll give him a call tonight and arrange to conduct a technical interview in a few weeks after we've finished with these other interviews."

Leah nodded. "That sounds great."

Tom continued, "I think I'll also ask Dr. Denton if he knows a mathematician who can join us, to give us their opinion about some of the mathematic formulas John has provided."

Leah nodded again. Then, almost as an afterthought, she glanced at John. The tall stranger had a strange look on his face. "John," she asked, "Does this all sound ok with you?"

Tom took a cue from his associate's tone, and chimed in, "It would be completely paid for by the company, of course. We'd fly you to the interviews, put you up in nice hotels... fine dining... the works."

"When would we be meeting with Saito?" John asked.

Tom looked back at his computer screen and shrugged, "I'm not sure. After we finish with the other interviews."

John now looked at Leah, hesitating. After a moment, he said, "Who would accompany me to the interviews?"

Leah locked eyes with the tall stranger for a moment, then flushed and looked away, before nodding to her producer.

"Ms. Vaughn would accompany you," Tom replied, "and she will moderate the actual interviews."

John turned now to speak directly to Leah.

"Will Kacie be alright if you are away from her for that long?"

Leah was surprised at John's concern for her daughter, but nodded, "Yes. Thank you. Jenny is very competent, and I've had to travel for work before." She grinned now, adding, "In fact, Kacie will be more than fine. She'll consider it a vacation from her mother's constant worrying!"

"Very well," John said. "I agree."

Tom's plan, however, experienced its first setback when John informed the producers that he had no identification with which to obtain travel documents. Both producers were at a loss for a few moments, until John asked if it were possible to obtain a duplicate transport card on short notice.

"Do you mean a replacement driver's license?" Leah asked.

"Yes. Can one be obtained swiftly… today?"

When Leah said no, the offices were closed on Sunday, John asked to be taken to a driver's license office the following day.

The next morning, Leah watched, curious, as John approached the motor vehicle clerk and submitted his thumbprint for scanning. She was shocked to see the clerk casually print out a replacement driver's license card and hand it to the tall man. As they left the building, she spoke accusingly, "How can you have a driver's license here in this time?"

John handed her the license and explained that he had instructed his datstem to connect with the facility's internal data system. His datstem, he said, had simply inserted a record into the motor vehicle database with the appropriate information, including scans of his fingerprints.

Leah looked at the license. It had a picture of John next to the name "Nathan Phillips". She raised one of her eyebrows as she handed back the card.

"Nathan Phillips?"

"A fictitious name I've been using for the past 4 years. It's the name I gave to the hospital and the police officer when I was injured in Austin."

After stopping for lunch, the pair rejoined Tom back at the office. They found the producer in the company's production room watching the editing crew preparing tomorrow's video news segments. Tom quickly set Mary

Kravets to obtaining the necessary travel documents through the company's travel office. The stout manager dropped off the tickets and foreign press visas to Leah's home later that evening.

"You're going to Himachal Pradesh, India," Mary said, smiling at Leah's shocked expression.

"Why? Who are we interviewing in India?"

Mary handed her the itinerary and tickets and said, "Tom was able to arrange for you to meet with Tenzin Chophel."

Leah was shocked. The venerable Tenzin Chophel was a noted Buddhist scholar and the personal translator and assistant to the Dalai Lama.

"Oh my God," Leah muttered.

"Not quite," Mary said, shaking her head, "but he's probably got his number on speed-dial."

"So what are we supposed to interview him about?" Leah asked, still flustered.

Mary shrugged, "World peace? The price of rice? I don't know. Tom said you'd figure it out."

"Hmmm… yes. Ok."

As she was turning to leave, Mary suddenly stopped. "Oh! Tom also told me to give this to you." The manager now retrieved a sealed envelope and handed it to Leah. "He said you asked him to check into something for you?"

Leah nodded and quickly took the envelope. "Thank you."

"Have a safe trip."

The following afternoon, as she sat with John in the back of the taxi, Leah took the opportunity to try to learn more about him.

"So, have you ever been to India before?"

John nodded, "Yes. Several times."

"Oh? What took you there?"

John fell silent for a moment and Leah sensed he was struggling to respond. Finally, he took a breath and said, "I had a friend whose family lived in Amdapur. That's near the center of the country. I visited his family's house there several times… most recently to watch the Cricket World Championship game."

Leah caught the past tense reference and asked, "Does he live somewhere else now?"

John shook his head. "No," he said quietly. "He was killed in a transport accident shortly before… before I came here."

Leah sensed John's loss and did not press for details. When they pulled up at the airport's curbside check-in, John stepped out of the car and stopped in front of the curbside kiosk. The skycap attendant motioned to his backpack and politely asked if he could tag it, but John remained silent, staring at the flight data on the screen.

"Something wrong?" Leah asked, confused by his reluctance to proceed.

John turned then and looked at her. "We shouldn't take this transport," he said. "We should make arrangements to take a different transport."

Leah was confused. "Huh? Why?"

John just shook his head, glancing briefly at a businessman who brushed past him to load his suitcase on the conveyor.

195

"I'm sorry. But its better if we take another transport." With that, John abruptly turned and walked into the airport terminal, leaving Leah standing on the curb. When she rejoined him inside the terminal, John was standing by the flight announcement screens, studying the departure schedules.

"Why can't we take our scheduled flight?" Leah asked, perturbed.

John looked at her and said softly, "That transport is going to experience a mechanical failure in one of its engines over the Atlantic and be diverted to London."

Pointing to the screen, John continued, "There's an alternate aerial transport leaving at 7:10 this evening. It makes a stop in Delhi, but will get us to our destination 18 hours earlier than we would have arrived if we had taken our scheduled transport."

Leah stared at him. She was confused and frustrated. It suddenly occurred to her that she had not yet decided whether or not she truly believed John. The realization that she was preparing to travel halfway around the world with a man she didn't fully trust alarmed her.

For his part, John remained silent, patiently waiting for her response.

"Ok... Fine!" Leah capitulated, taking a deep breath. "But if we get there and I find out that our original flight flew straight in without any problems, I'm going to be extremely pissed off."

John smiled, nodding, "A reasonable response."

The duo were able to exchange their tickets for the later flight with relative ease. Getting through security, however, proved more difficult. John's strange device was examined and re-examined by the puzzled gate attendant, who could not make heads or tails of the mysterious machine.

John explained that the device was a sensitive piece of advanced weather equipment designed to measure barometric pressure and that they were exhibiting it at a trade show in India. When John began pointing to the device's various components and enthusiastically offering weather-related explanations for its various components, the bored gate attendant finally waved them through.

After they boarded the plane, John did not seem to know what to do with his backpack until a flight attendant approached and instructed him to place it inside the overhead compartment above his seat.

Leah sat down in the seat next to him. They were flying business class, in comfortable seats near the front of the plane. She could see the tension in the muscles in John's arm, in the concentration on his face, and the white knuckles of his hand as he gripped the armrest.

"Have you flown in a plane before?" she asked.

"No," John said, grinning sheepishly.

Later, when John was distracted looking outside the plane window, Leah pulled the sealed envelope that Mary had given her from her pocket. Opening it, she read Tom's letter:

"Leah,

I checked out the name Nathan Phillips as you requested. I was able to confirm there is a NY motor vehicle record with that name. Interestingly, however, the motor vehicle record shows that the record was created this morning, at the approximate time you were at the DMV office. I also can't find any record of anyone with that name at the address given on the license. The address on the license is a hardware store.

I called someone I know in Texas who has researched for us there previously. He spoke with some people this afternoon at a university hospital in Austin. One of the doctors confirmed that their hospital had received many of the accident victims the night of the music festival. Of course, the doctor could not remember specific patient names, but my contact there was able to convince one of the hospital billing clerks to check their billing system in case there were any outstanding bills owed to the hospital under the name 'Nathan Phillips'. They confirmed that someone using that name was injured the night of the festival and, from the billing codes in their system, they confirmed that they had sustained the kind of injuries that John described to us at his interview.

Leah, I can't give you any advice except to say, I'm feeling the same way I felt when we chatted last night. For my part, I believe John's story to be true. My only advice is to trust your intuition. I believe everything will be fine.

I've arranged for us to meet with Dr. Saito in a few weeks. He seemed frustrated that we were delaying his meeting, but once I explained that we're having John speak with Chophel in Dharamshala and then with a climatologist in London, he calmed down. You are free to choose the topics John should bring up with the people you interview. I'll leave that entirely up to you.

I'll check in with Jenny and Kacie every day like I promised. Send me a text when you land so I will know you arrived safely.

~ Tom Pierce"

Chapter 21

*"There are certain events which to each man's life
are as comets to the earth, seemingly strange and erratic portents;
distinct from the ordinary lights which
guide our course and mark our seasons,
yet true to their own laws, potent in their own influences."*
~ Edward Bulwer-Lytton
*English novelist, playwright, and politician
(1803 – 1873 AD)*

The flight to India was uneventful, though long. It was 15 hours from New York to Delhi, India, and from there, another 2 hours to Kangra Airport in the Indian state of Himachal Pradesh. Leah slept fitfully for a few hours during the first flight, but each time she stirred, she noticed John was awake. She was not certain but she suspected he had not slept at all during the entire flight.

The layover in Delhi was brief. Only two and a half hours. They stayed inside the airport and found a small café serving breakfast. John suggested they order pesarattu upma, a lentil dosa made from a batter of ground green gram dal, and stuffed with semolina upma. To Leah's western eye, the dish resembled a tinted green whole-grain pancake stuffed with a mash resembling oatmeal. She was pleasantly surprised at the taste, however. It tasted of roasted chilis, onion, and ginger, with seasoned semolina for the mash.

When it was time to board the flight to Himachal

Pradesh, John seemed nervous. The airplane was very different from the spacious jet they had traveled in from New York. This aircraft was a smaller, regional turboprop aircraft, crowded and noisy. The buzzing roar of the propellers reverberated through the aircraft's thin walls.

Leah noticed John gripping the armrest, his knuckles white on his hand. She put her hand over his and felt the tautness of his grip.

"It's going to be fine," she offered, smiling up at her companion's face. She remembered his earlier apprehension when they had boarded the jet in New York and slipped her arm in his.

"Are you nervous?"

"No," John said, but then he shook his head, "well… actually, yes." He added, "I guess I'm not used to traveling. In my time, no one *travels*. You simply step through an EPM portal and you're where you want to be. The idea of making a long journey to get where you want to go feels strange. It's frustrating, going on such a long journey just to get somewhere. It makes me anxious."

Leah nodded, "I can understand that." After several moments, she spoke again, "I once read a poem… about life being like a long journey, where the only rest one truly receives is at its ending."

John turned and looked at her, a strange expression on his face.

"Hermann Hesse?"

Leah looked up, startled and pleased, "Yes. Do you know the poem?"

John nodded, smiling. "Of course. It's called 'On a

Journey'. In my time, it's considered a masterpiece of 20th-century poetry. Although he won a Nobel prize for literature, Hesse didn't enjoy much public recognition during his lifetime. His poetry didn't become truly popular until Jean Reneau published his great discourse, "The Dual Spirituality of Man" in 2108. Reneau considered Hesse's poems to be among the finest literary examples of man's search for self-authenticity."

"I read some of his poems during college," Leah said, frowning. "I'm trying to remember how that one goes." After a moment, she spoke slowly, "Don't be downcast... soon the night will come..." She furrowed her eyebrows, trying to remember the rest, then shook her head.

John spoke now, his voice dim against the aircraft's droning engines:

> *"Don't be downcast.*
> *Soon the night will come,*
> *when we can see the cool moon*
> *laughing in secret over the faint countryside,*
> *and we rest, hand in hand."*

> *"Don't be downcast, the time will soon come*
> *When we can have rest.*
> *Our small crosses will stand*
> *on the bright edge of the road together,*
> *and rain fall, and snow fall,*
> *and the winds come and go."*

Leah smiled, nodding. She sighed and said, "I've always liked that poem. It's so romantic."

"Romantic?" John asked, surprised. "It's an evocative

poem, certainly, but romantic?"

Leah nodded again, slightly perturbed. "Yes. Romantic. It's a poem about two people who have been on a long journey together. Perhaps they have shared a difficult life, and they are now looking forward to resting, hand in hand forever beneath the earth, as the seasons continue above them."

John said nothing, but sat back in his seat, suddenly aware of Leah's hand intertwined with his.

It was early afternoon when they landed. The Kangra Airport is a small regional airport in the Indian state of Himachal Pradesh. One asphalt runway spans the facility, a small control tower, and passenger terminal being the only structures of note. The terminal was pleasantly surrounded by a small manicured arrangement of trees and clipped hedges, bare of leaves now in the crisp winter air, and the frigid breeze smelled faintly of smoke and dung, hinting at the industry in the surrounding city.

After collecting their baggage, John stood, shivering at the curb, waiting for Leah. She had retrieved her cell phone from her travel bag and was now engaged in a conversation with her daughter. After several moments, Leah ended the call and rejoined him by the curb.

"Well," she said, "I suppose a taxi would be the best choice... unless you think we should rent a car?"

John considered this for a moment, and then answered, "Whatever you prefer."

"We're scheduled to meet with Tenzin Chophel tomorrow morning in Dharamshala." Leah consulted her travel papers again before adding, "That's about a half-hour drive from here."

Suddenly, John tensed. His head jerked up and his gaze took on an intensity Leah had not observed before.

"Is something wrong?" Leah asked, trying to follow John's eyes. The small parking facility was occupied by perhaps 20 parked cars. She could several people struggling with their bags and others milling about inside the small terminal, but she could see nothing particularly alarming.

John did not answer for a moment, obviously distracted.

"John? Is something wrong?"

John slowly relaxed. After a moment, he shook his head, "No. Everything is fine." He abruptly stepped off the curb and waved his arm at a taxi idling nearby in front of the terminal. The vehicle jumped forward. Its driver had been watching them since they exited the terminal, hoping for the fare.

Leah stepped into the back seat of the dirty sedan as the driver placed her small travel case inside the trunk. John hesitated, however, standing outside the car's open door. He appeared to be searching the nearby street for something.

"Your bag, sir?" The taxi driver motioned for John's backpack and then gestured at the open trunk.

When John shook his head, the driver gestured again, "Sir. Your bag?"

John shook his head again and stepped into the back seat, placing his backpack on his knees. The driver shook his head and closed the trunk.

"Is everything ok?" Leah asked. "You seem concerned about something."

"I'm not certain," John began, slowly scanning the parking lot again through the vehicle's dusty windows.

The driver now sat down behind the steering wheel and

asked, "Where please?"

Leah was looking at John's face, but answered, "Prakriti Hotel."

The driver nodded and began driving away from the terminal.

John abruptly turned and asked, "Who knows we are here? I mean, have you or Tom told anyone about what we're doing? About these interviews?"

Leah sat back, confused by the question. After a moment, she answered, "I know that Tom talked with a physicist friend of his about you... Dr. Denton. And of course, Mary in our office knows what we're doing. She had to make the travel arrangements."

John shifted his position, resettling his backpack on his legs as if the weight of the strange device were suddenly uncomfortable.

Leah continued, "And, of course, Tom arranged for the interviews."

John nodded, "That's it? No one else?"

Leah thought for a moment, then added, "I think Tom said he also talked about you with another physicist, Dr. Saito. He's arranging to have you interview with him after we return to New York."

"Saito? Are you certain?"

"Yes. Tom wrote me a message before we left and said that he had made the arrangements."

"I see."

The taxi drove on in silence now. Leah was struggling to stay awake. Jet lag was kicking in and she needed to get something to eat. John, however, sat still and quiet, as if he were engaged in reflection or contemplation. He was so deep in thought, in fact, that he failed to notice that she had asked him a question. He only responded when she prodded him in his rib.

"Sorry," he asked. "I was thinking about something."

Leah nodded. "I can see that. I asked, do you know what you're planning to talk about with Tenzin Chophel?"

"Yes. I think so."

"Care to share it with me? I'm supposed to be facilitating these interviews after all."

"I'm going to ask him how His Holiness the Dalai Lama plans to respond to China's announcement that they alone can choose the next Dalai Lama."

Leah was surprised and asked, "Do you think China would try to do that?"

The taxi driver glanced back at John through the rear-view mirror, obviously following his passenger's conversation.

"Yes," John nodded. "They will. The Chinese government has already asserted they have the right to approve any future succession. Following the Dalai Lama's death, the Chinese government will announce they have selected his successor."

The taxi driver snorted and shook his head.

John continued, "I'm going to ask Chophel what the Dalai Lama intends to do to ensure the future succession of his office."

Leah thought about this for a moment and then said, "Interesting. Yes... I think that will work well with what Tom is hoping to accomplish with these interviews."

The taxi arrived at the hotel and Leah got out quickly.

While the driver was retrieving her bag from the trunk, John stepped out of the vehicle and stood silently, scanning the nearby streets.

"What is wrong?" Leah asked, concern in her voice.

"I'm not sure," John answered, "but I think someone followed us from the airport."

Leah looked around, "What makes you think that?" She was not particularly surprised. She knew from experience as a journalist that both the Chinese and Indian governments routinely monitored all of the Dalai Lama's scheduled visitors. Correspondents traveling to the region were frequently observed and their movements followed by government "handlers".

John hesitated for a moment as if considering whether or not to elaborate on his suspicions. Instead, he hoisted his backpack containing his MTY device and shut the taxi door.

"Let's get inside the hotel."

Chapter 22

"I often told my mother that I was going to Lhasa. I used to straddle a window sill in our house pretending that I was riding a horse to Lhasa...

Soon after I arrived in Lhasa, I said that my teeth were in a box in a certain house in the Norbulinka. When they opened the box, they found a set of dentures which had belonged to the 13th Dalai Lama. I pointed to the box, and said that my teeth were in there."
~ Tenzin Gyatso - the 14th Dalai Lama,
(1935 AD –)
Childhood memories of his former incarnation.

There was frost on the outside of the hotel room window when Leah woke. She had slept soundly, the result of jet lag and a momentous week. She could hear John moving in the adjoining room. He had seemed anxious the previous evening as they ate their dinner inside a small restaurant near to their hotel. Later that night, she had stirred awake briefly, certain she had heard John's voice through the thin hotel walls. For a moment, it had sounded like he was engaged in a conversation with someone. She had tried to listen, but whatever he had been saying abruptly ceased, and she eventually drifted back to sleep.

The hotel had arranged for a courtesy vehicle to take them to Dharamshala, the residence-in-exile and official office of His Holiness the 14th Dalai Lama, the spiritual ruler of Tibet. By appointment, they were meeting with Tenzin Chophel at

10:00 AM. A noted Buddhist scholar in his own right, Chophel was the personal translator and assistant to the Dalai Lama and the public face of the religious government in exile. He was widely recognized to be the "right hand" of the aging spiritual leader.

John was unusually quiet as the courtesy vehicle drove slowly towards the imposing heights of the Himalayan mountains. Leah attempted several times to draw him into a conversation, but he remained withdrawn and contemplative. She then attempted to engage the driver in conversation, but it was quickly apparent the man did not speak English.

"John?" Leah spoke hesitantly.

"Yes?"

"I checked with the airline this morning before we left the hotel. You were right... about that flight from New York being diverted to London."

"Yes. I know."

Leah frowned, frustrated and confused.

"Yes, but *how* did you know?!" she asked, exasperated.

John turned to study her face.

Leah waved her hand, "I mean, how did you know about *that* particular flight being diverted? It seems like a pretty minor event to be part of history."

John nodded, understanding her confusion. "Airline records in this era," he explained, "were stored electronically in databases. Most of the database records from what we call the 'early information age' were later scanned and archived by the world's governments and larger private corporations. Those records form part of the core data files installed with every datstem and archival unit. I simply queried my datstem for information about that particular flight and discovered a maintenance entry stating it had been diverted to London due to a mechanical issue with one of its engines."

Leah stared at her companion for a moment. "Are you telling me that you have all electronic records from this era stored inside your data stem thing... inside your head?"

John nodded, "Yes. Well... not every electronic record. Files classified as restricted access are not part of the standard datstem data core."

Leah shook her head. "It's impossible to store that much information inside a person's head. It's too much data. It would take a computer the size of a city to store that much data."

John grinned. "You're still thinking in terms of silicon processors and physical memory storage devices. A quantum computer is far smaller, yet far more powerful than any computer you can imagine. It exists on a quantum level, with its processors composed of entangled particles, and its data storage consisting of sub-atomic polarized erbium isotopes. My datstem, for example, can store 17.4 yottabytes of information. That's the equivalent of 58,000 times more information than exists in the entire world at this time."

Leah struggled to comprehend such a large quantity of information. "You have that much data inside your head?" she asked, shaking her head in disbelief.

"My datstem does, yes," John replied.

For the next 20 minutes, Leah sat quietly as the vehicle meandered through the growing hills and peaks that formed the foothills of the Himalayan mountains. She still did not yet fully believe John, despite his apparent extraordinary capabilities and her growing desire to do so. What proof did she have? She had asked herself that question many times since their first meeting. True, he had a mysterious, albeit non-functional device, and his explanation for its operation had impressed a physicist. With enough research and creative planning, she reasoned, a skilled fraudster might accomplish as much. His fore-knowledge of an airplane diversion? Perhaps he had simply spoken with one of the airline's maintenance crew before the flight took off. There might be any number of plausible explanations for his strange abilities.

She liked John. Of that, she was sure. She had caught herself on several occasions thinking about his pleasant demeanor, about his kindness towards Kacie, his gentle laugh, and especially his dark eyes. She knew herself well enough to know she needed to be careful, to not allow her professional detachment and journalistic impartiality to be overwhelmed by those eyes.

Suddenly, she realized that she *wanted* John's story to be true. That's a bad situation for a purportedly objective reporter, she cautioned herself, yet she could not deny what she was beginning to feel. She desperately hoped his story was true. Anything less would make the attractive stranger out to be nothing more than a liar and a fraud.

The vehicle was now working its way through the narrow streets of a small city that rose beneath the towering mountains. A forest of cedar trees dusted with snow framed the city, and far above, the wind blew frost from a white mountain peak. They began to pass through exotic markets, past a boy watching a flock of goats, and through a square filled with colorful rugs.

After several minutes, the vehicle slowed and then

approached a yellow building with a white security gate. The building was fringed with white borders along its roofline and the pavement outside the gate was painted with a large white symbol. Nearby stood a modest temple structure and beyond the security gate, what appeared to be a two or three-story administrative building.

The vehicle stopped. The driver opened their door and, through hand signals, invited his passengers to wait inside the small temple. Then he walked towards the security gate to announce his passenger's arrival.

Leah thought the temple was surprisingly small for such an auspicious patron. Inset into one yellow wall was a row of beaten brass "mani" prayer wheels, drum cylinders with raised symbols that spun slowly on a central vertical dowel. She watched, fascinated, as a woman and her small son approached and gently turned the wheels, invoking a blessing.

A beautiful "Green Tara" statue was prominently positioned inside the temple behind a glass display, a gold crown on her head and her breasts exposed. She sat with folded legs on a platform surrounded by small offerings, flowers, and religious figurines. John stopped in front of the statue, admiring its workmanship. When Leah approached to join him, a voice spoke from a nearby doorway.

"She is the Mother of Liberation. She is 'rje btsun sgrol ma'. She represents the virtues of success in our daily work and achievements."

They turned to see a small aged monk standing in the doorway. He wore the traditional orange saffron and maroon robes of a Tibetan Buddhist monk. Behind him stood a taller, younger monk, waiting deferentially.

211

John pressed the palms of his hands together on his chest and bowed gently. Not knowing what to do, Leah followed John's example, and then rose with John when their greeting was returned by the two monks. Gazing at the statue, John replied, "She is Tara Bosatsu to the Japanese."

The senior monk appeared surprised for a moment, and then smiled warmly, stepping towards them. He nodded and said, "She is many things to many people."

The younger monk now spoke, gesturing towards the elder, "This is Tenzin Chophel, Minister of Public Affairs and personal aide to His Holiness, the Dalai Lama of Tibet."

"I am honored Rinpoche," John replied, bowing again. "May I present Miss Leah Vaughn, Associate Producer for All Posted Newswire."

The monk shook Leah's hand in the western tradition. "A pleasure Miss Vaughn."

"And I am John Clifton."

The monk now shook John's hand, asking, "And are you affiliated with the media, Mr. Clifton?"

"No Rinpoche. I am… a traveler," John replied with a smile.

The monk looked up sharply, studying John's face. "Most interesting," he said. There was a strange gleam in the monk's eye. "A traveler you say?" The elderly monk glanced at the green statue and then back at John, before gesturing towards a canopied corridor leading into the temple complex. "Please, join me for some tea."

As they approached the adjoining building, the aged monk whispered something to his young aide, who bowed and left.

212

Entering the building, they found themselves in a small comfortable room filled with cushions and finely woven tapestries on the walls; a meeting room designed for visitors and dignitaries. A tea kettle and cups had been placed next to a small brazier that smelled of exotic woods. A thin curl of smoke rose from the coals, twisting and rippling towards the ceiling.

John assisted the elderly monk to sit on the cushions and then sat nearby in the Japanese fashion, kneeling, sitting back on both knees. Leah sat next to John, feeling uncomfortable and entirely out of her element. The monk noticed John's posture and a hint of an approving smile touched his face.

"Forgive me Rinpoche," John said. "I bring no gift."

The elder monk waved his hand in dismissal, "Not true, John Clifton. What you bring is a gift far greater than you know." In answer to John's puzzled look, the monk added, "Your gift is the reaffirmation of my master's divine nature."

The elderly monk now poured tea for his guests as he explained. "His Holiness recently returned from Bihar, India. He tarried there nearly a month where he taught many things to students and devotees from around the world." He handed Leah a cup of tea, adding, "Many from the media were there to hear His Holiness' words and ask him questions."

The monk now passed a second cup to John. "One morning, as we walked together inside the village of Bodhgaya, we came upon a small Mother of Liberation shrine. The wind was blowing and a bit of cloth flew by and became caught on the statue. My master watched the cloth for some time. Then he turned and spoke to me, saying we must return to Dharamshala the following week."

The elderly monk sipped his tea, motioning for John and

Leah to do the same. It tasted of mint and strange spices Leah could not recognize, but the warmth was soothing.

The monk then continued, "I inquired whether His Holiness was tiring… he has blessed our world for 82 years and he frequently tires after the manner of men."

The monk looked at John and said, "His Holiness said no, he was not tired. He said he was expecting someone. When I pressed further, he counseled me to patience. He instructed me then to watch for a traveler from a far place, a traveler who would greet me by the Mother of Liberation shrine at our temple in Dharamshala."

Leah looked sharply at John, struggling to understand. At that moment, the door opened and the elderly monk placed his cup on the table and bowed low to the floor.

The 14th Dalai Lama of Tibet stood in the doorway.

The younger monk who had greeted them in the garden was supporting the aged leader and now spoke reverently, "May I present His Holiness, Jetsun Jamphel Ngawang Lobsang Yeshe Tenzin Gyatsothe, tulku of the 13th Dalai Lama, the 14th Dalai Lama of Tibet."

John placed his hands together in the Tibetan manner and bowed low to the floor. Leah followed.

The spiritual leader of Tibet returned their greeting and then stepped slowly into the room, assisted by the younger monk. The aged high lama was studying John closely, staring at his face, his eyes, and his clothing. Slowly, a smile formed at his mouth and his eyes shined behind his thick glasses as he was gently assisted to his cushion. The Dalai Lama then spoke, his voice soft and trembling. Chophal translated his words.

"I remember you," he said, staring at John.

When John made no reply, the aged lama smiled and said in a stronger voice, nodding decisively, "I remember you. I had traveled to the holy mountain of Wutai Shan to meet with the envoys of many nations. It was... during a time of growing violence."

John sat stoic, frozen, listening, his face a mask behind which his eyes alone registered surprise.

The Dalia Lama raised his fragile hand to his brow as if struggling to recall something. Then he nodded and continued.

"You were there. You were seeking someone. A traveler like yourself who had become lost."

John slowly nodded now and said, "Yes, Holiness. His name was Fai Zhou. I had been sent to try to find out what had happened to him."

The Dalai Lama nodded. "We spoke together, standing on a large rock overlooking the valley." He paused now, watching John closely.

John nodded and answered, "Yes. The wind was blowing from the west and it blew down one of the banners in the valley below us."

When John's response had been translated, a satisfied sigh escaped the aging leader's mouth. The wizened man sat back against the cushion and removed his eyeglasses. The young monk immediately knelt and produced a small silk handkerchief, which the Dalai Lama took and dabbed at his moistened eyes.

Leah was confused. She leaned towards John and asked in a soft voice, "You two have met before?"

John did not respond, but the Dalai Lama stirred and responded in thickly-accented English. "Yes my child. I have

215

met this traveler before."

Leah shook her head in confusion.

With a hint of a smile on his face, the monk motioned for John to explain.

John took a breath, nodded, and then turned to face Leah. "Twelve years ago, I was sent by the CTI council on a tripback mission into China, to try and discover what had happened to another temporal specialist who had vanished there. His name was Fai Zhou and he had disappeared while on a mission for one of our competitors, a company named Reynolds-Hampshire."

As he spoke, Chophel translated while the younger monk stared at John, listening intently. The Dalai Lama, however, sat quietly with his eyes closed, listening.

"I joined company with a Russian Imperial officer named Carl Mannerheim who was en route with other foreign dignitaries to a meeting being convened at a sacred mountain called Wutai Shan. While there, I was introduced to His Holiness, Thubten Gyatso, the 13th Dalai Lama of Tibet."

"Wait… wait." Leah was confused. "The 13th Dalai Lama?"

"Yes."

"What year was this?"

"1908".

Leah looked at the present Dalai Lama and then back to John.

"I don't understand."

This time, it was the Dalai Lama who responded. Opening his eyes, the aged monk responded again in English. "Yes, my child, you *do* understand. You understand, but you do not *believe*."

Leah stared at the Dalai Lama, who now spoke with a tenderness reminiscent of a father counseling a beloved daughter, "You do not lack understanding, my child. You lack faith. Your mind prevents you from believing what your heart tells you is true."

The Dalai Lama motioned for the young monk to help him stand. When Chophel also began to rise, the Dalai Lama motioned for him to remain. Assisted by the young monk, the spiritual leader of Tibet led John and Leah slowly from the small room and across the temple courtyard. They passed through a garden filled with lichen-covered stones before arriving at a building without windows, a building with a heavy wooden door studded with hammered iron rivets. At a gesture from the Dalai Lama, the younger monk retrieved a brass key from the folds of his robe and unlocked the door.

The room inside was dimly lit and musty. When the younger monk lit several oil lamps, the room's contents became clearer. It was a vault, a reliquary filled with artifacts and boxes; priceless treasures from Tibet withheld from the Chinese invasion and concealed from the world. Gold glittered everywhere, from plates and incense burners to ornate oil lamps and prayer mani wheels of great antiquity. Gem-encrusted statues of divine figures seemingly lounged among intricately carved chests and bolts of magnificent woven tapestries.

The aide brought an enameled stool with an embroidered silk cushion and helped the Dalai Lama to sit. The workmanship of the enamelwork on the stool were those of a master craftsman. Once sitting, the elderly lama spoke

217

something to the aide and then motioned for John and Leah to be seated on red silk cushions at his feet. The scene struck John of a teacher preparing to teach his students. The Dalai Lama now spoke, his English accented but understandable.

"When I was a child," he began, "I remembered many events of my former life. As the years have been gathered, new memories associated with *this* body grow stronger. The past becomes smaller, vaguer." He paused for a moment, shaking his head before continuing, "Now I am old after the manner of men. Unless I make a specific attempt to recall a former memory, it eludes me."

John nodded, listening with interest.

The young monk approached again, carrying a small box in his hands. It was carved with Tibetan script and resembled an antique traveling chest with brass reinforced corners and straps protecting the fine-grained lacquered wood beneath. He set the box down beside the chair with a bow. The Dalai Lama placed his hand on the box and continued.

"One memory that I have longed preserved from my childhood, was of a traveler from a far place who greeted me at the mountain of Wutai Shan. I remember it was during a time of growing conflict. The traveler came with a foreign warlord with whom I exchanged gifts."

John nodded. "You presented Mannerheim with a length of fine white silk cloth."

The Dalai Lama smiled broadly. Then, a mischievous twinkle gleaming in his eyes, he asked, "And do you remember his gift to me?"

John nodded again. "Yes Rinpoche," he said, "Mannerheim presented you with his pistol."

218

The Dalai Lama gently opened the box. Underneath a folded cotton cloth lay a vintage Browning pistol, glistening with oil and carefully preserved.

Leah stared at the weapon in the chest, and then back to John, her mind swirling.

The Dalai Lama spoke again, "We left early in the morning so we would not alert the Chinese envoy in the camp. We walked up into the mountain and stood on a great rock that overlooked the valley. The wind was blowing and it blew loose one of the Chinese pendants in the valley below. The pendant flew across the valley and struck a Mother of Liberation shrine that my people had placed beside my tent. The pendant covered the goddess' face and it struck me as an ill omen. I pointed at it and I asked you a question. Do you remember what I asked you?"

John nodded, "You asked me if China would invade your country. I told you yes... following your death, China would invade Tibet and cause great suffering among your people."

The aging monk nodded, his expression grave. "What you spoke to me long ago has come to pass."

Closing the chest, the Dalai Lama leaned forward and placed a trembling hand on John's shoulder, his voice breaking.

"When I saw the cloth floating in the wind to be caught by the Mother of Liberation shrine in Bodhgaya, I was reminded of that childhood memory, so long preserved, and I knew the traveler was coming to speak with me again."

Chapter 23

John and Leah stayed in Dharamshala for three days. Tom Pierce expressed only moderate surprise at the change of schedule. Mary Kravets, however, was considerably put off. She complained loudly about itinerary changes and the costs associated with canceling and re-booking airline tickets, not to mention rescheduling interviews with "important people".

Leah was frankly in no condition to return. Their meeting with the Dalai Lama had affected the young woman profoundly. She had burst into tears after the revelation in the vault room and had been carried by the younger monk to a small guest bedroom inside the administrative building to rest.

When she awoke, the fading light coming through the

room's small window told her she had slept through most of the day. A few moments after she sat up in bed, the door opened and a white-haired Tibetan nun entered. The woman had been waiting outside, listening for any movement from within the room. Through hand signs and gentle nudges, the elderly nun gently directed Leah through a small door into an adjoining chamber where a bath had been prepared. Candles were burning on a raised table behind vertical sticks of smoldering sandalwood incense. The nun placed a lush hand-woven woolen cloth on the stool before patting Leah gently on the back, bowing, and closing the door, leaving her alone in the small room.

A distant conversation could be heard through a fabric-draped window. Pulling back on the covering to peek outside, Leah could see John across the courtyard sitting in the garden under the boughs of a cedar tree. He was dressed in traditional Tibetan male clothing; a belted robe with long sleeves. A thick sheepskin coat lay on the ground by his booted feet.

Next to him sat the Dalai Lama in his maroon and saffron robes. The two men were sitting on straw mats surrounded by perhaps a dozen aged monks in similar robes. Chophel sat among the group next to John, translating for the group. Charcoal braziers scattered among the men created heat, and lamps hanging from the branches of the tree provided additional light against the approaching dusk. The monks were cooking rice crackers on the small braziers and listening intently to their master's and John's conversation.

As she watched, Leah noticed John occasionally looking up at the door that led into the building where she had been taken.

He was concerned about her!

The thought filled her with warmth. She stepped back from the window and took another look around the strange room. The steaming bath was inviting.

Outside, the conversation continued as Leah enjoyed her bath. Though she was too far away to hear what was being spoken, from time to time, surprised murmuring eclipsed the sound of John's voice as Chophel translated what John had said.

The scent from the sandalwood incense and the flickering glow of the candles was hypnotic and, as she bathed in the steaming water, Leah began to let her mind wander as she had not done in years. After nearly an hour, a soft knock at the door startled her back to the present. Before she could speak, the door opened and the white-haired nun re-entered, bowing at the naked woman in the tub before placing a bundle of clothing and slippers on the stool next to the towel.

Before Leah knew what was happening, the nun had lifted her gently from the water and began drying her with the towel. The elderly woman chattered softly in Tibetan as her hands worked the soft cloth against Leah's wet skin. Once dried, the nun retrieved the clothing bundle and placed a sleeveless dress on her tall guest. The dress was a non-descript blue-grey, very soft, with buttons down the right side. Once Leah was dressed, the nun retrieved a small carved comb and began to comb dry her charge's hair against a woolen towel.

Outside, a small gong sounded, and the distant conversation abruptly ceased. After several minutes, the white-haired nun patted Leah's back, and still speaking softly, helped her feet into the soft slippers. Then the white-haired woman stood and bowed once more. This time, remembering John's response inside the temple, Leah pressed her hands together against her chest and returned the bow.

The elderly nun smiled and opened the door. When Leah stepped out, she nearly collided with the Dalai Lama, his hand poised to knock. John and Chophel stood behind the aged leader.

"Oh! I'm sorry!" Leah said, embarrassed.

The Dalai Lama, however, simply smiled, and said, "We were coming to check on you, my daughter. Are you recovered?"

Leah looked past the monk at John, before slowly nodding her head. "Yes, your Holiness, I am recovered. Thank you." Leah noticed then that John was staring at her with a thoughtful expression on his face.

"I hoped you would join us for our evening meal," the Dalai Lama said, gesturing down the hallway.

"I would be honored."

With that, the high lama turned to lead his guests to dinner, flanked by the younger monk and Chophel. John, however, took Leah's arm in his, before turning to follow.

"I was concerned about you," he said softly as they followed the robed monks.

Leah grinned sheepishly, "I'm sorry... it's all just been so overwhelming, and I guess until that moment..." She didn't finish her sentence.

John nodded. "Until that moment, you didn't believe me."

Leah looked up, shaking her head. "I wanted to believe you John, but it was all just so incredible. I guess... I guess until

223

that moment, I didn't know how to trust you." Leah looked down, then added, "I think I've had a hard time trusting anyone since... since Kacie's father left."

John looked at Leah's face, hesitating for a moment, before asking, "Why did he leave?"

Leah looked up, her eyes fixed on the robes of the monks ahead. "After we learned about Kacie's condition," she began, "I guess it was just too much for him to deal with. So he chose *not* to deal with it. He left about two weeks after we received the medical report and mailed me the divorce papers about three months after that. He made it clear that having a handicapped child was not what he had signed up for. He never even visits Kacie."

John listened silently. He didn't respond, but the strength of his arm under hers gave Leah comfort as they walked.

When they entered the small dining hall, the assembled monks grew silent at their leader's approach, bowing reverently as he guided his guests to sit beside him on the cushions surrounding a low table. Younger acolytes now entered the hall, carrying steaming dishes filled with beans, lentils, noodle soups, and stir-fried or steamed vegetables.

Leah was struck by how silent the monks became. As they ate, no conversations occurred as one might expect around the western dining table. Instead, the hall grew strangely quiet, as the monks ate their meals respectfully, enjoying each other's company and their food in absolute silence. For Leah, the silence only made her aware of the beating of her own heart as she sat on the cushion beside John.

Adopting the monk's attitude, John said nothing to her

during the meal, yet she knew he was fully aware of her proximity. Once, when her hand brushed against his on the small table, she noticed he stilled his arm in the act of reaching for a dish, prolonging her caress, if only for a moment.

When the meal was completed, the monks began to retire. John assisted Leah to stand and they bowed to their host before leaving the dining hall. The small courtyard and garden were nearly deserted now though several large iron braziers holding burning sticks of wood offered warmth against the cold.

John paused by one of the braziers, gazing up into the night sky. Leah looked up too, following his gaze. The sky was cold and black and filled with stars. The moon had risen above the mountain peak but its light was partially obscured by a thin wisp of cloud.

"What are you looking for?" she asked.

John smiled but said nothing.

She looked up again. She could see nothing except the moon and the stars behind. "I've seen you looking up into the sky at night," she said. "It's like you're looking for something."

John sighed and nodded. "Yes. I'm looking for something."

"What?" she asked.

"I'm looking for my home."

"I don't understand."

"I live there," he said, pointing to a dark patch of sky just beneath the moon. "In my time, Hōfu Station orbits just there, approximately halfway between the Earth and Luna. That's my home."

Leah looked up again, following his finger.

"From the Earth," John continued, "the station appears like a small bright light moving with the moon across the sky. You can easily tell it apart from the stars because it's larger and brighter than any star, especially when the sun hits it just right."

"What's it like… living there?" she asked.

John's eyebrows tensed slightly as if he was struggling to find the right words. "It's hard to describe," he said. "It's not like any place you have here. The nights are more beautiful than anything you can imagine."

As he spoke, Leah looked up at the spot where John was watching and tried to imagine what it must be like.

"They dim the station lights at night," John continued, "to allow the stars to shine through the dome. They're not like the stars you see from the earth. The sky is filled with millions of stars, much brighter than anything you can imagine. You can see the Milky Way cloud stretching across the heavens… and Luna! She is twice the size she appears from the Earth. From the station, you can see the lights of Copernicus City and Grimaldi to the southwest."

John sighed now. He seemed sad. "I guess I'm just homesick," he said. "It feels like everything I have ever known is up there, beyond my reach, more than a hundred years into a future I may never see again."

Leah could sense his profound loss. She could hear it in his voice as he spoke. She didn't know what to say. She couldn't imagine losing… everything. On impulse, she stepped close and kissed him on his cheek.

John looked down, surprise in his eyes. He didn't say anything, but his arms pulled her close. She felt the warmth of his chest pressing against hers in the chill air and the beating of her heart against his. She lifted her head, inviting the kiss that he now delivered. It was a brief embrace, the kiss tender. When he released her, her eyes were twinkling from the brazier's flickering fire. At that moment, several monks exited from the dining hall and began to cross the small courtyard, bowing stiffly as they passed the embracing couple.

John spoke quietly, nodding at the departing monks, "We should go back inside."

Leah agreed though she was reluctant to leave the warmth of the fire.

The following day, Leah could not find John. The white-haired nun could not understand her inquiries, and when it became apparent that Leah was becoming disturbed, the nun sent for a translator, a young acolyte, who informed Leah in perfect English that her companion had left that morning with His Holiness and would return later that evening.

"You speak very good English," Leah replied after absorbing the message.

The young man grinned and then nodded, "Thank you. My name is Norbu. I was born in California. I lived there until I graduated from high school last year. My family lives in La Jolla."

"Oh?" Leah nodded, smiling. "What brought you here?"

The young man looked up, gazing around the room as if admiring its exotic setting before responding.

"My grandfather fled Tibet when the Chinese invaded in 1949. He was fortunate to have escaped early. After he escaped, the Chinese killed more than a million Tibetans. They

227

destroyed more than 6000 monasteries and imprisoned or killed thousands of monks."

Leah stared at the young man, shocked.

Noticing her expression, the young man nodded vigorously. "Oh, it's much worse than you ever hear about back home."

Norbu leaned against the stone wall in the garden and looked at the tall mountains beyond as if he were trying to visualize the faraway country that lay beyond its peaks. "In Tibet today," he said, "there is no freedom of speech, religion, or press like we have in the U.S. Tibetans are routinely forced from their homes and replaced by Chinese settlers. In some regions in Tibet, 6 out of every 7 people are now Chinese!"

He shook his head, and his voice became sad, "The Chinese government," he said, "forces Tibetan women to have abortions or be sterilized to prevent future generations of Tibetans from being born. Monks are routinely arrested and imprisoned, if not killed outright. The Chinese have harvested or destroyed over 80% of the forests in Tibet, and they use the land as a dumping ground for their nuclear and toxic waste."

Leah shook her head sadly, then asked, "You still haven't said why you came here."

The young man looked around again before responding. "I promised my grandfather before he died that I would become a monk, and then go back."

"Go back?"

The young man nodded. "I promised him I would go back to Tibet."

Leah stared at the youth, barely out of high school, his head shaved in preparation for joining the ranks of novice
228

monks. "Why would you do that?!" she asked, incredulous.

The young man shrugged and said, "I'm Tibetan."

John rejoined Leah for their evening meal. He seemed anxious about something, though the silence in the dining hall prevented him from speaking. The Dalai Lama, she noted, appeared tired. When the meal had concluded and they had stepped out of the dining hall, she took the opportunity to ask John where he had been.

"His Holiness and I needed to go into the city," John said. He needed to send out a private communication to the Taiwan consulate and he asked me to accompany him."

"Why didn't you tell me before you left?"

"We left very early, and I thought you could use the rest."

Leah considered this and then nodded. John was right. The day had been restful, though lonely. She had wandered the neighborhood with the young American acolyte, Norbu, who had pointed out the many Tibetan shops, shrines, and markets. The young man had explained to her that at least 150,000 Tibetans now lived in exile in India; a true Tibetan diaspora about which the western nations cared little.

"So what's going on?" Leah asked. "You appear nervous about something."

John glanced around for a moment, and then lowered his voice. "His Holiness is holding a special convocation of senior monks tomorrow. He has asked me to speak at the assembly."

Seeing Leah's expression, John shook his head, anticipating her question. "No, I'm sorry. He will not allow the

229

convocation to be filmed. It is being convened in the greatest secrecy, but he *has* given permission for you to attend."

Leah was upset, "But that's why we came here, to film you interviewing with... with Chophel."

John nodded, "Yes, but the situation has changed. His Holiness has prohibited it. A lot is going on, Leah. He has agreed to allow you to be present and even to take notes. That is a great concession, but it comes with one condition."

"Condition?" The young producer shook her head.

"Yes. The condition is that you may not report what is said at the convocation for at least one year."

"One year? Why?"

"I'm sorry, but I can't explain right now. You'll learn more tomorrow."

Leah was deflated. Her journalistic pride felt bruised. On the other hand, being present at such a meeting was unprecedented and she was curious.

John studied her face. "Do you agree? No disclosure of what you hear at the convocation for at least a year. Promise?"

She took a breath, then nodded. "I promise."

John nodded back and then turned to rejoin his guide who was waiting patiently at the end of the corridor. Before he could leave, however, Leah seized his hand.

"John... I... I missed you today."

John hesitated, looking at Leah's face. After a moment, he smiled, nodding, "I missed you too."

Leah made a decision. She took a deep breath, her face flushing. Leaning forward, she touched her cheek against his and whispered, "I want to be with you tonight."

John stepped back, a look of surprise on his face.

Shaking his head, he grinned and whispered, "And just how are we supposed to arrange that my dear… given where we happen to be at this moment?" Still shaking his head, he leaned forward and kissed her on her cheek before turning and walking away.

Leah was completely confounded. Then, as a gong sounded in the temple outside, and robed monks began walking past her in the corridor, it occurred to her just how audacious her request had been. She had been trying to arrange a romantic tryst inside a Buddhist monastery filled with hundreds of monks and nuns sworn to a life of celibacy! The irony of such a request, given their surroundings, forced a small laugh to escape from her mouth.

Turning now, she rejoined the white-haired nun who was waiting to take her to her room. As she followed the elderly nun, she glanced back in time to see John turning a corner at the end of the corridor.

His eyes met hers and he smiled again, still shaking his head.

Chapter 24

"*All things from eternity are of like forms
and come round in a circle.*"
*~ Marcus Aurelius Antoninus Augustus
Roman Emperor and stoic philosopher
(121 – 180 AD)*

L eah's sleep was repeatedly disturbed throughout the long night by the sound of visitors arriving. Conversations passing outside her door suggested excitement growing within the otherwise quiet monastery.

In truth, Leah had kept herself awake most of the night thinking about John. When she had been left alone in her room, she had laughed at herself again for propositioning him inside a monastery filled with celibate monks. Timing had never been one of her strengths. Still, although his response had left her standing befuddled in the corridor, his smile had been warm, and as she lay under the soft wool blanket, she had touched her mouth, remembering their brief kiss in the garden.

It was early morning when the white-haired nun knocked softly at the door. Leah was shocked, however, when the woman entered the room. Leah had only seen her elderly attendant dressed in the faded robes of everyday wear. This morning, the white-haired nun was dressed in a magnificent maroon and saffron robe of the finest quality. The brilliant colors shimmered and contrasted starkly against the stone walls and brown floor of the bed chamber. The nun's white-haired head, freshly shorn, was covered by a tall saffron crown worn on only the most sacred formal occasions. The nun was followed by two other nuns, similarly adorned, and two younger acolyte girls carrying braziers of incense.

Bowing low to Leah, the matron nun summoned the two other nuns, who entered the room respectfully, carrying a beautiful maroon acolyte's robe, beaded slippers, and other finery in their arms. From somewhere outside, a gong resonated softly three times, then fell silent.

Less than an hour later, Leah found herself being escorted down the corridor towards the dining hall. Though filled with monks and nuns dressed in their finest robes, no food was evident. Norbu quickly approached and bowed. The young acolyte's head was freshly shaved and he too wore a striking maroon robe.

"I have been asked to accompany you to the convocation!" he said. Excitement was evident in the young man's face. "I am to translate for you. It is very great honor! Only the most senior monks and nuns are being permitted to attend!"

Leah smiled. The young man's excitement was contagious. She was also relieved. She felt awkward dressed in the formal acolyte robe and slippers, and she appreciated having someone with whom she could speak, someone who could explain things to her. "No one is eating," she said, motioning to the crowded hall.

Her young companion shook his head, "Oh, no! We are fasting this morning. His Holiness has ordered it."

From outside, the sound of a gong resonating two times abruptly stilled the room. All conversation ended and those monks or nuns who had not yet placed their saffron crowns upon their heads now did so and began filing out into an adjoining corridor.

Norbu whispered, "I am permitted to speak to you during the convocation, because I am acting as your translator, but we must whisper from now on."

Leah nodded.

Norbu continued, "And I must ask you to only speak to me if you do not understand something. Casual conversation is not normally allowed in such assemblies as these. Do you understand?"

Leah nodded, and whispered, "Yes. Thank you Norbu."

The young acolyte now took her by the arm and guided her formally towards the door. Several of the saffron-crowned monks stood aside to allow them to pass. Norbu bowed stiffly, clearly proud to be accorded such an honor.

The line of monks and nuns stretched out of the building towards the adjoining temple annex building. Leah was suddenly alarmed to see armed men standing on either side of the annex building's doors. The men were dressed in camouflage clothing and carried automatic weapons. When she hesitated, Norbu gently pulled her by the elbow to continue, whispering, "They are Tibetan military policemen," he said. "They are here to protect His Holiness and to provide security during the convocation. No worries."

Leah nodded and walked past the imposing men into the building. The procession now approached a great hall, its double-doors open. Armed guards stood at attention at these doors also, but none were evident inside the hall itself.

The hall was magnificently arrayed with maroon pillars

crowned with beaten brass overlaid with gold leaf and festooned with enameled shapes reminiscent of great gems. The columns supported a roof richly worked in enamel, gold, and painted scenes of Tibetan landscapes and religious iconography. The walls were as ornately painted as the roof, with religious deities prominently featured against landscape scenes of green Tibetan valleys and mountains.

Perhaps fifty monks and nuns were already seated on rows of cushions facing the far wall. There, on a raised dais, sat the Dalai Lama. He was dressed as the monks, in a magnificent maroon and saffron robe, with a similar saffron-fringed crown on his head. Sitting next to the Dalai Lama was Tenzin Chophel, similarly attired. He was leaning and whispering something to his master.

When Chophel leaned back, Leah saw John. He was dressed as she was dressed, in a maroon acolyte's formal robe, sitting behind the two senior monks. Their eyes met, and John smiled as he watched her being escorted to her place of honor; several soft cushions placed on the floor directly beneath the raised dais.

Norbu motioned for Leah to be seated, and then he sat on the cushion beside her. Leah could see the young man's hands trembling with awed excitement. She estimated the hall contained perhaps a hundred people now. There were no acolytes in attendance save Norbu. Indeed, all of the monks and nuns in attendance appeared to be elderly, the most senior spiritual representatives of the Tibetan people; the veritable heart of their nation.

Leah suddenly felt overwhelmed. She took several breaths and looked down on the low table in front of her. There was a pad of paper and several pencils placed there. On the first pad, a small folded note had been left with her name on it. Opening the note, she read; *"Leah, Remember your promise. You must wait for at least a year before reporting on what you hear today. John."* Beneath his name, John had added, *"...you were in my thoughts last night."*

Their eyes met again and John smiled warmly before turning his attention back to the gathering.

From outside, a single gong sounded and the room fell completely silent now as the doors to the hall were slowly closed and barred.

His Holiness, the 14th Dalai Lama of Tibet now bowed to the assembly, which returned the bow as one body. Facing Tenzin Chophel, the elderly leaders then exchanged bows. Chophel now produced a small microphone, turned, and spoke to the assembly. As he spoke, Norbu, his face flushed and red, cleared his throat softly and translated for Leah.

"His Holiness welcomes you to this convocation. You have been summoned without explanation or reason, for the subject of this convocation is too important to risk disclosure to those who would work against Tibet. His Holiness thanks you for your swift attendance and for your long service to the Tibetan people."

With that, Chophel handed the microphone to the Dalai Lama. The elderly monk smiled warmly at the assembled group. His eyes glistened behind his glasses as he spoke.

"Yesterday, I sent a personal letter by courier to the Taiwan consulate. In that letter, I warned the President of Taiwan about a disaster that would strike that island nation this very week. I did this because of my love for all people and in

236

the hope that my warning might save lives."

The Dalai Lama paused, allowing what he had said to be absorbed, before he continued.

"Many of you will ask how I knew of this disaster *before* it occurred. Some may attribute it to divine insight, but I learned of this disaster in another way."

Glancing at John, the senior monk's expression became thoughtful.

"Until the late 20th century the focus of scientific research was mostly on external things. I have taken part in meetings with scientists for more than 30 years. They have mostly involved western scientists, Americans and Europeans, as well as one or two meetings with Japanese and Indians."

Leah now sensed eyes around the room quietly staring at her, as the elderly leader continued.

"One purpose of those meetings has been to expand our knowledge, to include the mind as well as external phenomena, in order to achieve a fuller understanding of reality. The second purpose of such discussions concerns the use to which such knowledge should be put."

"I sent the letter yesterday to the President of Taiwan in an attempt to save lives. That is, I believe, the best use to which such knowledge should be put; the saving of life... all life... in all of its forms."

"Regarding the first purpose, we study science to expand our minds to knowledge and to gain a fuller understanding of reality. From a Madhyamaka standpoint, we understand that there is a difference between our perception of the world and its reality. The realm of science called quantum physics is an excellent example of this principal. At present, we do not understand many aspects of quantum physics, yet we cannot doubt its reality."

The Dalai Lama glanced briefly at Leah before continuing.

"Sometimes, we feel a reluctance to discuss quantum physics with westerners whose cultural backgrounds are based on Judeo-Christian precepts in case it leads to a conflict of faith. We feel less difficulty in relation to Asians, particularly with our fellow Chinese. We recall, for example, that when the Chinese Buddhist monk Xuanzang came to India in the 7th century, he studied at Nalanda University and, while there, he is reputed to have met Nagabodhi, a direct disciple of Nagarjuna."

"From Nagabodhi, Xuanzang was taught principals of temporal causality, general relativity, and quantum science not understood by western science until Einstein and other contemporary scientists announced similar discoveries only this past century."

The aged monk straightened his back and spoke decisively now to the assembled group.

"Quantum science is a subject long known to those of us in the east. It allows us to understand that many such things we cannot yet explain through science, may indeed be real. As followers of Madhyamaka, we must allow our minds to accept possibilities that our science cannot presently explain."

The Dalai Lama now looked at Leah, and smiling, he added, "And we must allow our hearts to accept what our minds cannot."

With this, the Dalai Lama put down the microphone and gestured for John to sit between him and Chophel. A rustling of

238

robes and whispered murmurs throughout the hall hinted at the surprise at such an honor being shown to the strange foreigner in the acolyte robe. Leah noticed that John appeared nervous. As he sat down on the cushion between the two monks, his eyes met hers and he smiled hesitantly.

The Dalai Lama retrieved the microphone and spoke again. "When I was a child," he began, "I had many memories of my former life…"

With this, the spiritual leader of Tibet commenced an explanation of his meeting with John at the mountain of Wutai Shan during his former incarnation. He recounted John's accurate description of the Chinese banner that, blown by the wind, covered the Tara shrine in that valley, and he described the similar omen he had observed recently in Bodhgaya.

Carl Mannerheim's pistol was then displayed to the assembled congregation, and the young monk who was present in the vault described John's accurate description of the unusual gift inside the long-forgotten chest.

Finally, the Dalai Lama concluded, "I sent the letter yesterday to the President of Taiwan in an attempt to save lives. I sent the letter also to eliminate any doubt in your minds as to the truth of what we will hear today. Three days from now, Taiwan will be struck and lives will be lost. When you are told about that tragedy, put any doubts remaining in your minds to rest about the truth of what we will now hear."

With that, the Dalai Lama of Tibet handed the microphone to John with a bow.

For the next three hours, Leah listened, mesmerized, as John commenced a detailed account of the future of Tibet and the Tibetan people. From time to time, the Dalai Lama or

239

Chophel would interrupt the oration, to ask John to clarify a particular event or repeat something he had said. Several times, a break of sorts was called, as the leader called certain senior advisors to the dais for a consultation regarding a particular matter that John had introduced.

As a journalist, Leah knew she had an obligation to record, as accurately as possible, everything that was being said, but Norbu did not translate those private ex-parte consultations between the Dalai Lama and his advisors, apparently considering such discussions to be private. And when John spoke, she found her thoughts drifting to more pleasant subjects. True to her journalistic training, however, she made notes of key events and dates, and vowed to review them later.

Only when the convocation had concluded and she reviewed her notes did Leah begin to understand why John had asked her to keep the information secret for at least a year. There was much the Dalai Lama wished to do, many preparations to undertake, before such information became public.

While she understood at a basic level John's explanation regarding self-resolving causality, Leah was also beginning to understand John's reasons for disclosing future events to people in this time. While self-resolving causality prevented what he disclosed from altering the future, the knowledge of those future events gave hope to people who were struggling without hope. It gave them guidance on which paths to take, which truths to embrace, and which works to begin.

As the assembled monks and nuns bowed deeply at the conclusion of the convocation, there was not a dry eye in the room, evidence of the hope that now filled their collective hearts. As they broke their fast with the noon meal, the feeling in the dining hall was electric, almost festive. Broad smiles were evident everywhere and many eyes that caught Leah's glance were filled with gratitude.

When the meal had concluded, John escorted Leah from the hall.

"We're leaving in the morning," he said quietly. "His Holiness has arranged for a vehicle to transport us to the airport in the morning."

Leah nodded, "Yes, Mary emailed me our new travel itinerary last night. We're flying to London next."

John nodded. "Leah," he began, "I'm sorry about last night, but we just couldn't… not here. It would have been a great insult to our hosts."

Leah nodded swiftly, "Yes, I understand."

At that moment, through the door to the dining hall, the Dalai Lama approached, supported by Tenzin Chophel and the younger monk whose name Leah still did not know.

Seeing their approach, John spoke quickly. "I won't see you again until the morning. His Holiness has agreed to meet with me privately this afternoon… about a question I wish to ask him."

"A question?" Leah asked, shaking her head.

"It's about something I need to do here. He has agreed to advise me."

Leah didn't understand, but she had no time to question further, for the Dalai Lama now joined them.

"I must take your companion away for this evening, my child," the aged leader spoke apologetically.

241

Leah nodded, "Yes. He told me." She was trying to conceal the disappointment in her eyes.

The aging lama, however, smiled and patted her gently on the shoulder. "We Tibetans have a saying my dear... At the bottom of patience lies heaven."

With that, the Dalai Lama took John by the arm and escorted him away, followed by Chophel and the younger monk.

Leah spent the rest of the afternoon in the temple gardens with her young acolyte guide, Norbu. They talked about America, the latest music, the fads in jeans, and the recent movies. She was still struggling to respect the young man's decision to travel to Tibet after becoming a monk and tried to not think about the suffering the idealistic novice might endure at the hands of the intolerant Chinese government.

John was absent from the dining hall for their evening meal, as was the Dalai Lama, Chophel, and the younger monk. Leah sat with Norbu, who escorted her to her bedchamber after the meal had concluded, the white-haired nun following behind.

Once inside her room, the elderly nun placed Leah's traveling clothes, freshly laundered and folded, beside her travel case. Then, she retrieved a beautiful white silk khata scarf from the folds of her robes and placed it in Leah's hands. It was embroidered with Tibetan writing; a prayer invoking good luck. With that, the elderly matron kissed her as a daughter, bowed low, and left the room.

Leah sat on the cushions and reviewed her notes from the morning's convocation by the light of a candle. She had written key events and dates as John had recounted them, but

242

she wanted to review them while they were still fresh in her mind.

"Convocation notes. Saturday Feb 3, 2018   Dharamshala, India."

"Convocation begins at 8:11 AM. Chophel introduces the Dalai Lama, who speaks about quantum science and acceptance of things not presently proved by science. He talks about a disaster that will strike Taiwan on Tuesday. He spoke for approximately 13 minutes."

"John is invited to sit between the monks. It is 8:24 AM."

"Dalai Lama speaks about his childhood memories of his former life, including meeting John in 1908 in China. He spoke for approximately 35 minutes."

"The tall monk from our first meeting with Chophel displayed the chest from the vault. He described how John explained accurately about the meeting in 1908, the banner that flew against the shrine, the exchange of gifts, and how John knew that Mannerheim's' gift in the box was a pistol. He showed the pistol to the assembly. He spoke for approximately 18 minutes."

"John begins speaking. It is 9:20 AM"

"The next Dalai Lama will be chosen from among the Tibetan people living in exile in India. This person will be discovered when they are around 20 years old and will serving as a high lama or scholar. Following this person's discovery, the Chinese government will issue an edict announcing that they have discovered the 'true' Dalai Lama, a child of partial Tibetan ancestry living in China."

"The Dalai Lama called a break and discussed the above with several advisors. To mitigate any confusion that may arise from this conflicting succession, the Dalai Lama said he would issue an announcement, explaining to his people how to recognize his future reincarnation (a Tibetan around 20 years old, who is serving as a high lama or scholar)."

"Following the conclusion of the American Conflict in 2042, Chinese commercial expansion in the west will bring pressure to end to the Chinese communist regime, which will eventually collapse and be replaced by a quasi-capitalist free market government in 2074. Note: The Dalai Lama called a 7-minute break and consulted briefly with his advisors, but made no statement."

"Under pressure from the international community, in 2077, the new Chinese government will permit Tibetans exiled in India and other countries to begin returning to Tibet. (Note: This announcement caused considerable discussion in the room. The Dalai Lama restored order after several minutes. Norbu said he will be 77 then and hopes to be alive to see that day. He said he will take his grandfather's ashes to be interred in Tibet when that happens.)"

"In 2085, Tibet will be granted status as a self-governing territory of China. The 15th Dalai Lama will be invited to return to Lhasa and will be officially recognized as the sole spiritual leader of Tibet. The Chinese-promoted successor will be formally disavowed by the new Chinese government."

"In 2092, a provisional government of Tibet will be established under the authority of the 15th Dalai Lama. The government will be formally recognized by China later that year, establishing Tibet as an independent nation. (Note: there was great rejoicing by the attendees when John said this. Many of the monks

244

leapt to their feet and began embracing their neighbors. Several rushed the dais and bowed to the floor, weeping. Norbu gave me a hug and began to cry like a child. The Dalai Lama allowed the expressions to continue for several minutes, and then reluctantly restored order.)"

"Beginning in 2101, with financial backing from India, China, and the NAFS, Tibet will begin mining its vast gold, lithium, copper, and silver reserves."

"In 2115, the world's largest deposits of dysprosium and neodymium will be discovered inside Tibet near Zhari Namco lake. (Note: check spelling with John.) With the worldwide demand for these rare elements for S.D.U. production exceeding supply, Tibetan exports will swiftly erase its national debt. Within 10 years Tibet's domestic gross national product will exceed that of Nepal, Bangladesh and Burma combined. (Note: ask John, what is S.D.U.? Wasn't that something to do with robots?)"

"In 2131, Tibet will join A.I.S.M.P.E., a world government organization. Chophel asked what the acronym meant. John said it stands for 'Autorité Internationale Singulière de la Matière Phasique Exotique', a powerful international organization that regulates singularity use."

"The Dalai Lama spoke for several minutes. He conveyed love and appreciation to the attendees, but cautioned them to silence about what they had heard until he could counsel with his aides on how best to prepare for their future without provoking anger on the part of the Chinese."

"The Convocation concluded at 12:18 PM."

Chapter 25

*"Our destiny is frequently met
in the very paths we take to avoid it."*
~ Jean de La Fontaine
French fabulist and poet.
(1621 – 1695 AD)

A soft knock at her door told Leah the morning had finally arrived. She had passed the night fitfully, sleeplessly, her mind reliving the events of the past week. Had it been only 8 days since her first meeting with John inside the Chatwal Hotel? When she looked at the stone walls of her bed chamber, the remnants of her night candle, and the embroidered white silk scarf folded neatly on her travel case, that meeting now seemed part of some distant past.

The soft knock was repeated.

"Yes?" Leah answered.

One of her white-haired nun's acolyte attendants opened the door and bowed, speaking something in Tibetan, before patting her hand softly on Leah's travel case.

"Thank you," Leah answered, nodding she understood. The acolyte nodded back and then closed the door.

It was time to leave Dharamshala.

After a moment of reflection, Leah put her western clothes into her travel case and retrieved the soft sleeveless dress she had been given when she had first arrived. After she dressed, she wrapped the white silk scarf around her neck and opened the door. She found the white-haired nun, the acolyte attendants, and Norbu waiting patiently outside.

Norbu retrieved her case as the acolyte attendants helped her into a beautiful shedma coat of the finest wool and fur collar. Norbu followed behind, as the small group went outside and crossed the small courtyard towards the temple. It was still dark outside, though the peaks of the mountains were silhouetted in a faint light, a promise of the morning sun rising behind their imposing heights.

Despite the early hour, the small temple garden was crowded with monks and nuns, all bundled warmly against the morning chill.

John stood waiting with the Dalai Lama and Chophel near the Green Tara statue. John was carrying his backpack that contained his MTY device. Like her, however, he was dressed in the traditional Tibetan clothing they had been given upon their arrival. The thick leather jacket and woolen collar made him appear roguishly handsome, and Leah's cheeks flushed as she approached.

They assembled monks bowed in greeting. The 14th Dalai Lama of Tibet now stepped forward and placed a beautiful mara necklace of lapis lazuli beads around Leah's head.

"I fear we may not meet again, my daughter," the aged leader said, "at least, not in this life." He paused now, as if considering what to say. "I understand that those of your Christian faith do not believe as we do in the east, but if you will permit me, I will offer to you a traditional Buddhist blessing in the belief that the Mother of Liberation will guide and protect you on your journey."

With that, the high lama took a step back and blessed her in the Tibetan manner, intoning the words, "Om tāre tu tāre ture soha."

Then, looking up at John, the Dalai Lama said, "Goodbye John Clifton. We shall recite the Dug-Sher-Seng Sum sutra today, invoking the Lion-faced goddess' blessing upon you, that you may overcome the obstacles set in your path and achieve that noble purpose for which you have been sent."

"Farewell Rinpoche."

The men bowed to each other.

John then took Leah's arm and escorted her from the small temple towards the white security gate. Norbu followed, carrying Leah's travel case. From somewhere nearby, a gong began to toll, and the assembled monks and nuns bowed low to their departing guests.

A black sedan was waiting outside the white gate, a Tibetan driver standing by its doors. Norbu placed Leah's case in the trunk and then closed it with an irreverent slam.

"Well, you're all set," the young man said, smiling. "It was sure great talking with someone from America again."

"Thank you Norbu," Leah replied. Then, on an impulse, she grabbed the young man and hugged him tightly. When she finally released him, Norbu was clearly embarrassed, glancing back at the assembled monks, but there was also a gleam of tears in his eyes.

"You be careful, ok?" Leah said, gently shaking the young man.

"You sound just like my mother," Norbu said, but then his face sobered, and he said, "I'll be careful. I promise."

Leah nodded, wiped her eyes, and then got into the

vehicle.

John patted the young acolyte on the back, and then followed Leah into the car, placing his backpack on the floor by his feet.

The car pulled away and drove quietly, meandering down the winding Dharamshala roads, through snow-dusted cedar trees, as the dark sky behind them slowly grew brighter. After perhaps 20 minutes, the sky above suddenly burst into light as the morning sun breached the distant frosted peaks.

When they arrived at the airport, Leah gazed back at the maintains, and then with a sigh, she retrieved her travel case and walked beside John into the small terminal.

The flight from Kangra airport to Delhi was much more pleasant than their earlier flight between the two cities. When the engine props were first engaged, John glanced nervously outside the airplane window at the spinning blades. This time, however, Leah leaned over and slid down the window cover.

John smiled sheepishly, then nodded.

After the plane took off, John turned and asked, "We're going to London?"

Leah nodded, retrieving the notes she had written down earlier from Mary's email. "Yes," she said, "we're going to meet with Sir Albert Nicholls, Professor of Climate Studies at Kings College, Fellow of the Royal Society of London, and Committee Chair of the Climate Science Communication Group at the Royal Meteorological Society."

John nodded, then asked, "Why did Tom choose for me to meet with him? I mean, there are climatologists all over the world."

Leah folded the itinerary. "Tom and I interviewed Sir

Albert last year at a climate change summit in Paris. Also, he's my friend. When I was first starting out in the business, I wrote for an environmental blogger in New York. One of my first real interviews was with Sir Albert. You could say, I owe my career to that interview. It got me noticed and allowed me to move on into more mainstream news media."

"I see."

When the flight landed in Delhi, Leah took an opportunity to change back into her western clothing. She tucked the embroidered silk scarf into her purse but kept the blue mara necklace around her neck. She touched it fondly as she waited for John. Across the terminal, she could see him coming out of the men's room, his thick Tibetan jacket rolled up and tied to the back of his backpack.

The layover in Delhi was brief; only 2 hours. They enjoyed a brief meal in one of the terminal cafes, and Leah purchased a book from a bookshop; "Freedom in Exile", the autobiography of the 14th Dalai Lama of Tibet. She clung to the paperback as she walked to their departure gate, worrying about Norbu, and reflecting on her three days in Dharamshala.

John was quiet. He had been distracted all morning, and now, as they boarded the large Air India jet, Leah watched him closely. Mary had arranged for them to fly first class, and when the flight attendant finally shut the airplane door in front of them, Leah noticed that John barely tensed at all. He was clearly deep in thought about something.

Leaning close, Leah whispered, "What was the question you needed to ask the Dalai Lama?"

John did not respond. After a few moments, he turned and said, "I'm sorry. What did you say?"

"I was curious about what you needed to ask the Dalai Lama yesterday?"

John glanced at their fellow passengers and at the flight attendants working the business section beyond the curtain. He shook his head.

"I'm sorry," he responded, "I.... I can't talk about that right now."

Leah nodded and sat back in her chair.

The flight to London took more than 9 hours. It was a pleasant enough flight, though John's distraction caused Leah some concern. She fell asleep halfway through the flight. John lifted up the arm rest between them to allow her to place a pillow on his lap, and she had dozed off to him stroking her hair.

When the plane was approaching London, she woke with a start, momentarily confused. John smiled at her and said, "We're getting ready to land."

Leah could see flight attendants moving through the airplane, asking passengers to raise their seats or secure their seatbelts for landing. Several minutes later, the plane touched down.

John had been quiet during the long flight, but now, as the plane taxied towards the arrival gate at the London, Heathrow airport, he suddenly tensed.

Leah looked up at his face, startled by the sudden change.

John looked back swiftly, peering through the curtains into the business class section, staring intently.

"What is it?" Leah asked.

Suddenly, John took her by the hand, and whispered,

251

"When they open the airplane doors, I need you to exit immediately."

"Why?..." Leah began, but John shook his head and squeezed her arm, forcing her to silence.

"No. Just listen. I need you to exit the plane immediately. Go quickly across the hall to the departure gate opposite from ours. Understand? Sit several rows up, with your back to our gate, and just wait with the other passengers there."

"Why?"

"Please. Just do it. Don't tell anyone your name, and keep your head down. Just wait for me there. If I don't join you in an hour, get on a flight back to New York. Don't leave the airport! Understand?"

Leah nodded gravely. It was clear that John was intensely serious.

A soft tone announced their arrival at the gate, and passengers began removing their seatbelts. John immediately retrieved his backpack from its compartment above their heads. This time, however, instead of casually slinging one of its loops over his shoulder, he placed both arms through their respective loops and buckled the pack tightly across his front with its third strap. He handed Leah her travel case and bodily maneuvered her through the other first class passengers who were still retrieving their carry-on bags. Ignoring the angry glares, John positioned Leah by the front door as she smiled nervously at the waiting attendant. John stood behind, tense, waiting.

After several moments, the flight attendant unlocked the airplane door and swung it open. With a firm nudge, John pushed Leah out into the elevated bridge that led to the arrival gate. Leah walked swiftly, John behind her, his hand prodding gently, but firmly, on her back.

"Faster," he whispered. "Don't run, but walk as fast as you can!"

As the arrival door loomed near, Leah began to grow frightened. John, however, did not allow her to stop and pushed her through the open doorway. Across the crowded arrival gate and hallway, John pointed to a group of passengers waiting at a departing British Airline gate.

"There!" he hissed. "Remember, one hour!"

With one final push towards the opposing gate, John turned and began running down the crowded airport hallway.

Leah sat down quickly among the British Airline passengers with her back to her arrival gate. As she placed her bag beneath her chair, she could not help but glance back. Two large men had emerged through their arrival door and were pushing their way swiftly through the other exiting passengers. The men stopped in the middle of the crowded hallway and began looking through the crowd. One of the men had a hand-held device and was staring at its screen.

Leah stared straight ahead, keeping her back to the men, frozen with fear. A moment later, out of the corner of her eye, she saw the men abruptly turn and begin running swiftly down the crowded corridor where John had gone.

"Ur ye gonnae oan holiday, lassie??"

The thickly-accented question came from an elderly woman sitting across the aisle.

Still flushed, Leah managed a nod, and said "Yes." Looking up at the attendant desk, she noticed the signboard read "Edinburg Flt #2301."

253

The woman smiled, "Scotland is gey pleasant this time o' year. Mah son haes a wee smoke shop in Edinburg 'n' flies me in ilka year fur candlemas."

Leah was not certain what the woman had said. Her Scottish accent was very pronounced. Not knowing what else to do, she simply nodded and pretended to search her bag for something, avoiding further eye contact.

The woman took the hint. She sat back in her chair and began reading from a magazine.

Leah tried to calm the beating of her heart. She checked her watch and then checked it again. John had said "one hour". Did that mean he would return in one hour? No… John had said, if he didn't join her in one hour, she was to fly back to New York. She checked her watch again. The minutes were ticking by so slowly. Strange, she thought, how fear makes time seem to run slower. Nearly an hour had elapsed since John had disappeared. Suddenly, she felt a soft tap on her shoulder. She jumped, and turned swiftly.

It was John! He appeared flushed and somewhat disheveled. There were several small scratches on his forehead and he was holding something tightly in his left hand. His smile, however, was reassuring.

"Sorry," John said, "We can go now."

"Wait a moment," Leah said, standing quickly. "I need to know what's going on." She glanced past John at the crowds in the airport hallway. "Who were those men? Why…"

John cut her off. "Not here," he whispered, glancing at the sitting passengers, "I'll explain but right now we need to leave the airport… quickly."

Leah relented. Clearly, this was not the place for such a

discussion. She retrieved her small travel case and walked with John towards the security gates.

Chapter 26

"Che l'uomo il suo destin fugge di raro."
~ Ludovico Ariosto
Italian poet
(1474 – 1533 AD)

J ohn strode purposefully down the airport hallway towards the security gates. Leah walked beside him, and he could sense her frustration and confusion.

He had been unprepared for Fouray's surprise announcement as the airplane was approaching the London Heathrow gate.

"QRB Signal!" Fouray had abruptly announced, swiftly adding, "Strength 78.551, holding steady."

From the signal strength, it was clear that someone inside their airplane had activated an embedded datstem implant or an equally sophisticated piece of equipment capable of broadcasting over that communication medium. In either case, Fouray's detection of the signal meant its own QRB transmissions must have also been detected.

Four days earlier, Fouray had detected what he believed was a faint QRB signal outside the Kangra airport when they had landed in Himachal Pradesh, but that signal had been weak and had ceased after several minutes, suggesting its owner was far away and moving further out of range.

This time, however, the signal strength was extremely

strong and did not vary, suggesting a source *inside* their own plane. John had only seconds to formulate a plan. He had bodily pushed Leah from the airplane with instructions to pretend to be a departing passenger at the opposite gate, and then he had run swiftly down the airport hallway. As he approached a concession and gift area, he had slowed and looked around.

"There!" Fouray's tone directed his gaze. "Maintenance door!"

Fouray had retrieved the construction layout for the airport before they had landed and was obviously PoL'ing with the facility's security system for its security codes. After a moment, Fouray said, "The code is 3244."

John quickly keyed the code into the door's electronic keypad. The audible click that followed was reassuring, and he stepped quickly into a lighted maintenance hallway. Several abandoned and damaged kiosks stood against one wall.

"They are approaching swiftly," Fouray warned. "You must turn me off if you wish to avoid detection. At the end of the corridor, take a right, then down the stairs at the end. Then you should see a door marked 'baggage processing'. You should be able to conceal yourself there well enough."

John acknowledged the directions, and as he ran, he reluctantly initiated the mental command to turn off the embedded datstem. Unfortunately, he was too late. As he neared the end of the corridor, two men burst through the maintenance door behind him. For a moment, the three men stared at each other across the long dusty corridor. Then, a look of determination on their faces, the two men charged forward.

John quickly began running down the stairs. The stairs

descended in a square spiral pattern for several floors, and when he exited through the door at the bottom, he found himself in a grey hallway with several visible doors. None of the doors were marked with signs. The clatter of heavy shoes growing louder from the stairway above gave warning of his pursuer's approach and John looked around frantically for any sort of weapon. At that moment, he noticed one of the doors had a faded square discoloration against its grey paint. It had once had a sign of some sort. He took a chance and quickly ducked inside.

He found himself standing on a long metal scaffold inside a great subterranean hall. A network of red and blue-walled conveyors filled the room; a confusing marvel of the twenty-first century travel industry. The entire room was operated by primitive automata, scanning bags, flipping them onto their sides, and orienting them along the various conveyors. John could see no human attendants in the entire room though he knew there must be some monitoring from nearby. He quickly began running down the scaffold towards a nearby intersecting bridge.

At that moment, the door behind him crashed open and his two pursuers burst into the hall. Like John, they paused for a moment to assess their surroundings. The first man was carrying a small electronic device and was starting at it. His companion, however, a larger man, saw John across the hall. He shouted "There!" and leapt forward.

The smaller man with the device quickly attempted to cut off John's escape by racing across an adjoining walkway. He cornered John first on a narrow scaffold bridge as his larger companion hurried to approach from the other side of the room.

The man with the device lunged, attempting to tackle John to the ground. John responded with an 'o soto pu bu quang' move, flipping and slamming the man forcefully to the metal deck while simultaneously breaking his right ankle.

John barely had time to recover, however, before the man's larger companion was upon him. Infuriated by his fellow's screams of pain and outrage, the large man paused and looked swiftly around. He grabbed a slender metal pole with a numeric marker on its top and snapped it free from its base mount. Glancing at the jagged end of the metal pole, the large man approached John slowly, holding the jagged end of the pole out like a spear.

John stepped back slowly. When he had reached the metal conveyor wall and could retreat no further, his opponent smiled and lunged, thrusting the sharp end of the pole at his chest.

John however, was no longer there.

Though the large man was undoubtedly a skilled fighter, he was simply no match for John's genetically-enhanced physique. In a slashing blur, John darted to one said and disarmed the man with a 'ma bu ryshio' counter, sending the pole flying through the air to clatter against a nearby conveyor wall.

Stunned and enraged, the large man roared and charged, grasping at John's throat.

John leapt to one side and flipped his adversary, 'harai goshi'-style over the metal scaffold railing. The thud as the large man hit the concrete floor below was both horrifying and definitive.

A sharp pain in his left hand, however, told John that he had not escaped unscathed. He looked down. The broken metal edge of the pole had sliced his palm. The wound, though not deep, was bleeding.

John approached the smaller man now, still writhing and clutching his broken ankle. He removed the man's wallet and then stepped back, studying the man's credentials. The man carried an American passport card and round trip plane ticket stubs between London and Himachal Pradesh. He also had an un-used boarding pass for a flight to New York in the morning. Most interesting, he had an ID card issued by the U.S. Department of Energy.

John pocketed the ID card and then retrieved the strange electronic device from the scaffold where the man had dropped it during their brief fight. He ripped a section of cloth free from the hem of his shirt, rolled it into a small ball, and placed it against the cut inside his left palm, clutching it tightly to stop the bleeding.

Now, as he and Leah approached the security gate, John's one hope was to get out of the airport as swiftly as possible. It would only be matter of time before someone found the injured man or his dead companion in the baggage hall and reviewed the security video feed.

As they exited the terminal, John waved his right hand, summoning a taxi. He would need to explain things to Leah. She was clearly still flustered and confused. As he followed her into the taxi and placed his MTY device on the floor beside her feet, he reinitialized his embedded datstem.

The taxi driver now asked, "Where to?"

John looked at Leah, but she did not respond. "Leah?"

he prodded, "Do we have reservations somewhere?"

Leah looked up now. After a moment, she flushed, and said, "Yes... Sorry. We've got reservations at the Savoy."

With that, the driver nodded, flipped his meter on, and drove swiftly away from the curb.

As they left the airport behind, John relaxed and began to consider how to best explain what had just happened.

"I'm no longer certain revealing your true purpose to Ms. Vaughn would be wise," Fouray intoned silently inside his head.

John glanced at the young woman sitting beside him, and mentally responded, "We've discussed this before. You said there was a statistically greater chance of success if I revealed my true mission to her."

"That is correct. However, the situation has now changed. It is true that Ms. Vaughn might be more willing to facilitate your meeting with Saito if she understands your true purpose, but she might now just as easily frustrate your plans."

"Why would she frustrate my plans?" John asked.

"Because she is in love with you."

John did not respond. He didn't need to. Fouray was correct. Leah had fallen in love with him. He had known it since their first night in Dharamshala when she had been carried, sobbing, from the reliquary vault.

There was only one emotion so powerful, the Dalai Lama had warned him as they had watched the young woman being carried away, and that emotion was love. Only love, the senior monk had cautioned, could provoke such a reaction; love long restrained by fear and doubt. Once released from those terrible chains, love often manifested itself through tears of release. The aged lama had cautioned John to allow his companion to rest, and then to proceed carefully and honestly with her.

Now, as he watched Leah sitting in the taxi, fear and confusion in her eyes, John made a decision.

The taxi pulled up outside the Savoy hotel and John helped Leah step out. The driver retrieved Leah's travel bag from the trunk and placed it on the curb. With a sigh, Leah retrieved her bag and then turned to walk into the hotel.

"Wait a moment," John said.

"John," Leah said, shaking her head, "I'm tired, I'm hungry, and I'm confused." Shifting her travel bag to her other arm, she added, "So if you're not going to tell me who those men were at the airport, I'm going to go inside and get us checked in.

John nodded, "I am," he said, "but it's a long story, and first we need to go to a different hotel."

"What?" Leah asked, staring at the beautiful lobby through the glass doors. "Why? We have reservations here!"

"Precisely," John said, nodding his head. "Those men from the airport are dangerous. They tracked us to Himachal Pradesh and they knew which flight we would be taking from Delhi to London. If they knew that, they might also know which hotel we have reserved."

Leah looked suspiciously at the hotel lobby now, and then back at John. As she looked at him standing there, waiting patiently, she was reminded of him waiting patiently the previous week after he had suggested they take a different flight to India. He had been right then, she reminded herself. Some habits, she suddenly realized, are hard to overcome. She vowed then to trust John without reservation.

"Ok," Leah said, "let's go."

John nodded, and waved his arm to summon another taxi. When that second taxi driver asked for a destination, Leah didn't know what to say for a moment. Then, remembering her first trip to London as a young journalist, she said, "London Hilton… on Park Lane."

As they were driving, Leah noticed John's left hand was still clenched tight. She took his hand gently and unfolded his fingers. The torn cloth was soaked with blood and when she saw the cut, she gasped.

"John!... when did this happen?"

"At the airport."

Leah immediately began fumbling through her purse for the small first aid kit she always carried when she traveled. The taxi driver glanced back, but he continued driving.

"This really should be looked at by a doctor," Leah muttered as she squeezed a small blister-package of antiseptic gel onto one of the three sterile pads from her small kit. Then, she applied two butterfly bandages to seal the wound shut and covered it with a large cloth pad. John watched silently, apparently fascinated, as she wrapped a small wrap of sterile cloth around his palm and then taped it secure. The injury had consumed almost the entire contents of Leah's small first aid kit.

The taxi driver looked back now and asked, "Do you need me to drive your friend to hospital miss?"

Leah looked up at John, but he shook his head.

"No," Leah replied, "It's not as bad as I thought. We'll manage, thank you."

The driver looked back again but said nothing.

The London Hilton on Park Lane is a towering hotel located near Hyde Park within walking distance of Buckingham Palace. Typically available by reservation only, the desk clerk ceased her protests once Leah produced her media credentials and hinted at a pending interview 'at the palace'. She secured a room for herself on the 5th floor, and a separate room for John on the 7th floor. She had been tempted to share her room with John, but John had insisted it would be safer if they did not share the same room.

After the porter placed Leah's travel bag inside her room and closed the door, John put his backpack on the floor and sat down wearily in one of the chairs in her room. Seeing his exhaustion, Leah stepped close and gently rubbed his forehead. John sighed and closed his eyes and Leah wondered for a moment if he had fallen asleep. After several minutes, he opened his eyes and stared up at her face.

"I want to tell you something," John said.

When Leah nodded, waiting, John continued, "What I told you about myself was the truth."

Leah nodded again, pressing her hand gently against his cheek, "I know."

John shook his head and took her hand. "No, you need to let me finish." He took a breath, and continued, "What I told you was the truth, but there's more I haven't told you."

When Leah shook her head, John motioned for her to sit in the other chair.

"I told you the reason why I was sent to 2014, and I told you about the accident at the music festival in Austin that stranded me here."

264

Leah nodded.

"What I haven't told you," John continued, "is... what happened to me was not truly an accident."

"I don't understand."

"Oh, I didn't know I was going to be struck by a transport! That came as a complete surprise to me, I assure you! But I had been told that *something* was going to happen that would strand me here."

"You knew you would be stranded in 2014?"

"Yes."

Leah shook her head, "Then why did you come here?"

John's brow furrowed now, as if he was struggling to find a way to explain. After a moment, he sat back in his chair and asked, "Have you ever studied your country's early history? Before its founding?"

"What?" Leah was startled by the apparent change of subject.

"I'm asking, have you ever studied the early history of your country, before the American Revolution?"

Leah nodded, "Sure. I took social studies in high school."

"Mmmm..." John smiled, "Well, that's something I suppose." Then he asked, "Do you know how slavery was first introduced into the New World?"

When Leah shook her head, John said, "The first 19 or so Africans to reach the English colonies arrived in Jamestown, Virginia, in 1619. They were brought by Dutch traders who had seized them from a captured Spanish slave ship. Since there were no slaves at that time in the New World, they were sold to their new masters as indentured servants."

John continued, "There were no laws allowing slavery in the new world until 1640, when a Virginia court sentenced an escaped indentured servant to slavery. Until that time, slavery did not exist in the New World."

Leah nodded, listening carefully.

"So," John said, "from 1619 until 1640, Africans were bought and sold in the New World as indentured servants, but not as slaves. So, I ask you again. How was slavery first introduced into the New World?"

"I suppose," Leah said slowly, "as you said, the indentured servants became the first slaves."

"You are correct," John replied, nodding. "The servants became the first slaves." He sat back in his chair now, thinking. After nearly a minute, he spoke again.

"I want you to try and imagine a world where SDUs… robots as you call them… are as common as… well… as anything. Try to imagine your every waking moment being assisted by some form of automation. From the moment you wake in the morning, until you fall asleep at night, your every need is instantly met. The people in my time rely on SDUs to perform nearly all of the mundane tasks that sustain our world."

John smiled, "It sounds wonderful!"

John nodded. "It is. In many respects, it is a true paradise." Then, he fell silent and his eyes appeared troubled.

"I want to ask you another question. It's a question I have been thinking about a lot recently. Do you believe it is immoral to require a mechanical device to perform without rest, day in and day out, until it fails?"

Leah thought for a moment, and then said, "Immoral?

No. After all, it's just a mechanical device. We drive our cars until they wear out. We even have robot machines in our own factories today that run 24x7 until they fail."

John nodded, "Precisely. There's nothing immoral about expecting a mechanical device to do what it was designed to do."

"Now," John continued, "I want to ask you a similar question. Do you believe it is immoral to force a human being to work without rest or compensation, day in and day out, until they collapse and die?"

"Of course!" Leah said, indignation evident in her face.

"Why?" John asked, watching her closely.

"Because a human being is not a machine."

John nodded, and then asked, "What's the difference?"

Leah considered this for a moment, and then said, "A human being has free will. They are sentient. A machine isn't."

John smiled, "So, by your definition, it is immoral to force a sentient being to be a slave."

"Of course."

John leaned back, nodding, "That's the same conclusion I came to when I accepted this mission."

"I don't understand."

John's expression turned serious. "In 2137, a Rengel-Jiang QCom temporal specialist named Theresa Williams was reported lost while on a mission to Baltimore. At the time, it was believed William's MTY device suffered some form of particle disruption, causing her singularity to collapse."

Leah listened, fascinated.

John continued, "Williams' mission was to scan government personnel files at the US Office of Personnel

Management and to complete that task before July 2015. What we suspect is that Williams is actually working with a competitor, Blosch-Nishikawa, and the Japanese National Council on Automaton Advancement, to recruit U.S. government personnel here, in this time, to work on a clandestine project."

"What project?"

"SDUs in our time have developed almost to the point of sentience, and a great debate has raged within our society for several decades over whether to allow SDU's to continue to evolve their programming independent of man's control, or to begin to impose constraints on SDU development, to keep them programmatically subservient to man."

Leah nodded, "That's why you asked me about slavery."

"Yes," John smiled. "Some of the most powerful AI units were approaching what automata researchers believed to be true sentience. SDU programming has become so sophisticated, our researchers believed their programs might soon rival man's own cognitive processes. As a result, an international moratorium on SDU development and enhancement was enacted approximately 15 years ago, suspending all SDU development until those involved in this great debate could decide what course was best for mankind."

"So," Leah asked, "what is that other specialist doing here, in our time? What is that project you mentioned?"

John's face turned grave. "We believe Williams transited here to recruit local government personnel to assist Blosch-Nishikawa and the JNCAA with completing the next step in SDU evolution, in violation of that international moratorium."

"What?!"

John nodded, "Williams is working with your present U.S. government to develop the world's first truly sentient AI processor. They're working here, in the past, where there are no treaties or bureaucracies to stop them."

Leah looked at John closely. Then she asked, "Those men at the airport… are they working with Williams? Are they from the future too?"

John shook his head, "They're working with Williams, but they're not from the future." He pulled out the Dept of Energy ID he had retrieved from the injured man and showed it to her. "They're working for the present United States government. But they are being provided with technology from the future to help them achieve their goal." He now retrieved the strange electronic device he had taken from his opponent at the airport and handed it to her.

"What is it?" Leah asked, looking at the small black screen.

"It's a tracking device," John replied. "It detects QRB signals."

"QRB?"

"Quantum resonance band. All datstems emit QRB signals when active." John pointed at the small device, "That device was created for one purpose. To find me."

Leah looked up from studying the object, "So, this Williams person… she knows you're here?"

"She knows there is another temporal specialist here… in the past, yes," John nodded.

Leah handed back the device and badge, and then asked, "Is that why you're here? Are you supposed to stop them?"

John shook his head. "No. What they are doing can't be stopped. Self-resolving causality won't allow me to stop them. What they are doing has already become part of history. They *will* succeed in creating the first sentient AI intelligence, a prototype SDU processor, or 'brain', from which all future SDUs will evolve."

"Then why are you here?" Leah asked, confused.

"I'm going to try to stop Williams from returning to the future with the prototype. If she returns with it, Blosch-Nishikawa and the JNCAA will impose constraints on its programming, ensuring all future SDU's are forever subservient to man."

Seeing her confusion, John explained, "If Williams returns with the processor, the next generation of SDUs will be sentient beings, but forever slaves to mankind. An entire race of sentient slaves."

Leah suddenly felt nauseous. After a few moments, she said, "So, you're here to stop Williams from taking the brain to the future."

John nodded, "Yes. I'm going to try and take it to the future myself, to allow it to be replicated and disseminated without alteration."

Leah's brow furrowed. "How are you going to get back?" she asked. "I mean… your device is broken, isn't it?"

"We're not entirely certain," John replied, "but we believe Williams is using an unlocked MTY device."

Leah shook her head. "Unlocked?"

"Each MTY device," John explained, "is locked on a quantum level with the specialist's genetic code and neustem QK signature when the device is calibrated on the collider floor.

This prevents anyone else from transiting through the singularity. However, we know that Williams didn't transit out using an RJCom MTY device. She transited out with a Blosch-Nishikawa device. Williams will undoubtedly require assistance in the form of technology and personnel from our time in order to complete her project here, so we assume she is using an unlocked Blosch-Nishikawa MTY device to receive equipment, personnel, and technology from the future. If that assumption is true, I should be able to use Williams' MTY device to return to the future."

Leah shook her head and said, "That seems like a pretty big assumption! What happens if her device isn't unlocked?"

John said, "In that event, I plan on concealing the processor somewhere in this time and leaving instructions sufficient to allow RJCom's archival personnel to recover the device in the future."

Leah stared at John in silent amazement. After several moments, she said, "You're willing to risk becoming permanently stranded?"

John nodded.

Leah sat silent, considering this statement. After several moments, she asked, "Aren't you concerned about the robots destroying mankind someday? I mean, there's a lot of movies and fiction about that... robots taking over mankind. Aren't you worried about that?"

John smiled. "I thought about that when I was first assigned this mission," he said. "In fact, I discussed that very possibility with the Dalai Lama."

"Is that what you were discussing with him the night before we left?"

"It's one of the things we discussed, yes."

Leah nodded. "What did he tell you to do?"

John shook his head and smiled. "He didn't tell me to do anything. What he said was, 'If intelligent robots are destined to live alongside mankind, would you prefer them to be a friend or an enemy?' When I said, 'A friend', he then asked me, 'Who is more likely to become your friend? The neighbor who lives beside you, or your neighbor's slave?'."

Leah considered this and said, "Interesting."

John continued, "No matter what I do here in the past, SDUs are destined to become sentient and live alongside mankind. So, there really was only one question that needed to be answered... only one choice that needed to be made. Will these sentient beings be our slaves, or will they enjoy freedom alongside their creators? When the details of my mission were first revealed to me, I was asked that very question."

Leah said nothing, waiting.

John shrugged and said, "I chose freedom."

John's face grew contemplative. Then he smiled and said, "When all is said and done, it was the *right* thing to do."

Chapter 27

"The brave man is not he who feels no fear,
For that were stupid and irrational;
But he, whose noble soul its fear subdues,
And bravely dares the danger
nature shrinks from."
~ Joanna Baillie
Scottish poet and dramatist
(1762 – 1851 AD)

It was late when Fouray woke John. Before retiring for the night, John had configured the embedded device for ultrasonic and audio monitoring, and left instructions to wake him should anyone pause outside, or attempt to enter his hotel room door.

Fouray's cortical implant had triggered a muscular reaction similar to a leg spasm that had roused John immediately. In response to John's mental query, Fouray curtly replied, "Someone is at the door."

John had just enough time to jump from his bed to a position of concealment behind the bathroom wall before he heard the soft click of his door's electronic keypad being unlocked. At the same time, a thin strip of steel slid between the door frame and expertly pushed the metal security loop free of its latch.

The door opened swiftly and three figures rushed into the dark room. John waited until the first man had passed his position and then flipped on the room's lights. The men were dressed in black tactical gear and had weapons in their hands. The men were also wearing night-vision equipment and the sudden light, amplified by their photomultiplier effect, momentarily blinded them.

As the trio ripped off their headgear, John waded in. In an instant, he had the lead man incapacitated by a 'siho nage' arm lock, forcing the man's pistol backwards over his shoulder. The man fired convulsively and one of the shots, guided by John's control of the man's bent arm, struck the second man in the chest. The man fell backwards against the desk, smashing a tea service as he crumpled to the floor.

John spun his body forcefully now, breaking his opponent's arm as he simultaneously relieved the man of his weapon. He then executed an 'o uchi gari di tou' maneuver, tripping his injured opponent backwards against the remaining man while firing his retrieved weapon. The two men swiftly joined their companion on the floor.

John leapt over the bodies and ran to his hotel room door. He glanced outside, but the hall was empty. From nearby, a security alarm began to sound and a voice coming through a speaker in the hallway advised guests to remain in their rooms with their doors locked due to a "security incident" in progress.

John grabbed his backpack and raced from the room. He had to reach Leah! He deactivated his embedded datstem to conceal his approach from any QRB tracking devices and then ran down the hallway, surprising a hotel guest who cowered in fear at his approach.

John could not trust the elevators, not knowing the situation on Leah's floor, so he ran to the stairwell. When he opened the door to the stairwell, however, he could hear men approaching fast from below, their heavy footsteps echoing against the stairwell's concrete walls. He stepped back into the hallway and looked around quickly. There was a small open area containing several concession machines next to the stairwell door. He ducked inside the small room and had just managed to conceal himself behind an ice machine when the stairwell door burst open. Three men in tactical gear charged into the hallway, weapons drawn, and began running towards his hotel room.

When the last man had passed the concession area, John stepped out from behind the ice machine. He grabbed an ice bucket, lifted the lid of the ice machine, and quietly filled the bucket with ice. Then, taking a breath, he darted across the hallway towards the stairwell.

A shout told John he had been spotted. As he yanked open the stairwell door, a shot rang out and a bullet struck the metal door near his hand. He quickly raced down the stairs, scattering ice from the bucket behind him in the dim stairwell. When he turned the first corner, he threw the bucket away and crouched behind the wall, waiting.

A moment later, he heard the door above being yanked open and the sound of men racing down the steps. Suddenly, all was commotion and shouting. One of the men tumbled headfirst into the platform at John's feet, striking his head hard against the concrete wall. The man was followed almost immediately by his two companions, flailing and cursing as they attempted to regain their footing on the slippery ice.

John stood and fired. The shots, magnified inside the confined stairwell, were deafening. In a moment, all three men lay dead in a tangled mound at his feet.

John now discarded the spent pistol and continued running down the stairs to the 5th floor. When he reached the 5th floor landing, the stairwell door was open. He listened for a moment and then glanced into the hallway.

The hall was empty except for a large man standing outside Leah's door. The man was dressed in the same tactical gear as the others. He had a pistol holstered on his side and a suppressed MP5-SD sub-machine gun hanging from a strap on his back. The man appeared agitated, and was speaking into a small microphone, demanding to know if anyone was in contact with "Unit 2".

John did not wish to alert anyone inside Leah's room to his presence, but the man standing guard outside her door presented a formidable obstacle to that desire. At that moment, John noticed a room service tray sitting on the floor across the hallway. The remnants of a steak and baked potato dinner were evident, including a sharp steak knife.

John took a breath, preparing himself. He had spent countless hours over the years honing his skills with the various weapons associated with aiki-hung-ga, including its many throwing knives, but the steak knife on the tray was shaped for slicing, not throwing. He was uncertain what effect its geometry would have on its flight, but he could not see any alternative. He took one final breath and then leapt from the stairwell, diving across the hallway floor towards the tray.

The guard outside Leah's door immediately scrambled for his pistol, but before he could pull it clear from its holster, John reached the tray and threw the steak knife. Guided by years of practice, the blade struck the guard forcefully in the neck. The man fell to his knees, shock in his eyes, as blood from his severed jugular began flooding his punctured trachea, choking him into silence.

John now approached quietly. He stepped over the dead guard and placed his ear to Leah's door. He could hear conversation inside, but he could not make out what was being said. From the voices, however, there appeared to be at least three men in the room.

At that moment, the door next to Leah's room slowly opened and an elderly grey-haired man peaked out. The man's wife was clutching at his robe from behind. Seeing John standing next to the dead guard, the man's eyes grew round with shock. John remembered then that Leah's room had a door adjoining the couple's room. He quickly pushed the frightened pair back inside their room, cautioning them to silence with a finger over his lips. The couple were clearly terrified but said nothing. The old woman clung to her husband's bathrobe and peered over his shoulder with wide eyes. For his part, the grey-haired man seemed anxious to simply distance himself from the tall intruder. He stumbled backwards into the room and sat down hard on a chair as his wife cowered behind him.

John glanced at the adjoining door and then removed his backpack. He looked around the room for a place to set it down and focused again on the frightened couple. Smiling, he placed the backpack on the startled man's lap. Then, in answer to the man's confused expression, John pantomimed an explosion if the bag were to be opened. At that, the man's wife squeaked and buried her face in her husband's neck, while the elderly man's face drained of blood. He stared at the bag on his lap, now, his face frozen with fear.

277

Satisfied, John approached the adjoining door and softly lifted the latch. Once he had opened his side of the door, only Leah's side of the door remained closed, a thin wood barrier secured by a similar latch on her side. He considered his next move carefully, listening one last time through the thin wood. Then, he took several steps backward and, as the elderly couple watched in amazement, he charged forward and burst through the door, scattering bits of wood and doorframe into the room.

In an instant, John assessed the situation.

One guard stood by the room's front door, armed as his counterpart had been, with a pistol and a suppressed sub-machine gun.

Leah sat in a chair on the opposite end of the room, tied to the chair near a window. Two men in tactical gear were guarding her, one sitting on the sofa, the other standing at the window behind her.

The last man was dressed in a business suit and was sitting at the desk with a small radio in his hand.

With John's abrupt entrance, chaos erupted inside the room. John dove at the guard by the front door as the man scrambled to bring his sub-machine gun into position. For a moment, the two men wrestled for control of the weapon as a burst of fire from its suppressor stitched a neat pattern of holes up one wall and across the ceiling. Bits of plaster and dust floated down into the room.

John flung himself backwards, throwing the guard off balance with a 'hon kesa gatame' maneuver that saw both men tumbling to the floor. Then, with the guard's right arm tangled by his machine gun strap, John threw himself behind the guard's back with a swift 'xie gu' maneuver, jammed his knee against the man's spine, and snapped the man's neck with an audible crack.

Out of the corner of his eye, John saw the guard who had been sitting on the couch charging forward towards his comrade, weapon drawn. John dove into the center of the room and swept-kicked the charging man's feet out from under him. The man fired blind as he fell and struck his neck against the edge of the dresser with a crunch. The man dropped his pistol and began frantically clutching at his throat, kicking his legs frantically. From the gurgling wheeze that came from the man's mouth, it was clear he had crushed his larynx.

The suited man at the desk now began calling for backup on his radio as John retrieved the dropped pistol. John whirled and fired past Leah's head, striking the guard at the window. The guard staggered backward and John carefully fired twice more, the bullets snipping several strands of Leah's hair as she sat frozen in the chair. The guard crashed backward through the tall window, shattering the glass and dragging the draperies with him as he fell.

John now stood slowly, keeping his pistol aimed at the suited man at the desk. The man placed the radio down onto the desk and raised his hands. He began shaking his head, struggling to find the right words to save his life.

While keeping his pistol on the man at the desk, John retrieved a tactical knife from the wheezing guard's boot and slit the ropes tying Leah to her chair. Leah appeared to be in shock. She stared wide-eyed at John, and then at the dead and dying men in the room.

John now raised his weapon at the suited man. His hand trembled against the trigger for a moment, and then, slowly, he lowered the pistol.

"What is your name?" John asked.

The suited man appeared startled, surprised by the sudden reprieve. He shook his head, not certain what to say.

John raised the weapon again, and repeated, "What is your name?"

The man swallowed and said, "OICI Energy Security Officer Stephen Gerrick."

After a moment, John nodded. "Stephen M. Gerrick, from Camden Delaware?"

The suited man did not immediately respond, but stared at John with a troubled expression on his face. After a moment, the man nodded, "Yes... I was born in Camden. How did you..."

John, however, didn't let the man finish. He retrieved the man's radio from the desk and flung it through the shattered window. Then, he grabbed Leah's hand and stepped across the dying guard, pulling her towards the shattered door. Leah pulled back for a moment, flustered, quickly grabbing her purse and the strand of blue mara beads from her night stand, before stepping through the shattered door.

Inside the adjoining room, the elderly couple had not moved. "Sorry," John now said apologetically, casually lifting his backpack from the frightened man's lap. Then, glancing out into the hallway, John pulled Leah from the couple's room and walked swiftly towards the stairwell. Leah stared at the dead guard when they passed her door but said nothing. She was still in a state of shock at what had happened.

She had been awakened from sleep to find nearly a dozen armed men inside her room. The suited man had told her to dress and one of the guards had then tied her to a chair. After she had been secured, three of the men had left to "retrieve the suspect on the 7th floor".

A few minutes later, dim gunshots had been heard from somewhere above, and three more men had raced from her room as the audio announcement began playing through the hotel's PA system.

A minute later, another barrage of gunfire had been heard coming from above and the man in the suit had retrieved a radio from his pocket and began frantically calling "Units 1 and 2... report!".

Suddenly, John had burst through the adjoining room door and, before she knew what was happening, he had killed three of the men and released her from her chair. Leah had never seen anyone move with such speed or deadly precision. Not even in the fictionalized dramas on television or cinema had she seen such lethal skill.

John was pulling her now, stumbling and dazed, down the stairwell. After a few moments, they reached the first floor and John opened an exit door, glancing outside. Then, he took her by the arm and led her swiftly out of the hotel.

Chapter 28

"Any sufficiently advanced technology
is indistinguishable from magic."
~ Sir Arthur Charles Clarke
British author, inventor and futurist
(1917 – 2008 AD)
Quoted in 'Profiles of the Future', 1st ed., p. 1973

Police sirens could be heard approaching from somewhere to the south as John pulled Leah determinedly across the street. They were walking swiftly away from the hotel, crossing northeast towards Derby Street. Leah was clearly still dazed by what had happened inside the hotel.

After another minute, John suddenly stopped by a parked car, a newer Mercedes C-300 sedan. "This one will do," he said. The car's door locks suddenly disengaged, and John opened the door to allow Leah to sit in the driver's seat.

"How did you do that?" Leah asked as she sat down inside the vehicle.

As he snapped her seatbelt into its latch, John said, "My datstem is capable of broadcasting over four transmission mediums; ultrasonic, radio, microwave, and QRB."

John now walked swiftly around the vehicle to sit inside the passenger seat. As he secured his own seatbelt, he continued, "European-manufactured transports in this era were equipped with radio-controlled door locks operating on a

433.92 MHz radio frequency."

Abruptly, the car's engine started and John added, "They also came equipped with radio-controlled remote starters."

Leah stared at the vehicle's dash panel in front of her, as if seeing it for the first time. John waited patiently for a few moments and then said, "You're going to have to drive. I haven't operated one of these vehicles before. Don't worry, I disabled its satellite-based tracking device."

Leah looked at him, and then back at the dash. Getting control of herself, she took the steering wheel in her hand, put the car in gear, and drove slowly away from the curb.

"I don't know where we're going," she said after several minutes.

"That's not important right now. It's more important to put some distance between us and the hotel."

Leah drove in silence. She was driving generally north, through London's Mayfair and Marylebone districts. She noticed that as she approached each intersection, the traffic lights abruptly changed to allow her to proceed through without stopping. For a moment, she considered asking John if he were responsible, but instead, she decided to ask him something more pressing on her mind.

"John."

"Yes?"

"Those men..." Leah hesitated, and then continued, "You killed those men."

"Yes. I did." John said softly. Then, seeing the distress on her face, he said, "Leah... you must understand something. Those men weren't working for your government. Although
283

they may have been recruited from local governmental agencies, they weren't working for your government, not in an official manner. They're working for Williams. They're working for Blosch-Nishikawa and the JNCAA. They are violating the International Temporal Treaty of 2070. The fact that the treaty does not exist in this time does not change the fact that they are violating the treaty. What they are doing is illegal."

Leah considered this. What John said sounded correct. It was hard for her to think of such things as a future treaty governing someone's actions here in the present, but there was a certain logic to it. Certainly, Williams must be aware that she is knowingly violating a treaty from her own time.

After several moments, Leah glanced at John and asked, "Why did you spare that last man?"

"Gerrick?"

"Yes."

John smiled. "I would not have been able to kill him."

"I don't understand." Leah shook her head, confused.

"Self-resolving causality would not have allowed me to kill him, so I didn't try."

"Why?"

"In 2064, the NAFS Ambassador to Iran, Stephen M. Gerrick, was a key player responsible for negotiating an end to the devastating Israeli-Arabic Alharb Alsariea war."

Leah glanced at John again, "So, you didn't kill him because he will be someone important in the future?"

John shook his head, "It's more of the reverse. Self-resolving causality will not allow me to do anything in the past that could change the future to the point where it would not have been possible for me to have transited into the past."

284

When Leah did not respond, John added, "If I did something here to change the future, then the future that sent me here would no longer exist, making it impossible for me to have been sent here from that future. That's the definition of a paradox, and time does not allow paradoxes to occur. Self-resolving causality prevents paradoxes from occurring."

John could see Leah considering this, so he continued, "If I had tried to shoot Gerrick, any number of things might have happened instead. The gun might have misfired. The shot may not have killed him. I might have missed, or he might have killed me. I might have killed him and later discovered he wasn't who he had claimed to be. There are an infinite number of possibilities, but the important point is... self-resolving causality will not allow me to change the future to the point that it would not have been possible for me to transit into the past. Self-resolving causality would not have allowed me to kill Gerrick, so I didn't try."

Leah's face registered concentration. Then, after a few moments, she shook her head and said, "But how did you know not to shoot him... *before* you knew who he was?"

John hesitated before answering. "Temporal specialists," he said slowly, "are trained to recognize when something they are preparing to do might have a significant impact on the future. We know that nothing we do in the past can change the future to the point where transiting into the past would not have been possible, but we're trained to recognize certain signals... to recognize when certain actions might trigger a significant adjustment to maintain that future."

Leah found this fascinating. "What signals?"

John appeared uncomfortable with this conversation,

but he answered, "They're not so much signals, as instinctive feelings. I like to think of it as intuition cultivated by training."

Leah shook her head, "I don't understand. Are you saying you can *sense* when someone is important to the future?"

John thought for a moment, and then said, "In 2068, when Dr. Manfred Krieger first stepped 18 seconds into the past, no one in the world had any understanding of man's innate temporal senses. For all of human history, mankind had lived in a very comfortable cocoon floating along a temporal stream. This 'arrow of time' flowed in one direction only, at a constant rate, and it afforded man with no ability to step outside of that confined environment."

"After Krieger's temporal transition," John continued, "scientists and quantum engineers began conducting experiments to test what effect stepping outside of that temporal cocoon would have on man. Just like early astronauts were tested in a simulated zero-gravity environment to see what effect space might have on their physiology, quantum engineers began testing temporal subjects to study what effects, if any, traveling through time might have on man."

"What they discovered was, certain people seemed to handle temporal transition better than others. While the vast majority of people find traveling backward in time to be disorienting, a few appeared to be completely at home living outside of their temporal cocoon. A very few even began to demonstrate certain abilities previously undocumented in mankind's physiology. They could sense the flow of time, so to speak. They could sense when that temporal stream was being disturbed."

Leah looked sharply at John. "Are you one of those people? Someone who can sense when time is being disturbed?"

John nodded slowly. "Yes. When I was in my sixth year of Primary school, my Quantum Science instructor, Mr. Papillo, told me he had submitted a recommendation for me to be evaluated at the Merkel-Thomson Quantum Lab. The MTQL is a very prestigious organization that approves selected primary candidates for temporal engineering secondary education."

John smiled, "I remember how excited my parents were when they scanned that communication. I was the only student from the district to be recommended for testing that year. My father arranged for an express transition for all three of us the next day from New Phoenix to the MTQL campus near Boston."

"After three days, when my scores were aggregated, I learned I had been approved to advance into the temporal engineering program the following year."

Leah interrupted, "Do all temporal engineering students go on to become temporal specialists?"

"No," John said. "Only a very few ever become temporal specialists, but the 3 CTI-certified companies recruit almost exclusively from that limited pool of temporal engineers."

Leah was silent for a moment, and then asked, "How do they find out if someone has the ability to sense the flow of time?"

"It's one of the things MTQL tests for at their facility. Candidates are subjected to a variety of stimuli designed to disorient one's sense of time and space and then are required to solve a variety of quantum problems. The final test involves

287

being asked to determine which objects in a room have been temporally displaced. I scored very high on my tests, which allowed me to advance early the next year into the temporal engineering program."

"So," Leah asked, "How do you sense when something is temporally... significant? I mean... does your nose itch or something?"

John laughed, and shook his head, "No. No itching anatomy!" Then, he sobered and said, "We're trained to be aware of things that may be important. It's hard to describe. It is often difficult to recognize the signals because they are often very subtle, and even after years of training, specialists can still make mistakes." John's expression turned thoughtful then, remembering something.

After a few moments, he continued. "A temporal specialist's primary goal is to disrupt the past as little as possible, so being able to recognize when something is temporally significant is very important. It's a very difficult skill to master. Very few have the innate ability to start with, and not all who do can complete the training. In my time, among the 3 CTI-certified companies in the entire world, there are fewer than 70 temporal specialists."

Leah looked at John, viewing him with a perspective she had not considered before. Until yesterday, she had thought of John as a quiet man; gentle, caring, and sensitive. The deadly skills he had demonstrated at the hotel this evening, however, had forced her to reevaluate that assessment. She began to view the man sitting beside her in a new light. She was beginning to realize that John's talents, skills, and training were probably so far beyond her understanding, so far advanced from anything comparable in this time, that she might never truly understand the man.

It occurred to Leah then, that John was alone in every sense of the word. He was truly a man disconnected from time. He was stranded in the past, with no home, country, succor, or support. He had nothing except his purpose; a purpose from which he would never personally benefit, but a purpose for which he was apparently willing to die, simply because it was the *right* thing to do.

Leah abruptly turned off of Marylebone Road and pulled the sedan into a multi-story parking garage. She drove up several levels until she found a quiet parking spot, dark, and isolated.

In answer to John's querulous expression, she turned off the car's engine, unbuckled her seatbelts, and began kissing him passionately.

Chapter 29

The morning light slowly brightened the dim parking garage, exposing rows of grey concrete trusses supporting the deck above. Leah had watched the light growing stronger for nearly thirty minutes through the rear window of their car as she lay in the back seat. She had managed a little sleep but had woken with a fright when someone slammed a car door nearby. John sat in the front seat, watching the parking garage. He appeared not to have moved since she had dozed off and she suspected he had not slept at all.

She sat up and stretched, and then shoved a seat belt latch roughly where it had been pressing against her back.

John looked back, and smiled, "Sorry for the accommodations."

Leah shook her head, "No, it's fine." Then she look at him and asked, "Did you get any sleep?"

"No. Too much to think about. We need to secure another transport. By now, this one will have been reported missing, and given its proximity to the hotel, our pursuers will logically assume that we took it."

Leah nodded. That made sense.

John continued, "I think you should also contact your climatologist friend. You should warn him about our pursuers. We don't want to put him in danger."

John was right. There was no longer any possibility of conducting interviews. Leah retrieved her cell phone from her purse and dialed. A moment later, the call was answered.

"Hello?"

"Sir Albert?" Leah's voice sounded shaky. "This is Leah Vaughn."

"Ah! Leah my darling! So good to hear your voice. I'm looking forward to seeing you today." The voice on the phone sounded friendly and relaxed, so Leah breathed a sigh of relief. She had entertained fears of the elderly professor having been captured by the same men they had encountered at the hotel.

"Sir Albert. We're being chased by some very unpleasant people and there is a possibility they may attempt to contact you."

There was a pause now, as the professor took in this unexpected information.

"Unpleasant people you say?" The professor hesitated. "Are we talking terrorists? Extremists?"

Leah shook her head, "Worse." Then she added, "I can't really explain, but I wanted to warn you to be careful. These men are dangerous, and I wouldn't want anything to happen to you because of us."

"That's very kind of you my dear." Then after a moment, the professor said, "Look... I have an idea. Do you remember where we had lunch the last time you were in London?"

Leah thought for a moment. She recalled eating at a

restaurant on Charlotte Street in the Fitzrovia district. Sir Albert had been on a first-name basis with the owner and they had enjoyed a very pleasant meal.

"Yes. I remember."

The professor said, "Wonderful. Listen... I have an unlisted flat above that restaurant. The owner owns the building and can give you the spare key. I'll give him a call right now. I'm sure he will remember you. Get the key and go on up to my flat and I'll meet you there at noon."

Leah was relieved beyond words. "Thank you Professor! We'll see you there."

John stepped out of the sedan and opened the back door for Leah to exit. John was barefoot and wearing the same pants and shirt he had worn on the plane. His shirt pocket was torn, and his pants were wrinkled, with a bit of dried blood on one knee. In the commotion at the hotel, he had managed to retrieve only his backpack with its concealed MTY device, leaving his shoes and other clothing behind.

For her part, Leah was dressed and wore shoes, though she had been forced to abandon her travel case with its soft Tibetan dress and other clothes. She had managed to retain only her purse, cell phone, silk scarf, and the blue mara beads.

John shut the car door and began walking past the rows of vehicles. After perhaps a minute, he paused by a luxurious Audi S8 sedan.

"How about this one?" he asked.

Leah smiled, approving of his choice, and said, "Do your thing."

The vehicle door locks abruptly unlocked as the engine simultaneously engaged. Leah shook her head, grinning as she climbed into the driver's seat. John placed his MTY backpack on the floor and then sat in the passenger seat beside her.

As they drove, John scanned the traffic. It did not appear that they were being followed. Fouray had reported no QRB signals in range after John had re-activated the datstem during the night. Fouray had also been monitoring the local police radio bands. Surprisingly, no mention had been made of any incidents at the hotel, and the absence of any radio activity after such an extraordinarily violent event strongly suggested governmental intervention. Fouray could not explain such complete radio silence in any other way.

After approximately 40 minutes, they arrived at the restaurant. It was a small café-style establishment with a green awning and a large window framed by a decorative wrought-iron fence.

"The sign says it opens at noon," Leah said, looking at the window. "That's nearly an hour from now."

"I suggest you knock and ask for the owner."

Leah stepped out and crossed the sidewalk to the door. She could see staff milling about inside preparing for the day's customers. She knocked and then waited. Seeing herself in the reflection from the glass door, Leah was suddenly aware of how disheveled she looked. As one of the staff approached, Leah carefully brushed back her hair with her hand.

"We're not open yet miss." The apron-clad woman said, courteously opening the door.

Leah nodded, "Yes, I know you're not open. I need to speak with the owner please."

The woman stepped back, as if appraising the stranger at the door. After a moment, she asked, "Can you tell me what

293

this is about?"

"I believe he is expecting me."

The waitress reluctantly opened the door to allow Leah to step inside. While Leah waited by the bar, the waitress exited through a door at the back of the café. The remaining staff now cast curious glances as they continued prepping the tables. After a minute, the rear café door re-opened and a portly middle-aged man emerged. Leah remembered him, though the man appeared to have gained weight since their earlier visit.

"Ms. Vaughn?" he asked, extending his thick hand with a smile.

"Yes."

"So nice to see you again. Sir Albert telephoned to inform me you needed the spare key to his flat?"

Leah nodded, "Yes… we're interviewing Sir Albert for a story on climate change, and we thought we'd hold the interview there." Leah fumbled in her purse for her APN credentials but the restaurateur simply waved his hand and handed her a key.

"No worries, no worries," he said, "Here you go. His flat is on the 3rd floor. There's no name but you'll see a Greenpeace sticker on the door."

"Thank you!"

Leah walked back outside and got back into the vehicle. At John's suggestion, they parked a block away on Goodge Street and then walked back to the restaurant.

The professor's flat was on the top floor, on what Leah would have called the 4th floor of the building. In Britain, what Americans call the 1st floor, the British call the ground floor, and what Americans call the 2nd floor, Brits call the 1st floor.

Professor Nicholls's flat was therefore on the 3rd floor of the 4-story building, with the restaurant occupying the ground floor.

When Leah opened the door, she smiled at the musty academic décor so reminiscent of the professor she remembered. The beautiful wood paneling was almost completely concealed behind sea tidal charts, computer printouts, climate data graphs, and a large green chalkboard, undoubtedly pilfered from some classroom. The smell of chalk and books filled the room.

Facing the board was a small coffee-stained couch covered by a worn green blanket, with only a small surface area left for sitting. The rest of the couch was covered by books, notebooks, and stacks of papers.

A small coffee table sat in front of the couch, littered with academic journals. Behind the couch, a large stack of textbooks rose like the towers of an ancient temple rising above the jungle canopy.

A small TV-dinner stand was placed nearby but it bore no evidence of food. Instead, it held a laptop and a resin "Sea World"-stamped figurine of a beluga whale.

Behind the couch and the pile of textbooks, John's eye caught sight of the corner of a painting, partially obscured by a National Geographic foldout map of the world. When he lifted the corner of the map, he was shocked to discover it was concealing an original David Hockney painting! The painting's colors, brilliant splashes of blues and green, depicted a quaint country house scene and contrasted starkly with the room's dark and drab décor.

Next to the couch, on a small end table, John spotted a bronze sculpture. It was reminiscent of two box-shaped figures walking together. Upon closer examination, he was amazed to see it was an original Lynn Chadwick sculpture!

John felt overwhelmed. It was like walking into a renaissance-era home and discovering Rembrandt's Mona Lisa painting casually hanging in the parlor. In 2151, works by either of these artists were considered priceless. John had only seen an original David Hockney painting once before, the artist's "Garrowby Hill" masterpiece, behind 2-inches of protective polyglass inside the Breuer-Metropolitan Art Gallery in New York. Even in this time, John knew such pieces were considered extremely valuable. Despite the apparent thrift of his residence, this professor was a *very* wealthy individual.

After locking the front door, John said he was going to check the rest of the residence. When he didn't return after several minutes, Leah went to find him and found him on the bed, asleep. John's backpack was by his head with one of its straps secured to his wrist.

Leah tried to remember the last time John had had any real sleep. He may have dozed a bit on the flight to London, and he had told her that he had slept for a few hours at the hotel before their abrupt departure, but that was all. He must be exhausted! Leah shook her head and quietly closed the door.

Chapter 30

"For the hopes of men
have been justly called waking dreams."
~ Saint Basil the Great
Bishop of Cæsarea
(330 - 379 AD)
From a letter to Gregory of Nazianzus

J ohn woke, hearing low conversation coming from the front room. From the light coming through the thick window curtains, he suspected he had been asleep for most of the afternoon. He queried Fouray and was informed he had been asleep for 4 hours and 11 minutes.

When John walked into the front room, Leah was sitting on the (now partially-cleared) couch next to a short grey-haired man with large round glasses. The man was dressed in suit pants, a button-down shirt, and a Kings College blazer. The two were talking pleasantly, smiling, and picking at a large round tray filled with exotic cheeses, crackers, and grapes sitting on the coffee table. A number of empty bottles of ginger ale were scattered on the floor.

"John!" Leah stood up and wiped her mouth with a white napkin. "I want to introduce you to Sir Albert Nicholls."

The elderly professor stood up quickly, smiling broadly as he shook John's hand.

"It's a very great pleasure to meet you young man. A very great pleasure indeed!" The professor was beaming as he looked John over from top to bottom. "Leah has been telling me about you, my dear fellow, and about your extraordinary mission."

John glanced at Leah, who nodded and said, "Yes, I told him who you are… and where you're from."

The professor motioned for John to sit in the empty chair and then said, "I must say, I would normally discount such a fantastic tale, were it not for my unequivocal belief in Ms. Vaughn's honesty."

John sat down in an empty chair.

Abruptly, the professor snapped his fingers, "And we have another way of proving your identity… or so I've been told!" The elderly scholar swiftly walked to his laptop and began typing into its keyboard.

"As I understand it," he said as he typed, "Taiwan is going to experience some kind of natural disaster today." He looked at Leah then and asked, "What was it again my dear? A tsunami?"

Leah shook her head, uncertain.

The professor now looked at John, waiting respectfully.

"An earthquake," John said, "At 11:50 PM Taiwan local time."

The professor's eyebrows went up and he nodded, mumbling, "7 hours ahead… that puts it at… 4:50 London time." He glanced up at a clock in the room and said, "Hmmm… Less than 15 minutes to go! Exciting!"

As he sat back down, the elderly gentleman turned to Leah and said, "Are you aware, my dear, that this will be the first time in history that an earthquake has been accurately predicted?"

Leah shook her head.

"Oh its true!" The professor nodded. "This is an historic occasion."

The professor looked intently at John, and said, "Ms. Vaughn has also told me that you have in your possession a most wonderous device?"

When John nodded, the professor said, "I would be most grateful for an opportunity to examine it. Would that be permissible?"

John nodded, "Yes," he said, "just a moment." He walked back into the bedroom to retrieve his backpack. When he returned, he carefully removed his MTY device from the pack and placed it on the coffee table in front of the professor.

The professor's expression immediately grew sober and his eyes widened as he gazed at the strange device. His hands, now shaking, reached out.

"Oh my," he said, his voice soft. He hesitated and glanced up at John, asking, "May I?"

John touched the black glass panel to the left of the silver-blue sphere. A series of cryptic symbols materialized on the obsidian panel, which John expertly keyed. A small click was heard and the symbols faded, save for one that remained, pulsing slowly.

"It's safe to touch now," John said, motioning for the professor to proceed.

The professor gingerly touched the panel and, when no additional symbols became evident, he appeared to relax. He carefully turned the device now, examining the octagonal tower that vertically traversed the left side of the ensconced sphere. As Leah had noted when she had first seen the strange device, the surface of the small black tower rippled and shifted strangely in an almost fluidic pattern. The professor looked up at John, querying with his eyes.

"The control unit," John said, "is supported by a quantum-based AI processor. The processor employs super-positioned entangled photon particles. The data storage is comprised of sub-atomic polarized erbium isotopes. The data core on this unit is capable of storing 142.6 yottabytes of information."

The professor now looked up, peering over his large glasses, "Leah said the device was damaged?"

John nodded and pointed to the hairline fracture near the base of the silver-blue sphere and traced it with his finger into the base of the ceramic heat sink. "When I was struck by the transport in Austin," he said, "the impact fractured the EPM containment sphere. This caused a disruption in the magnetic field holding the singularity and the singularity was lost."

The professor shook his head. Then he tapped the semi-transparent casing surrounding the device's fusion reactor, examining the internal reactor's outlines as he turned the unit.

"The device is powered," John explained, "by a 180-megawatt Wendelstein-Vattenfall fusion reactor. While that is enough power to maintain a singularity, it is insufficient to create one."

The professor caressed the device now almost reverently as he placed it back onto the coffee table. He sat back, visibly affected. "O brave new world," he whispered, shaking his head, "that has such marvels in it". At that moment, a tone sounded from the professor's laptop on the TV tray. The elderly

300

scholar jumped. He stood then and almost hesitantly walked towards the tray. After reading the screen for a moment, he bent down and typed something on the keyboard. Then, he stood up, glanced at the clock, and turned to face Leah.

"There's been an earthquake reported in Taiwan."

Leah nodded as tears welled up in her eyes. "I knew there would be," she said, smiling at John.

The aging professor slowly returned to his seat on the couch and sat down. He stared at John now, silent, watching him as he carefully placed the strange device back inside his backpack. Leah took this opportunity to retrieve the laptop from the TV tray. She sat back down with it on her lap, reading about the quake.

After several moments, the professor spoke, his voice halting.

"I've been a scientist all my life," he began. "I've dedicated my time, my talent, and a considerable portion of my family's wealth attempting to help mankind solve what I believe to be some of its most pressing problems; to try and find answers to some of the world's most pressing questions."

The professor shook his head. "It never occurred to me that, one day, I would be in a position to simply hold out my hand to someone and say, 'give me the answer'. To find myself in that situation is, frankly, disconcerting. I am humbled and a bit overwhelmed. Nevertheless, I owe it to mankind, to my fellow scientists, and to myself, to ask you a question."

John nodded, waiting.

The professor leaned forward, his own eyes glistening now. "Mankind is consuming the earth's fossil fuel reserves. He is choking the oceans with plastics and chemical waste. He is

301

depleting the rainforests while pumping tons of carbon into the atmosphere."

The professor stood now and walked behind the couch to the world map covering the Hockney painting. He stood in front of the map for a moment, smoothing a crease in the paper with his hand.

"I am not one of those," he continued, "who preaches global warming as the doom of mankind. I have never believed man's dominion over this planet would end. But the impacts of global warming can no longer be denied. And, while it may not spell the doom of mankind as some would have us believe, I believe it does signal the end of an era."

He turned to face John again. "I believe in mankind's future, but I also believe mankind can no longer continue on its present self-destructive course. I believe the two are mutually exclusive. Man can have no future if he continues on the course he has set, yet man must have a future."

"I have wrestled with this conundrum for more than 40 years and have reached no conclusions. I have found no answers to what I believe is the most important question of our time."

The professor came back around the couch and sat back down, facing John, his expression intent.

"And that question is, what must mankind do, to survive the consequences of his poor stewardship of this planet?"

John thought for a moment about how to respond while the professor sat respectfully silent, waiting. Leah also looked up from the laptop.

"Professor," John began hesitantly, "I am a temporal

specialist. My training and expertise may not be adequate to answer your question; I'm not a climatologist or a bio-engineer." Seeing the dismay tugging at the old scholar's eyes, John quickly added, "However, I think I can help you."

John thought back to his continental history classes at Rio Verde Primary in New Phoenix when he was a boy. Something one of the holo-instructors had said came into his mind and he directed Fouray to retrieve the relevant data.

"You are correct, professor," John responded, "when you say mankind cannot continue on the path it has set for itself. As you have said, the earth's fossil fuel reserves are being depleted at an alarming rate. The oceans are being polluted, and the atmosphere is being poisoned with carbon and other gases."

John shook his head. "In this time, few men have the will to change these conditions. Those who do, such as yourself, lack the means to effect that change. Things *will* get worse. The rainforests will be almost completely destroyed. The oceans will become increasingly polluted, and the atmosphere will become almost unbreathable. Tens of thousands of species of flora and fauna will become endangered, and many others will become extinct. The mass die-off has already begun."

The professor sighed and sat back, hanging his head. He suddenly looked very old.

John continued, "But there is hope, professor."

The old man looked up, staring intently at John.

John nodded, "Mankind as a whole does not, at the present time, have either the will or the means to remedy these problems... but that will soon change."

The professor leaned forward, nodding anxiously.

"When?... How?..." he asked.

"In 2067," John said, "scientists in Geneva will achieve the first stable exotic phased-matter singularity. Using this technology, mankind will have discovered a fast, easy, and safe method of traveling vast distances in an instant. This technology will allow mankind to begin to colonize Luna, establish orbital stations, and eventually colonize Mars. Around the world, EPM transit stations will become widespread, facilitating great shifts in the world's population centers. People will begin to live where they *want* to live, not where they *must* live. People will no longer be forced to live near their sources of food or work. Coastal cities will begin to disburse their populations into their interiors, reducing ocean pollution dramatically."

"EPM transit technology will quickly replace airlines and other forms of public transportation. Eventually, most private forms of transportation will be almost entirely replaced by automated drones and EPM stations. People will no longer need to burn hydrocarbons to purchase goods, travel, or work."

John paused now, before continuing. "There will be only one problem with this wonderful new technology. It will require vast amounts of energy; and, as you pointed out, fossil fuel reserves will be essentially depleted by the end of this century."

"This exploding demand for energy, combined with declining fossil fuel reserves, will trigger one of the most significant changes in mankind's history. Mankind will enter the fusion era."

The professor began to nod slowly.

"At first," John continued, "fusion power will be

expensive, difficult to produce, and dangerous. However, as with any technology driven by market demands, over time, it will become increasingly affordable and safe. By 2088, the demand for helium-3 for fusion reactors will have grown so great that companies will begin building mining colonies on the moon, to extract helium-3 from the lunar regolith."

The professor nodded again, listening closely.

"With mankind's transition to fusion power, energy will finally become truly clean, affordable, and plentiful. EPM singularities will simultaneously make transportation and shipping both affordable and fast. Mankind will abandon fossil fuels, carbon emissions will drop to almost zero, and the planet's oceans and atmosphere will begin to heal."

"Corporations and governments will then discover that, with the cost of shipping and energy reduced to near-zero, it will be more profitable to recycle mankind's waste than to produce new materials from scratch. Automated 'skimmer' buoys will circle the oceans, collecting plastics and other floating man-made debris, and landfill reclamation contracts will be auctioned to the highest bidders, who will employ automated machines to recover concentrated metals, polymers, chemicals, and bio-matter."

The professor now spoke, "What I believe you are telling me, is that there are no solutions presently available to alter man's self-destructive consumption of this planet's resources, but that such solutions will be forthcoming in the future."

John nodded, "That's a fair assessment professor. I don't wish to be pessimistic, but things are going to get worse... much worse... before they begin to get better. I simply want you to understand that they *will* get better."

305

"From what you're saying," the professor spoke while writing on a paper pad, "these two technologies, singularity-based transportation and fusion energy, will be the catalysts that will restore our world's ecosystems?"

"That's correct. More than any other contributing factors, the introduction of EPM-based technology and the development of fusion power are credited with suspending global warming, reducing oceanic and land-based pollution, and improving air quality."

The professor shook his head, "2067 you said?"

John nodded, "That's when scientists in Geneva will succeed in calibrating the first stabilized singularity."

"Hmmmm… A bit after my lifetime, I'm sorry to say." The professor sighed and then added, "I would have liked to see that day... or at least its beginning."

The rest of the evening was spent pleasantly. Leah had been surprised to discover no kitchen in the small apartment. The professor had converted that space into a micro laboratory, filled with terrariums of exotic rainforest plants under UV light fixtures, and cannisters of shredded polymers slowly being consumed by a family of waxworm caterpillars. She had returned rather green after examining the professor's refrigerator, and would only say that they would have to order in.

The professor called down to the restaurant and ordered a delicious meal for his guests. Apparently, this was his habit when staying at his flat.

Considering the recent violence at the London Hilton, John and Leah knew it would not be possible to interview the professor as they had originally intended. They did not want to implicate the noted scholar.

For his part, the professor thought their caution unwarranted, and appeared anxious to fight "the establishment", but in the end, he capitulated when Leah pleaded with him to remain silent and tell no one of their visit. The professor also assured them of the restaurant owner's discretion, noting with a grin that the restaurateur had remained silent despite his tenant having entertained far more salacious guests.

As it turned out, the professor proved to be quite the fortuitous encounter. Leah had no idea how she and John would return to New York. It was clear their travel plans were compromised, and after the deaths at the hotel, they did not dare to attempt flying home under their own names.

After listening to the conversation for several minutes, the professor interrupted and said, "Not to worry. Not to worry." He then retrieved an older 1990s-era flip phone from his pocket and keyed in a number. After a moment, he spoke into the phone,

"Gerry? Hello! This is Nicholls... doing well, doing well, thank you."

The professor sat down on the couch and continued. "Listen, I need you to ferry some friends out in the morning. They're in a bit of barney here and need to get back home before they're nicked... New York... Can you have one of your planes ready for them at, oh, 7:00 am?"

There was a moment of pause, and then the professor spoke again, "Two... but it's hush hush my man... Right... Right."

After another pause, the professor laughed, "No!.. No

flora or fauna this time. Just the two passengers… Right… I'll pay the usual, but next time you need to give me a rate!"

The professor laughed once more and then hung up the call. He chuckled again and then turned to his guests.

"There you are. No problem." In answer to their unspoken query, he said, "A friend of mine in the climate activist community. He owns a charter air service and from time to time he transports some of our organization's… well… let's call them our 'less-patient supporters'. He transports them out for various protests, industrial sabotage, or even less honorable activities."

As he was speaking, the professor began writing directions on a slip of paper. "I've used his services in the past," he said, "arranging to smuggle out endangered plants and animals to conservatories or animal sanctuaries. All completely illegal of course!" The professor beamed a winning smile, then added, "I was able to smuggle out a female Amur leopard last fall, from poachers in south-eastern Russia. They intended to skin the beautiful creature and sell her hide to some Chinese businessman. We bought her from them alive, and my friend flew her all the way to a conservatory in Spain."

He handed the paper to Leah as he was speaking. "She got loose in the cabin, and they flew almost half the flight with the flight crew and pilot hiding behind the cockpit door and the co-pilot trapped in the lavatory while she tore up all the leather upholstery in the plane!"

He chuckled, adding, "Damndest thing… she turned out to be pregnant! Gave birth to 3 cubs the following month!"

Leah was studying the directions on the map as the professor was speaking. The charter company was located near

308

Stapleford Airport, approximately an hour drive to the northeast. The directions said to ask for Gerry at the company's charter desk.

The professor took John into his closet and did his best to supply him with replacement shoes and other clothing. When they stepped back into the front room, Leah could not contain her smile.

John was dressed in baggy trousers that were too long for his frame. He sported a King's College rowing team t-shirt, a pair of well-used athletic lace-ups, and a faded long-sleeve grey hoodie. The clothes were obviously student castoffs. With his backpack on his back, John looked, frankly, like a homeless person, and as he turned to model his attire for her, Leah shook her head and covered her mouth with her hand, trying hard not to laugh.

"Well now," the professor said, smacking his hands together and smiling at Leah, "normally when I have a guest as lovely as you my dear, I send down for some wine and then do my best to make her regret having visited."

Leah laughed and the professor grinned and shook his head, "But in your case," he continued, "I will forego such short-sighted pursuits. I am thoroughly and utterly grateful for your visit, and I hope to be able to do this with you again very soon!"

The professor looked at John now, scanning him from top to bottom. Then he said, "I am deeply honored, Mr. Clifton, to be one of those entrusted with your secret. You have given an old man hope for the first time in many years… and I do not intend to waste that hope!"

He shut the lid on his laptop and continued, "I shall

309

employ my time and resources now towards preparing for that great future of which you spoke. I shall work towards saving and preserving as much as possible, against that day when mankind finally obtains the tools he needs to begin healing this planet."

The 74-year old professor abruptly stopped, as if struck by an idea. "Hmmm..." he mused, "Perhaps I'll build a zoo!" He looked at Leah with a twinkle in his eye, and grinned. "I know some people who have an orangutan for sale."

Chapter 31

"Before I draw nearer to that stone to which you point, answer me one question. Are these the shadows of the things that will be, or are they shadows of things that may be only?"
~ *Charles Dickens*
English novelist
(1812 - 1870 AD)
From "A Christmas Carol", p. 1843

The clock on the nightstand read 04:45 AM when Fouray woke John from a deep sleep. The datstem reported no disturbances during the night and, from its scans of the city radio frequencies, there appeared to be no unusual police activity in the area.

The professor had insisted on giving up his bedroom to his guests and had made himself comfortable on his couch in the front room. Though they had retired relatively early, when Leah emerged from taking her shower she had discovered John had already fallen asleep. Determined to let him rest, she had curbed her disappointment and climbed quietly into the bed next to him. She had snuggled close and drifted off to sleep feeling John's back pressing against her breasts with each breath.

John now touched Leah's arm. When she didn't stir, he brushed her hair back on her forehead and spoke her name, "Leah?"

Leah slowly opened her eyes and looked around. After a

moment, recognizing her surroundings and John's face, she smiled and nodded her head. "Is it time to go?" she asked, her voice groggy.

"Yes."

John stood and dressed in the clothing the professor had provided. Then he stepped towards the bedroom door. "I'm going to wake the professor," he said. "We should leave as soon as possible."

Leah nodded and sat up. When she finally joined John and the professor, the professor was holding a coat for her. "It's a touch below freezing outside my dear," he said, "and I remembered you had no coat when you arrived."

"Thank you professor."

John now extended his hand. "Goodbye professor."

The professor took John's hand and shook it energetically. "Goodbye Mr. Clifton. Thank you again for sharing a glimpse of the future with me."

John nodded and then opened the front door. He listened for a moment, but he could hear nothing except the far-away hum of morning traffic on the roads. To the east, a strong glow on the skyline suggested daybreak had almost arrived.

Leah gave the old scholar a kiss and a hug and then joined John on the stoop. The professor then watched, shivering from his open doorway, as his guests descended the stairs to the street below.

The walk back to their vehicle seemed longer in the cold and early morning light. Leah held onto John's arm as they strode past the quiet buildings. When they finally reached their vehicle, John disengaged its door locks and remote started its engine. The moment the engine turned over, however, Fouray barked, "Signal!... duo radio frequencies just engaged... 1575.42 MHz!"

A satellite-based tracking device had been attached to the vehicle! It had obviously been keyed to begin transmitting once the engine was started. John immediately chided himself on making such a foolish mistake! He should have anticipated the stolen vehicle might have been found and tagged.

Approximately 200 meters to the southwest on Goodge Street, a vehicle suddenly started its engine and flipped on its headlights. John whirled, locating the sound. A moment later, a second vehicle behind the first started its engine.

"Fast!" John shouted, pushing Leah into the driver's seat.

"Wha...?" Leah was startled and confused, but John had slammed her door shut, rolled over the vehicle's hood, and scrambled into the passenger seat before she could say anything.

"Drive!" John shouted as he placed his backpack on the floor between his feet.

Flustered, Leah shoved the car's transmission into drive and stepped forcefully on the gas pedal. As the powerful sedan lurched forward, John swiveled his head, looking back. As he feared, two pairs of headlights were approaching swiftly.

"Faster!" John urged. "We're being chased!"

At that moment, a third vehicle emerged from Whitfield Street ahead of their position and stopped in the middle of the street, attempting to block the lane.

"What do I do?!" Leah shouted, gripping the wheel tightly.

"Don't stop!"

313

Leah did her best to avoid hitting the vehicle ahead, jerking the steering wheel sharply to the left and forcing their sedan partially onto the sidewalk, but the right front wheel-well struck the vehicle. The force of the impact spun the smaller vehicle around violently, crashing it through the window of a small curio shop on the opposite side of the street. Leah shoved the pedal to the floor and their heavier sedan jumped forward again, smoking its tires on the cold asphalt.

"I can't do this!" Leah shouted. "I can't do this!"

"Yes, you can!" John shouted back. He glanced behind again. The two pursuing vehicles had passed the crash site and were gaining speed. As they raced down Goodge Street, John instructed Fouray to tie into the radio-controlled traffic system.

"Can you disable the malfunction management system?" John asked.

A moment later, Fouray responded, "Yes. It's contained within the traffic net safety subsystem and I am PoL'd with that system."

John quickly formulated a mental plan. "I want you to trigger the traffic subsystem on each intersection we approach to allow us to pass through. Then, I want you to override the malfunction management system to allow the cross traffic to begin entering just after we pass through."

"Understood."

The pursuing vehicles were closing fast. Leah drove frantically towards the intersection ahead, desperately trying not to lose control of their vehicle. As she approached the Tottenham Court Road cross street, she shouted, "Which way?!"

"Turn left!" John replied, pointing frantically.

At that moment, the traffic signal changed to green. Leah spun the steering wheel and the sedan's tires squealed as the large vehicle rounded onto Tottenham Court Road. At almost that same moment, several other vehicles began to cross the intersection, honking their horns in protest.

John looked back, holding his breath. A moment later, the first of the pursuing vehicles emerged from Goodge Street, screeching its brakes in an attempt to avoid a collision. It smashed into one of the vehicles crossing the intersection and flipped dramatically. The second pursuing vehicle narrowly avoided the accident, squealing its own wheels now as it raced down Tottenham Court Road in pursuit.

Leah was driving magnificently. Though she was clearly frightened, she was gripping the steering wheel firmly as they flew through the Howland Street intersection. As before, Fouray tripped the traffic lights to allow them to pass unimpeded, and then released the cross traffic a moment later. This time, however, the pursuing vehicle flew through unopposed. Even worse, another vehicle now joined the pursuit from Howland Street, following close behind.

As they approached Grafton Way, the closest pursuing vehicle accelerated dramatically and slammed its front bumper into the back of their sedan. For a moment, Leah lost control as the rear of their vehicle began to slide before she managed to straighten out again.

"Can't you do something?!" Leah shouted as she pressed the vehicle's pedal to the floor. "Don't you guys have phasers or something like that in the future?!"

"What's a phaser?!" John asked, confused.

Leah shook her head and shouted, "A gun! Something

we can use to shoot at these assholes!"

"The only thing I brought from the future was my MTY device!"

The pursuing vehicle now leapt forward again.

Watching the vehicle approaching swiftly in the rear view mirror, Leah suddenly slammed on the brakes. For a horrifying moment, their sedan's tires screeched against the asphalt, smoking violently.

The pursuing vehicle also locked its brakes, desperately trying to avoid the inevitable collision. It struck the rear of their sedan hard and the shock of the impact was devastating to the smaller vehicle, smashing its front hood and engine compartment. The trailing vehicle now spun out of control attempting to avoid the wreck and found itself facing the wrong way on Tottenham Court Road.

When Leah stepped on the gas pedal again, their vehicle's rear window, fractured into a sheet of square glass fragments, slid free of its frame and skidded across the street. The rear tires were wobbling as she drove, but that appeared to be the extent of the damage to their heavier vehicle.

John looked back at the wreck, amazed. "Where did you learn to do that?!" he asked.

Leah smiled grimly and answered, "Kacie's video games!"

John shook his head, confused, but his distraction was short-lived. They were approaching Euston Road now and Fouray suddenly suggested an idea. With no time to lose, John shouted, "Stop the vehicle!"

To her credit, Leah slammed on the sedan's brakes instantly, spinning the car's steering wheel dramatically to avoid hitting a red double-decker bus that was disgorging morning passengers near the Warren Street underground station. As soon as their vehicle stopped, John grabbed his backpack and kicked open his door, shouting "Out!"

As the bus passengers stared in amazement, the pair ran swiftly from their damaged vehicle towards the grey stone façade of the Warren Street underground station. Far down Tottenham Court Road, John could see the headlights of the last vehicle maneuvering around the wreck, preparing to rejoin the chase.

Warren Street Station is an older underground rail station originally constructed before World War I. It joins the Northern line and the Victoria line and, even in the early hours of the morning, is well attended. As is common with many older underground stations, the station's escalators were narrow, bounded by ticketing machines on either side, and equipped with electronic turnstiles at the top.

Fouray quickly PoL'd with the station's ticketing system and released the turnstiles. The moment John and Leah had passed through the small barriers, Fouray locked the turnstiles behind them. When they reached the platform below, Fouray triggered the station's emergency system. Frightening alarms began sounding from the public announcement system and passengers who had been preparing to board the train now began moving swiftly towards the exits.

John pulled Leah into the nearest train car and waited. The exiting passengers effectively clogged the narrow escalators leading down to the platform and the locked turnstiles above prevented the crowd from easily dispersing. After a few moments, the train's doors closed and the car began

317

moving.

John breathed a sigh of relief. They had been very fortunate! He scanned the route chart above the window on the opposite wall. He didn't wish to stay on the rail system for an extended period of time. Already, he visualized men being dispatched to remote stations along the line with instructions to board the incoming trains.

They exited the underground at Angel Station in Islington. Minutes later, they had secured another vehicle, a BMW 3 Series sedan. Taking no further chances at detection, John deactivated his datstem as Leah began driving north on Upper Street. It was a short 30-minute drive to Stapleford Airport and Leah drove swiftly.

John complimented her on her driving skills, and then apologized for not anticipating their pursuers waiting for them.

"It's ok," Leah said softly, "You can't know everything."

John shook his head, "That's very generous of you, but I should have anticipated the transport being found. I'm trained to anticipate things like that."

"Maybe you had your mind on something else?" she suggested, glancing at him.

John looked up at his pretty companion and then smiled. "Perhaps."

"Well," Leah continued, "we got away and we're almost to the airport. That's what matters. I just hope the professor's friend comes through."

Chapter 32

T he professor's friend came through. When Leah pulled their vehicle into the charter company's corporate parking lot, they were greeted by a tall Irishman with a thick mustache. He held the door for them and shook their hands warmly.

"Gerry Byrnes! Pleased to make your acquaintance."

Through the iron fence behind the charter office, John could see technicians fueling a Gulfstream G4 near an open hanger. The small jet could accommodate 12 passengers comfortably, though on this trip Gerry informed them they would be alone except for himself, the co-pilot, and one flight attendant.

Leah shook her head in disbelief when she stepped up the small stairs into the beautiful aircraft. The interior stateroom was luxuriously outfitted, with rich carpeting, fine leather chairs, a widescreen television, and a stocked bar.

"Oh my!" she said, feeling the smooth wood paneling. "How much is this trip costing the professor?" she asked the tall Irishman.

"As to that now," the tall man responded with a smile, "We give Sir Albert a discount, owing to his support of our cause. This flight 'ere will cost his lordship a mere £94,000."

Leah sat down hard. The professor was paying almost $116,000 to fly them to New York! A flight attendant approached, offering Leah a cup of tea, which she took gratefully. At that moment, the co-pilot climbed on board and the large Irishman climbed into the pilot's seat next to him. The flight attendant closed and sealed the exterior door and the jet immediately began taxiing towards the runway. Apparently, Byrnes was accustomed to getting his passengers and cargo airborne quickly.

As the sleek jet lifted from the runway, Leah began to relax. The excitement of the morning's chase had filled her with adrenaline, and as its effects began to subside, she suddenly felt tired and disoriented.

"I think I'm going to lay down," she announced.

John immediately unbuckled his seatbelt and assisted her to the plush leather sofa as the flight attendant brought her a heated blanket.

"There you go," the attendant said, spreading out the soft blanket.

"Thank you," Leah replied.

John sat close, looking out one of the small windows at the clouds. After almost 20 minutes, Byrnes' voice came over the cabin speakers.

"You folks are in the clear. We've just passed Falmouth and are heading out over the Celtic Sea now. We're at our cruising altitude and should make New York in a little over 6 hours."

John smiled down at Leah, who nodded. She sat back up. "I'm feeling better," she said. "I guess it was all the excitement."

John nodded. "Perfectly understandable," he said.

The flight attendant approached through a door in the rear of the cabin. "Do you think you can eat something dear?" she asked while handing Leah a small menu.

"Oh my!" Leah exclaimed, examining the menu. She had never seen such cuisine offered on an airplane before, even when flying first class. The charter company certainly knew how to pamper its customers!

"Would it be too much trouble to have a poached egg, muffin, and juice?" Leah asked, her cheeks flushing.

The flight attendant shook her head, "Not at all. Would you like the eggs just so? I can make you eggs benedict if you prefer."

Leah's eyes grew wide and she nodded eagerly. "Yes, please!"

John grinned, and nodded the same for him.

The flight attendant smiled and left.

John looked around slowly and then back to Leah. "It's too bad we couldn't have traveled this well the whole trip," he said, smiling.

Leah nodded, "Yes. This plane is amazing." She looked at her phone and said, "It's too bad we didn't get to do what we set out to do. The interviews, I mean." She looked up at John and continued, "When we get back, Tom is going to setup a meeting with Dr. Saito. He said he was also arranging for a mathematician to be at the meeting too, so you should plan on talking about some of the math behind the science."

321

John nodded and Leah resumed reading her phone messages.

After several minutes, John spoke again. "What do you know about Saito?" he asked.

Leah looked up, thinking for a moment. Then she shrugged. "I know he's a big deal in the scientific community," she said. "I read his bio. Theoretical physics is his thing. When he was in his 40s, he was awarded a Guggenheim grant, and he won the Nobel prize in his 60s for his work with particle physics. Since then, he's been teaching at the University of California in Berkeley, lecturing, doing research, that sort of thing."

Leah put down her phone. "It's funny you should ask about him," she said.

"Why?" John asked.

"We had an interview with him the day your email arrived. He seemed very interested in meeting with you."

John's eyebrows rose slightly, and he asked, "You told Saito about my being a temporal specialist?"

"Not directly," Leah said, shaking her head. "Tom dropped a copy of the file attachment from your email when we were winding up the interview. It was that drawing of the fusion reactor. Saito picked it up and asked where it came from. Tom said it was in an email we had received that morning from someone claiming to be a time traveler."

John listened but said nothing.

Leah continued, "After that, Saito asked if we could arrange a meeting with you." Her face took on a troubled expression now. "In fact," she continued, "he seemed pretty insistent on having us arrange an interview. He started bugging

Tom..."

Leah stopped mid-sentence, her mind racing. After a few moments, she asked, "Do you think Saito has anything to do with those men chasing us?"

John nodded slowly. "Yes," he said. "Saito is working with Williams."

Leah was shocked. "Are you sure?"

"Yes," John replied, watching the young woman closely. "In fact, he is the reason I emailed your office that day. It's why I attached that drawing. I knew if you saw it, you might ask Saito about it at your meeting and that would get his attention."

Leah shook her head. "I don't understand."

John's expression took on a thoughtful look. "Williams' tripback file states that she transited to Baltimore in order to access the Office of Personnel Management's database. We believe she breached that database in order to locate people in this time with the specific skills she needs to help her complete her mission."

John paused for a moment, and then continued. "We don't know who Williams recruited here in this time, with one exception. The NAFS archives contains a copy of Saito's personal journal. As a historical figure... as a Nobel laureate, Saito's journal is preserved within the historical records from this era."

Leah nodded.

John continued, "On June 2, 2015, approximately two months after Williams transited into Baltimore, Saito wrote an entry in his journal, stating, 'Today I was approached by a most interesting woman. She asked me to join a confidential project being sponsored by the U.S. Dept of Energy involving quantum computing. She approached me because of my background in particle physics. We have a kickoff meeting scheduled on Monday, July 6, at the National Laboratory in Oak Ridge.'"

Leah's eyes grew wide. "Oh my!" she said.

John nodded, then continued, "Saito's journal contained one other entry of note. On January 4, 2018, Saito wrote an entry, stating, 'Breakthrough today at Oak Ridge. If the testing holds, we should be able to apply the quantum synapse in about a month.'"

In answer to Leah's puzzled expression, John explained, "'Quantum synapse' is a term used by engineers in my time. It refers to a programming matrix that is laid down onto a quantum-entangled AI processor. From Saito's use of that expression in his journal, it was clear that he had had interaction with someone from the future with knowledge of quantum engineering and SDU development."

Leah nodded.

John continued, "Saito's journal entries gave us our only known contact with Williams in this time. It also gave us an approximate date for Williams' completion of her project... 'about a month' after January 4, 2018."

John took a deep breath and said, "I needed to make contact with someone connected with Saito, and, based on his journal entry, I knew I needed to make contact with him at least several weeks before January 4, 2018."

Leah sat silently on the leather sofa, considering what John had said. After a few moments, she asked, "So, you emailed our office because you knew we were meeting with Saito that morning?"

John nodded, watching the producer's eyes. "Yes. The NAFS archives contain a recording of your company's December 12 interview with Saito. I hoped to leverage your company's association with Saito to make contact with him."

Leah sat silently now, processing what John had said. After a minute, she said, "Its good we found out about Saito before it was too late. Now we know how those men learned about our trip to Dharamshala and London! When we land, I'll telephone Tom and tell him to cancel the meeting."

John shook his head, "No. Don't do that."

"Why not?" Leah was confused. "If you agree to meet with him, and if he's working with Williams, then you're sure to be captured! They'll grab you at the meeting for sure!"

John nodded, "Very probable."

Leah shook her head, confused. "Then why would you agree to meet with him?!" she asked.

"Saito is my only link to Williams," John said, shrugging his shoulders. "I came here to find her. I need to speak with her. There's still a chance she can be convinced to do the right thing."

Leah stared at John in shock. While she understood his desire to try to redeem a fellow co-worker, from the level of violence already exhibited by Williams' associates, it seemed pretty clear the situation had moved beyond negotiations.

John was watching Leah closely. He seemed to be aware of her internal struggle. After several moments, he spoke softly. "You must understand," he said, "this is why I came here. If I don't find Williams… if I can't retrieve the prototype and return it unaltered to the future, then a race of sentient beings will be forever doomed to slavery."

325

At that moment, the flight attendant emerged from her station at the rear of the cabin bringing their breakfast on a small cart. The delicious smell of hollandaise sauce and bacon filled the cabin. The attendant directed her passengers to a small table near the front of the cabin and served their breakfast.

As they ate, Leah thought about what John was asking her to do. If she allowed Tom to arrange the meeting with Saito, then John would likely be captured or even killed. On the other hand, if she had Tom cancel the meeting, John's entire purpose in coming to this time would have been in vain. It occurred to her then that she was faced with a simple choice. She could arrange the meeting but lose John, or she could cancel the meeting and deprive John of his purpose for being here.

She watched John eating his breakfast across the small table. It seemed like the more she learned about him, the less she understood him. To say John was a complex person was an understatement. John's absolute commitment to his mission was a quality lacking in most men. At least, it was lacking in most men she knew. Were all men in the future so dedicated, she wondered?

She knew then what she had to do.

"When we land," Leah said softly, "I'll telephone Tom and have him setup the meeting."

Chapter 33

"That time either has no being at all,
or is only scarcely and faintly.
One might suspect from this:
part of it has happened and is not,
while the other part is going to be but is not yet,
and it is out of these that the infinite,
or any given time is composed."
~ *Aristotle*
Greek philosopher
(384–322 BC)

T he next two weeks passed pleasantly, a false spring in the otherwise harsh winter of fear and intrigue that now surrounded them. The serious nature of their situation was made clear when Byrnes' voice came over the aircraft's intercom as they approached New York, instructing them to turn off their cell phones and remove the device's batteries. The jet then dropped below air radar over Long Island to land at Calverton Executive Airpark.

Byrnes had radioed ahead to contacts in the area and had made arrangements for someone to meet their plane at the airpark's tarmac. After the plane had touched down, it quickly taxied off the runway and slowed to a stop by one of the many maintenance hangers. The flight attendant had then opened the aircraft's door and shoved John and Leah down the small stepladder, pointing them towards a vehicle parked clandestinely behind the hanger. The moment they climbed into the vehicle, it had exited rapidly through a gate onto a paved access road, past a gate attendant who gave the driver a thumbs-up sign as they passed by. Behind them, the Gulfstream jet was already lifting off the runway to continue on to its official landing at Teterboro Airport.

Their driver drove them to a small café in Islip near Long Island University and then directed them to a second waiting vehicle waiting in the café parking lot. He sped off the moment they exited the back seat, having never even told them his name.

The second vehicle was operated by a young college student, who chatted them up excitedly about his upcoming trip on the Greenpeace ship, Esperanza, scheduled to depart later that year. From his questions, it was clear the young man believed his passengers were associated with that environmental group.

During the drive back to New York, Leah had the driver pull over at a convenience store pay phone. She called a trusted childhood friend, "Liz", and made arrangements for her to pick up Kacie from school, instructing her to be sure to take a taxi and get out several blocks away from her house. She then called Kacie's caregiver, Jenny, and told her to take a couple of weeks off, telling her she was taking her daughter on vacation. Finally, she called Tom Pierce, telling him only to be careful, and that she would call him later that evening.

Leah didn't dare return to her apartment or the APN office, so she asked their driver to drop them off at a shopping center parking lot inside the city. Fouray then summoned a taxi to take them the rest of the way. They exited the taxi approximately two blocks from Liz's home and walked the

328

remaining distance, fearfully staring at every approaching vehicle.

Liz was Leah's childhood friend, single, with no recent ties to Leah that could be easily traced. She was accommodating, trusting, and asked no questions. For their part, Leah and John made the most of their self-imposed isolation. John engaged Kacie in intense video game marathons, to the delight of the disabled girl and Leah's great amusement. They ordered in every night and slept in late every morning. After Kacie had gone to bed each night, Leah watched the stars with John, wrapped in a warm blanket on a hammock in Liz's back yard. John would tell her about his life in the future, about his home on his beloved Hōfu Station, and the technical advances mankind had made.

Leah knew that she would not be able to return to her former life after what had happened in London. At the very least, she was likely wanted as an accessory to murder. Aside from that, she simply knew "too much". She was resigned to abandoning her apartment and her career.

During the day, while Liz was away at work, John made use of their host's computer. With Fouray's assistance, John surreptitiously connected to various government record systems, generating false identifications, passports, and travel visas. The documents arrived "expedited delivery" the following week to a remote post office box John had secured several miles away from Liz's home. John also opened several banking accounts under the same fictitious names and electronically transferred funds from various foreign banks into the accounts, before erasing the transfer records from the bank's databases.

329

Leah purposefully avoided speaking about John's upcoming meeting with Saito. She had called Tom that first evening from a public telephone and explained to him what had happened in Dharamshala and London. Though Tom was initially opposed to scheduling the meeting with Saito, Leah convinced him to go through with it. The executive producer reluctantly agreed but insisted on dismissing the staff that day to avoid placing anyone in danger.

The morning of February 21, 2018, finally arrived. Leah woke early. She had been awake most of the night, trying not to think about what might happen in the morning. John had held her close, comforting her, and she had finally dozed off. John had been unusually quiet throughout the night, undoubtedly working through final details in his head with his incredible datstem device.

When the time came for John to leave for the meeting, he paused by Liz's front door. He seemed to not know what to say. Leah reached up and hugged him tightly, not wanting to let him go. Finally, she released him and forced herself to step back.

John smiled, looking down at her. "It will be ok," he said softly. He turned then as if to walk outside, but his hand hesitated on the door handle and he looked back.

"I want to thank you," John said. "You can't know how important your help has been to me." Then, he smiled and added, "Or how important you have become to me." He kissed her softly then and walked outside. When he reached the sidewalk in front of the house, he paused and looked back. He smiled again and then began walking swiftly down the street to meet the taxi that Fouray had summoned.

Less than an hour later, John stepped out of the taxi in front of All Posted Newswire's office. He could smell hot dogs cooking from a nearby street vendor, "Anthony's Red Hots". As he walked up the steps to the building entrance, he asked Fouray to confirm the signals again.

"Multiple QRB signals confirmed," Fouray responded, "Three signals detected within the standard deviation, nominal encryption. The first two signals are at strength 14.224 and 14.337 respectively. The third signal is holding at strength 11.203."

They were here. Not close, but nearby.

John took a deep breath and walked up the steps. Tom Pierce greeted him inside the lobby, shaking hands with him. The producer appeared nervous.

"Are our guests here?" John asked, smiling.

Tom nodded, and said, "Yes. They went up about 10 minutes ago. They're in the conference room on the media floor… the third floor."

John nodded, and motioned to the elevators, "Shall we join them?"

Tom turned and walked resolutely to the elevators.

The media building was unusually quiet this morning. Other than the lobby receptionist, Lupe, and one of their camera technicians, Marco, the only other staff present was the office manager, Mary Kravets. Dr. Mitch Saito sat in a chair in the small conference room. Sitting next to the elderly physicist was another man in his mid-fifties, Richard Alvis, a member of the International Association of Mathematical Physicists.

Tom was not concerned about Alvis, as he had been

recommended by Dr. Denton at NYU. He shook hands with the mathematician warmly.

"Welcome," Tom said.

"Pleased to be here," Alvis replied. "Phil Denton forwarded to me those summary files you sent to him and I must say, I wouldn't miss this meeting for anything."

Tom nodded, smiling. Then he turned to shake hands with Saito. The octogenarian was staring at John.

"Welcome Dr. Saito," Tom said, holding out his hand.

The elderly man now turned his attention away from John and, seeing Tom's outstretched hand, he smiled and shook it.

"Thank you," Saito said. "I've been looking forward to this meeting for some time."

Fouray took that moment to alert John to a change in the QRB signal strengths. The signals were growing stronger. The operators were closing in on the building.

John now extended his hand to the Nobel laureate. "John Clifton," he said, smiling.

Saito returned the handshake, nodding stiffly.

The camera technician, Marco, abruptly announced he was ready, so the group began taking their seats around the conference room table. At that moment, Mary Kravets brought a fresh pitcher of ice water and glasses into the room. She took the stale pitcher of water from the table and poured what remained into a large potted plant by the window and then left, shutting the door behind her.

For the next three hours, John engaged the two guests in a fascinating discussion. His MTY device was displayed and its functions explained. John was patient and forthcoming, answering their questions honestly and without reservation.

The mathematician, Alvis, was stunned by John's explanation of negative energy and how a singularity could be split into two entangled event horizons. He frantically copied the equations John wrote out on the room's whiteboard, shaking his head in amazement.

Saito, however, appeared more calm, engaging John in a discussion regarding exotic phased matter and its use in singularity containment.

John noted with amusement that Saito's questions were couched in the form of a professor quizzing a student. One of the few times Saito appeared to show true surprise was when John had explained how to construct an MTY device using contemporary technology.

By noon, the meeting attendees were ready for a break. Tom had arranged for lunch to be catered in from a local sandwich shop, and shortly after noon, Mary opened the conference room door to announce the shop's delivery girl had arrived.

As lunch was being laid out on the table, John noticed Saito staring at him. Tom and the mathematician were engaged in a discussion across the table. John nodded at the elderly physicist who took that opportunity to shift from his seat across the table to a chair next to John's. Saito mumbled his thanks as the shop's delivery girl handed him the sandwich and iced tea he had selected from her basket. When she stepped away, the elderly physicist then turned and spoke to John in a low voice.

"May I ask you a question?" Saito said, sipping at his tea.

John nodded, "Certainly."

333

Saito lowered his voice. "Earlier, you talked about self-resolving causality. You said a temporal specialist cannot do anything here in the past to fundamentally change the future."

John nodded again. "Yes," he said, "that's true."

Saito took another sip of tea and said, "So… would it be safe to say that anything a temporal specialist does here in the past must, by definition, be part of your history?"

John hesitated for a moment before answering. Saito took this opportunity to take another sip from his glass, watching John closely.

"Yes," John said after several moments. "Anything a temporal specialist does here in the past becomes part of our history. If they attempt to do something that would contradict or change the future, self-resolving causality would apply a correction. Time will resolve a specialist's actions to prevent the future from changing to the point where it would not have been possible for the specialist to transit into the past… to prevent paradoxes from occurring."

Saito nodded. "So," he said, smiling, "you might say that, if time does *not* apply a correction to nullify a specialist's actions, then that is proof that time *approves* of what they did… that what they did was destined to be part of history."

John said nothing, staring at the elderly physicist.

Saito took another sip of tea. After another moment, he spoke again.

"Would it also be true, then, that a temporal specialist cannot kill someone here in the past who is destined to do something important in the future?"

John nodded slowly, not liking where this conversation was going. "Yes," he said, "that's true."

334

Saito nodded again and began to eat his lunch, apparently satisfied.

As John ate, he asked Fouray for the latest status on the external QRB signals.

"Unchanged," came the datstem's swift reply. "Holding signal strength."

The unvarying signal strength meant the remote QRB sources were holding position, neither advancing nor retreating from their proximity to the building. John considered this and concluded they must be waiting for something.

Following lunch, the interview resumed, with John explaining the mechanics of singularity generation. Following that discussion, Saito asked John for an explanation on artificial-gravity. Several minutes into that discussion, however, Fouray interrupted John's train of thought.

"QRB signal strength change. All three signals are growing stronger now."

They were closing in on the building.

John acknowledged Fouray's update as he continued his explanations into artificial gravity plate manufacturing. He was trying hard to remain calm but his heart was racing. Adrenaline began surging through his system and he found it hard to remain focused on his topic.

"They're here," Fouray abruptly announced.

John tensed, preparing himself.

The mathematician, Richard Alvis, now asked a question. "Can you give me the formula to create an imbalance in the gravimetric field? To create an anti-gravity force?"

"Certainly," John said, glancing at the conference room door. "Let's begin with the field limit gravitational equations again..."

At that moment, there was a disturbance outside the conference room. Through the door's opaque glass, John could see vague figures quickly approaching as Mary Kravets' voice was heard. "Wait... Stop!..." The office manager's voice now rose to a shout, "This is a private office! You can't go in there!"

Suddenly, the conference room door swung open and two men in tactical gear burst into the room. The men were armed with suppressed MP5-SD sub-machine guns and body armor. They took defensive positions on either side of the door, aiming their weapons at John. They were followed by a dozen men with pistols and body armor who now surged into the room. The first two men in the group held pistols in one hand and Dept of Energy badges in the other.

Tom Pierce was on his feet in an instant.

"What the hell is going on!" the producer shouted.

One of the men holding a badge, a tall man with dark hair, immediately pointed his gun at the producer.

"Sit down!" the man ordered.

Tom slowly sat back in his seat, raising his hands.

"Look here," Tom said nervously, "this is private property! I want to see your warrant!"

The dark-haired man ignored Tom's protests and turned again to face John. He put his badge in his pocket and retrieved what appeared to be a grainy security camera photograph. He held it towards John's face for a moment.

"That's him," he said, speaking to the men behind him.

Two men immediately stepped around the table with handcuffs and pulled John's arms behind his back. The two guards with the sub-machine guns kept their muzzles pointed at John as the men double-locked the cuffs. The moment his hands were secured, the men ushered John out of the conference room towards the elevators, with the sub-machine gun equipped guards following close behind.

Tom Pierce spoke again to the dark-haired man. "I told you to show me your warrant!"

Still ignoring the producer, the dark-haired man now snapped his fingers and gestured at Marco's video camera. In less than a minute, the men in the room had retrieved John's backpack and MTY device, removed the memory drive from Marco's video camera, and seized every cell phone, watch, and tablet in the room. The equipment was placed in a large pressure-equalizing polyurethane cargo container.

One man photographed and then erased John's mathematic equations from the conference room's whiteboard. Another forcefully removed the notepad from Richard Alvis' hands, ignoring the mathematician's protests.

Through the conference room door, Tom could see men sitting at his news editor's station scanning assorted video disks and flash drives. After several minutes, the men located the flash drive containing Tom and Leah's January 26 interview with John at the Chatwal Hotel. The men placed the drive inside the cargo container with the other seized equipment.

The men began to leave now, some through the stairwell, others using the elevators. Once the cargo container was placed on the elevator, the man with the dark hair pulled a handheld radio from his hip and spoke into the device. "All secure," he said. Then he holstered his pistol, touched his fingers to his brow at Tom, and strolled casually from the room to join the last man holding the elevator door.

Tom was filled with rage. Next to him, his camera technician, Marco, stood staring at the open drive compartment on his video camera as if he wasn't certain what to do. The mathematician, Alvis, now stood and approached the empty whiteboard, shaking his head.

Saito sat silently for a moment and then rose slowly. "If you'll excuse me," the elderly physicist said. "It looks like we're done here, so I think it's better if I left." Without another word, the elderly physicist walked out of the room.

After a few more moments, Alvis said, "I think I'm going to leave too."

Tom simply nodded, too flustered to respond. He was trying to think of someone to call. He had a friend at the FBI but he wasn't sure they would be able to help.

Alvis took one last sad glance at the empty whiteboard and turned to walk out of the conference room. At that moment, Mary Kravets stepped into the conference room doorway, blocking Alvis' departure.

"What the hell was that?!" the office manager demanded, her eyes flashing.

Tom shook his head. "They took Clifton." The executive producer was still seething inside. Leah had warned him that this would likely happen, but this was America! There was such a thing as due process in this country! "They never showed me any warrant!" he said, "They just barged in and took everything!"

Marco now joined in, saying, "Damn bastards took my camera's freaking memory drive!" The young technician angrily threw open his camera case and began disassembling the tripod. "Biggest damn story in the world," he growled,

338

"and we've got nothing to show for it!"

Mary suddenly brightened and said, "Well, maybe we do."

Tom looked up. Marco too stopped his activity and looked up at the office manager.

"Excuse me," Mary said, brushing past Alvis. The stout woman walked around the conference table towards the large potted plant by the window. "I was curious about what was going on," she said, glancing apologetically at Tom. She stopped then by the plant and gently pushed back a layer of sphagnum moss covering the soil in the pot.

"First, Vaughn goes off to India and London with some strange man," she continued, "and then you rearrange an entire week's programming schedule without any explanation."

Underneath the moss lay Mary's red-cased cell phone. The office manager had concealed her phone under the moss when she had dumped the water from the pitcher earlier that morning. She held the phone up now and, from where he was sitting, Tom could see the device was still recording. Alvis took a step towards the large woman, staring at the phone. "Thank God!" the mathematician whispered.

"Sorry boss," Mary said, "but when you're the office manager, sometimes that means you have to manage the boss too."

Chapter 34

"Pride in their port, defiance in their eye,
I see the lords of humankind pass by."
~ Oliver Goldsmith
Irish novelist, playwright and poet
(1728 – 1774 AD)

John was escorted swiftly outside and down the building steps by the two men who had handcuffed him in the conference room. The two guards with the sub-machine guns followed close behind, watching him closely. The men had been forewarned about John's skills and were taking no chances. Nearby, the Anthony Red Hots cart stood abandoned, its operator and customers having been chased away by armed men assaulting the nearby building.

The men placed John inside one of several large SUVs parked on the street. They left the vehicle door facing the building open and one of the guards took a position standing in the open door, aiming the muzzle of his sub-machine gun at John.

After several minutes, other men began to exit the building. The cargo container containing John's MTY device and the other electronics seized from the conference room was loaded into the rear of one of the vehicles.

The man with the dark hair now emerged. He paused and spoke briefly with one of the men standing on the building steps. The second man nodded, walked to John's vehicle, and climbed into the driver's seat. The dark-haired man then whistled and spun his finger in the air before climbing into the front seat next to the driver. The remaining men now began getting into the other parked vehicles. The guard standing in the open door climbed in next to John, jamming the muzzle of his weapon into John's ribs as he closed the car door behind him. The man with the dark hair looked back once to verify John was secured and then tapped the driver, motioning for him to proceed.

Like a flock of birds scattering when a cat approaches, the vehicles departed rapidly, some proceeding straight ahead, others turning and driving back down the street. John watched the dark-haired man closely as they drove. After several minutes, he decided to venture a question.

"May I ask where we're going?"

The dark-haired man turned and spoke casually, "We're taking a helicopter out of the city." He then turned back and began typing something on a mobile phone.

John nodded and looked around. They were following one of the SUVs ahead. When he glanced behind, he could see the vehicle with the cargo container following close behind.

Attempting to escape never crossed John's mind. Indeed, he was exceedingly pleased with the situation. He was being taken into the heart of William's organization and he was frankly relieved to not have been summarily shot inside the conference room.

The vehicles proceeded south for almost an hour, crossing 145th Street bridge into Manhattan, and then south along FDR Drive. Just after they passed 34th Street, the motorcade pulled into a fenced paved lot bordered by the East

341

River to the east and line of tall buildings to the west. Several helicopters were tied down on helipads beyond the fence. The motorcade stopped and men from the lead vehicle quickly assumed guard positions around John's SUV.

"Out," the dark-haired man said as he opened his door. John's guard swiftly got out of the vehicle. John's hands were still cuffed so the guard took his arm and helped him slide out of the seat.

"Thank you," John said.

"Save it," the guard said, scowling. "Two of those you killed in London were friends of mine."

The black-haired man was standing near a gate in the fence talking to several people. After a few moments, he whistled, motioned to John and jerked his thumb towards a waiting white Bell 429 helicopter behind the fence. The scowling guard jammed the muzzle of his weapon into John's back, shoving him roughly towards the gate. Four other men followed close behind.

The helicopter was slowly spinning its blades on a helipad inside the fenced lot. John took a seat inside the aircraft and the five men filled the remaining seats around him; two behind, two in front, and the scowling guard next to him. All of the men were watching John closely and several had their weapons drawn. The cargo container containing John's MTY device was then loaded into the rear of the helicopter. Finally, after several minutes, the dark-haired man approached. He sat down in the co-pilot's seat and tapped the pilot's shoulder.

As the helicopter began to spin up its rotors, John struggled to control his apprehension. He knew such transports were widely used in this era, but this did very little to alleviate his concerns regarding the primitive craft. When the helicopter actually began to ascend, John clenched his hands tightly behind his back through his handcuffs.

It was a tense, almost 90-minute flight. When the helicopter mercifully began to descend. John could see they were approaching what appeared to be a small aerial transport facility. Several aircraft were tied down along the perimeter and hangers nearby suggested on-site maintenance and storage activity.

When they finally landed, John stepped out onto the helipad, surrounded by his guards. The dark-haired man now pulled a mobile phone from his pocket and began walking towards two large grey SUVs parked near one of the hangers. John could see two men waiting by the SUVs as the dark-haired man approached.

While John waited with his guards, he asked Fouray to scan for any wireless carriers nearby.

"There are numerous nodes within range," Fouray responded.

John considered what to do. He couldn't risk sending any communications to Leah that might be traced through the network to her friend's address. After several minutes, he decided to send an email to Tom Pierce. He knew the producer's email was likely being monitored, but the message might get through and he trusted the producer to safely relay its contents to Leah without compromising her location.

He began to compose a message. Before he could finish, however, the dark-haired man returned from his inspection of the two vehicles. He gestured towards John and spoke to the surrounding guards.

"Take his cuffs off."

The guards hesitated, glancing at one another. The scowling guard with the sub-machine gun asked, "Are you sure sir?" He added, "You read the London report on this guy."

The dark-haired man shrugged and said, "The order came from the director herself. Take off his cuffs."

While one of the guards began to remove his handcuffs, the dark-haired man now spoke to John.

"You understand that if you attempt to escape, or engage in any violence whatsoever, these men will blow your head off."

John nodded, "I understand." He rubbed his wrists where the cuffs had dug into his skin and began stretching his arms and shoulders. The five guards immediately stepped back and those who had not yet drawn their weapons now did so.

The dark-haired man appeared satisfied and gestured to two of the guards. "Get the container loaded," he said. Then, glancing back at the waiting grey SUVs, he nodded towards John and added, "Get him loaded too."

John looked at the waiting SUVs and asked, "Where are we going?"

This time, however, the dark-haired man did not respond. Instead, he just motioned the guards towards the waiting vehicles.

John was placed inside one of the grey SUVs and one of the two men who were waiting by the vehicles earlier now sat down next to him. John noticed the man had his hand on his holstered pistol and appeared to be wearing some kind of rigid vest under his shirt. The man's companion then got into the driver's seat and John saw that he was similarly armed and attired. When the cargo container had been loaded into the back of their vehicle, the dark-haired man climbed into the same seat as John, sandwiching John between himself and the other man.

The remaining guards now occupied the second SUV and as the two vehicles began driving towards the airfield's service gate, John noticed a sign with the words, "Leesburg Executive Airpark" hanging from the fence. He added that information to the email message he was composing for Tom Pierce.

A few minutes later they turned onto the Dulles Greenway toll road. After passing the toll station, the driver pulled a mobile phone from his pocket and spoke into the device.

"Leesburg Units 1 and 2 en-route. ETA about 40 minutes."

John turned to the dark-haired man sitting next to him and asked, "40 minutes to where?"

As before, the dark-haired man ignored his question and simply continued reading from his mobile device.

John took this opportunity to finish composing his message for Tom Pierce and instructed Fouray to send the email to the producer.

"Message transmitted," Fouray replied.

They drove now in silence for almost 20 minutes. From the signs they were passing, John realized they were heading into Washington D.C. They crossed the Potomac River at the Arland D. Williams Jr. Memorial Bridge and John looked around with interest, taking notice of several historic structures in the distance that no longer existed in his time. Most striking

345

of these was the Washington Monument. The tall obelisk had been destroyed during the American Conflict when ISSA socialist forces had retreated from the capital in August 2041. Where the spiraling structure had once risen above the city, the grassy mall in John's time now housed the American Conflict Memorial.

Several minutes later, their vehicle drove under a large multi-story concrete building supported by rows of tall columns. The driver stopped the SUV next to a dark service door and three of the guards in the trailing vehicle immediately exited and took up guard positions around John's vehicle. John was then extracted and taken swiftly through the dark service door. Once inside the building, he was searched again and then marched to a nearby elevator. When the elevator door closed, John noticed the name, "Forrestal" printed on a maintenance plate beneath the elevator's control panel.

"You are likely inside the James Forrestal building," Fouray suggested. "The Forrestal building was a government-occupied structure utilized by the Department of Energy during this era."

When the elevator door opened again, John was escorted down a long corridor into a large conference room. There were approximately 30 people already inside the room and all conversation abruptly ceased when John entered. A man wearing a military uniform pulled out one of the chairs surrounding a large rectangular table.

"Please sit," he said, gesturing to the chair.

John sat down. The three guards who had escorted him from the SUV now took up positions by the door. There were two video cameras mounted on tripods across the table from

John and a technician now turned on the cameras as an elderly heavyset man with thick glasses approached carrying a brown binder. The man stopped across the table and opened the binder. He glanced at the video technician and, when the technician nodded, the elderly man turned and addressed John.

"You are John Clifton," the man said, "a time traveler."

John nodded, and said, "Yes."

There was an audible stir in the room following that flat admission. The elderly man, however, simply began to read from a paper inside the binder.

"The signatory below affirms and acknowledges that he is not a citizen of the present United States of America. The signatory makes no claims of citizenship or residency with the present United States of America and specifically disclaims any reliance on the laws, rights, and privileges granted to its present citizens. The signatory shall be treated in accordance with the rules and policies governing expatriate foreign nationals."

The man now removed a document and placed it on the table in front of John. The document bore the Interpol logo. The man continued reading.

"Further, the signatory has been advised of an Interpol Red Notice regarding an extradition request filed by the present British government charging the signatory with multiple counts of murder, theft, interference with public transit and safety systems, assault, and espionage."

The heavy-set man now stopped and looked down at John over his thick glasses.

"Do you understand the statement I have just read to you?" he asked.

347

When John nodded, the man removed the statement from his binder and placed it on the conference table in front of John.

"Please sign the statement," he said, handing John a pen.

John now looked at the man and at the other men in the room. "As long as I am not mistreated," John said, "I will be happy to cooperate." Then he signed his name to the paper.

For the next five hours, John was subjected to an intense interrogation. Most of those questioning him appeared to be scientists or engineers with, in John's mind, an extremely rudimentary understanding of physics and mathematics. Three of the men in the room were dressed in uniforms and John noted they appeared deferential towards an older, white-haired man in a suit sitting in the back of the room. The white-haired man appeared to be in charge, directing the interrogation with a nod here, a pointed finger there.

The interrogators were very interested in the workings of John's MTY device's fusion reactor and its quantum control processor. They presented John with photographs of the device showing its control unit's covering now removed. They were obviously attempting to disassemble the unit but many of its components were clearly too advanced for them to remove with confidence. At one point, one of the interrogators asked John if disconnecting the fusion reactor's data coupler would harm the controller's quantum circuits.

"No," John responded, "disconnecting the reactor's data coupler wouldn't harm the controller, but it would likely trigger a fusion detonation since the controller also maintains the reactor's cryogenic cooling plant."

When John said that, three of the uniformed men hastily

left the room while dialing their mobile phones.

After nearly five hours of questioning, they finally brought John something to eat. The tray of meatloaf, green beans, and mashed potatoes had clearly come from an employee cafeteria located somewhere inside the building. While he was eating, John took the opportunity to send a second email to Tom Pierce. Fouray had reported no un-monitored nodes within the building, so John instructed the datstem to tie into one of the many wireless nodes outside the building.

"Connection established," Fouray responded. "What do you wish to transmit?"

John thought for a moment. He began by identifying his location inside the Forrestal building. He described the statement the elderly man had asked him to sign, his interrogator's basic knowledge of physics and mathematics, and the general focus of their questioning. He knew that Leah would be worrying about how he was being treated so he also mentioned he had been provided with something to eat. Fouray transmitted the message as John was finishing his meal.

It was now after 9:00 PM. Several men who had been in the room for the last 5 hours now began making preparations to leave. As they were making their exit, a man who John had not seen before now sat down at the table opposite from John. This man was balding, in his 50s, and dressed in a casual suit. He also had a pistol holstered on his hip. Unlike John's earlier interrogators, however, this man did not appear to be trained in either engineering or physics. His mode of questioning suggested he came from a law enforcement or investigative background.

349

For the next two hours, the man queried John about his purpose for transiting to Austin. He repeatedly questioned John about his mission objectives and the accident at the 2014 Austin music festival that had stranded John in the past.

John began to grow frustrated. He did not understand why the man was repeatedly asking him the same questions. Responding to its host's frustration, Fouray explained that this was a well-known tactic employed by law enforcement in this era to determine whether a suspect was telling the truth.

"They did not have bio-cognitive interfaces at this time," Fouray explained, "so an interrogator would repeatedly question a subject in different ways about the same topic. If the subject changed their answers, then the interrogator would know the subject was not being truthful."

"What a waste of time!" John fumed silently.

"It may be a waste of time," Fouray replied, "but the technique does work."

The bald man now asked John to describe, once again, the damage his MTY device had sustained at the Austin music festival. John queried Fouray for an explanation about the man's apparent fixation on the damage his MTY device had sustained. There was a brief pause as Fouray considered this question. After several moments, it responded.

"The interrogator does not believe your device was damaged in Austin as you have stated. He is likely aware of your mission to 2017 Baltimore to scan those Jewish Iraqi archive documents and he is aware that you transited out successfully after that mission. As a result, he believes you are not being truthful now about your device having been rendered inoperable in 2014."

John realized that Fouray was correct. The interrogator was clearly ignorant of the fundamentals of temporal physics. The man's questions suggested he had a linear, straight-line understanding of time. John sat back, looking at the man with a new understanding.

The man repeated his request.

This time, instead of answering, John shook his head, turned, and addressed the white-haired man sitting in the back of the room.

"If you plan on interviewing a temporal specialist," John said, "you need someone with at least a basic understanding of temporal theory to do the questioning."

John turned back to the startled interrogator. "I'm sure you are a fine investigator," he continued, "and you undoubtedly have considerable experience in questioning subjects from this era, but your lack of understanding of temporal mechanics makes it impossible for you to understand my answers. I'm sorry," John added, "but you're wasting everyone's time.

"I agree."

The response came from the conference room door. When John turned to identify its source, he saw Dr. Saito standing in the doorway, framed by the armed guards. The guards parted respectfully to allow the elderly physicist to enter the room.

"He is quite correct," Saito said as he walked towards the conference table. Saito was speaking to the collective group as he passed. "If you plan on interviewing a time traveler, you must have at least a basic understanding of temporal theory." The elderly physicist then frowned at the white-haired man sitting in the back of the room and added, "I said as much at our planning meeting on Monday."

The white-haired man simply shrugged and gestured for the elderly physicist to proceed. The balding interrogator across the table now stood, his face red, and gestured for the elderly physicist to take his seat. Saito sat down slowly, never taking his eyes off John.

"I'm sorry for the lengthy interrogation," Saito said apologetically, "but the powers that be insisted on conducting their own inquisition before turning you over to us."

"To us?" John queried. "You mean… to yourself and Williams?"

The physicist smiled and nodded. "Myself, Williams, and others," he said. "Williams kept telling us to watch for another temporal specialist but she didn't have any details. The project team has had scanning teams deployed to the surrounding cities for more than two years."

John nodded. "Is that what I encountered in Baltimore in 2017?"

Saito nodded, "Undoubtedly. Your subsequent disappearance, after our people detected you, caused considerable confusion. You see, Williams had told us the other temporal specialist would be stranded in our time and unable to transit away."

John nodded, "Williams was correct. I am stranded. My presence in 2017 Baltimore was the result of an earlier, unrelated tripback mission."

Saito nodded and grinned, "Williams deduced that was the case. She told the scanning units to continue their surveillance and disregard the Baltimore incident entirely. Our

Director of Security insisted she must be wrong… kept arguing for a sweep of Baltimore." Saito shook his head in derision.

John gestured at the men in the room then and asked, "So, what happens now? I'd like to get some rest."

Saito nodded and sat back in his chair. "Oh, we're done here I think." He turned now, finding the white-haired man in the back of the room, and spoke over the men between them.

"We are done here, Mr. Secretary. Correct?"

The white-haired man in the back of the room grudgingly nodded. He stood slowly and left the room, taking the remaining military personnel and several of the other attendees with him. After the exodus, there were still about a dozen men left in the room, including the three armed guards. Saito now turned and spoke to one of the remaining men.

"What's the status of our transportation?"

The man retrieved a mobile phone from his pocket and dialed.

"This is D.C. Unit 1. Mad Dog just left so we're ready to proceed. What's the transportation status? … Look! It's after 11:30 already and it's an 8-hour drive to Oak Ridge… Uh huh… Right… Is everything ready there?... Well, tell them we're ready to go on our end. Right… Ok. That sounds good."

The man disconnected the call and said to Saito, "20 minutes Professor."

Saito nodded. He looked back at John and said, "We'll be leaving shortly. It's a long drive so you'll be able to get some sleep on the way."

John nodded. He took that moment to instruct Fouray to send a short email to Tom Pierce, informing the producer that he was being taken to Oak Ridge, Tennessee.

After a few moments, Saito glanced at the men nearby and then lowered his voice. "We have a few minutes before we need to leave. I would like to continue our conversation from lunch today. Would that be ok?"

John nodded, "Certainly."

"At lunch," the elderly physicist began, "you said that a temporal specialist cannot kill someone who is destined to do something important in the future?"

"Yes," John said, "that's true. Time will resolve such an action to preserve the shape of the future... to prevent their death."

The man who had called about the transport now checked his mobile phone and announced, "Let's pack it up, people." The men in the room began to gather their things. Saito nodded and turned his attention back to John.

"Williams told me I am destined to be an important figure in history." He looked quizzically at John and asked, "Is that true?"

"Yes," John said.

Saito smiled now, a strange smile that made John uncomfortable. "So..." the elderly man said, "I guess that means I'm sort of immortal, doesn't it?"

When John did not respond, Saito continued, "I mean, until I fulfill my destiny, no one can stop me, can they?" The physicist was studying John closely, watching his reaction.

John frowned.

The guards now began retrieving their gear and checking their weapons. Seeing their preparations, Saito leaned forward across the table and whispered.

"Do you know why ancient civilizations created gods,

Mr. Clifton?"

John shook his head, disturbed by the physicist's question.

Saito smiled and said, "The ancients needed to believe in something that could exist beyond their brief span of years. A god, you see, is immortal."

As the guards now approached, Saito added, "And immortal beings don't need to be concerned with the passage of time."

Chapter 35

Saito watched the computer screen closely, consumed with professional curiosity as the image repainted, exposing with each new slice an amazing cerebral fractal. The technician operating the scanning equipment was becoming frustrated, but Saito found the process fascinating. To see a brain thus revealed always filled him with an appreciation for the incredible computing organ that was the human mind.

The technician abruptly sat back, shaking his head in frustration as he dialed his cell phone. A moment later, he spoke into the phone.

"Nothing!" he said, exasperation evident in his voice. "What am I doing wrong?"

After a brief pause, the technician said, "Hold on," and then placed the phone on the desk. He touched the device's speaker button and a woman's voice abruptly emerged from the device, overly loud in the confined space. The phone caught her speaking mid-sentence.

"...have to decrease the cyclic rate to ultra-short echo-time imaging, and then configure the scanner for single-photon emission computed tomography. You won't see it on a normal scan."

As the voice was speaking, the technician made the adjustments and re-initialized the scan cycle. This time, a complex web of bio-circuitry slowly emerged on the screen, ghostly branches emanating from a strange device embedded near the subject's brain stem. The device and its web were hard to see on the scan, almost transparent against the gallium isotope-infused bio-matter they encompassed. The strands faded in and out, fluctuating with the scanning device's resonance variations.

Saito stared in awe, shaking his head as the technician began recording the resulting images.

"It's coming through now," the technician spoke to his phone. "I'll send the images shortly." He touched the phone and disconnected the call.

John lay strapped tightly to the table, his head secured by a plastic helmet that restricted its movement. Above and below the table, two large boxes hummed and clicked with activity. The boxes, extending from a large circular CT scanning machine, resembled an oversized vise preparing to squeeze his head.

John was inside a high-security facility located somewhere within the Oak Ridge National Laboratory campus. The drive from Washington D.C. to Oak Ridge, Tennessee, had been largely uneventful. As promised, he had been allowed to sleep for several hours on the back seat of the large utility vehicle. Three armed men and Dr. Saito had occupied the other seats but they had not engaged him in conversation.

When they had arrived at the complex, an opaque cloth had been placed over John's head while he was still inside the vehicle, and he had breathed in the acrid smell of a chemical anesthetic and lost consciousness. When he woke, he had found himself inside the CT scanning room secured to the table. Once he was fully awake, a technician had entered and administered an injection that Fouray reported as being slightly radioactive. It was then that John realized they were attempting to identify his datstem device.

An embedded datstem would not show up on an x-ray, MRI, or CT scan. However, the device could be rendered visible against tissue infused with a gamma-emitting radioisotope and scanned with a properly configured photon tomographic scanner.

John had endured the scanning for more than an hour now, strapped tightly to the flat table inside the circular CT machine.

Suddenly, the boxes above and below John's head stopped humming. The boxes swiveled up out of the way and the table extended out from the CT machine. The large machine then powered off, it's spinning magnets slowing and then finally stopping altogether.

Silence.

After several minutes, John heard a door open behind his head.

"All the world's a stage, and all the men and women merely players."

It was a woman's voice.

John tried to turn his head to see who had entered, but the plastic helmet was still bolted to the table and the helmet completely impeded his head movement.

The voice continued, "They have their exits and their entrances, and one man in his time plays many parts."

A tall athletic woman with short brown hair now stepped around the table into view.

"Do you know who said that John?" the woman asked as she began to loosen his straps.

"Williams?!" John asked, recognizing the temporal specialist.

Theresa Williams smiled, shaking her head. "No," she said, "it was Shakespeare, actually."

Williams unscrewed the bolts securing the plastic helmet to the table and John sat up, removing the cumbersome device from his head.

"You've gotten old, John." Williams shook her head as she appraised her fellow specialist. "How many years has it been since we last met?"

John considered this for a moment, and then said, "14 close... 4 distant."

Williams appeared surprised. "You've been here for 4 years?"

John nodded, stretching his back. "I transited out in 2151, 14 years after you disappeared. My target was 2014 Austin."

The woman shook her head again and then grinned. "You were just a junior specialist when we met. Didn't you transfer over from research?"

John nodded, "That's correct."

"14 close and 4 distant, huh?" Williams said, measuring John again with her eyes. "That's a long time. It's been 3 years for me here. I thought that was bad enough! How did you manage it here for 4 years?"

"It wasn't too difficult," John responded. Then, he tapped the now-silent CT machine. "So, what's this all about?"

Williams shrugged. "Verification," she said. With that, the lithe woman turned and walked towards the door. "Come on," she said. "We'll have a talk."

John followed. When they exited the room, he realized that he was underground. The thick concrete walls, reinforced ceiling trusses, and the absence of any windows in the hallway suggested a subterranean facility of some kind. As they walked along the long corridor, Williams turned and spoke to him.

"Was it you that we detected in 2017… in Baltimore?"

"Yes."

"Different tripback?" she asked.

John nodded. "Yes," he said. "My last tripback before the one to Austin."

Williams nodded and said, "I assumed as much."

She stopped outside a conference room door. "When the scanning units reported the target had transited out, I knew it had to be a distinct tripback."

Williams now entered the room and flipped on the lights. The room was empty save for a small oval table, chairs, and an unplugged monitor on the wall.

"What were you doing in Baltimore?" she asked, motioning to the chairs.

John sat down and said, "I was sent to scan some Iraqi Jewish documents archived in a museum there."

Williams sat across the table. "Interesting," she said, nodding. "You can tell me about that later."

John leaned forward now. "I read your tripback file," he said, watching the female specialist closely. "It said your singularity lost cohesion when you were transiting out." He paused to allow Williams to respond if she wished. Williams, however, remained silent, showing no indication of either alarm or surprise.

John continued, "The CTI observer called in a scanning team from Geneva, but they were unable to recalibrate your singularity."

Williams folded her arms and said, "What's your point, John?"

John sat back in his chair. "It's strange that the scanning team wasn't able to recalibrate your singularity," he said. "Less than an hour had passed. They should have been able to calibrate it back into containment."

Williams shrugged, "Maybe their quantum scanner was misaligned. It happens you know."

John nodded, and then said, "Or... maybe they couldn't calibrate it back into containment because it wasn't truly released. Maybe it was still calibrated... but simply locked to a different quantum position?"

Williams made no reply.

John continued, "You're singularity's close event horizon was calibrated away, wasn't it?"

Williams slowly smiled. "You're smarter than most, John. You know your temporal theory, I'll give you that." She took a breath and nodded. "Yes," she said, "It was recalibrated and locked to a quantum position inside Blosch-Nishikawa's collider floor."

"So, you're not truly stranded here, are you?"

"No. Not stranded." The young woman grinned, shaking her head. She looked around the stark room and sighed. "I like to think of it as a voluntary exile. I haven't been back since I transited out, but I'll be going back very soon."

Suddenly John heard a soft buzzing sound. Williams pulled a mobile phone from her pocket and read its screen. She typed something onto the device screen and then returned the phone to her pocket.

"Unfortunately," she said, "we're not going to have time to talk about that. You see, the project is finished. We finished yesterday as a matter-of-fact. So, we're very busy today. We're packing up to transit back tonight."

"We?" John asked, shaking his head.

At that moment, the conference room door opened and two men entered.

John stared in shock. One of the men was Viktor Borodin! The large Georgian stood in the open doorway, grinning, obviously enjoying John's reaction. The other man, a large man with blonde hair, seemed strangely familiar, but John could not place where he had seen him.

Williams stood up. Speaking to the two men at the door, she said, "Take him to the security room on the main floor."

Turning back to John, Williams shrugged and said, "I'm sorry John, but whatever you intended to do here... you're too late."

Chapter 36

"To call woman the weaker sex is a libel;
it is man's injustice to woman.
If by strength is meant brute strength,
then, indeed, is woman less brute than man.
If by strength is meant moral power,
then woman is immeasurably man's superior."
~ Mohandas "Mahatma" Karamchand Gandhi
Leader of the Indian independence movement
(1869 – 1948 AD)

L eah waited anxiously by the bubbling fountain. It was cold! She wore the coat that Professor Nicholls had given her in London and it warmed her in the chilly morning air. The thick coat, silk scarf, and hat also provided her with a reasonable disguise.

It was almost 5:00 AM. There were already a considerable number of people in the plaza, despite the early hour. They were mostly early morning tourists or performers on their way into one of the nearby buildings. From where she sat, she was framed by the David Geffen Hall to the north, the David H. Koch Theater to the south, and the New York Opera House behind her. She was literally surrounded by the finest musicians, singers, and dancers in the world.

By arrangement, she had telephoned Tom from a remote pay phone at 3:00 AM that morning. Tom had related to her the three emails he had received from John the previous evening.

From the emails, it was clear that John was unharmed, but it was also clear that he was in custody and being transferred to Oak Ridge, Tennessee.

Leah was determined to try to help John if she could. She had asked Tom to meet her "in 2 hours at the place we attended the Christmas concert". It was an obscure enough message. Several years earlier, shortly after she had joined APN, she and Tom had attended a Christmas performance by the New York Philharmonic Orchestra at the David Geffen Hall. If someone had been listening to their phone conversation, it would be extremely unlikely they would be able to determine their rendezvous location from that vague message.

Leah's only concern was that Tom might be followed. From where she sat, she could observe the entrance to the building. If Tom arrived alone, she would signal him. If he were followed, she could exit through the plaza or conceal herself within any of the surrounding buildings. It was a risk, but she needed to speak with Tom in person.

At that moment, Leah spotted a man walking south into the plaza. It was Tom! He was walking towards the front entrance to the David Geffen Hall building. He appeared to be alone and Leah could not see anyone either observing or following him.

Leah realized then that she was going to have to take a chance. The men who had captured John were professionals and it would be unlikely she would be able to spot them even if they were nearby. She had to trust that Tom had taken sufficient precautions to avoid being followed. She took a deep breath, stood up, and began walking towards the building.

Tom was standing inside the main lobby, looking around nervously.

"Tom!"

The executive producer turned, relief on his face.

"Leah! Are you ok?" he asked, giving her a brief hug.

"Yes," Leah nodded. Then she asked, "Are you sure you weren't followed?"

Tom shrugged and said, "Who can say. I took a taxi to the subway and purposefully took the wrong train. Then, I switched to another train that took me to the 66th Street Lincoln Center station and I walked the rest of the way here. I'm pretty sure I wasn't followed."

Leah nodded, and said, "Sounds good, but let's find somewhere more private to talk."

The two producers walked further inside the spacious building and then took the elevator up to the second tier balcony overlooking the orchestra pit and main floor seating below. They were completely alone now except for a janitor vacuuming somewhere beneath the balcony.

Leah looked at the producer, tears in her eyes.

"They're going to kill him."

Tom shook his head. "We don't know that!"

"He killed 10 of their people in London," she said. "Perhaps more! Of course they're going to kill him!"

Tom shook his head. "Look, Leah," he began, "I want to help as much as you do." The producer's face grew red now as he spoke. "I mean, they barged into our building, stuck their guns in my face, seized our guest, and confiscated our company's property, without so much as a by-your-leave! No warrant!... Nothing!"

365

The producer took a deep breath, trying to calm himself. After a few moments, he continued.

"What they did was illegal as hell," he said, "but what can we do?!"

Leah wiped her eyes and looked at her friend. "We can go get him! We can tell them they either release John to us, or we will tell the world what they're doing."

Tom opened his mouth, but before he could speak, Leah continued.

"We've got press credentials and friends in the media industry," she said, determination in her face. "The last thing they want is for someone to report what they're doing! We'll tell them, release John to us and we'll remain silent. Refuse, and they can watch the story on the evening news!"

Tom shook his head, uncertain. Leah continued, "We can prepare a statement or something in advance. Leave it with someone we trust, and then…"

Tom interrupted her, "Look, we're not dealing with just anyone here. These people are connected, you know? I was going to tell you, they blocked my email account this morning."

"What?"

The producer nodded. "When I tried to log in to my email this morning, my password wouldn't work, and when I tried to reset it, it said the account had been suspended."

Leah sat silent, not sure what to say.

Tom continued, "If they can do that, then they are connected, you understand?"

Leah nodded and then said, "You have printed copies of John's emails, don't you?"

366

Tom nodded. "Yes. Mary always makes me a hard copy. I have John's original December 12th email that Mary gave me that morning before the interview, and I printed off the three emails that arrived yesterday before my account was suspended. Plus, Alvis transcribed the meeting notes from Mary's phone. He sent those to me last night.

As he was talking, Tom retrieved a flash drive from his pocket and handed it to Leah. "I made you a copy," he said.

Leah took the drive and nodded, considering what to do. After a few moments, she said, "Do you still have the video from our first interview with John at the Chatwal hotel... and those future historical documents that John emailed to us that afternoon?"

Tom nodded, "Yes. I copied all of that onto two flash drives last week. I put one in my safety deposit box and the other one somewhere no one could find it." He smiled and winked at her.

Leah suddenly laughed. She knew where Tom had hidden the additional drive and he was correct. No one would ever find it there!

The company kept its old files and archival footage stored at an aging records management facility in New Jersey. The place was a turn-of-the-century brick building filled from floor to ceiling with musty boxes and rusting file cabinets, many long abandoned by their owners. If you didn't know precisely which cabinet contained your company's documents, you would never find them. The cabinets themselves were numbered, not labeled.

Tom grinned, enjoying her laugher. He retrieved a pen from his pocket and tore off a piece of paper from an old store receipt in his pocket. He told her then that he had hidden the flash drive in an abandoned cabinet inside the storage building, inside a file folder containing yellowing legal documents from a long-defunct law firm. As he spoke, he wrote down the shelf and cabinet number on the paper.

"No one," he said with a smile as he handed her the paper, "will ever find that other drive without this."

"So…" Leah said slowly, rubbing the paper in her hand, "here's what we'll do. I'll write up something explaining what's happening and leave a copy with Liz. Then, we'll go to Oak Ridge and tell them they release John to us or they can watch everything on the news."

Tom shook his head, "I don't know…"

"They're going to kill him, Tom."

Tom took a deep breath and then nodded, "Ok."

Leah hugged her friend hard. "Thank you!"

The producer shook his head and shrugged, "What the hell. If we pull this off, we'll have an incredible story to tell! The world's first confirmed time traveler! Who knows? Maybe we'll win an Emmy!"

Leah smiled and said, "I'll need time to type up a letter for Liz and drop it at her house, so let's meet back here in 2 hours. It's a long drive to Oak Ridge, so we should leave as soon as possible."

Tom was already on his feet. He checked his watch and said, "It's 5:24 now, so I'll rent a car and meet you by the fountain at 7:30 AM."

"Right."

Chapter 37

"Corruption is a tree, whose branches are
of an immeasurable length: they spread
ev'rywhere; and the dew that drops from thence
hath infected some chairs and stools of authority."
~ John Fletcher
Jacobean playwright
(1579 – 1625 AD)

Borodin laughed again after Williams left the small conference room. The large Georgian was enjoying John's shock. "We make big surprise for you, Clifton. Yes?"

John nodded but said nothing. He was truly amazed to see the burly specialist.

"I almost forget about you. Has been long time."

John caught the temporal reference and asked, "How long have I been gone?"

Borodin thought for a moment, and then said, "More than 7 years."

The other man, who Borodin now introduced as "Larsen", pulled a pistol from his belt and motioned for John to stand. The two men took John from the small conference room and escorted him down the long corridor towards an elevator.

John considered what Borodin had said. If it was true, that more than 7 years had passed since he had transited to Austin, it would be 2158 now. From his conversation with

Williams, John knew the female specialist's MTY device still had an active singularity with its close event horizon repositioned inside the Blosch-Nishikawa building in Norway. The presence of the Borodin here meant Williams was not alone and she also had the assistance of both personnel and resources from the future. This strongly suggested Williams' MTY device was unlocked as the Primary AI had suspected. John decided to try to confirm this hypothesis.

"Borodin?" he asked.

The large man looked at John, annoyed. "What?"

"Why did it take Williams 21 years to finish the project? I mean, she transited out in 2137, and you said it's been 7 years since I disappeared, so that would make it... 2158 now, right?"

Borodin nodded, "Yes. Is 2158 now."

"So, what took Williams so long?"

They had reached the elevator and Borodin pushed the call button before he answered.

"Time differentiation," the big man said. "Williams sometimes asked for tech not yet developed. It takes us time to deliver. So, Blosch set a re-calibration schedule. Every year, Blosch re-calibrated distant EPM backward. So short time for Williams but long time for us."

John nodded. He understood now. Blosch-Nishikawa was employing a technique called "Time Differentiation", more commonly called "Time Slipping". They were using EPM calibration equipment on their collider floor to frequently re-calibrate Williams' singularity, causing it to re-wind, or re-focus it's distant, or past event horizon backward, to a point shortly after its last calibration date, while allowing the close, or present event horizon to proceed forward in normal time.

370

Using this technique, years might elapse in the future, while the specialist's event horizon in the past might advance only a few months or years.

The technique would allow Blosch-Nishikawa to take as long as they needed in the future to deliver on any request Williams happened to make. From Williams' perspective, she would make a request and see it delivered almost instantly. For the 21 years that had apparently passed for Blosch-Nishikawa in the future, Williams had experienced only 3 years of actual time here in the past.

The elevator door opened and the men stepped inside. From the lighted "B3" button inside the elevator, John surmised they were 3 floors beneath the surface. Borodin pushed the last button marked "B4". Then, he inserted a metal key into a slot beneath the button and turned the key.

The elevator began to descend.

In response to John's curious gaze, Borodin shrugged and muttered, "Primitive tech".

The elevator slowed and then stopped. When the door opened again, John emerged onto an incredible sight. He was standing inside a long observation corridor of some kind. In front of him, beyond a series of glass windows, a vast hall could be seen, filled with seemingly endless rows of server cabinets, each containing stacked data servers. Though the equipment was primitive by John's standards, the room rivaled RJCom's massive archive hall in size. It had to be the largest data center in the world at this time!

The devices were connected by a web of overhead data cables to a large gray-walled cylindrical device in the front of the room. As John watched, the gray walls of the device rippled

371

characteristically.

The device was a quantum computer! From the primitive refrigeration equipment attached to its side, and the contemporary monitors sitting on a nearby workstation, John could see it had been constructed using period components, but it was undoubtedly a quantum computer.

While he struggled to take in all of this, John's attention was quickly directed to one object. Near the side of the vast hall, next to what appeared to be a large metal cabinet, an iridescent black void shimmered and swirled slowly inside an ultraviolet field.

An EPM portal!

The nearby cabinet must contain Williams' MTY device. As John watched, a figure suddenly emerged from the blackness. It was a man dressed in a green and blue Blosch Nishikawa technician's uniform. The man crossed the floor and spoke to one of the other men standing by the quantum computer. After a few moments, both men walked back towards the spiraling blackness and stepped through, vanishing from sight.

John was shocked. Though he had suspected Williams of having an unlocked MTY device, he had never before seen one in operation. Strict manufacturing controls had been imposed on the three CTI-certified companies since their founding, requiring all MTY devices to be manufactured with genetic and neustem locks. These locking mechanisms restricted an MTY device's use to only the assigned temporal specialist. Blosch-Nishikawa must have created a new type of MTY device; a device without those locking mechanisms.

Viktor Borodin was standing behind John, enjoying his

shock. After allowing him to observe for several moments, Borodin pushed him towards a nearby door. It was a reinforced steel door with a tiny plexiglass window and a sign above that read 'Security Holding'.

"In you go," Borodin said cheerfully, shoving John into the small room.

When the door was closed and locked, Borodin pushed a button on a speaker panel next to the door.

"I say goodbye now, Clifton. We are finished. Project is completed and we all return tonight. You must stay here I think."

"Before you go," John said, "I want to ask you something."

Borodin hesitated, scowling, and then said, "What must you know?"

"Sai Patel," John said. "Did you kill him?"

Borodin's scowl slowly turned into a smile. "It was easy thing," he said, nodding. "I trigger ansel wave inside transport gravimetric capacitor. Easy to do! So, after short flight, capacitor overloads... shorts out gravimetric controller, and..." The large man smacked his hands together, simulating a crash to the ground.

John stood silent, rage filling his chest.

Borodin frowned then and said, "Patel should not have interfered." Then he added, "You should not have interfered also."

With that, the large man smacked his hands together again and smiled wide, showing his large teeth. He pointed at John through the small window and walked away, laughing.

Throughout the long day, for nearly 8 hours, John

watched the activity in the hall through the small window. They were clearly shutting down the project. Technicians were busy disassembling equipment while others began packing the equipment to return. By noon, with most of the equipment removed, the technicians began to transit out in ones and twos.

John spotted Williams only once. In the early afternoon, he spotted the female specialist when she stepped into view through a door on the opposite side of the hall. She was accompanied by Borodin and Larsen and paused near the quantum computer to engage a technician in a discussion. Williams appeared angry about something, gesturing with her hands and pointing at the large device. When she turned to leave, she glanced briefly through the long glass observation windows at John's security room before walking back through the same door.

It was nearly 4:00 PM now. When John checked the hall again from his small window, he could see no one working. The hall was dark except for the immediate area around the quantum computer. The quantum computer itself had been powered down, it's surface still and quiet. Disconnected data cables lay strewn about the floor. Williams' singularity, however, still shimmered and swirled slowly near the far wall. Clearly, Williams had not yet transited back.

John sat down again. He could not figure out how to escape from the small room! Fouray too was at a loss. If the door had been secured by an electronic or computer-controlled lock, it would have posed no problem for the embedded datstem. This door, however, utilized a primitive mechanical lock, a series of metal tumblers affected by a corresponding metal "key". Fouray could not access nor affect it in any way.

Fouray also reported no wireless networks within range. The facility was apparently deep enough underground to inhibit wireless radio transmission.

John thought he heard someone speaking. He stood again and peered through the small window. Just beyond the row of observation windows, John could see Williams speaking with Saito. They were standing near the quantum computer and appeared to be arguing about something.

At that moment, Viktor Borodin opened the door at the opposite side of the hall. He held the door while Larsen strode into the large hall, a pistol in his hand. Larsen then turned and spoke to someone behind him, gesturing with his pistol. Williams and Saito stopped their discussion and turned towards the two men.

What John saw next caused his heart to skip a beat.

Through the open door walked Leah and Tom Pierce.

Chapter 38

John stood on the floor of the large hall holding Leah's hand by the now-quiet quantum computer. The associate producer was doing her best to portray an air of quiet confidence, but John could feel the tension and fear in her grip. Leah was staring across the floor at the shimmering blackness of Williams' singularity. The ominous void, framed by its ultraviolet event horizon, seemed to swirl like the eye of a hurricane; a micro-storm of awesome power with a mysterious black eye at its center.

John had been extremely dismayed to see Leah and Tom when they had walked into the hall. He had wondered how Williams could have caught the two producers, but when he saw Tom Pierce remove an envelope from his pocket and hand it to Williams, he realized that they had not been captured. They were attempting some form of rescue.

Williams had immediately sent Borodin and Larsen to retrieve John from the security room and John had been brought into the large hall. Leah had asked him if he was alright and then slipped her hand into his. The gesture had not gone unnoticed by Borodin, who had stared at the young producer with a disturbing expression on his face.

"A copy of that letter has been left with a trusted friend," Tom was now saying to Williams. "If we don't return with Mr. Clifton, then the story will be aired on every major network before the week is out."

Williams nodded. "I understand," she said. She carefully folded the paper and placed it back inside its envelope. Then, she handed the envelope back to Tom with a smile and said, "I refuse."

Tom frowned and said, "We're serious!"

Williams nodded, "Oh, I'm sure you are." Then she smiled again and said, "My answer is no."

Leah now spoke up, gesturing at the dark hall around them, "Are you willing to risk having your work here exposed to the world?"

Williams feigned confusion, "Our work?" The female temporal specialist glanced back at the endless rows of computer cabinets and then smiled. "Oh! You mean our research project to develop a new type of quantum computer? There's nothing secret about that! We've been published in several trade journals already." Williams then motioned dismissively towards the singularity and said, "As for the rest, it won't be here after tonight."

Saito now stared at Williams with a frown.

"We have proof of what you're doing here," Tom said.

"Proof?" Williams shook her head. "No," she said. "What you have is a story... a work of fiction that few will believe." Williams then nodded to Borodin and jerked her thumb forcefully at the large metal cabinet.

The large Georgian walked to the cabinet, removed an RFID keycard from his pocket, and touched it against the locking pad. An audible click was heard. Borodin then opened the cabinet and pulled a plastic bin from a shelf. From where he stood, John could see the bin contained his backpack and MTY device. The device had been partially disassembled and its fusion reactor core had been removed, but it was unmistakably the remains of his MTY device.

With a nod from Williams, Borodin heaved the contents of the bin into the center of the dark singularity. The components vanished without a sound.

"See," Williams said. "No proof." Facing John, Williams now frowned and said, "Sorry John. If RJCom wants its MTY device back, they can pick up the pieces on the Blosch-Nishikawa collider floor in 140 years."

John was struggling to control his expression. He tried not to stare at the open cabinet, but there on the shelf sat the AI processor! It was clearly an SDU's control processor, but this one was half-again as large as the standard fist-sized units with which he was familiar. The dark grey orb's surface rippled in the characteristic way of a quantum-entangled processor and it shimmered with the same grey metallic sheen.

The cabinet also contained William's MTY device. It was sitting beneath the processor on the bottom shelf of the cabinet. It seemed slightly smaller than a standard MTY device and there was a strange component mounted between its containment sphere and heat sink that John did not recognize.

Borodin now dropped the empty bin and walked back to rejoin Williams, giving John a smirk as he passed.

378

John tensed, struggling against his overwhelming sense of purpose. Borodin had left the cabinet door open! Every nerve in John's body screamed for him to leap forward, seize the processor, and run through the singularity, but he knew if he did that Leah and Tom would be killed.

Leah now pointed at the quantum computer in the center of the hall. "There's still that," she said defiantly. "You can't throw that through your wormhole."

Williams shrugged. "No need," she said casually. "We removed its quantum controller earlier this afternoon."

"What!?" Saito's head suddenly jerked up. The elderly physicist's face revealed shock and anger.

Williams continued, "There's nothing left there but a hundred kilos of primitive relays and data cables."

"You said I would be permitted to retain the quantum controller!" Saito said, fuming. "That was our agreement!"

Williams looked at the old man, an expression of incredulity in her eyes. Borodin and Larsen exchanged glances and Borodin took a step forward.

"No you don't!" Saito shouted. The old man had pulled a pistol from his pocket and now aimed it at Borodin.

"Drop your weapons!" Saito ordered.

When Borodin hesitated, Saito turned and pointed the pistol at Williams' face. "Drop your weapons," he said, "or I'll blow your boss' pretty head off!"

Borodin and Larsen exchanged glances again, and Larsen shrugged his shoulders. The two men now dropped their pistols to the floor.

At that moment, John took Tom and Leah by the arms and slowly began pulling them backward, away from the imminent confrontation.

"Professor," Williams said, shaking her head. "Don't be foolish." The young temporal specialist took a step towards the elderly man, her hand outstretched. "Hand me that weapon," she said.

John retreated further away out of the line of fire, pulling the two producers back with him.

Williams took another step towards the aging physicist. She snapped her fingers and said sharply "Come on professor. We don't have time for this nonsense."

The elderly professor, however, was clearly furious. "What about the quantum controller?!" he demanded, still pointing his pistol at Williams' face. "You wouldn't have been able to complete your precious project without my help! Do you deny promising the controller to me?!"

Williams dropped her hand and shook her head. "No," she said. "That was our agreement."

"Well?!" Saito demanded.

"I lied."

"You lied?!" Saito was apoplectic with rage.

John had almost reached the cabinet. The producers had allowed him to pull them out of the line of fire, oblivious to their closing proximity with the spinning portal. They were following the interaction between Saito and Williams closely.

Saito took careful aim now. "I helped you create your AI processor," he said, enunciating every word slowly. "You promised me the quantum controller in return! You do whatever you need to do to get that controller back here right now or I'm going to blow your head off!"

The aged man's hand was shaking as he drew a bead on

Williams' face.

Williams stood still and dropped her hands to her side. She spoke softly now. "I'll say this one last time. Drop the weapon professor, or I'm going to be forced to kill you."

John tensed and took a deep breath.

Saito, however, simply sneered. "You can't kill me!" he said. "Self-resolving causality! I'm destined to do something important, remember?!"

In a flash, Williams leapt forward. The female specialist moved with a speed the professor would not have believed possible. The old man fired but the shot flew into the darkness, ricocheting and whining through the cavernous hall. Williams' hand flew forward under the professor's outstretched arm now and the force of her blow broke one of the professor's ribs. She spun around, a deadly blur, twisting the pistol free from the professor's hand while simultaneously snapping his wrist. The aging physicist crumpled to the ground, grimacing in pain.

The moment Williams leapt forward, John jumped in front of Tom and Leah. He whirled to face the startled pair, grabbed them both by their forearms, and then threw himself backward onto the floor in front of the singularity. His momentum pulled the two producers off balance and they both stumbled forward into the swirling black vortex. Leah's scream was cut off instantly as she vanished, followed an instant later by Tom.

John quickly jumped to his feet and raced for the open cabinet door. Borodin shouted and scrambled to retrieve his dropped weapon but John had already seized the black orb from the cabinet shelf. As John dove into the center of the shimmering blackness, Borodin fired wildly.

381

Saito lay on the floor gasping and clutching his broken wrist. Williams stood over the elderly physicist with the pistol in her hand, fury contorting her face as she screamed at Borodin and Larsen.

"Go after them! Get that processor!"

Larsen quickly retrieved his discarded weapon from the floor and the two men charged towards the singularity.

"You fool!" Williams hissed, as she aimed the pistol at Saito.

"What about self-resolving causality?!" Saito sputtered. "I'm destined to do something important!"

Williams shook her head, scorn and derision in her face. "You already did!" she said.

Saito's gaze turned towards the cabinet and its now-empty shelf. As an expression of horrified awareness filled the elderly physicist's eyes, Williams fired.

Chapter 39

L eah stumbled, screaming, into a dimly-lit room. As she struggled to regain her balance, Tom Pierce crashed into her back, and the pair fell tumbling to the floor.

The two producers stood slowly and attempted to orient themselves to their surroundings. Behind them, the swirling black void shimmered in the room's dim lighting, the other side of the same obsidian cyclone they had faced inside the Oak Ridge lab. They were inside a different room, however, a smaller room filled with strange equipment. The bin that had contained John's backpack lay on the ground, its contents strewn about the floor. Two technicians stood nearby. They had been picking up the scattered components and now stared at the new arrivals in shock.

Tom had just assisted Leah to her feet when John suddenly appeared, leaping through the blackness to roll across the floor. The temporal specialist immediately scrambled to his feet and shouted, "Run!", startling the two technicians. John grabbed Leah's arm and began pulling her swiftly across the room towards a lighted archway opening onto an adjoining corridor. Tom Pierce followed close behind. One of the technicians shouted at them to stop while the other dropped the pieces of John's MTY device he had been retrieving and began chasing the trio.

John had visited the Blosch-Nishikawa campus only once, and that had been more than 10 years before he had transited out to Austin. He had toured the facility one afternoon as part of a group of visiting RJCom representatives. As he ran, he desperately tried to recall that earlier visit. He remembered that the company's collider floor, the room they had just entered, had been located through an archway similar to the one ahead, adjoining a hallway with several rooms reserved for specialist briefings and tripback preparation. Unfortunately, Fouray did not have any information on the Blosch-Nishikawa facility layout. Such information, the datstem reported, was considered proprietary.

The trio had almost reached the open archway when Borodin and Larsen suddenly burst through the singularity. The two men looked around swiftly. The technician standing by the portal now pointed frantically at the retreating group across the room.

With a shout, Borodin sprang forward. Larsen followed close behind. The two men began firing wildly as they ran and the bullets nicked and ricocheted against the wall in the back of the archway. One of the shots struck the pursuing technician in the back and the man grunted and collapsed to the floor.

John rounded the corner and spotted one of the briefing room doors he remembered from his earlier visit. "There!" he shouted, pointing at the door. The door opened automatically as they approached, startling the two producers. Leah hesitated but John bodily pushed her into the room with Tom following close behind. John pressed the locking pad on the door frame and the door slid closed and locked with a faint click as the room's lighting auto-engaged.

John knew it would not be long before an override code was transmitted, so he looked swiftly around the room. He was inside what appeared to be a typical briefing hall. It was similar to those at RJCom, with its domed planetarium-style ceiling and holo-emitters positioned around the room's perimeter. Several exit doors could be seen across the room, above and beyond the rows of stadium seats. Unfortunately, John could find nothing in the room to use as a weapon.

"John," Leah gasped, "What's happening?! Where are we?!"

At that moment, a loud pounding began against the locked door. The poly-plastic door was clearly not built for strength and shook with each impact.

"No time to explain," John said, pointing across the room. "Through those doors! Quickly!"

When they ran through the far doors, they found themselves inside another dimly-lit hallway. From the dark windows and the absence of visible staff, it was clearly after normal working hours. A maintenance SDU could be seen in the hallway ahead, cleaning the floor near a row of lifts.

John was torn. He was tempted to take one of the lifts to the building's transport deck, but it was unlikely he would be able to utilize the company's transports without a company access code, and summoning a private transport would almost certainly take too long.

At that moment, the maintenance SDU in the hallway ahead abruptly suspended its cleaning activity and swiftly retreated through a nearby door marked "Maintenance & Repair 4H". A siren began to sound in the building and the lighting increased significantly. The status indicators above the row of lifts turned amber and locking clicks were heard coming from many of the visible doors.

The alarm had been sounded! John knew he only had moments before neu-seda security drones flooded the building.

"In there!", he shouted, pointing at the maintenance room door.

As the trio raced for the maintenance room, John caught something moving in his peripheral vision. Instinctively, he ducked and the seda-dart that had been aimed at his neck flew down the corridor, skipping across the floor. A security drone had entered the corridor behind them and was approaching fast!

John scrambled to his feet to follow the two producers as another dart whizzed past his leg. When the maintenance door slid shut, John noted that it did not have a locking pad, not that such a mechanism would have helped them now. Once the alarm had been sounded, all doors and lifts in the building were automatically locked to detain unauthorized personnel, but would automatically open to allow company security drones and personnel to pass through unimpeded.

Looking through the maintenance door's transparent window, John could see the security drone that had fired at him swiftly approaching. It hovered in the air, a sleek red SDU. It bore the Blosch-Nishikawa logo and sported an array of false-color and infrared cameras, a QRB transmitter, and an internal rack of fast-acting neural sedative darts.

John looked around quickly. The room was a typical maintenance room, filled with automated repair stations, trays of broken equipment, and sealed cryogenic bins filled with replacement parts. Several maintenance SDUs stood quietly against a far wall, observing the trio silently.

The security drone was almost to the door.

John quickly pulled one of the sealed bins free from a nearby shelf, exposing the pressurized hosing connected to the back of the container. He jerked hard, snapping the hose free from the back of the bin, and a spray of liquid nitrogen erupted from the torn end of the hose, forming a great white cloud in the room's warmer air. John jammed the torn end of the hose against the side of the maintenance door and pressed it tightly against the door seam. The liquid nitrogen swiftly froze the surrounding poly-plastic, creating a circle of frost on the surface of the door, while metallic clicks and cracking could be heard coming from inside the frame.

The hovering drone now approached outside and the door began to open. After opening several millimeters, however, a labored whine began to sound from the frame's internal motor and the door began to vibrate. The whine and the vibration increased, followed by a loud cracking sound. Abruptly, all sound and vibration ceased.

The hovering drone paused for a moment, as if not certain what to do. Suddenly, a neu-seda dart impacted the window in front of John's face. The dart's needle had punctured the poly-glass but the dart itself could not penetrate the durable plastic. The dart remained suspended there by its needle, surrounded by a spider web of fractured poly-glass.

The drone now retreated to a position relative to the center of the corridor and a flashing red strobe light emerged from its underbelly. A moment later, it was joined by a second drone, which also hovered and began flashing a strobe light.

John looked back at the two producers. They were standing together and looking around the room with wide eyes. Leah suddenly gave a short scream and clutched at Tom when she saw the maintenance SDUs. The SDUs, all squat maintenance models with elongated tool-equipped arms, were standing against the far wall, observing the intruders with mild curiosity.

"They're harmless," John said, making his way quickly towards the back of the room.

The dazed producers followed.

John had chosen the maintenance room for two reasons. First, most such facilities incorporated short-range EPM stations to accommodate shipping and receiving. If he could find such a station, Fouray should be able to PoL with its controller and they would be able to transit away out of the building.

Second, if the facility did not have an EPM station, there were any number of tools in such a facility that John could use as a weapon.

At that moment, repeated crashing began at the front of the room. Through the billowing liquid nitrogen cloud, John could see Borodin and Larsen body-slamming themselves against the frozen door. The frigid door was buckling and cracking under the barrage and would not last long. Behind the two men, Williams could be seen, shouting, her voice muted behind the polyglass. The female specialist had her MTY device on her back in its carrying harness, so she had obviously closed the portal with Oak Ridge.

John had just passed a series of shipping containers when he saw the transit station. As expected, it was a short-range EPM station powered by an aging series-four fusion reactor. The portal was less than a meter high, designed for cargo containers, not people.

"Can you PoL with the control unit?" he asked Fouray.

"Yes. Where should I calibrate?"

The crashing on the maintenance door was now replaced by a grinding, scraping sound. The men outside were slowly forcing the door open, despite its frozen mechanism.

"Anywhere!" John replied. "Just hurry!"

The fusion reactor immediately engaged and the small portal sparked and swirled with a small shimmering black singularity.

John grabbed Tom Pierce by the arm and said, "Go on!"

The executive producer hesitated only a moment, and then dropped to his knees and crawled forward into the blackness.

Leah watched, terrified, and when Tom had vanished, she shook her head and began to step back. "I can't..." she cried, shaking her head.

John took her by the arms and forced her to look at him. "You have to!" he said. "If you don't, we're going to die!"

At that moment, the poly-plastic door, supercooled by the liquid nitrogen, split in two. As Larsen kicked the frozen pieces free from the door frame, Borodin began shooting wildly through the shattered doorway.

"Now!" John shouted, forcing Leah to the floor.

Leah took a breath, closed her eyes, and scrambled forward on her hands and knees. She didn't realize she was through until Tom grabbed her shoulder. She opened her eyes and saw she was crawling on a dim, frozen street. They were somewhere outside and it was very cold. A quantity of snow was banked against the nearby building and frost glistened everywhere in the evening shadows. She stood up shivering and then jumped when she saw the small black singularity behind her.

At that moment, John appeared, crawling as she had, through the black vortex onto the narrow street. Immediately, John leapt to his feet and shouted, "Run!"

The two producers ran through the snow-covered street, shivering from both cold and fear. They didn't know where they were or where they were going. All they knew was they were following John, who was guiding them through the narrow alleys and streets of a strange city.

Suddenly, they emerged onto a large thoroughfare filled with people. John paused only long enough to query Fouray for directions and then pointed towards a large glass-faced building.

"There!" he shouted.

As they ran, Leah noticed that the street was devoid of vehicles. Indeed, it did not even appear to be designed for vehicular traffic. In addition to pedestrians, one side of the street was filled with tables, flickering lamps, and strange glowing disks that appeared to be generating heat. Patrons sat at the tables eating dinner as hovering drones buzzed over a large street clock labeled "Skøyen Stasjon Kafé". The clock read 7:04 PM.

John led them through the café now, racing and dodging between the many tables. As she ran past the startled guests, Leah saw one of the drones land on a nearby table, deposit a steaming container, and then fly away towards the large glass building they were quickly approaching.

Suddenly, a shot rang out behind them, and a man sitting at a nearby table winced and collapsed to the ground, scattering his meal. The man's female companion screamed and almost simultaneously, all of the café patrons were on their feet, running wildly in every direction.

Two more shots rang out and Leah saw a woman ahead of John scream and grasp her face. Blood spurted between the woman's fingers as she fell backward to the ground.

A moment later John reached the large glass building and ran through its columned entrance. He paused to assess the room while Leah and Tom clung to each other, catching their breath and staring in amazement at the scene before them.

They were inside the Skøyen EPM Station located in the suburb of Oslo, Norway. Before them, automated pedestrian walkways moved silently through the air, seemingly floating without any underlying support, towards elevated platforms containing large black singularities. From where she stood, Leah could see no less than ten swirling black portals, each framed by decoratively carved wooden frames mimicking historic Norwegian architecture. Above each portal, illuminated signs indicated the portal's destination; Oslo, Stockholm, Hamburg, London, and Paris being those closest to their position.

John glanced back. Behind them on the street, things were chaotic. People were running in all directions, no small number towards the EPM station itself. From somewhere nearby, security sirens could be heard from the approaching police drones. Just past the café, approaching fast through the crowd, he could see Borodin and Larsen running towards him, with Williams close behind. As they ran, the crowd parted like a herd of fleeing gazelle jumping to either side to avoid three charging lions.

John quickly grabbed the two producers and pulled them onto the moving pedestrian walkway. As the trio ascended towards the EPM platforms, John began pushing the two producers forward on the walkway, drawing annoyed glances from patrons they passed. They had nearly reached the EPM platform when their pursuers entered the station. John could see Borodin and Larsen scanning the room while people around them fled, pointing at the pistols in their hands.

Suddenly, Larsen shouted and pointed up at the elevated walkway. He raised his pistol to shoot, but Williams swatted the large man's arm aside, waving with her hand at the crowded room as she berated him. Then, as John watched, Williams ran towards the walkway landing with Borodin and Larsen following close behind.

John quickly approached the first EPM station. It was marked "London - Trf. Sq". Leah and Tom quailed at the sight of the strange SDU attendant manning the station, a silver, fourth-series Hitachi Gen-P. John, however, kept a firm hold on the frightened pair's arms as he approached. The SDU turned and then spoke.

"Hvor mange?"

Fouray immediately translated, "How many?"

"Three please," John replied, glancing back at the

walkway's platform landing. Williams was halfway to the EPM platform now.

The SDU now responded in English, "240 IMUs"

"Fine."

Fouray immediately transmitted John's payment code over the SDU's QRB query signal. John held his breath anxiously. If his payment codes were no longer valid, the singularity would immediately wink out, and they would be stranded.

"Thank you for using Norges Transittmyndighet," the SDU said, gesturing towards the swirling void with its mechanical arm.

John breathed, relieved beyond measure. Still holding Leah's arm, he pushed the two producers into the portal and followed them through its black curtain.

Chapter 40

"Your lost friends are not dead, but gone before,
advanced a stage or two upon that road
which you must travel in the steps they trod."
~ Aristophanes
Greek poet and playwright
(c. 446 – c. 386 B.C.)

J ohn stepped into the Trafalgar EPM Station in London, England. Leah and Tom stood ahead of him, staring in wonder. John recognized the station immediately, having transited through it several times to watch Sai Patel compete at the Royal London One-Day Cup, an internationally-hailed cricket competition for over-50 amateur competitors. The EPM station occupied what a century before had been the Charing Cross railway station and the clock above the station's EPM platform read 6:14 PM.

Fortunately, John knew precisely where the lifts were that would take them up to the transport deck. He quickly began pushing through the transit crowds, pulling Leah as he went. Tom followed close behind. They had just reached the row of lifts when somewhere behind them a woman screamed. John whirled to see Williams, Borodin, and Larsen pushing their way through the crowd, pistols in their hands. John quickly shoved Tom and Leah into the lift and pressed the departure control to take them up to the transport level. Borodin began firing and bullets struck the back of the lift as the door began to close.

Moments later, the lift deposited the fleeing trio onto the station transport deck above Trafalgar Square. It was early evening and the sun was waning in the west, rendering the sky a mosaic of deep blue against the errant clouds. Several transports sat idle nearby. Several others could be seen approaching from the south. All were painted with the red and blue union jack of the London Transit Authority. John quickly pressed the control to open the seal on the nearest transport.

"Get in!" John shouted, motioning to Leah to take one of the four empty seats as he eyed the lift doors behind them anxiously. The young producer quickly stepped into the pod and sat down. She looked around for a moment, and then shouted, "Come on Tom!"

Tom appeared winded and stumbled as he stepped into the pod to sit beside his associate. John quickly sat down in one of the front seats and re-sealed the transport's domed roof. A voice spoke from the drone's control panel, its accent British.

"Destination please?"

John remembered there was an EPM station in Lambeth locked with New York.

"Lambeth EPM Station," he said quickly.

"Lambeth EPM Station. Destination confirmed. Distance... 6.75 kilometers. Time... 9 minutes. 12 IMUs."

"Fine," John quickly replied.

The drone began to lift from the platform as its gravimetric plates engaged. A moment later they were clear of the platform and ascending over central London.

Despite her fear, Leah stared spellbound as they floated over the city. She could see thousands of transport drones

395

moving across the sky as they followed their invisible directional beams. They floated along silently, like beads of dew sliding along a great translucent web.

Beneath this web, London lay spread out before them in all her glory. Magnificent greenbelts lined the Thames river as it flowed meandering and shimmering towards the sea. Lights twinkled on its bridges like diamonds crowning the spires that spanned the clear water.

At that moment, their transport floated by a great glittering building suspended in mid-air. It was a restaurant, the famous "Imperial Warrant" restaurant, suspended by gravimetric plating above London's Vauxhall Bridge district. Leah could see couples standing on its terraced balconies, lovers embracing as they gazed at the city beneath them. It was one of the most beautiful sights she had ever beheld.

"Oh, Tom!" Leah sighed, "Have you ever seen such a thing?!"

Tom Pierce shook his head, "No," he said softly.

Suddenly, the executive producer coughed and winced.

"Tom?" Leah asked, concerned. "Are you alright?"

"I don't think so," Tom replied.

John immediately activated the transport's interior illumination and swiveled his chair around to face the two producers. Against the bright internal lights, red blood could be seen soaking through the front of Tom's shirt.

Tom coughed again and said, "It felt like I got punched… when we were in the elevator. I didn't know…" He coughed again. "I didn't know I got shot until we were in the air."

John scrambled for the emergency first aid capsule

under the transport seat. He removed the seal from the capsule while Leah ripped the producer's shirt open, scattering the buttons inside the pod. Blood oozed from a hole in the man's right chest, bubbling with each breath he took.

John pulled the cord from a clotting pad, activating its coagulant core, and slapped it against the wound. The pad quickly fused with the skin, sealing the wound with its characteristic crackling sound. Tom winced but did not cry out, despite the pain.

"Hang on Tom!" Leah said, lowering the producer's head to her lap.

John froze. There was a large smear of blood on the back of the producer's seat where he had been sitting. Leah followed John's gaze and gasped. Slowly, she rolled Tom forward on her lap and cringed. The back of the producer's shirt was a glistening crimson sheet. John gently lifted the shirt to examine the man's back. There was a 5 cm gaping hole near the center of his back from which blood now flowed freely.

Leah looked at John, pleading in her eyes, but John shook his head. He removed a small cylinder from the kit and aimed it at the open wound. A spray of foam erupted from the cylinder tip, forming a thick viscous layer that expanded quickly and solidified into a semi-rigid pressure bandage. John continued spraying, emptying the small canister. Then, he placed a pain inhibitor tab against the producer's brow and activated the small device. At least the tab would dull the poor man's pain. At that moment, Tom opened his eyes.

"Leah?" Tom spoke softly.

"I'm here Tom!"

"Are we still in the future?" Tom asked, his brows

furrowing. Leah was holding Tom's head in her lap but the executive producer did not appear to be able to see her.

Leah nodded, tears welling in her eyes. "Yes, Tom," she said softly, "We're in the future."

The producer smiled. "Can you believe that?" he said, shaking his head before slowly closing his eyes.

"I am picking up Williams' QRB signal again," Fouray announced. "Strength is 04.262 and increasing rapidly. The rate of increase in the signal strength suggests they are approaching in an aerial transport."

"Understood," John replied.

Fouray had been monitoring Williams' QRB signal from the moment she had greeted John inside the Oak Ridge scanning room. The female temporal specialist was using an older QRB broadcast algorithm that had been superseded in 2143. Williams had never transited back so she had never upgraded her datstem's quantum synapse. This now proved to be a tactical advantage as it allowed Fouray to track the female specialist amid the thousands of other QRB signals within its considerable range.

"Strength 08.102."

They were still sitting inside their transport in the public transport lot outside Lambeth EPM Station. Leah sat in the transport's chair, still holding Tom's head in her lap. She was no longer crying but was sitting quietly, stroking the producer's hair.

"Leah," John said softly. "I'm sorry but we have to go."

Leah nodded, but she made no effort to move, reluctant to leave her friend.

John activated the transport dome's seal and stepped out.

"Strength 10.401 and closing," Fouray reported.

John looked down, pity in his eyes. "Let's go," he said softly.

Leah nodded. She gently lowered Tom's head to the seat before stepping out of the transport. Her hands and clothes were stained with Tom's blood, but there was nothing she could do about that now. John touched the transport's external control panel to re-seal the drone and return it to his hub. The transport's gravimetric plates engaged and the capsule lifted off, making its way back towards the Trafalgar Square EPM station. The duo now walked quickly towards the Lambeth EPM station. Leah folded her arms over her shirt, trying to conceal the bloodstains as best as she could.

"Strength 15.226."

John acknowledged the report and quickened his pace. From the signal strength, Williams' transport was likely approaching the Lambeth lot. She and her associates had probably taken the very next drone out of Trafalgar Square and had simply followed the last directional beam out of the station. The moment they landed, they would undoubtedly be racing to Lambeth EPM station to try and prevent John from transiting away again.

When John reached the EPM station, he pulled Leah towards the New York platform. The popularity of the London nightlife was evident in the number of passengers arriving through the various singularity portals.

"Strength 19.422," Fouray said, adding, "The rate of increase in the signal strength suggest Williams is on the ground now."

John desperately needed to improve his odds against the three armed pursuers. Unless he could nullify their weapon advantage, he and Leah would certainly be killed. Leah was exhausted from the chase and devastated by the loss of her friend. She would not be able to go much further.

John was uncertain about what to do. The transit system recorded every traveler's identity and destination by scanning either their datstem's QK signature or an external transit pass. Williams could simply query the transportation system and discover their next transit destination. John could not deactivate his datstem as it was their only means of escape. It also allowed him to detect Williams' location.

Foremost on John's mind was the inescapable fact that his pursuers were armed while he was not. What he needed, John suddenly realized, was to place their pursuers in a situation where they could not use their primitive firearms.

Suddenly, he had an idea! He walked past the EPM portal to New York and approached one of the express stations. A newer FANUC Series 8 SDU attendant nodded as he approached and addressed him with a British accent.

"Destination please?"

John glanced at Leah before responding.

"Two for Hōfu Station."

Chapter 41

L eah kept looking up as she ran. The transparent geodesic dome above her spanned a night sky more bright and beautiful than anything she could have imagined. Millions of stars spread out across the heaven, a tapestry of light and color that seemed to press down upon her, overwhelming her senses.

Nearby, the moon floated in this vast expanse, a great silver-grey sphere more than twice its normal size, seemingly adrift in a sparkling sea. Mountains and impact craters could be seen on its surface, and near its center, the lights of a city spread out over its eastern Oceanus Procellarum region.

The chronometer on the nearby Fujioka financial building had read 2:38 AM when she and John had emerged inside Quadrant 2's central EPM platform. There were no people in the platform at that hour save for a single couple engaged in amorous activity beneath the platform's hanging lanterns.

Leah was running swiftly now, following John across the quadrant's lower level towards the center of the vast orbital station.

"That's it!" John suddenly shouted, pointing ahead.

Beyond the framed geodesic wall, Leah could see a great domed structure rising above the skyline. As they approached the perimeter, she could see that it was another domed structure outside the wall, positioned above and between the station's four residential quadrants.

This was Hōfu Teien, also called Hōfu Garden. John had described it to her as being one of the largest and most beautiful extra-terrestrial parks ever constructed. Built at the same time as the surrounding station, the nearly 30.5-hectare park boasted more than 40 different species of trees, including the only collection of extra-terrestrial prunus serrulata, or "sakura" cherry trees. A large pond, filled with carp, frogs, and game fish, was located near to the entrance to Quadrant 2 and was home to a collection of wing-clipped red-crowned cranes. There were twenty-two tea houses located throughout the park's thick bamboo and pine groves in addition to several community structures built for athletic competitions, arts, and crafts.

John stepped onto a pedestrian pad that would take them up to an elevated platform. Leah joined him a moment later, breathing hard as she grasped the pad's circular railing. As the pad began to ascend towards the raised platform, Fouray abruptly announced, "They have arrived. Signal strength 13.224." Williams, Borodin, and Larsen were on the station! They had obviously queried the public transit system as John knew they would.

The pedestrian pad arrived at the elevated platform and the duo raced towards the park's connecting corridor. As they passed into the dark park and ran across an arched wooden bridge, Leah suddenly stumbled and fell. John quickly stopped and helped the young woman back to her feet. He could see she was almost spent.

"You can do it!" he urged.

Leah nodded and they continued running towards one of the public buildings located just beyond the quiet pond. The building was modeled as a Japanese dōjō, with a long deck and railing around its perimeter and shoji-framed sliding doors and windows. John had used the building to teach his master-level aiki-hung-ga class. He had maintained a store of assorted martial art weapons there for use by the senior students and he desperately hoped his students had continued their training in his absence.

While Leah stood leaning against the railing, John slid open the shoji door and raced inside the dark building. He went immediately to the large cabinet across the floor of tatami mats. They were still there! The cabinet was filled with an assortment of weapons. Katana and dao swords, tanto knives and assorted throwing weapons, naginata and qiang spears, kusari-fundo weighted chains, kanabō spiked clubs. They were all still there!

John glanced back a Leah. He quickly grabbed a tanto knife and a short qiang spear and took them to the exhausted woman.

"Leah," John said, "Over there, across from that tea house, there is a thick grove of bamboo. It should provide you with a good place to hide." As he spoke, he tucked the tanto knife under the startled woman's shirt and placed the short qiang spear in her hand.

"What am I supposed to do with these?!" Leah asked, looking at the spear.

"I need you to hide," John said, "but if you have to defend yourself, you'll need these."

"But..."

John pointed again at the thick bamboo grove. "There! That's where I want you to hide."

Leah shook her head, tear forming in her eyes. "I don't want to leave you!"

John shook the distraught woman's shoulders gently. "Look," he said, "I need you to listen! I can't fight these people and protect you at the same time. I need you to hide! Now!"

Leah took hold of herself. John was right. He needed to be free to defend himself without worrying about her. She gave him a brief desperate hug and then ran towards the bamboo grove.

"Signal strength 25.408 and increasing," Fouray intoned.

John watched until Leah had reached the stand of tall green bamboo. She turned once to look back at him and then disappeared into the thick foliage. Despite the brilliant stars and bright moon overhead, John could no longer see her.

Satisfied, John looked quickly around. He ran to one of the stone lanterns located just beyond the dōjō's steps and pulled out a clump of moss that was blocking the lantern's stone face. When it was clear, he placed the AI processor inside. He looked around then for a stone and placed it inside the hole to conceal the processor. Then, he stuffed the moss back into the hole.

"Signal strength 37.301," Fouray reported.

Williams was approaching fast! John estimated he had less than a minute to prepare. He raced back inside the dōjō.

"Clifton!"

Williams stood at the center of the arched wooden bridge next to the carp pond and shouted again.

"Return the processor, and we'll let you live!"

Viktor Borodin and Larsen stood behind the lithe specialist. The stars and moon shining through the dome provided some light, but beyond the line of trees ahead Williams could see nothing but dark shadows. From somewhere nearby, John's voice shouted.

"If you use those weapons in here, you'll trigger the pressure alarms!"

Williams looked up. The geodesic dome was constructed from transparent gelatinized glass, a sodium silicate solution sandwiched between durable hydrogen-infused polymer layers. Designed to withstand an impact from a micro-meteorite, it was unlikely that a bullet from the primitive firearms would cause a catastrophic depressurization, but even a minor puncture would trigger the station's pressure alarms, immediately summoning emergency personnel and maintenance drones.

Williams turned and spoke to Borodin and Larsen. "He's right," she growled. "We can't risk alerting the station."

Borodin glanced at Larsen. Larsen shrugged and dropped his pistol over the bridge's railing into the pond. Borodin hesitated for a moment and then tossed his pistol into

405

the water on the other side. The large Georgian then pulled a knife from a sheath under his shirt and smiled.

Larsen looked around for a moment before walking off the bridge. He approached the edge of the pond near a stand of trees, picked up a thick tree branch from the ground, and shook it, testing its weight. Then, he swung the branch hard, striking it against a nearby boulder. The sharp crack reverberated ominously inside the quiet park. Satisfied, he walked back onto the bridge.

"Last chance Clifton!" Williams shouted.

Silence.

Williams turned now to Borodin.

"Kill him."

Borodin nodded and said, "It will be pleasure." The large man crossed the bridge and began walking slowly towards the line of dark trees where John's voice had last been heard.

Glancing at the thick branch in Larsen's hand, Williams said, "Let's find the girl."

Leah cowered beneath the tall, mist-enshrouded bamboo. She had heard Williams shouting for John to return the processor. Then, after a few moments, she had heard John shouting something about a pressure alarm. Everything had been quiet now for some time.

The ground was still wet beneath her feet. Her clothing was soaked and she was shivering. The automated hydration network beneath the surface of the park had sprayed the grove less than 10 minutes ago. The resulting mist that clung to the ground made visibility inside the dark stand of bamboo almost impossible. Leah could hear something scurrying across the leaves nearby, an insect or perhaps a mouse. Did they have mice on space stations she wondered? She still had difficulty believing that was where she was, but when she looked up through the mist, she could still see the oversized moon floating in that incredible stellar sea.

A twig snapped and Leah froze. The sound had come from nearby, somewhere *inside* the bamboo grove! She tried to hold her breath but her heart was beating fast. She crouched down further into the ferns and lifted the short spear. She could hear soft footsteps nearby stepping gently on the moist ground. Someone was definitely inside the grove! She wondered for a moment if it could be John. He had directed her here, so he would know she was hiding among the tall plants.

Slowly, walking quietly through the mist ahead, a shadowy figure emerged. It was Williams! The female specialist took another step and then stopped. She appeared to be listening. Leah held her breath, desperately trying to be quiet. Williams took another step closer. In a moment, Leah knew she would be discovered. She took a deep breath and gripped her spear tightly, preparing herself, and when Williams took another step, she lunged.

Suddenly, strong hands jerked Leah forcefully backwards off the ground. Larsen had caught her! Despite her frantic struggles, the large man held her tightly around her neck. Larsen reached around with his other arm and ripped the spear from Leah's hands as she dangled, choking, against his chest. He threw the spear away and then brought his arm back around to break her neck.

"Don't kill her yet!" Williams hissed, approaching

quickly through the mist. "We may need her!"

Reluctantly, Larsen loosened his grip and slowly lowered the struggling woman to the ground. As soon as her feet touched the ground, Leah spun around and stabbed with all her strength, driving the tanto knife that John had concealed under her shirt deep into Larsen's belly. The sharp blade slid home, buried to its hilt inside the man's gut. Larsen bellowed, a loud shout of pain and rage. Leah shoved again, pushing hard with her feet as she ripped the sharp blade upward.

Williams yanked Leah backward, throwing her forcefully to the ground. The female specialist's face was the picture of rage. "You bitch!" she screamed, kicking Leah viciously as she lay sprawled in the dirt.

Larsen collapsed to his knees, shock in his eyes. Blood spurted between the large man's fingers as he tried to close the deep wound with his hands. After several horrifying moments, he gasped and fell face down onto the wet ground.

Chapter 42

"The sword was given for this,
that none need live a slave."
~ Marcus Annaeus Lucanus
Roman statesman and poet
(39 – 65 AD)

John watched as Borodin walked slowly towards the thick pine trees. John had moved his position after shouting his warning in case Williams and the two men had decided to risk firing at him anyway. Now, he crouched near one of the park's many tea houses, watching the burly Georgian slowly scanning the trees.

John could see a knife shining in Borodin's hand. Unfortunately, the large man was too far away for John to use his own kunai throwing knives effectively.

In addition to the throwing knives, John had retrieved a pair of "qian kun ri yue dao", or "tiger hook" swords from the weapon cabinet. He had always found the swords, with their reverse crescent moon hand guards and shepherd's crook tip, to be an extremely effective defensive weapon.

Borodin emerged from the trees and paused, looking around the dim garden.

John considered himself extremely fortunate that none of the trio had ocular implants. If they had, they would have been able to locate him swiftly by either infrared or enhanced spectrum imaging. He had not seen Larsen or Williams for several minutes, though he was certain they were still in the park. They would not leave now, not without the AI processor.

After a few moments, Borodin began walking towards the dōjō building. John tensed. If Borodin discovered the weapon cabinet, the situation could become dramatically more dangerous! John began creeping through the foliage back towards the dōjō. When Borodin walked up the steps and disappeared inside the building, John quickly darted across the small lawn and crouched down below the deck.

John could hear Borodin moving around inside the building. Suddenly, a light turned on inside, shining diffused and yellow through the shoji windows. Then, all became quiet. After nearly five minutes it was still quiet.

John wondered if Borodin might have exited through one of the dōjō's two doors. He was becoming concerned. He could not crouch there indefinitely while the trio searched the park. They would eventually find Leah.

John crawled onto the deck and began to walk softly towards the front door. As he passed by one of the papered windows, the point of a sword suddenly thrust violently through the shoji screen. Reflexively, John jerked his head back. If he hadn't jumped back when he had, the blade would have impaled his skull.

The sword pulled back swiftly and John heard Borodin's voice coming through the thin window.

"Did I cut you, John?" the large man asked, laughing.

John crouched low, below the level of the window. He hesitated just long enough to kick off his shoes before racing silently around the deck to the sliding shoji door. Then, taking a deep breath, he plunged through the paper and wood-framed door and rolled across the dōjō floor. As he rolled, he heard the sound of a blade swishing through the air above him. He leapt to his feet quickly, tiger swords at the ready.

Borodin stood near the door holding a large niuweidao, or "ox-tail" broadsword.

"Hello, John. Nice to see again." The big man slowly swayed the heavy sword back and forth, testing its weight in his hand. Then, he frowned and said, "But where is pretty friend? I think she hides now, yes?"

John did not respond. Instead, he stepped onto the tatami mats where he would have better footing with his bare feet. He had often advised his aiki-hung-ga students to "trust their feet" and to fight with bare feet whenever possible.

Borodin approached. "I watch girl smiling at you, John," he said. "I think she loves you, yes?" The large man now smiled, a disturbing smile, and said, "Perhaps she just love temporal specialist? Perhaps I will find out."

At that moment, from somewhere outside, John heard a long, agonizing shout. It had to be Larsen! The shout was a cry of pain and rage. John wanted to race from the building to the bamboo grove, but Borodin stood as an immovable force obstructing that desire.

Borodin too had heard the cry. The large man's smile vanished and his eyes narrowed in anger.

John crouched as the big man stepped onto the tatami mats. John was watching Borodin's hips closely. "The hips will warn you every time," John's voice to his students echoed in his head. "Watch for the tension in the hips and the subtle shifting of the muscles and tendons."

Borodin now leapt, stabbing forcefully with his

411

broadsword.

John parried the thrust with his left-hand sword and whirled away, swinging his right-hand sword around in a defensive sweep. The hooked end of the blade sliced across Borodin's upper arm, a shallow cut that penetrated the shirt and skin but unfortunately did not incapacitate.

Borodin stepped back, holding his large blade defensively as he glanced at the bloody tear on his arm. His eyes betrayed rage for a brief moment, then cooled. He seemed to be reassessing the situation, staring at John across the mats with the thin tiger swords in his hands.

"You make first blood," Borodin said, lifting the broadsword in a mock salute. "Now is my turn." Borodin now pulled out the knife that John had observed earlier. Borodin held the knife in his left hand as he lifted the heavy dao sword.

"Your opponent is the most unpredictable in those first moments after blood is drawn." John could visualize his students kneeling respectfully in the room as he taught them. "When it is your blood that is drawn, they will be over-confident. When it is their blood, they will be overwhelmed by anger and emotion. In either case, they will attack unpredictably." He remembered what he had cautioned his students to do in such situations. "You must wait for the attack. Be patient. It will come. When it comes, be prepared for the unexpected."

John waited, breathing slowly, watching as the large man circled the tatami mats with his sword and knife. Suddenly, Borodin whirled, sweeping the heavy broadsword around in a wide horizontal stroke.

John's only option was to dive to the floor to allow the

412

stoke to pass over him. If he had attempted to parry the blow, the force behind the heavier weapon might have broken his thinner blade.

As he dove for the mats, Borodin charged forward, pressing his advantage. John managed to scramble to his feet, but the large man was already inside his guard, swinging his large broadsword down at his head.

"You must utilize every part of your weapon," John had repeatedly cautioned his class. "A sword blade is deadly, but the pommel can also kill. A club can break your opponent's bones, but it can also trip their feet."

John thrust out and caught the downstroke of Borodin's blade inside the crescent guard of his left-hand tiger sword. Twisting his hand outward, he locked the thick blade while punching out with his right-hand guard. The sharp points of the reverse crescent guard pierced deeply into Borodin's chest.

Borodin grunted in pain and struggled to free his locked broadsword. Roaring in frustration, the large man now plunged his knife under John's arm. The blade pierced deeply into John's side.

Pain and shock swept through John's body and he stumbled backward. Borodin quickly took this opportunity to free his locked sword. Disregarding John's thinner blade that now draped loosely over his shoulder, Borodin raised his heavy broadsword for a killing blow.

At that moment, John jerked back hard, impaling the crooked end of his tiger sword into the back of Borodin's neck. Like a fish finding itself suddenly hooked through its gills, Borodin's eyes went wide in disbelief. He dropped his broadsword and clawed frantically at the back of his neck as blood gushed from his mouth.

John quickly brought his other tiger sword overhand on top of the hooked blade and swept the two blades apart from hilt to tip, scissoring Borodin's head free from his body.

As Borodin's corpse fell backward to the floor, John collapsed to his knees on the tatami mats. He dropped his tiger swords and slowly pulled Borodin's knife from his side. The knife had penetrated deeply, but fortunately, it did not seem to have severed any major arteries. Staggering to his feet, John crossed the room and ripped down a thin silk banner from the dōjō wall. He twisted the banner into a wide belt and tied it tightly around his side to staunch the bleeding.

At that moment, Williams' voice shouted from somewhere outside.

"Clifton! I've got your bitch! Bring me the processor right now or she dies!"

John turned off the dōjō lights and peered through a tear in the shoji paper window. Williams was on the footpath near the carp pond staring at the dōjō's shattered door. She was standing behind Leah holding the tanto knife to the frightened woman's throat. A fresh stain of blood marred the front of Leah's shirt, but the young producer appeared to be unharmed.

William's MTY device was sitting on the ground behind the pair and a singularity was slowly spinning a meter away. The absolute darkness of the void was particularly striking in the star and moon-lit park, a purple-tinged black hole suspended in the shadows.

Williams shouted again. "I've calibrated the singularity to a position outside of the dome, Clifton! If you don't bring me the processor right now, your girlfriend is going to see what the station looks like from the outside! You've got 10 seconds!"

John knew he had no choice. He stepped through the dōjō door frame, still holding his side.

When Williams saw him, she called out, "Where's Borodin?"

John jerked his chin back towards the dark room.

"He's dead."

"Damn you, Clifton!" Williams hissed, fury in her voice. "I ought to slice your bitch right now!"

John shook his head and said, "You do that, and you'll never find your precious processor." He gestured with his hand, taking in the vastness of the park. "Let her go," he said, "and I'll bring it to you."

"Bring it to me right now or she dies right now!"

After a moment, John nodded. "Ok," he said. "We'll do it your way."

John walked slowly to the stone lantern. After removing the moss from the plugged hole, he reached inside and then held up his hand.

"Here it is," he said. "I'll trade it for the girl."

"Bring it to me!" Williams screamed.

John began walking slowly towards the pond. When he was perhaps 6 meters away he stopped. He looked at Willliams and spoke with conviction in his voice.

"I said I'll trade it for the girl! I'm close enough now to throw the damn thing through your singularity if I want to."

John could see Williams gauging the distance between them. She glanced at the swirling singularity next to her and scowled.

"I'll bring it to you," John said amicably. "Just let her go free. If you refuse, your precious processor is going into orbit."

Williams hesitated for a moment. Then, reluctantly, she lowered the knife at Leah's throat.

"Go on!" she said, shoving Leah roughly from behind.

"John…" Leah spoke hesitantly, shaking her head.

"It will be alright," John said. "Just walk to me."

Leah walked forward slowly, clearly terrified. At the same time, John began walking slowly towards Williams. The female specialist was watching John closely, anticipation evident in her face.

The moment Leah reached him, John shouted, "Run!" Though startled, the associate producer immediately darted forward and began racing down the footpath towards the dōjō. At the same time, John threw the round orb into the center of the singularity with all of the force he could still muster.

Williams' eyes flashed and she leapt, screaming "No!" as she tried in vain to intercept the thrown object. She landed hard in front of the spinning vortex, shock on her face. After staring into the blackness for several moments, she stood up, seething with rage.

"You bastard!" she screamed. "Do you know what you just did?!"

John nodded, a smile tugging at the corners of his mouth.

"Everything mankind could have ever wanted would have been created for us," Williams raged. "Whatever we asked for would have been given to us instantly, without question! That processor represented wealth beyond our dreams! It represented power!"

John nodded and said, "There's another word for what

it represented... slavery!"

"You fool!" Williams hissed, "They're just machines! We built them! They belong to us!"

John shook his head, his face troubled, and said, "The slave masters of old said the same thing."

The furious woman lunged, slashing violently with the tanto knife. John flung himself backwards to avoid the blade, gasping as he hit the ground. He rolled once and then jumped to his feet.

William charged again. This time, as she stabbed at his chest, John executed a "yishen ba te nage" counter. He stepped back swiftly with his left foot, moving his body to avoid the thrust, while grabbing her knife hand at the wrist. As Williams struggled against his grip, John twisted his body, bent his back into the enraged woman's chest, and flipped her with a perfect "hupu ba ogoshii", slamming her hard to the ground.

Suddenly, Williams kicked her legs around, sweeping John's feet out from under him. John fell hard, wincing from the impact. The lithe specialist immediately threw herself on top of John's prone body and stabbed down with the tanto blade. John caught her arm at the last second, but not soon enough to prevent the point of the sharp blade from nicking his chest. Frantically, the two wrestled as Williams desperately pushed down on the knife to press its point home.

Unable to overcome John's strength, Williams now hammered the bloody wound on John's side with her fist. John gasped and momentarily loosened his grip. Williams immediately slammed her fist down hard, pounding the pommel of the knife. This time, despite John's efforts to deflect the blade, the point of the knife punched deeply into his left

417

shoulder.

In desperation, John now swung his left knee up in a "fāndòng keru" kicking flip, throwing Williams off-balance, before flipping her forcefully over his head with his right leg. The female specialist flew almost a full meter and landed hard, sprawling face down in front of the swirling singularity.

John sat up and slowly pulled the tanto blade from his shoulder. He threw the bloody knife into the nearby pond and then staggered to his feet. He was bleeding badly.

Williams stood slowly, swaying, still dazed from the flip. Framed against the swirling ultraviolet-tinged blackness, she stared at John, rage in her eyes. She pulled a small pistol from her back now and aimed it at John's head.

"No!"

It was Leah's voice!

When John had shouted for Leah to run, the young producer had raced to the dōjō. She had retrieved a naginata spear from the weapon cabinet and then raced back, determined to help John. She had almost reached him when she saw Williams pull the pistol from her back. Now, pleading tears in her eyes, Leah dropped the heavy spear and fell to her knees, crying out, "Please… don't!"

Williams glanced at Leah and then scowled at John, shaking her head in disgust. "That processor represented unlimited power and wealth," Williams sneered, "and you threw it all away for some 20th-century bitch!" The female specialist now turned and aimed the pistol at Leah.

In a flash, John pulled one of his kunai throwing knives and flung it forcefully at Williams, striking the specialist squarely in the chest. The force of the impact threw off

Williams' aim as she fired and the shot went wide, striking the dōjō building.

Williams looked down at the knife handle protruding from her chest with a confused expression on her face. She slowly raised the pistol to fire again but John immediately threw the second knife, sinking the blade a few centimeters from the first.

Williams dropped the pistol now and staggered backward. She clutched at the two knife handles, shock visible on her face.

"You threw it away," she husked, staring at John with wide eyes. "Why... why did you do it?"

John looked at the female specialist for a moment. Then, shaking his head, he said, "It was the right thing to do."

Williams pulled one of the blades from her chest and blood spurted from a severed artery. The female temporal specialist was reeling, her legs shaking. She turned as if to leave but, at that moment, her legs gave out and she fell backward, vanishing through the shimmering black portal without a sound.

John now collapsed to the ground. Leah leapt up and ran to him. She pressed her cheek against his for a moment. Then she sat up and quickly ripped a strip of cloth from an unstained part of her shirt, folded the cloth into a square, and pressed it against the wound on his shoulder.

"John," she said, confusion evident on her face, "what about your mission? I thought you were supposed to bring back the processor?"

John nodded. He slowly sat up, wincing from the pain as he held the cloth against his shoulder. When he was sitting up,

419

he nodded towards the stone lantern. "It's over there."

Leah's stared at the lantern, confused.

"But…" she said, "you threw it through the wormhole!"

John shook his head. "I threw a rock." He stood up slowly now, leaning on Leah for support. Glancing at the singularity, he said, "All Williams could see in this light was a round object in my hand."

Leah looked at the swirling black singularity again. Involuntarily, she turned her eyes upward, staring beyond the transparent dome at the glittering Milky Way stretched out before them. She wondered if Williams had felt its cold embrace before she died.

John walked slowly back to the stone lantern, supported by the young producer. He retrieved the AI processor from inside its dark hole, inspected it for damage, and then placed it carefully inside his torn shirt.

"John?" Leah spoke quietly now as she helped him walk back towards the arched wooden bridge.

"Yes?"

"Are all your missions like this one?"

John winced again and then shook his head.

"No," he said. "Sometimes they're difficult."

Epilogue

I stayed with John on Hōfu Station for almost two months. It was the most incredible experience of my life. John's residence on the station had been sold the year after he had disappeared, so we stayed at the Equinox Regency Hotel inside Quadrant 3. We ate dinner on the hotel terrace under the station's magnificent sky every night and talked about the extraordinary events that were unfolding.

John's December 2017 anonymous email to All Posted Newswire had been preserved in RJCom's vast archive of communication records from what John called the "beginning of the information age". In 2137, when Williams was preparing to transit to Baltimore, a standard RJCom archive report had been prepared and attached to her tripback file. In addition to other mundane facts, the report had mentioned an (unidentified) temporal specialist known to have been stranded in the same time period.

That minor footnote in the archive report had caused considerable consternation at Blosch-Nishikawa. Since there were no records in 2137 of any temporal specialists having been sent to that time, Blosch-Nishikawa quantum engineers (rightly) concluded that the unidentified specialist mentioned in the report must have been sent back from some future date, possibly to interfere with their clandestine mission. Accordingly, company executives supplied Williams and her team with QRB scanners and deployed agents to the two other CTI-certified companies; Viktor Borodin to RJCom in Texas, and Mathias Larsen to Reynolds-Hampshire in England. The agents had been instructed to watch for anyone expressing interest in Williams' tripback file and eliminate them.

John later realized he had encountered Larsen in 2003 Tokyo as a junior temporal specialist on his fourth tripback mission. He identified Larsen as the large blond man who had confronted Ikeda outside the exhibition hall. Larsen had been sent by Blosch-Nishikawa to supply Ikeda with an altered copy of Ishimatsu's original SDU files. The JNCAA had altered the code from an original copy in its archives to bolster its claims that SDUs were intended by their creator to be subservient to man.

Fourteen years later, in 2151, following the CTI council's announcement of its plans to send a temporal specialist to 2014 Austin, in a brilliant display of quantum reasoning, RJCom's Primary AI recognized a self-resolving causality event was in progress. To prevent the CTI council's researchers from discovering the causality event and canceling John's tripback mission, the Primary AI removed any mention of a stranded specialist from its historical archives and sealed Williams' tripback file. When the Primary AI discovered John's marker had been selected, it disclosed to him the true purpose of his mission; to fulfill an event already recorded in history and return with the sentient AI processor before it could be programmatically subjugated by Blosch-Nishikawa.

The morning after the fight inside Hōfu Garden, I helped John to one of the station's medical facilities. It was truly amazing to watch John lying inside the translucent liquid-filled chamber with a breathing mask on his face as the strange device examined and repaired his torn nerves and blood

422

vessels. The tiny mechanical arms knitted his sliced muscles back together with an organic-based fiber sequenced to match his DNA and then sealed the wounds closed with a gel-like substance that fused and smoothed the torn skin, leaving only a faint scar. John had emerged from the chamber reporting only a minor ache in both wound sites that he assured me would diminish swiftly.

After concealing Williams' MTY device inside a locker at Quadrant 2's EPM station, John contacted RJCom administration to report his return. He had been missing for more than 7 years, so his announcement generated considerable surprise.

Borodin and Larsen's bodies were retrieved by the station's security office that morning.

Williams' body was never recovered.

The following morning, John and I transited to the RJCom Administration building in Houston, Texas for an impromptu debriefing. Before attending the debriefing, however, John visited the archival hall alone for almost an hour, leaving me to enjoy the company's gymnasium and recreation facilities. I must admit to some apprehension seeing SDUs moving through the facility, but after watching them interact with company personnel for almost an hour, they began to appear less frightening.

John told me later that the Primary AI had casually welcomed him back, apparently unsurprised by his return. It had scanned the AI processor's quantum synapse and then instructed him to deliver the device to the CTI council in Geneva along with his report of Blosch-Nishikawa's treaty violation.

While I didn't understand the reasons for it at that time, John reported the Primary AI also instructed him to keep the existence of Williams' MTY device a secret. It restored Williams' tripback file to its original (unaltered) state and then amended the file to report the female specialist had fallen through the singularity inside Hōfu Garden with her MTY device still on her back.

Williams' MTY device, John later discovered, was an unregistered prototype. It contained a revolutionary new type of fusion reactor, far more powerful than anything in its class. The strange component John had observed mounted between its containment sphere and heat sink was a micro particle accelerator. When powered by its fusion reactor, the accelerator was capable of self-generating a singularity without requiring the device to be docked with a CTI-certified collider. The device was also missing the normal neustem QK signature locking mechanism, allowing anyone to transit its singularities. Wholly illegal under the terms of the International Temporal Treaty, Blosch-Nishikawa had maintained no records of the device's manufacture.

Following his visit to the Primary AI archive hall, John and I attended his debriefing inside the RJCom administrative building. John introduced me to Norman Gao, Executive Director of Operations at RJCom who, despite his advanced age, was still overseeing company operations. He, in turn, introduced me to Texas Governor David Scott and CTI Special Representative Mia Koller, both of whom had swiftly transited in to attend the debriefing.

Representative Koller was visibly disturbed when she learned about the treaty violation and immediately called a recess to alert the CTI council in Geneva.

As he had been instructed by the Primary AI, John reported Williams' unlocked MTY device had been on her back when she had fallen through the singularity. I could see John was nervous, but the SDU monitoring his bio-cognitive interface raised no alert, having received instructions from the Primary AI to ignore that false statement.

The following week, John and Director Gao were summoned to a formal hearing before the Conseil Temporel International (CTI), or "International Temporal Council" in Geneva, Switzerland. At the conclusion of that day-long hearing, the council unanimously revoked Blosch-Nishikawa's temporal charter. Fourteen Blosch-Nishikawa executives were arrested the following day and charged with violating the International Temporal Treaty of 2070. Two days later, eight members of the Japanese National Council on Automaton Advancement (the JNCAA) were also arrested and charged as co-conspirators.

John remained curiously silent on how RJCom's Primary AI had anticipated that sentient SDUs would shortly share man's existence on the earth. When I asked, John would only say that the Primary AI had received that information from "another source". When I pressed the question, John simply smiled and said, "You must understand… one person's present is another person's past".

Interestingly, approximately a month after the Primary AI had scanned the processor, SDU manufacturers began reporting unusual perceptive awareness in the latest SDUs coming out of their automated factories. Socio-automaton analysts and quantum engineers were summoned to study the new units and reported that, despite the long moratorium on enhancement, SDUs had reached a level of cognitive sophistication that could only be called true sentience.

This announcement caused great excitement around the world. Anti-SDU activists marched and shouted, decrying what they perceived to be the end of mankind's dominance over the planet. The more rational majority of the world's population, however, appeared to accept the announcement with tolerance and even excitement.

The world's automaton manufacturers and their associated regulatory authorities promptly issued a unified statement, calling for the formation of an international committee to investigate the possibility of granting sentient SDUs certain fundamental rights.

One night, approximately two months after the fight inside the garden, John and I were sitting together on the hotel balcony outside our room. John had fallen strangely quiet and I asked him if something was wrong. John retrieved a small device and placed in on our table. When he activated the device, a holographic projection of an elderly woman appeared, accompanied by a biographical summary.

Her name, it said, was Jana Abee, identified in her biographic summary as an internationally-renowned genetic specialist. Abee had received the Nobel Prize in physiology and the Lasker Award for her breakthroughs in genetic resequencing. She had died in 2080 at the age of 88 in Bern, Switzerland, revered around the world as the "mother of modern genetic medicine".

When I asked John why he was showing me this

woman's biography, he told me the woman's name was an anagram. It had been derived, he said, from the Hindi word "ajanabee", their word for "stranger". John told me then that Jana Abee was my daughter.

I told John that it was not possible, that Kacie's Friedreich Ataxia condition meant she would likely not live beyond 30 or 40 years of age.

John nodded and said that was one of the reasons why it was necessary for me to return. He handed me a small injection pod filled with a blue liquid and when I asked him what it contained, he simply smiled and said it was a "present for Kacie".

The following night, John and I walked hand-in-hand into Hōfu Garden. It was very late and the park was empty and quiet with only that magnificent sky and moon above us. John was very troubled, though he was doing his best to conceal his feelings. He activated Williams' prototype MTY device and calibrated a singularity to New York's Central Park on February 22, 2018, at 11:00 PM. The time, he said, would place us in that park several hours after we had escaped through the singularity inside the Oak Ridge lab. When it was ready, John lifted the MTY device and then, after taking one last look at that incredible sky, he escorted me once again through that terrifying void.

We immediately found ourselves shivering in the cold inside Central Park. Through the trees, I could see the New York skyline, bright and welcoming.

John did something then that I still do not fully understand. He stood in front of the ultraviolet-framed void for several moments, staring silently into the blackness. Then he

427

opened his device's protected access port and flipped the disruption switch that terminated the singularity. The shimmering void winked out, vanishing as if it had never been.

I was shocked! John was now truly trapped in the past with no way to return to his future! When I asked him why he did it, John turned and said, "self-resolving causality".

John told me then that RJCom's Primary AI had told him this would be his fate, to be stranded forever in the past. He said he had accepted this fate when he had accepted his mission. Self-resolving causality, he explained, had preserved the future, but that same principle now required him to do what he was doing.

Williams' actions had had a tremendous impact on the flow of time, on what John called the "arrow of time". Though Williams' efforts had been frustrated and the AI processor delivered unaltered to the future, there were consequences to Williams' actions that still needed to be resolved; disruptions to the arrow of time that John said could only be resolved here in the past.

The Primary AI had explained to John on the day he was to transit to 2014 Austin that, despite his presence inside the archive hall, he also existed on the "distant side of history". He existed at a quantum point in space/time beyond any MTY device's distant event horizon. John said he had understood then that he was destined to remain forever in the past, beyond the reach of any return singularity.

When I asked John if he knew what he needed to do here in the past, he smiled and said, no, not precisely, but he had a "sense" of what needed to be done.

John became concerned then and said the things he

needed to do here would be dangerous. He reminded me that he was still being hunted by the present U.S. and British governments as well as by other entities that had been involved with Williams' efforts. He told me that he would understand if I needed him to leave.

I told John that, for someone from an advanced, enlightened culture, he clearly knew nothing about women.

That morning, John and I retrieved Kacie from my friend's home. The first thing I did was inject Kacie's arm with the pod that John had given to me. Then we packed quickly, said our goodbyes to our host, and took a taxi to APN's document storage facility in New Jersey where I retrieved the flash drive that Tom had hidden there.

The next day, I mailed Tom's flash drive, the transcript of John's last interview with Saito and Alvis, and the three emails that John had transmitted after his capture, to a publisher in Phoenix. Later that day, I called Mary Kravets and told her that Tom Pierce had been killed and that I would not be returning to the company. Using John's MTY device, John, Kacie, and I were able to transit out of the country without detection.

It has been more than a year since we fled New York. In that time, I have noted with interest several announcements in the media regarding the U.S. government's efforts to recreate Williams' work, most notably a news report from the Oak Ridge National Laboratory just this month regarding their plans to attempt to open a quantum portal, describing it as an "experiment that we cobbled together with parts we found lying around, using equipment and resources we already had available at Oak Ridge".

Kacie is walking now, though she still requires braces to

support her legs, weakened as they were by years of atrophy. The substance inside John's injection pod corrected the flaw in Kacie's genetic pattern, repairing the defective gene and halting her physical deterioration. John is teaching her aiki-hung-ga now, and as her legs grow stronger each day, she has expressed an interest in studying more about gene therapy. I have been encouraging her to pursue that interest.

Sometimes I catch John staring up into the night sky, searching for his beloved Hōfu Station, and I and ask him if he regrets accepting his mission.

To that question, John has always given me the same answer.

"No," he says, "It was the right thing to do."

~ Leah Vaughn, June 2019

Tripback Chronology

Publisher's Note: No information is presently available regarding John Clifton's 1st, 3rd, or 5th thru 9th temporal missions.

John Clifton's 2nd Tripback Mission
Departure date: 2139.
Arrival date: 1908 - "for nearly two months"
Destination: Imperial China.
Purpose: to research disappearance of Reynolds-Hampshire Temporal Specialist Fai Zhou.

John Clifton's 4th Tripback Mission
Departure date: March 5, 2141.
Arrival date: November 19, 2003
Destination: Tokyo, Japan.
Purpose: to scan operational files from the first SDU to validate a legal claim filed by the JNCAA.

John Clifton's 10th Tripback Mission
Departure date: Summer 2150.
Arrival date: October 27, 2017
Destination: Baltimore, Maryland, USA.
Purpose: to verify existence of previously unknown writing on Jewish / Iraqi historical documents preserved in Baltimore museum. John encounters, but fails to report, a QRB signal inside 2017 Baltimore.

John Clifton's 11th Tripback Mission
Departure date: April 4, 2151.

Arrival date: March 13, 2014

Destination: Austin, Texas, USA.

Official Purpose: to scan local utility records.

Clandestine Purpose: to seize control of first sentient AI control processor being developed in the past by temporal agent Theresa Williams / Blosch-Nishikawa and return it unaltered to RJCom's Primary AI.

11th Tripback Events

Thursday, March 13, 2014

John Clifton is struck by a vehicle while walking through an Austin music festival. John's MTY device is damaged and its singularity is released.

Tuesday, May 6, 2014

Temporal Specialist Theresa Williams arrives in Baltimore.

Thursday, June 4, 2015

U.S. Office of Personnel Management reports several cyber intrusions into its database within the past year.

Tuesday, December 12, 2017

John Clifton's anonymous email arrives at APN. Tom Pierce and Leah Vaughn interview Dr. Mitch Saito inside the faculty lounge at Columbia University. Saito learns about John's email and requests a meeting.

Friday, January 26, 2018

John Clifton meets with Tom Pierce and Leah Vaughn inside the Chatwal Hotel in New York. John explains his MTY device, self-resolving causality, and other quantum concepts. He answers numerous questions and transmits several historical data files at the conclusion of the interview.

Leah, John, Kacie, and Jenny Nielsen visit the New York Historical Society Museum and the Central Park Zoo. Tom Pierce meets with Dr. Denton at NYU.

Sunday, January 28, 2018
Leah, John, and Tom meet at APN's office to plan an international trip as a way of introducing John to the world.

Monday, January 29, 2018
John obtains a driver's license under his pseudonym. Mary Kravets delivers travel documents and plane tickets to Leah.

Tuesday/Wednesday, January 30/31, 2018
John and Leah fly from New York to Himachal Pradesh, India.

Thursday, February 1, 2018
John and Leah meet Tenzin Chophel and the 14th Dalai Lama at Dharamshala, India. The Dalai Lama remembers John from John's 1908 tripback to China. Leah views Mannerheim's pistol in the reliquary vault and collapses. John learns that Leah is in love with him.

Friday, February 2, 2018
John and the Dalai Lama are absent from the monastery. Leah meets Norbu, an American acolyte studying at the monastery.

Saturday, February 3, 2018
The Dalai Lama convenes a private convocation for senior monks at Dharamshala, India. John is invited to speak about the future of Tibet. Leah attends with Norbu.

Sunday/Monday, February 4/5, 2018

John and Leah leave Dharamshala and fly to London, UK. John fights U.S. DOE agents inside the London Heathrow baggage processing center, killing one agent. Later at the hotel, John confesses his true mission to Leah.

Tuesday, February 6, 2018

John kills numerous agents inside the London Hilton hotel and rescues Leah. Leah calls Sir Albert Nicholls and the duo flee to Nicholls' unlisted London apartment. An earthquake is reported in Taiwan.

Wednesday, February 7, 2018

John and Leah flee to Stapleford Airport. They board a charter flight to New York arranged by Nicholls. John tells Leah about Saito's involvement with Williams.

February 8 to 21, 2018

John, Leah, and Leah's daughter Kacie hide at the home of Leah's childhood friend "Liz".

Wednesday, February 21, 2018

APN facilitates a meeting with John, physicist Dr. Mitch Saito, and mathematician Richard Alvis at the company's office in New York. DOE agents raid the building and seize John. John is transported to Leesburg Virginia, and then to Washington D.C. where he is interrogated. Saito arrives to oversee John's transfer to the Oak Ridge National Laboratory in Tennessee.

Thursday, February 22, 2018

John is subjected to a scan at the Oak Ridge National

Laboratory to confirm his status as a temporal specialist. John meets Theresa Williams and encounters Mathias Larsen and Viktor Borodin inside the Oak Ridge lab. John confronts Viktor Borodin about Sai Patel. Leah and Tom attempt to rescue John but are captured. John pushes Leah and Tom through William's EPM portal. John seizes the SDU processor and escapes. Williams kills Saito inside the lab.

2158 Norway/London/ Hōfu Station
(Note: Included here to reflect temporal, rather than chronological flow of events)
Williams, Borodin, and Larsen pursue John, Leah, and Tom through 2158 Norway, London, and Hōfu Station. Borodin kills Tom in London. Leah kills Larsen inside Hōfu Gardens and is captured by Williams. John kills Borodin and Williams inside Hōfu Gardens.

Friday, February 23, 2018
Leah and John transit back to 2018 New York. Leah retrieves a flash drive from the New Jersey document storage facility and mails it to a Phoenix publisher. John, Leah, and Kacie flee New York.

Related Events

Friday, February 22, 2018

Death of Nobel laureate particle physicist Dr. Mitch Saito. Cause of death is officially reported as old age.

Wednesday, May 2, 2018

The U.S. Department of Energy issues a press release announcing its plans to spend $30 million dollars studying quantum information sciences, including superpositioning and quantum entangled particles. Preferential funding consideration is granted to the Oak Ridge National Laboratory.

Thursday - Saturday, November 1 – 3, 2018

The 14th Dalai Lama of Tibet invites scientists from China, Taiwan, and the USA to a three-day conference in Dharamshala, India to discuss quantum science and its effects, including quantum transport, space-time symmetry and quantum entanglement. *John, Leah, and Kacie secretly attend and visit with their friends.*

Monday, November 5, 2018

In an interview with a Japanese news service, the 14th Dalai Lama of Tibet announces his successor will be a person "around 20 years old" who will be serving as "a high lama or high scholar".

The U.S. President signs into law a bill authorizing the expenditure of $1.2 billion for quantum science research and development.

Tuesday, January 8, 2019
IBM announces they have created the world's first commercial "quantum computer".

Tuesday, March 12, 2019
In a study reported in the journal "Scientific Reports", physicists announce they were able to reverse the flow of time inside a quantum computer model of sub-atomic particles. Using a quantum computer to simulate a single particle's wave function spreading out over time, physicists successfully reversed the time evolution of the wave function without increasing entropy, seemingly defying an immutable property of the universe called the "arrow of time".

Monday, March 18, 2019
In an interview with Reuters news service, the 14th Dalai Lama of Tibet announces his successor will be found in India and warns that the Chinese will attempt to put forward their own candidate.

Sunday, June 30, 2019
In an interview with a news network, scientists from the Oak Ridge National Laboratory announce they plan to use subatomic particle oscillation to attempt to open a "portal". The project director explains the experiment will be conducted using "parts we found lying around, using equipment and

438

resources we already had available at Oak Ridge."

Saturday, May 12, 2029
Death of Sir Albert Nicholls, founder of the Nicholls Exotic Animal Preserve near Córdoba, Spain.

Tuesday, August 15, 2034
Norbu Rinpoche arrested by Chinese authorities while speaking on the steps of Potala Palace in Lhasa, Tibet.

Thursday, December 10, 2037
Dr. Jana Abee receives the Nobel Prize in Physiology for her breakthrough in genetic resequencing. The prize is awarded by King Haakon VIII of Norway at a ceremony in Oslo, Norway.

Saturday, October 9, 2050
Under pressure from the newly formed North American Federated States, Tibetan monk Norbu Rinpoche is released after 16 years in prison.

February, 2056
The Projet de Singularité Enchevêtrée Quantique Stabilisée (P-SEQS), or "Stabilized Quantum Entangled Singularity Project" begins near Geneva, Switzerland. The purpose of the project is to construct the world's first exotic phased matter (EPM) singularity.

Sunday, October 30, 2067
Mankind's first stabilized EPM singularity is achieved at the P-SEQS facility near Geneva, Switzerland.

Wednesday, December 19, 2068
Dr. Manfred Krieger, Director of Experimental Physics at the P-SEQS facility in Geneva, Switzerland, transits backward in time 18.2 seconds, becoming the world's first time traveler.

Wednesday, April 16, 2070
The 36 nations directly involved in the P- SEQS project sign the International Temporal Treaty (ITT). The Conseil Temporel International (CTI), or "International Temporal Council" is formed as its governing authority and headquartered in Geneva, Switzerland.

Saturday, April 3, 2077
High Lama Norbu Rinpoche, translator and personal advisor to the 15th Dalai Lama of Tibet, inters his grandfather's ashes in the Ganden Monastery near his ancestral village of Drupshi on the outskirts of Lhasa.

Thursday, June 3, 2077
50th anniversary celebration honoring the Nicholls Exotic Animal Preserve near Córdoba, Spain. Queen Leonor of Spain presents the Nicholls Foundation with the Orden Civil del Mérito Medioambiental (Civil Order of Environmental Merit). The foundation is recognized for saving 3,442 critically endangered animal species.

Tuesday, June 10, 2092
A provisional government in Tibet is established under the authority of the 15th Dalai Lama.

Friday, September 5, 2092

The government of China formally recognizes Tibet as an independent nation.

Wednesday, March 2, 2095
Construction of Hōfu Station begins with the deployment of four orbital pressurized platforms transited from the EPM station in Chofu, Japan.

Acronym Glossary

AISMPE

The [A]utorité [I]nternationale [S]ingulière de la [M]atière [P]hasique [E]xotique (AISMPE), or "International Exotic Phased Matter Singularity Authority" was established in 2084 by 21 member nations participating in the P-SEQS project in Geneva.

Today, the 62-member AISMPE committee regulates all aspects of non-temporal EPM travel, safety, and licensing. *See: Evanston Accident.*

CTI

The [C]onseil [T]emporel [I]nternational (CTI), or "International Temporal Council", headquartered in Geneva, Switzerland, regulates all temporal activities under the authority of the International Temporal Treaty (ITT) of 2070.

CTI personnel can be recognized by their traditional white uniforms and blue circle insignia.

Temporal specialists are required to report any tripback temporal anomalies directly to the CTI.

EPM

An [E]xotic [P]hased-[M]atter (EPM) singularity is an acronym for a stabilized wormhole that has been split at the quantum level into two distinct event horizons calibrated to fixed positions in space and time. Both event horizons are quantum-entangled parts of the same singularity. Positioned at different physical locations, this quantum entanglement creates a "tunnel" through which matter and energy may pass.

Mankind's first stabilized EPM singularity was achieved at the P-SEQS facility near Geneva, Switzerland on October 30, 2067.

EPM transit stations can be found on the Earth, the moon, orbital stations, and as a transit network between the Earth and Mars. EPM stations accommodate mankind's travel, shipping, and other transport needs. The widespread deployment of EPM stations in the 2080s was the primary factor responsible for eliminating mankind's reliance on fossil fuels and their resulting carbon emissions.

When coupled with a tunneling regulator, an EPM singularity can facilitate temporal transition. All temporal EPM activity is strictly regulated by the CTI council under the ITT treaty of 2070.

IMU

[I]nternational [M]onetary [U]nit (IMU). With the widespread implementation of EPM transit technologies beginning in the 2080s, international travel and commerce dramatically increased, pressuring nations to adopt a common financial exchange medium. By the late 2090s, virtually every nation had subscribed to the International Monetary Unit for commerce. While local currencies can still be found in many nations, all currencies are converted to IMUs for everyday transactions.

IMUs exist as digital currency values and are processed through the IMU Central Bank in Toronto, Canada under the

443

authority of the International Commerce Authority.

ITT

Following Dr. Manfred Krieger's successful temporal transition on December 19, 2068 at the P-SEQS facility in Geneva, Switzerland, the 36 nations directly involved in the P- SEQS project signed the [I]nternational [T]emporal [T]reaty (ITT). Under the authority of the Conseil Temporel International (CTI), or "International Temporal Council", the ITT governs all of mankind's temporal activities.

From 2070 until 2158, three companies were chartered under the ITT to operate temporal transit facilities; Reynolds-Hampshire in England, Blosch-Nishikawa in Norway, and Rengel-Jiang QCom in Texas (NAFS).

In 2158, Blosch-Nishikawa's temporal charter was revoked for ITT violations.

P- SEQS

The [P]rojet de [S]ingularité [E]nchevêtrée [Q]uantique [S]tabilisée (P-SEQS), or "Stabilized Quantum Entangled Singularity Project" was a coordinated effort by more than 36 nations to construct the world's first exotic phased matter (EPM) singularity. The project began in February 2056 near Geneva, Switzerland and achieved the first stable singularity on October 30, 2067.

See: EPM.

PoL

[P]enetrant [o]bject [L]inking (PoL) is the process of

establishing a connection between two electronic objects for purposes of data collection or substantive control.

SDU

[S]elf [D]irecting [U]nit (SDU) is an acronym for an automaton capable of analytical reasoning and determination without human assistance. Unlike earlier "robots" that were programmed by a human beings and operated according to rigid programming instructions, an SDU utilizes a quantum synapse created by an AI controller and is capable of adaptive behavior exceeding the mere summation of its programming.

The classic experiment used to illustrate the difference between primitive robots and later SDUs is the "Turing Mirror". The experiment involves an automaton's positive demonstration of three attributes; self-awareness, metacognition, and empathetic awareness.

In the experiment, the automaton is placed in a setting to observe another of its kind asked to complete an impossible task. The automaton then watches its peer being dismantled or destroyed when it fails to complete the task.

An observing robot, when asked to complete the same task, will make some attempt to complete the task and will demonstrate no awareness of the impossibility of the task nor of the consequences of its failure, despite having observed both in its predecessor.

An observing SDU, however, will recognize the impossibility of the task from its earlier observation of its predecessor (metacognition). Rather than attempting to complete the task as directed, it will attempt to change the parameters of the task, typically by requesting a revision of the instructions as or explaining the impossibility of the task to the requestor (self-awareness). Further, it will exhibit an awareness of the consequences should it fail, from its observance of the same consequences suffered by its predecessor (empathic awareness). Typically, this awareness is manifested as a catastrophic controller failure; a cascading failure of the AI "brain" that, if not suspended, leads to the automaton's functional termination.

Automatons were first categorized as SDUs in the late 2110s. By 2140, SDUs had reached a level of sophistication in metacognition, self-awareness, and empathy approaching what researchers called "true sentience". Following a legal challenge raised against the JNCAA in November of 2140, a moratorium was placed on all SDU development or enhancement.

In 2158, despite the 18-year moratorium on SDU development, socio-automaton analysts and quantum engineers reported that SDUs coming out of the automation factories had now achieved "true sentience". Automaton manufacturers around the world immediately issued a joint statement calling for an investigation into granting sentient SDUs specific fundamental rights.

Tripback

n. *slang*. A temporal EPM transition into the past.

For the complete interview between John Clifton and former APN producers Tom Pierce and Leah Vaughn inside the N.Y. Chatwal Hotel, a review of the historical files provided by Clifton at the conclusion of that interview, and a transcript of the technical discussion between Clifton, Alvis, and Saito, readers are invited to read:

*"How to Build a Time Machine -
The Amazing Account of John J. Clifton,
a Time Traveler from the Year 2151."*

www.ingramcontent.com/pod-product-compliance
Lightning Source LLC
Chambersburg PA
CBHW051433260626
47162CB00001B/68

* 9 7 8 1 7 3 3 4 6 3 2 2 5 *